FALSE LIGHT

Peter Sheldon's portait in Valois costume, referred to on page 25.

FALSE LIGHT

BY
PETER SHELDON

with a foreword by
FRANCIS KING

Pulsifer Press
London

First published in 1993
by Pulsifer Press
PO Box 205
London WC2N 4BQ

Phototypeset directly from author's discs
by Discript, 24 Bedfordbury, London WC2N 4BL

Printed by Redwood Books, Trowbridge, Wiltshire BA14 8RN

Peter Sheldon is hereby identified as author of this work
in accordance with
Section 77 of the Copyright, Designs and Patents Act 1988

Foreword copyright © Francis King, 1993

A CIP record for this book is available from the British Library

ISBN 0 948849 01 0

FOREWORD

The story of how this autobiographical novel came to be written is both tragic and heartening.

Its author was born in Vienna in 1919, of a Jewish father and a gentile mother. Obliged to flee his native country soon after the *Anschluss*, he eventually arrived in Australia, where he took both Australian nationality and a name to go with it. Soon after the War he settled in Greece, where he earned a living, at first precarious and then increasingly lucrative, as an English teacher and a writer of guidebooks.

Five years before his death last spring, he was blinded in a motor accident. Unfitted to produce any further guidebooks and able to teach only with extreme difficulty, he then began to write this novel on a small, old-fashioned typewriter. The appalling difficulty of such an undertaking will at once be apparent. He had no way of seeing his mistakes, much less of correcting them. Friends offered their help; but the frustration of relying on people who could not immediately intuit his intentions would ignite volcanic rages. On a visit to Athens, when I spent a week working with him, such rages would frequently blast me. More than once I said to him, 'But, Peter, that just isn't English', to receive the scorching answer that the book must be written as he wanted it written, not as I did. In consequence, I have now made no attempt to impose a more conventional style where he himself never wished for one. To my pleas that firstly he should write the book in his native German and secondly that he should write it as an autobiography not as a *roman à clef*, he was equally unresponsive.

When he was not working himself into a fury over the book, Peter was often doing so over other matters. That week taught me precisely what it is that the blind must endure. When, for example, I had washed up the cups in which we had drunk our mid-morning Nescafé, Peter asked me: 'Where have you put those cups?' I replied that I had put them on the draining board. 'Idiot!' he shouted at me. 'How do you think I'm going to find them when I next need them? You *must* put things back *exactly* where they came from!' On another occasion, not thinking, I held out a sheet of the typescript to him: 'Why don't you put this paragraph before that one? Do you see what I mean?' He almost pushed the table over in his rage: 'How can I see what you mean? I can't even see what I've written.'

Eventually I came to recognise in his constantly frustrated but never relaxed efforts to get the book completed a metaphor for the novelist's vocation. Friendships were unimportant, his own happiness and peace of mind were unimportant. All that was important was somehow, with titanic, self-destructive effort, to get down on to paper what was within him.

Peter and I used to correspond with each other on tape. One day a tape arrived to tell me firstly that the book was now as good as he could ever hope to make it and secondly that by the time that I had received the tape he would have taken his life. I had indeed already received news of his meticulously planned suicide from sleeping pills. He went on to tell me that he had one last request to make of me: I must, please, please, do everything in my power to see that the novel was published.

I am glad to have been able to accomplish that for him. He was a friend as dear as he was difficult; but, no less important, he has written a book which tells of a fascinating life in a fascinating, albeit highly idiosyncratic, manner. It deserves to be read, not merely as a personal document but as a document of the exile which, like him, so many wholly innocent people of Jewish descent have been forced to endure in the course of our barbarous century.

Francis King
January 1993

DAWN

Karl occasionally pretended that an invasion of stallholders from Vienna's Food Market soon after his birth had caused his hatred of mobs. His mother had shown a slightly threatening deputation over the empty cellars of the Imperial and Royal Horticultural Society, till even the fishwives conceded that here was a bareness proper to the hungry capital. Their apologetic withdrawal stopped any resemblance to the assault on Versailles in the French Revolution, but an allusion to Marie Antoinette, an impressively tragic Habsburg, was hard to resist.

1

Karl's father, Dr Kurt Fechtner, had been recalled from the Italian front to take charge of the capital's food supply, a thankless task in fatal 1918. Facing alone two million famished Viennese required equal courage and more ingenuity than facing the enemy as captain in the Imperial and Royal Army's only Moslem regiment – officered, of course, by Christians.

During his military service he visited with fellow subalterns the Prater, Vienna's popular but respectable amusement centre. One of the lieutenants was related to the plumper of two pretty girls drinking chocolate with whipped cream on a café terrace. Introductions were made; the finely featured blonde and the dark officer in the Bosniak red-and-blue uniform looked and behaved like the young lovers in a Viennese operetta. Their subsequent memory of Léhar conducting a band at this first encounter was a creative embellishment, excusable by the composer's subsequent fame.

The romance blossomed without any second-act complications, though Adele's parents were unenthusiastic about a penniless officer from the Bukovina, the Empire's easternmost province. Her father, the headmaster of a high school in Upper Austria, had only reluctantly consented to her staying on with a schoolfriend in Vienna after the girls had finished their education at the Ursuline Convent, which dispensed manners and piety at the expense of worldly wisdom. Her mother expected the worst as the schoolfriend played battledore and shuttlecock 'all dressed in white, how vulgar'; the lieutenant did not fulfil the anticipated doom, since his doctorate in philosophy should assure a suitable position at the end of his military service. Dr Kurt Fechtner was undoubtedly bright, almost alarmingly so. Adele's determination overcame conventional objections, even to Kurt's insistence that the bride must adopt his own Lutheran persuasion; not from militant Evangelism, but because he resented the obligation to bring up his children as Catholics, as was required for mixed marriages.

Conversion and marriage took place in the Protestant Church of Vienna's fashionable Inner City. Kurt was engaged by the Horticultural Society, not entirely on the strength of his first-class degree in Botany but through high patronage. Students outstanding in political discussion rather than duels were favoured by the circle of would-be reformers round the Heir to the Throne. Archduke Franz Ferdinand advocated a federalism as abhorrent as his morganatic marriage to Emperor Franz Joseph, convinced that Austria could not stand radical changes.

Dr Fechtner, now on the fringes of the Archducal Court, was promoted Secretary of the Horticultural Society and lodged comfortably in its extensive grounds. The birth of a daughter did not interfere with her parents' social life as Herta could be entrusted to the Swiss nanny. Owners of gardens sought advice and reciprocated with invitations to receptions enjoyed by birth and talent in the certainty that the situation was desperate but hardly serious.

In June 1914 the situation became, however, desperately serious when the Archduke and his wife were murdered at Sarajevo. Franz Joseph was unable to prevent the war he dreaded; his death symbolised the end of Europe's oldest empire which disintegrated under his grand nephew and successor. Emperor Karl refused to abdicate and remained even in exile the ruler recognised by many Austrians.

———

The Republic was, however, a sad reality. Dr Fechtner had been decorated for his services on the Front and in the last Imperial government, but the revolution deprived him of the ennoblement that would have followed. Despite the official abolition of titles, the lack of even a simple *von* was resented by a family barred from deserved recognition.

Born in the last year of the monarchy, Karl had naturally been given the Emperor's name. Herta blamed the boy for diverting the affection of her parents who were already preoccupied with survival amidst the wreckage of all Imperial institutions. A flamboyant financier initiated Dr Fechtner into the currency speculations that ruined several countries and eventually most operators. Despite the financial losses, banking bridged the difficult period till the former under-secretary's endeavours were appreciated by his appointment to head a large trading firm.

In their fashionable flat in the Inner City the Fechtners received artists, intellectuals and politicians opposed to the ruling Socialists. On quiet evenings Mother played the piano, her parents' wedding gift, and sang Schubert as well as popular songs to the delight of the family and a few intimates.

Karl caught whooping cough from his sister. She recovered quick-ly but he nearly died, remaining prone to colds at a time when food was as scarce as medicine. Father's regimental doctor became a nominal uncle, following the Austrian custom of accommodating close friends with fictitious relationships. Mother had once referred to the few strands of hair plastered across the doctor's pate as 'Curly glory' and was horrified when Karl twisted these sparse remnants round his tiny fingers to a distinct repetition of her joke. The doctor had a sense of humour and also a sister who painted for a living. Sales were to and through the doctor's patients, amongst whom the Fecht-ners were the most promising; Mother commissioned the expected portrait.

Another uncle, the Colonel of the Bosniaks, had been awarded the Maria Theresa Order for gallantry; this highest military decoration conferred a knighthood recognised by the Republic which abolished all other hereditary titles. Uncle Colonel offered to adopt Karl, but a *von* before a Czech name was found insufficient. He first thrilled then bored the children with his war exploits, till Mother married him off to a wealthy widow.

Czech names were little appreciated, as most servants came from that part of the defunct Empire, where the aristocracy had been Germanised. A smattering of Czech gleaned from Cook was fun; but to be called in that language was another matter. Thanks to the Swiss nanny, kept throughout the war, the children spoke French as well as German. The English governess was, in the ways of Vienna, the daughter of a local Jewish haberdasher. Her family lived in the Grilparzer House, where Austria's outstanding dramatist had written several plays. The tenuous literary association bestowed on Margarete Horbitzer greater prestige than her first-class English Literature degree, yet from her traditionalistic background she expounded progressive ideas which slightly alarmed Mother and amused the Headmaster.

This headmaster had resigned in protest against the Socialist school reforms and moved to a flat in Vienna's historical Black

Spaniards Court. Affectionately called Ohli, Grandfather was very popular with his grandchildren. Usually even-tempered, he would not suffer fools and this impatience with stupidity was inherited by his daughter whose outburst might end in a slap, always justified to the recipient and therefore not resented.

From her mother Adele inherited an artistic taste and lovely Biedermeier furniture. For lack of space, Granny had parted with her drawing room and now contributed to the collection of cut glass originated by two Renaissance goblets, the wedding present of Kurt's sister. The display cabinet was greatly admired by the ladies of the weekly card party, especially by Granny's oldest friend, a Frau Hofrat. The title Court Councillor was in the Republic as ludicrous as Secret Councillor had been in the Empire, yet Frau Hofrat ranked a kiss on the hand while lesser councillors' consorts had to be content with mere words of polite greeting from Karl. The pretty blond child was fussed over and plied with chocolates hastily confiscated by Nanny before they could do too much harm. She was less successful at children's parties where chocolates, solid and liquid, gave Karl tummy aches and a diminishing appreciation of such delicacies.

———— ————

Nanny complained about the boy's clumsiness in catching a ball and his bumping into corners of tables. Negligence was excluded because of the pain, and the parents took over. Mother put a hand over his left eye and Father raised some fingers. 'How many?'

'Two, no, perhaps three.'

The fingers approached. 'Two, yes, two!'

Consternation, then Mother remembered, 'Uncle Ferdinand has something wrong in one eye. It couldn't . . .'

It was a rare hereditary weakness, usually restricted to males but transmitted in the female line. Vienna's leading oculist recommended covering the left eye for a year to force the right into a belated development; at the age of four there was still hope that he might eventually be able to count those fingers. Uncle Doctor considered the prospect too uncertain to deprive the child of sight and normal contacts; added care would have to be taken of the excellent left eye.

Uncle Ferdinand was consulted. He lived with his Swiss wife Marceline, called La Tante Vaseline, and his mother, whose jetblack tresses and antimacassars proved the efficacy of nut oil. Great-grandmother showed little interest in the children who disliked kissing her mummified hand and cheeks, but spent her remaining passions in vituperating against the Prussian Pigs, the murderers of her husband in the War of 1866. Her persistence had probably driven her son into the Pro-Prussian party, the Pan-Germans, but politics were avoided for the sake of his eyes. One apparently sufficed for most practical purposes, even for an engineer, besides securing him exemption from military service. Of no importance with the Republic's standing army of 30,000 men, but in another war . . .

The children felt no sorrow when Great Grandmother died and was buried near her parents in Lower Austria as her husband lay on some forgotten battlefield. The simple ceremony was attended only by the family and servants; her son and daughter seemed moved, her daughter-in-law relieved. On the drive home, Karl voiced disapproval of the unimpressive funeral. 'Since she couldn't muster more mourners from her own family, couldn't Ohli have brought reinforcement from his?'

'You do use the oddest expressions. No, my brothers live in Upper Austria.'

'Why don't we visit them?' Karl was anxious to enlarge the meagre family circle and, after receiving some vague assurance, turned to closer relations. 'What about Father's kith and kin?'

Had Father not excused himself, pleading an important conference, his reaction would have been different from Mother's. 'Ohli, please stop reading Nordic Sagas to Karl. He talks like an Icelandic bard. Father's only sister is married and lives in Germany. Another died before he was born.'

'His mother visited us when I was very small. She gave me a doll in a strange dress.' Herta savoured her familiarity with a dead grandmother. 'She said something about Karl.'

'You are an idiot, I wasn't even born.'

'I know that,' Herta was scornful, 'but there definitely was some Karl. Wasn't there, Mother?'

'Yes, he died . . . young.'

The boy had noticed the pause. 'What of?'

'Better ask your father.'

That same evening an answer was skilfully avoided. 'Who? . . . What do you know of Uncle Karl?'

'Coming back from the funeral, we were discussing family matters.' Karl had doubts about the adult expression under Father's stare. 'Ohli told me about his brothers we are going to visit.'

'Are we? Actually it's not such a bad idea, we might then drive on to Ohli's school.'

——— ———

Grandmother's curious pride in transmitting a hereditary 'frailty' found expression when Karl cut himself and it was difficult to staunch the bleeding. 'Think of the Tsarevitch and of the Spanish Royal family.'

'You are not Queen Victoria, mother, and Karl is not a haemophiliac.'

Granny's reference to princes of the blood made her popular with Karl. The two were sitting on the nursery balcony watching a procession of flower-bedecked horse carriages on the way to the Cathedral. 'Are you taking me in a carriage like these, Granny?'

'You are by far too young. These are candidates for confirmation. Aren't the flowers lovely, especially the lilac?' Flowers were easier to discuss than religion; Karl had again been sidetracked.

— — — —

The first holiday abroad was spent on the German Baltic coast where bags stuffed with banknotes were needed to pay for the smallest purchase. Karl believed icecream was worth its weight in money and seemingly most other articles too. Awareness of the inflation prepared him for the intelligence test which made possible an early start to education. Asked how he had come to the town hall Karl replied 'In my mother's car.' The inspector of primary schools looked out of the window at the uniformed chauffeur next to the Daimler and pronounced the boy remarkably intelligent.

— — — —

Margarete Horbitzer recommended a school founded by a feminist who added progressive ideas, arts and crafts to the three Rs to justify the expense. Gilding small baskets woven by older pupils pleasantly filled the weeks before Christmas.

The baskets flanked the crib below the richly decorated tree sparkling with candles and Bengal lights. Presents were heaped all around, for young, old and the servants. Books outnumbered toys, tin soldiers familiarised Karl with the uniforms of the Imperial Army's crack regiments, weaponry was excluded. The birthdays of Mother and the children followed too closely in January to rekindle a truly festive spirit, but the *Sachertorte* with the appropriate number of candles presided over such memorable presents as architectural building blocks and a rocking horse.

— — — —

Karl's introduction to operetta was Léhar's *Friedericke*, the story of a selfless girl abandoned by a selfish Goethe whose name, however, hallowed all misconduct. Mother had attended the first night and entrusted the boy to her parents; Granny and the child shed copious tears to the embarrassment of Ohli, whose eyes did not remain quite dry either on this enjoyable outing.

The Fechtners subscribed to the State Theatre's ten-month season for two front-row seats. Father and Herta favoured the Burgtheater, Mother the Opera, Charles loved both. The impact of Goethe and Schiller was further enhanced because the robust septuagenarian actresses had once pleased Emperor Franz Joseph.

The choice of a first opera was as seriously debated as the merits of a new minister. An acceptable libretto raised greater difficulties than suitable music. The *Magic Flute* might be offensively absurd, Puccini was too erotic, of Wagner only *Tannhäuser* was sufficiently melodious, while Christianity overcame the wrongdoings in the Venusberg. To Karl it was pure enchantment, medieval sagas come alive in a superb union of drama, singing and orchestra. The aural and visual pleasures combined admirably, Karl became an opera buff, but no performance ever equalled this first experience.

Unreality on the stage opened, perhaps, more than one new world. Nanny was chatting with her cronies on a bench in the Volksgarten while their charges were playing before the Empress Elisabeth Monument. The sunlight filtering through the trees hypnotised Karl who did not hear repeated calls and only woke from a trance when he was gently shaken. He was unable to answer Nanny's and later Mother's worried inquiries except by stating that he had been elsewhere. 'Elsewhere' was beautiful, indescribable, and he would like to go there again.

_____

Instead he went with mother and Herta to France. They all loved Paris and Karl felt strangely at home at the Louvre, especially the wing built by the Valois kings. Mother ascribed this to the Alexandre Dumas novels but secretly wondered why her small son was drawn to these empty apartments in preference to the grand galleries. Millions believed in reincarnation, but Karl was so eminently Austrian. Yet his French was more elegant than Nanny's, as La Tante Vaseline had remarked, and more natural than Herta's.

The bracing air of a Brittany beach swept away transcendental speculations. Father came to fetch them in the big open Mercedes driven by a former Bosniak NCO. Swaddled in dustcoats and hoods they motored back through Germany, which Herta preferred to France, contrary to her brother. Mother traced this back to Uncle Ferdinand who had recently shown some interest in the girl, but would be given no further opportunity to propagate his pan-Germanism.

The following summer Karl's wish to enlarge the family circle was fulfilled by meeting Father's sister, her husband and son at Lucern.

Uncle Siegfried Auer was manager of the Chemical Works at Wittenberg, where Aunt Rosa presided over the Luther Society. Surprisingly, this pillar of Protestantism was accompanied by a somewhat younger Catholic priest who paid noticeable attention to the son. Kurt was aged halfway between his cousins and therefore ill-suited to both. Yet all enjoyed 'this full family reunion'; no sooner uttered than meaningful glances exchanged by his elders warned Karl that he had said the wrong thing.

After the Auers' departure, the Fechtners rented a villa on Lake Zurich. Father had been offered the management of a large Swiss food concern but finally declined, influenced by a wife who found Zurich too provincial, missed her artistic friends and was alarmed by the results of irresistible creams and cheeses.

——— ———

The velvet pyjamas in which Karl kissed hands at Mother's card parties were immortalised when photographs of the Fechtners appeared in the *Salonblatt*, the Society magazine. An Imperial or at least a Royal Highness always graced the cover, with the inside pages given over to birth, position and wealth. The Fechtners' qualification was illustrated by the spread over two pages: Father and daughter in riding clothes justified by their winning prizes in sundry competitions; Mother's blond distinction was emphasised by a dark evening dress and a string of pearls; Karl was embracing a teddy bear he had long outgrown. It was rare for an entire family to be portrayed, but the Fechtners were photogenic, besides being good for a dozen additional subscriptions.

They were also suitably conservative, as proved by Dr Fechtner in a radio discussion with Prince Charles Rohan. Dr Fechtner stressed the necessity of a Danube Federation, an updated version of the Habsburg Empire; the proposal was economically too sensible to be politically acceptable despite the mounting evidence that none of the Succession States was viable on its own.

The double publicity inspired Karl to rewrite the story of the Trojan War in *Tales Retold* to the detriment of the quarrelsome Greeks. Not invulnerable Achilles but his brave opponent was the real hero and the Trojans deserved victory. This version based on merit pleased the headmaster as well as Karl's new friends at school.

——— ———

The newly-established comprehensive schools were not subject to age restrictions. Yet the reform had overlooked the possibility of transfer in the second year to a classical high school. Karl would then enter the Schotten Gymnasium, founded by Scottish Benedictines in the twelfth century, and remain the youngest pupil. He also learned that laws could be interpreted without bending them unduly. The transitory stay at the comprehensive limited his school friendships to the grandson of an Imperial minister and Felix, the bright offspring of a Jewish lawyer, both equally loyal to Emperor Otto in his Belgian exile.

The boys were traditionalists, the teachers innovators. The lowest form was to make a two-day excursion to northern Lower Austria, where the family of a pupil owned property. Karl considered it natural to be one of the four boys invited to spend the night at the castle, though he was no particular friend of Johann. That moon-faced boy called Karl aside a few days before the departure. 'There isn't enough room in our place.'

'Funny castle, if there isn't enough room for us.'

'It's OK for the other three. You see, the castle belonged to my grandfather, the founder of the Pan-German party.'

'So what? My Great Uncle is also a Pan-German.'

Moonface regained colour. 'Are you sure? That would change matters!'

'What has my mother's uncle got to do with it? This is perfectly crazy.'

'Oh, your mother's uncle . . . I'll try. No, it won't do. Ask your father.'

The totally bewildered Karl kept silent to his friends, anxiously waiting for an explanation at home. Telling his story, he did not miss the glance his parents exchanged.

'I suppose Johann's parents object to my broadcast advocating the Danube Federation as an alternative to Pan-Germanism. Had I known Johann's background, I wouldn't have allowed you to accept the invitation.' The half-truth seemed plausible in Austria's politically charged atmosphere. 'Johann is not to blame and don't involve your friends.'

'Felix was not invited. Johann said something about his being baptised standing up. Felix seemed annoyed but, as he didn't say anything, I didn't ask him. Christ was baptised standing in all the pictures in the Louvre.' Karl had started the diversion to safer grounds

Deus ex machina intervened the following morning. The teacher claimed credit for securing accommodation at a monastery hostel near a lovely baroque town. This was the first the boys heard about baroqu about which they knew little and cared less. The emphasis had been on the magic of the forest, which held some promise despite tiresome quotations from silly poets; and being all together in a hostel was hardly the fun the teacher made out with false jocularity. It was now Karl's and Johann's turn to exchange a quick glance, both convinced that the *machina* was homemade; the *deus* was, however, uncertain as neither Pan-Germans nor Protestants seemed likely recipients of instant monastic hospitality.

The excursion was a success as architecture was kept to an acceptable minimum. The two boys avoided one another as if guilty of the anti-Semitism underlying the episode.

———— ———— ———— ————

Awareness of undeserved enmity probably contributed to Karl's unusually high fever when he caught a chill. Uncle Doctor recommended removal of tonsils and adenoids by the leading ENT specialist Professor Neumann, who looked after and into the ears and throats of the King of Spain and the Prince of Wales. He rarely performed routine operations on ordinary mortals but was persuaded by a considerable fee. Karl felt no fear, since the necessity and painlessness of the intervention had been explained. Mother joked about his occupying the same room in the clinic in which he had been born. He counted bravely under the chloroform mask in the operating theatre.

Vomiting opened the wounds and Mother insisted that the Professor himself should staunch the bleeding. One gauze pad was missing from the tongs, obviously swallowed, nothing to worry about. During the week in the clinic Karl's breath became increasingly malodorous and at home so foul that even Granny ventured no more than a perfunctory peck. She was sitting at his bedside when the boy began retching and gasping for air. Granny rushed for unspecified help to the bridge party in the drawing room, but the drama resolved itself when a slime-encrusted ball of gauze emerged to stain the bedlinen. The boy was breathing noisily, but the worst was obviously over. His recovery was confirmed by the Professor. 'A misjudgement, but the gauze hardly ever lodges in the sinus. The gargling can now be stopped.' At this callousness Karl lost the awe in which Vienna held its chief medicine men; but his parents retained some, and promptly paid the hefty bill.

Compensation for the broken promise of painlessness was a railway with more gadgets than the trains envied at Felix's. The tracks extended across the nursery floor, had to be assembled and packed away, soon to make the joy of an orphanage. Like all his family Karl was bored by things mechanical or technical, scornfully dismissed by Ohli as ironmongery.

Increased attention was a more durable gift, but the end to the sore throat also ended the spells of uninterrupted reading in the warm bed. A running nose offered an opportunity for an experiment; he dipped the thermometer into the infusion he was to inhale at a temperature that shattered the quicksilver. He received his only serious beating as Mother was outraged at such clumsy deception.

———— ————

Every May Mother followed a strict diet at Marienbad, to lose the weight she had gained during the preceding eleven months. Favoured by Edward VII, the spa had long attracted the stout of the world, who were depicted on irreverent postcards running for the lavatories scattered throughout the lovely woods. Mother befriended some Scandinavians equally regular in reducing their girth, but less successful judging by photos showing the slim Viennese surrounded by portly Nordics. Despite the absence of other ladies they did not look rivals for Father.

Father too had to watch his weight; there was much talk about calories and fresh fruit instead of sweets at the rare meals without guests. *Man As A Factory* demonstrated the dependence of bodily functions on the right fuel; the diagram was sexless, leaving the embarrassing mechanics of reproduction to older schoolmates, the traditional source of enlightenment. Herta prepared for her first ball by dieting and taking Mother's slimming tablets; only Karl was kept outside the slimming whirl. Yet the concept was strengthened when he was excused from school to visit Mother at Marienbad.

At Vienna airport Father tipped the flight steward to assist at the change in Prague, but in the small local plane Karl was so violently airsick that he tried to jump out. The rattling of the doorhandle alerted the fellow passengers. A kind lady first comforted and then deposited the shaken lad into Mother's arms. He quickly recovered under her care and the attention of the stout Scandinavians who vied with one another to gain the son's approval by buying him all the delicacies they were forbidden. It was fun to eat under the envious eyes and not to drink the nasty water after one try. Slimming was too obsessive at Marienbad, it had to wait for the opposition in Vienna. When he finally confessed his suicidal misery, Mother arranged his return by rail. Father commented cuttingly on the ignorance of air pressure preventing the opening of the door, but the classmates appreciated the macabre heroism of the frustrated jump.

At Marienbad eating had been enjoyable, in Vienna fasting was meritorious. Karl became more preoccupied with calories than his sister; he shunned fats and starches, ate less and less, and became all skin and bones. Parental opposition to his asceticism increased in severity. 'Enough of this nonsense. No opera or theatre unless . . .' assured a reasonable food supply at family meals. In the absence of the parents, Karl ate under the surveillance of Granny or Mitzi, the maid, but with the dexterity of a prestidigitator he spirited the most nourishing morsels into a box covered by the tablecloth. Getting rid of the boxes proved more difficult, and a smell of mould led to the discovery of rotting food secreted behind books, in the toy cupboard and under clothes. The unexpectedness of this extraordinary treasure trove drove Mother to 'This lunacy has to stop.' Karl's determination was shaken by doubts of his sanity.

He shifted his pursuit of skeletal beauty. A friend of Mother had lost weight because of insomnia, so Karl reduced his sleep by reading into the early hours. A pleasure rather than a privation, but demanding as much cunning as the box trick. To prevent the light showing under the doors, he enveloped the table lamp in the curtain kept by hand at a safe distance. One night he fell asleep and a large hole was burnt into the contraption. This time Father exploded 'Besides ruining your one good eye, you almost burnt down the house. It's boarding school for you.' The horror of a dormitory and lack of privacy made him promise to behave like a normal boy, though judging by his classmates this seemed of doubtful desirability.

———— ————

Karl never shared his classmates' interest in cars; but he regretted the Mercedes given up, along with journeys abroad, during the Great Depression that hit early an Austria not recovered from its dismemberment. Dr Fechtner resigned from his directorship, which no longer warranted its emoluments. Such an unusual admission further enhanced his standing, and he was entrusted with the reorganisation of the largest food chain in six Succession States. Krainer had been a household name throughout the Empire, but inflation, tariffs and nationalism were beyond the experience of the elderly founder and president. With the thoroughness that justified his reputation, the General Manager presumptive started on the salary and under the working conditions of ordinary salesmen. The apprenticeship imposed economies, so that the summer vacations were now spent at Maria Wörth, an unspoilt village on Austria's warmest lake. Mother and Herta learned to ride bicycles, but the boy was considered too young for bloody knees; a curious decision, as he had been riding for some years. Nor did the grandparents join in the undignified wobbling, but Ohli swam unaccompanied the eight kilometres across the lake and back. Granny's ire at this rash exploit endeared him to the children who had inherited his predilection for swimming.

The Burgtheater's principal comedian was staying at the same hotel. His son, Ernst Häussermann, provided suitable company, since he was a pupil at the Schotten in the second form Karl was about to join. The boys swapped schoolyarns and Karl was initiated in the shape of things to come.

2

The Schotten Gymnasium had for centuries educated the scions of the ruling class. Stretching loyalty at the expense of credibility, Emperor Karl headed the memorial of pupils fallen for the fatherland. The narrowing of the fatherland's borders had forced the Benedictines into widening admission to include the middle class. No attempt was made to convert the few Lutherans who naturally participated in the *Pater Noster* at the start of the first period, but received religious instruction at the Evangelical School.

With quick judgement, the form-master seated Karl next to Count Otto Barovsky, named after the last Emperor's eldest son. He spoke the same Frenchified Viennese, most of the other pupils acceptable Austrian German, but those who tried too hard never achieved Christian-name intimacy. Simultaneous domestic upgrading elevated Karl to 'Young Master', and he received generous pocket money, largely saved.

For several months Dr Fechtner joined the shop assistants for the opening of the Krainer branch at eight a.m. In the evenings he studied the firm's management problems in different countries and, therefore, rarely found time for the Burgtheater or the Opera, to which subscription had been maintained as an essential part of life. When he finally emerged as General Manager, a Mercedes returned, as also the actors and artists to the Biedermeier drawing room. The Burgtheater Director was a well-known poet and thus provided a link with the leading Austrian playwrights, Arthur Schnitzler and Hugo von Hoffmannsthal, and Shaw's translator, Siegfried Trebitsch, whose marriage with a Russian princess illustrated the Viennese mixture of aristocracy and Jewish intellectuals in the Fechtners' approximation of a pre-war *Salon* under the approving eyes of the last Emperor's secretary.

For the next vacation the Wörthersee was likewise upgraded by a switch to the Lake's most elegant resort. Mother chaperoned Herta through Pörtschach's social life, while Ernst Häusserman was invited to talk school and theatre with Karl. When spicy behind-the-scene stories had paled after some weeks, Karl was content with his books and solitary walks in the surrounding hills. Public-minded by nature and upbringing, he was shifting a large stone from the path when faced by a viper ready to strike. For a moment Karl was tempted to imitate Luther who had vowed to become a monk if saved from lightning. Though paralysed by fear, the boy was too cautious for such a commitment but prayed fervently till the snake slithered away.

Instead of his perilous labours, he attended the rehearsals of the hotel's student jazzband. The band leader often patted his blond hair and once remarked 'You are too pretty for your own good'. Bewilderment was not solved by 'You'll find out soon enough, but not just yet'. Karl felt that Mother had better not be bothered for an explanation.

———— ————

With his experience as headmaster, Ohli had correctly foretold that his grandson would be top of the class in History, bottom in Mathematics. But in Latin and Ancient Greek the trilingual pupil fell behind expectations, because of the grammatical approach. To smooth his educational progress, Mother engaged private tutors and dispensed lavish gift baskets at Christmas and Easter. Father kept silent about this purposeful appreciation of the monks' zeal; Ohli inappropriately quoted 'Beware of Greeks carrying gifts' considering the gift was carried to the Greek Master. Herta's outrage was not moral but envious, as the Krainer cornucopia could not begin in the year of her *Matura* and she had to pass her final high school exams on merit only.

Self-reliance merited a fine new mare, and Herta's white gelding passed to her brother. He enjoyed cantering along the Prater avenues under what he imagined to be the admiring glances of mere pedestrians. He followed his sister in gaining bronze medals in showjumping, while Father won silver cups in dressage as Austria's only equestrian family trio. One day the gelding's hind leg caught on a hurdle, bringing him down on the rider. Karl's broken collar bone healed quickly but after that he shunned obstacles higher than fallen tree trunks. Father remonstrated half-heartedly in uncharacteristic reluctance to impose remedial daring. Mother was openly pleased at the end to a dangerous sport, favouring skating and swimming which she herself had mastered.

———— ————

In recognition of his successful reorganisation, General Manager Fechtner was appointed Vice President of Krainer. The opening of branches in Berlin afforded a starting point for a Scandinavian holiday, to the delight of Mother's Nordics. Herta opted for an

International Summer Course in Geneva before entering the Vienna Consular Academy. The whole family became airborne the same day, she to Switzerland, the others to Germany in a large Junker easier on Karl's stomach.

Aunt Rosa joined them at the Adlon, to accompany Mother on shopping expeditions while Father presided over board meetings. Karl went photographing. While he was trying to get the *Reichstag* into a single picture, a well-dressed and well-spoken youngish man offered advice. The kind helper proposed meeting again in the afternoon, as Karl had to return to the hotel for lunch. The account of his exploits was received with remarkable coldness and meaningful glances. Aunt Rosa's 'I'm afraid this is to be expected in Berlin' caused Mother's 'You really must not talk to strangers', countered righteously 'But I didn't, he only helped me with a difficult shot'. Father's 'We'll drive to Potsdam in the afternoon, it's the right weather for a carriage ride through the park' showed an unexpected enthusiasm for this kind of locomotion.

————

The Nordics were as welcoming in Stockholm as in Oslo and over the delicious *Smörgåsbord* Karl gladly renounced any lingering asceticism. The Fechtners embarked on a cruise through the Norwegian fjords to the North Cape and a drive in the midnight sun to Finland. Shipboard acquaintances fussed much over Karl, and were impressed by the youngest passenger's knowledge of Scandinavian history. Copenhagen excelled in hospitality and sites; Karl was allowed to roam through the park of Hamlet's Elsinore but forbidden the Tivoli Gardens on his own, which astonished him more than the Danish Uncle.

A new Mercedes with the old driver took them to the Auer villa at Wittenberg. The age difference between the cousins remained unbridgeable, and Kurt's good health was annoyingly stressed. His elder brother and sister were away, studying music, which seemed strange in August. An exchange of glances stopped further inquiries as Karl had learned that he would not be given a straight answer.

The Wartburg spectacularly surpassed the stage set for *Tannhäuser*; the stain made by Luther throwing an inkwell at the devil thrilled Karl by its historical implications. Weimar was synonymous with Goethe, exciting Father's emotion and intellect. But his admiration for the poet's 'Earn what you inherit from your ancestors' was not shared by Karl, to whom inheriting seemed sufficient.

————

Suspected of malingering before, Karl set forth to school one morning despite a distinct belly ache. The pain became so severe that he asked for permission to go home. This was granted; but he was despatched on foot, accompanied by Franz Schmidt, since his Father was a physician. The two boys wondered if the German Master believed medical know-how to be hereditary. They did not pluck up enough courage to hail a taxi though Karl had sufficient money in his pocket. A spasm of vomiting occurred shamingly outside the house of Maria Jeritza, a frequent guest at the Fechtners', luckily then at the Metropolitan Opera. Franz inexpertly held his charge's head while assuming an expression that he hoped would distance him from a nasty mess round which the kind-hearted Viennese made a wide circle.

Mother sent the car for Uncle Doctor who diagnosed acute appendicitis, and arranged an immediate operation while cursing the stupid delay of the walk home. In all the excitement Franz was not forgotten; he was served a large slice of cake and presented with the first book at hand. Half-read, *White Magicians* was about Pythagoras and his insistence on chastity, and therefore suited for a boy studying classics. Returning to school after a leisurely stroll, Franz impressed his classmates with descriptions of Maria Jeritza shaking her blond curls in disgust at the mess below her windows as well as the gratitude of the Frau General Direktor. The book was leafed through and the discovery of some mildly unsuitable passages caused admiration for the donor.

As there had been no time to entice a celebrity into performing the operation, no complications ensued, yet the near escape from peritonitis provided an exciting aura of danger. Karl enjoyed the flowers, exceptional for a boy as the nurses assured him, and delayed getting up as long as possible. He had been collecting stamps for some years; first attracted by exotic colonial issues, he had only recently followed Ohli's advice to concentrate on Europe. He was flattered to be asked his opinion of a beautifully ordered album that contained not only the complete issues of the Imperial Austrian Post but also most irregularities in colours, print and perforation. The unique collection became his the following Christmas when the extravagant gift was justified not only by past but also new threats to Karl's health.

The death of some twenty infants in Hamburg drew world attention as much to the danger of vaccination as of the disease; Karl's thinness might indicate tuberculosis. X-rays revealed a slight shadow on one lung, quite common in a rapidly growing child but demanding certain precautions and plenty of fresh air. Fresh air meant to the Viennese the nearby Semmering and to this fashionable mountain resort headed the Fechtner Mercedes and two rickety sports cars favoured by the few Consular Academy students who could afford them.

Herta was popular among the potential diplomats whose main asset was a coronet; but the joke that for her humans began with counts was an exaggeration. Baron Willi Hollthal seemed a privileged contender, and he now led the cavalcade of titled young men wishing to curry favour with a generous hostess, her presentable daughter and, one at least, with the good-looking son. After a hearty meal the escort left with much blowing of horns and kisses while the three settled down to a wholesome fortnight of boredom. Herta soon rebelled against the peace and tranquillity, longed for holiday parties with her friends and joined them before the New Year. No chagrin for Karl, happiest alone with Mother; they skated on the hotel rink, went on sleigh rides through the enchanted snow-covered forest, and once listened to a popular zither player, but did not appreciate folklore in a smoke-filled room.

—— —— —— ——

Karl's frequent absences impressed masters and pupils very differently. He never caught up in his weak subjects; yet he had travelled farther by more varied means of transport, had won prizes in show-jumping, had nearly died because of the German Master's parsimony, was acquainted with famous actors, singers, writers and politicians, had more pocket money, was sometimes driven to school in the latest Mercedes model, yet was the youngest in his form. When social background increasingly separated the boys, he was naturally preeminent in the Upper Chamber formed by the class-conscious third of the Fourth Form imitating an Imperial institution of which they knew only by hearsay. The parents' standing was a sufficiently flexible guideline to allow the admission of Franz Schmidt on Karl's grateful insistence. They met during the ten o'clock break in an out-of-bounds corridor of the vast old building. As all spoke English or French, discussions were sometimes in a foreign language till the rising tide of National Socialism put an end to unpatriotic behaviour as well as to the solidly Monarchist sentiments; Archduke Otto remained Emperor to a minority. Politics eventually determined the merits of a film, play or book, influenced by actor or author being Jewish. The repute of *White Magicians* declined as only Franz continued to believe in the magic powers of chastity. Yet sex was hardly touched on, despite boasts of hand squeezing or even an unlikely kiss with girls from the dancing school where a once-dashing Hussar officer taught social graces.

Karl's prestige reached its zenith with headlines announcing 'General Director Fechtner Buys Landtheater'. Anton Bluhm, the director of Vienna's largest playhouse, tried to balance the huge fees of German guest stars by employing cheap local actors; but, though achieving artistic success, he unbalanced the accounts. The Landtheater Association could not shoulder the mounting losses which were paid off by Dr Fechtner when he purchased a majority of membership certificates and confirmed the management of Bluhm, a controversial figure on and off stage.

The shadow on Karl's lung necessitated summer vacations in Switzerland. Maloja was lovely in every respect, except for the icy water of the lake. Interchanges of visits with Aunt Rosa and her son on an equally chilly neighbouring lake were more enjoyed by the sisters-in-law than by the cousins, as Herta rated Kurt a ridiculously young dancing partner at afternoon teas. The open carriage rides in the rarified air might have contributed to the severe pain in the chest and the irregular heartbeat felt by Mother. The doctor blamed the attack on an injection tried out at Marienbad which drastically reduced body liquid; but the patient recovered quickly and laughed off the children's fears.

As the doctor insisted on a reduction of altitude, Mother compromised on the Tyrol, while Herta rejoined the International School in Geneva. Usually fond of company, Mother showed no interest in the other hotel guests and for a whole happy month lived only for her son. They walked through the woods to a small lake where swimming was a pleasure, they took funiculars to the surrounding peaks, they discussed the books they were reading and planned the plays and operas for the winter. Their isolation was idyllic, and subconsciously they resented Father's coming for their return to Vienna.

The closeness of summer continued in Vienna on all levels. Karl accompanied Mother to her schoolfriend, who had married the Lieutenant making the introductions in the Prater café. The couple had lived in the country till the husband finally succumbed to a war wound and 'Aunt' Charlotte – a participant in the Fechtner union naturally became a relation – employed her artistic talents in restoring furniture. Three Pekinese puppies had learned to respect the chair tapestries while one adorable bundle of beige fluff showed a marked preference for the boy, who fervently reciprocated. Aunt Charlotte's 'Such mutual puppy-love at first sight is more unusual than between school girls and dashing lieutenants' prepared the transfer of Toki on condition that beds remained out of bounds. Mother's quick agreement was decided by the probability of a garden where the Pekinese could prove that he was indeed housebroken.

The once-spacious flat had become inadequate for the expanding number of guests at multiple social functions. Among the bankers and industrialists reappeared the flamboyant financier, who brought his daughter as playmate for Karl. The swarthy girl was heiress to the lovely large *palais* her ruined father had been unable to sell and acquisition by betrothal was in the best Habsburg tradition; a hefty mortgage combined with the girl's looks to squash Granny's idea of aggrandisement.

In the deepening depression there was no lack of lovely *palais* for sale and Mother expertly assessed the potentialities of what she intended to make into Vienna's *Salon* of the 1930s. On a final survey she consulted Karl and they settled on a Biedermeier mansion, a twin of the adjoining Swedish Legation; and facing the Liechtenstein Gallery which housed the greatest private collection of pictures; across the Liechtensteinstrasse was Europe's greatest private picture gallery while the back garden abutted on the Consular Academy. On the raised ground floor, the parents' apartments occupied one side, Father's panelled study, the family dining room and Karl's quarters the other. A marble staircase curved up to the large dining room with yellow silk hangings, the Louis XV drawing room where Mother's collection of cut glass blended harmoniously with the furniture among which imitations only slightly postdated the originals; the semi-circular music room opened into the columned and panelled library; a curtain divided Herta's living room and bedroom, and the huge pink marble tub in her bathroom was even larger than Mother's. The back stairs ascended from the porter's flat, the kitchen and ample service facilities in the basement to the servants' quarters on the second floor, to which Granny's Biedermeier furniture had to be relegated for want of space. Modernisation of the central heating and the installation of telephones in every room delayed the move for several months.

To bring together businessmen and politicians who would not qualify for the *palais*, Father founded the Austrian Club which duplicated the structure of the Krainer concern; the same President in the seat of honour and the same Vice President in charge, pulling strings on the economic and artistic stage, tentatively even in politics. Fortune so favoured the Fechtners that Ohli quoted the tag about the jealousy of the gods.

———— ———— ———— ————

Sex raised a primitive rather than ugly head in the fifth form. A well-developed lad imparted his basic experiment with pleasure to his classmates in the hope that the manifestation of virility might link him to the Upper Chamber from which he, son of a wholesale butcher, was excluded. Having achieved a wanking acquaintance with his more accessible betters, he generously offered to bring Karl up to date. Though pleasurably excited by the real-life demonstration, the apprentice refused participation, which he feared might produce no tangible result, as he was a year younger. He promised, however, 'To have a bash at it at home and keep in touch'.

This inadvertently ambiguous wording was not put to the test, as the disseminator of glad tidings displayed his ware to the forlorn white magician. Chaste Franz revealed to the Upper Chamber a secret gratefully shared by most members, yet they were too cowardly to resist the demand for summary punishment. In the general consternation over the exposure, Franz bludgeoned two once-so-willing victims into joining his denunciation to the Headmaster. After the departure of the virtuous deputation, Otto Barovsky dared an aristocratic frankness. 'We are a lot of bloody hypocrites. Moral outrage about what we've been doing anyway. As if that rubbish about depravity wasn't enough, that loathsome toad went on about the indignity of rubbing shoulders – the idiot can't even get the parts of the body straight – with a butcher's son. As if old Schmidt were a grandee.'

'Yes, it's my fault he was admitted. But he took me home when I was sick.' Karl weakly parried the implied reproach; while the following was unanswerable.

'Your mother would give that fanatical halfwit the *White Magicians*!'

The Headmaster was probably aware of a superior social organisation judging by his sarcastic use of titles when a pupil committed a misdeed. He cut short Schmidt's vituperation, interrogated the culprit privately, and made him apologise to an embarrassed class for his misbehaviour. He was then ordered out, and this unprecedented expulsion shocked the boys into unnatural wariness.

After the shaming failure of sex, the school lavatory was used for smoking, practised in a like retreat at home. Smoke drifted out when Karl emerged before Father. 'Odd place for a cigarette. Better try a cigar after dinner.' Father never joked idly and offered a finely wrapped Havana to his son who coughed, turned green and rushed to the retreat. The experience was sufficiently traumatic to preclude a repetition, but Herta could not be treated equally tolerantly; girls never smoked, so eventually she consumed two packets of cigarettes a day. Wine, however, was indispensable at a civilised meal where vintages of grapes and actresses were discussed with equal interest. Karl was allowed an occasional sip but a full glass only at the last Christmas in the flat, a subdued occasion despite the usual lavish gifts.

———— ————

The Austrian Club increasingly claimed its Vice President's evenings, which Mother spent at concerts or the Opera. Once she stayed at home and coming into Karl's room took him into her arms, but to his anxious questions only replied that he was too young to understand. Even a young man who smoked and drank could hardly tell his Mother that he was aware of matrimonial upsets. 'Why don't we go away, just we two? We were happy in the Tyrol.'

The unexpected intuition brought tears. 'No, Karli, running away is never a solution. After all, it's better than his brother . . .'

'Uncle Karl?'

'Has Father been telling you? Of course not. Don't worry, I'm just over-tired from arranging the house. I'm getting a cold and shouldn't have come so close. But as I have already kissed you I might as well do so again. You are wonderfully understanding and now I'll be able to sleep.'

That, Karl doubted in his own sleeplessness. Mother had turned to him in her grief, which, naturally, she could not spell out. Mistresses were common enough, not only in history but in Vienna society, excusable when wives were dull or ugly. Mother was neither, the very opposite; Father was inexcusable yet one adventure might be forgiven. An adventure with whom? None of the female visitors could compare with Mother. He remembered her description of an actress 'Elle a du chien' and his silly mistake in believing that she really had a dog. Just then Toki scratched reproachfully at the bed he was not allowed to enter. Exceptional circumstances justified an outlet for tenderness, all concentrated on Mother while the dog was cuddled. Why was the case of Uncle Karl worse? Obviously something to do with sex, surely nothing sordid like the lavatory experiments of the butcher's boy, but several famous historical figures, let alone actors, were inordinately fond of their friends. Toki gave up the kissing attempts and preceded his master into sleep.

———— ————

The move to the *palais* was scheduled for Mother's birthday, but she decided on a change to Karl's, four days later. In between Herta received a string of pearls for her twenty-first feast which silenced any objection; her stay would in any case be temporary as her engagement to Willi Hollthal was to be announced at the house-warming party. Alone with the beds and the grand piano in the emptied flat, Karl became depressed by so clearly visible an end to his happy childhood. He tinkled a Mozart sonata, badly but it went well with his being a marquis. The mob had plundered his ancestral home, he would be taken to prison, kiss once more the hand of Marie Antoinette and then mount the tumbril. The fascinatingly morbid daydreams were interrupted by a cough. Mother's cold had worsened as she disobeyed Uncle Doctor's orders to stay in bed. 'How can a son of mine play so badly?'

Instead of an impossible explanation, Karl told his tale of the guillotine. Despite Herta's hints at schizophrenia, Mother quite enjoyed the elaborate fantasies he never intruded into reality.

———— ————

Karl failed to blow out the fourteen candles in one breath, a bad omen; emotionally and physically exhausted, the family went to bed early. Mother felt worse in the morning, but insisted on getting up as there was still so much to be done. In the afternoon she was running a temperature and complained of earache. Uncle Doctor was very cross that his orders had been flouted and called in Professor Neumann for consultation.

'Very naughty of you to disobey Doctor's orders. You must have felt considerable pain for some days.'

'Well, yes, but I had to get the house ready for Karl.'

Her husband thought it odd that she failed to add 'birthday' but seemed to imply possession. Preoccupied with her illness he refrained from commenting.

'Heroic, but now you have an otitis. The pus must be drained off, a perforation of the ear, all over in five minutes. And then you will kindly stay in bed.'

The following morning Karl wanted to kiss Mother goodbye before going to school. She raised herself in the large Louis XVI bed, stretched out her arms and called three times, 'My little boy.' She had not used this expression for years. Her voice was weak, her eyes shone feverishly, and the bandage added to Karl's alarm. He panicked, turned away, but somehow got to school and through the five lessons. The masters, remembering their recent Christmas baskets, left the obviously distraught boy alone. His friends had to be satisfied with a laconic 'Mother is very ill' and he wondered why he had said 'very' as he had not been told so. He felt no wish to confide in Ernst or Otto that he had failed the appeal of those outstretched arms, though he was haunted by the image.

On his return he was told by Mitzi that the *gnädige Frau* had been taken to the clinic. The *gnädige Herr* had left strict orders that she was not to be disturbed. Racked with self-reproach, Karl contemplated disobeying, but went through the usual routine of private lessons. Over dinner Father explained with ominous gentleness that the inflammation had spread to the membrane of the brain, that meningitis was a very dangerous illness, but Professor Neumann was looking after her.

So now the 'very' had come true, and that increased Karl's feeling of guilt; his own experience with the Professor, world-renowned or not, hardly inspired confidence. He was only prevented from rushing to Mother when told that he would not be admitted, but perhaps the next day. He finally cried himself to sleep.

Mother died without regaining consciousness. It was thought advisable to dispense with the customary leavetaking after an attempted reasoning that the after-effects of meningitis might be worse than death had provoked a paroxysm of weeping. That death should be preferable to permanent mental or physical disability seemed blasphemous cruelty. Withdrawing into his private world Karl evolved a subtle pattern of daydreams in which he sacrificed his youth to the care of an ailing mother. Yet the ignoble desertion of those outstretched arms that would never again enfold him constantly broke through the noble makebelief.

The senior Lutheran pastor conducted the funeral service at the crematorium chapel of the Central Cemetery. The Imperial Family and the government were represented among the throng of mourners, 'Everyone who is anyone' according to the obituary notices which made the children laugh hysterically without bringing relief.

———

Dying suddenly at thirty-nine, Mother had left no will and the children had never heard of legal entitlements. Herta was content with a solitaire diamond ring added to her trousseau, while Karl knew that the whole house was to be his and no singling out of the cut glass collection or other valuables was even thought of. His generous pocket money was increased to an allowance, mostly saved till the accumulation of a goodly sum. Stamps, a costly hobby, were often presents for which occasions were not lacking.

For religious consolation Karl tried the Capuchines, guardians of the Habsburg tombs, but his prayers seemed lost in the severe authority of the Church. Equal bareness had alienated him from

Protestantism, the Gothic beauty of the Cathedral would be more congenial. In the semi-obscurity of stained glass, candles flickered before a *pietà*, but the Mother mourning the Son reversed the role. Suddenly a sunbeam revealed a medieval sculpture of the Virgin in a dramatic similarity to a recent production of *Faust* in the Burgtheater. The ray of light had then made the prayer to the *mater dolorosa* superbly poignant and now brought emotional release and relief.

He had learned to pray and to ask for celestial intervention before indulging in his nightly speculations. The matrimonial upset must have been worse than Mother had allowed him to see. When it became unbearable, she took refuge with the exiled Empress Zita in Belgium. A romance was not ruled out, not with Emperor Otto who was Herta's age, but with a more mature Archduke who had commanded armies during the war. Before the Imperial claim Father withdrew, which exonerated him from his earlier misdemeanour.

To masters and friends at school Karl was the inconsolable son whose preference for being left alone during the ten o'clock break must be respected. On his lonely round two boys from an upper form expressed their condolences and invited him to the cinema in the afternoon. Karl did not know their names and shook his head in surprise and smiled enigmatically, which evoked the comment 'Nefertiti'. He was not aware of his embarrassed smile and failed to understand the allusion to the Egyptian Princess whose bust he recalled. Strange and no one to consult.

Father grieved so sincerely that Mother looking down from Higher Regions – to which she moved from Belgium with great ease – could not but forgive and the son gladly followed. Father was not demonstrative, but now he often put an arm round Karl's shoulders or squeezed his hand to indicate understanding.

———   ———

Together they rejected angels, obelisks and *stele* for the corner plot in the Central Cemetery, but Karl regretted that Father removed the baroque clouds from the sketch submitted by Professor Engelhardt. This fashionable representative of the Academic School was commissioned and achieved with the white marble headstone surmounted by a cross and flanked by two urns the simple dignity of which Mother would have liked. After the graveplate had been lowered over the ashes, the Professor remarked casually, 'I'd like to do a picture of the boy.'

No less surprising was Father's reply, 'Let's talk it over at lunch tomorrow.'

By then Karl's extravagant idea had been accepted. Father's willingness implied a favour to the artist. 'He is obviously not very busy just now to finish the tomb so punctually. If he's an equally good painter . . .'

Karl grasped the opportunity. 'May I choose the costume?'

'Riding togs, I suppose. Plus fours look a bit dreary on canvas and your evening suit seems too dressy.'

'Valois, please Father. Like the Clouets in the Museum.'

'Ohli shouldn't have given you all that Alexandre Dumas. The whole of Vienna would be laughing at Fechtner royal pretensions.'

'You've told Granny more than once that you don't care what people say.'

The quick repartee earned a grudging 'True, within limits. I can't recall any picture of a boy in modern clothes and the Valois costumes are certainly becoming, if the Professor agrees . . .'

He agreed emphatically. 'It's a pleasure to paint beautiful materials and colours. Garments have never been so devastatingly uninspiring. Flowers are a help with ladies, but Karl could hardly be holding a rose.'

The *Rosenkavalier* seemed a legitimate precedent, but Karl could not raise the point as the tutor was waiting. Herta likewise excused herself, fed up with her brother's glorification, so that Grandmother felt free to remark, 'I find it curious, Professor, that you didn't suggest painting the girl.'

The painter was sufficiently famous for a blunt 'The boy is more interesting. He is not just attractive, that dreamy look in his eyes is a challenge.'

'Perhaps Karl should have been the girl,' Grandmother reflected. Why did her son-in-law look so annoyed by this observation? Strange man, but he had always behaved correctly and was obviously heartbroken over Adele's death.

———

Artist and model scrutinised the Valois portraits in the Museum. They agreed on pearl-grey velvet for the embroidered doublet and the trunk breeches slashed with the same violet satin as the lining of the court cape only the Burgtheater tailor was able to fashion. The blond hair under the cap with an ostrich feather had grown to the maximal length acceptable at school where any teasing was squashed with a haughty 'It is for my portrait'. This stirred the envy which replaced the sympathy for bereavement; who had ever heard of a schoolboy being painted, and in regal fancy dress?

The artist enjoyed the sittings; he could concentrate on his untiring model without the need to amuse him with gossip, while the tapestry behind the lifesize figure, hand on the hilt of a dagger, afforded a splendid range of colour interchanges. Father forbade the publication of photos, but the picture was praised by art critics and attacked in the Nazi papers. The young subject of these artistic and political discussions was proud of his Valois semblance, but kept his affection for the simple picture of Mother by Uncle Doctor's sister.

———— ————

Mourning precluded attendance at the dancing class but not at the Burgtheater or Opera, to which the prettiest girl was sometimes invited. Dolly von Freyer's mother coyly hinted 'Such a pretty pair, a bit young of course.' The Upper Chamber ungenerously attributed Karl's success to an over-supply of marriageable Freyer daughters and love of the theatre rather than of the boy.

Herta could not attend balls, only small private gatherings where her fiancé-in-waiting introduced Count Maximilian Tarburg, a spectacular society bankrupt. On coming of age he had received a large estate, which he sold to finance his motor racing mania. The costly Bugattis accumulated no prizes, perhaps held back by the driver's size or his crushing debts. Good manners and superficial charm insufficiently hid his little learning and less wit, yet Herta was so obviously impressed that Willi's mother had to deploy all her diplomacy to maintain her son's position.

———— ————

At Easter Karl accompanied Father on a business trip to Paris, sad with memories. They met Herta at Marseilles to embark for Algiers in search of new surroundings. A gale was blowing and no sooner had the ship passed the historical Château d'If than Karl was sick over the railing before rushing to their state cabin. In the stuffy air Father was soon equally prostrate on the opposite bunk. When Herta at last descended, she muttered something about Vikings. Certainly she looked convincingly dishevelled. Her tactless reference to the dinner gong provoked waves of nausea, but too shy to face the Captain's Table on her own she grumbled herself to bed in the outer cabin. A particularly violent lurch was followed by a dull thud and muffled unladylike exclamations. Father dragged himself to a rescue he was in no state to effect, while Herta extracted herself from the pile of luggage that had caused more shock than bruises. Karl cited Divine Punishment for her lack of compassion and began praying for the ship to sink; to which Father only objected because of the hundreds of passengers and crew involved. 'On the flight to Marienbad you only wanted to end *your* misery.' Karl apologised for being too weak to jump overboard and limit the watery grave to himself.

The horrors of the night vanished in the brilliant sun at Algiers where they drove to the St Georges; the pseudo-Moorish rooms looked over the splendid bay and the food was all the better after the enforced fast. A guide was engaged for the kasbah, which presented basic Arab exoticism to a fascinated Karl. The crammed noisy lanes where flies covered the stringy carcasses hanging outside the butchers' stalls and festooned the eyes of begging children repelled Herta and she hurried ahead. This worried Father, but he demanded no amplification of the guide's 'It's the boy who needs looking after'; however, he cut short the absorption of local colour after his son dropped all his francs into the bowl held out by three blind beggars. Blindness added to dirt spoiled the sexual ambiguity for Karl.

In the afternoon he swam in the hotel pool under the far-from-envious glances of his elders. 'The water is almost as cold as in the Swiss lakes.' Herta busied herself with the tea on the terrace. 'Willi's mother is a darling, but he . . .'

'To prefer the mother-in-law to the future husband is somewhat unusual. Willi is your choice, I don't believe in interfering, and anyway you are over twenty-one.'

Encouraged by this friendly neutrality Herta dared 'What do you think of Max Tarburg?'

'I neither do nor want to. His father went through an enormous fortune through singular foolishness. Both are bankrupt, and you are supposed to be an heiress.'

——— ———

Despite the warning, Max became a regular at the Liechti, Herta's sensible abbreviation for Liechteinstrasse forty-nine or the House Fechtner of the private telephone switchboard. At a family lunch he was mildly amusing about racing and shooting, which gave the hostess an opportunity for another attempt on Father. 'Poor Max had such bad luck.'

'That's not what inheriting a large estate is usually called. Youth and his father's example are a poor excuse for stupid waste. Old Count Rudolf now lives in the porter's lodge of the Tarburg he can no longer afford to heat, while his eldest son built Austria's largest country house since the war on another slope of the mountain they once owned. No wonder they aren't on speaking terms. Hardly a family to be recommended.'

——— ———

One afternoon Father cancelled Karl's lessons and sent him to the grandparents without explanation. In Ohli's absence Granny failed to satisfy the curiosity by stating pompously 'Countess Henriette Neunhaus is calling.'

'If I were sent away each time Father has a visitor, I'd better move in with you. She isn't a headhunter by any chance?'

'Rather a manhunter' was the amazing reply Granny tried to cover with, 'That book of yours on Borneo; the photos of shrunken heads give me nightmares.'

'If the Neunhaus can shrink heads she can earn a fortune. What's all the mystery?'

'She is married and lives in Berlin.' After a pause 'She is Max's sister.'

'Even in Berlin some people are married.' Karl was bewildered. 'I've met Max's brother, so why not his sister?'

'Skeletons abound in the Tarburg cupboard' sounded odd so that Granny concluded, 'Now do your homework. Ohli will help you with Greek.'

— — — —

Passing beyond conventional help, Father invited the dreaded Classics Master to Pörtschach, where Ohli was chaperoning his grandchildren. The two elderly masters indulged in their tutorial reminiscences undisturbed by Granny, who had remained in Vienna to look after Toki and her son-in-law, neither in particular need. Aunt Rosa acted as Mother surrogate, but her manifest goodwill strained under Germanic stiffness which also prevented any intimacy with Kurt. His older brother and sister had suffered nervous breakdowns from studying too hard, an odd admission when Karl was constantly urged to study harder. Curiosity aimed at a more intriguing relative. 'Auntie, what happened to Uncle Karl?'

'He . . . was brilliant. He died young.' Hesitancy was unusual for the Luther Society's President.

'What did he die of? And brilliant, how?'

The second question provided an escape from the first. 'His thesis *The Last Valois* won a prize.' She remembered Karl's portrait of which she had received a photograph. 'I wouldn't mention it to your father who remembers his brother with great affection for assisting him financially through the university. God knows how little poor Karl earned as tutor to lazy boys like you.' This called for defence, and distracted from the unanswered question as Karl realised too late. His easy victory in the costume battle had, however, found an explanation.

— — — —

Herta, still round-faced but now slim, had to sort out her suitors, who summoned the clans and friends for support. She was the centre of attention at the fashionable hotel, whose owner allowed the Tarburgs special reductions as the ruin of Carinthia's foremost family was too recent to tarnish the ancient glamour. Even more because they kept the Fechtner business tied up. Max's Bugatti returned briefly, because the creditors believed the display might decide Herta. It did not, since she, like all her family, had no admiration for things mechanical.

The White Russian mother of Karl's chief playmate held a certain attraction due to a fatal novel describing the Red Terror. Her Tsarist credentials were vague, but the lady used Karl's romantic notions to get him into her bed. He was thrilled as well as disgusted by the expert initiation she wished to keep secret. The hide-and-seek amused Max. 'So you are the Spider's latest victim, not bad at your age. No need to be gallant, the Spider has earned her name. Not with me, of course,' was added as a precaution.

Clever makeup almost redeemed the face but nothing could disguise the sagging breasts and the flabby flesh of a woman nearly three times her partner's age. The triumph of conquest faded with usage and she departed unlamented to her husband in Berlin.

The revulsion favoured highbrow Yvonne Venteser, never seen without a bulky tome. Her bulkier mother was a heavier handicap, since it caricatured the slim elegance of the girl. Aunt Rosa and especially Herta disapproved of the unprepossessing Jewess who wanted to show off what was not really her daughter's catch. Yvonne was, however, almost beautiful and amusing despite her predilection for German philosophers; she was excellent company in the bathing establishment and at afternoon tea, but not among Herta's set in the restaurant or bar.

Convinced that a sixteen-pointer would clinch his son's engagement, Baron Hollthal invited the Fechtner children to his hunting lodge. Karl enjoyed the role of chaperon and the excuse of his bad eye, but resented the cold and stillness of the lookout. Herta trudged willingly through the autumnal forest and was allowed the first shot. The magnificent stag retreated unharmed setting his would-be assassin an example.

——— ———

Only the families and a few intimates attended Herta's marriage to Max in the Lutheran Church. To the chagrin of the old Countess Tarburg, Father insisted on a Protestant ceremony and had made it quite clear that settling the considerable debts of the bridegroom did not buy an unbreakable link. Max appreciated this generosity coupled with the purchases of an estate where he might atone for the mismanagement of his own domain. Herta had visions of a medieval castle, but Father rejected the costly folly of dank dark dungeon. To minimise the damage of Max's incompetence, Father bought the Altenhof in his own name. The woods, well-stocked with game, extended round the large comfortable country house in a lovely district less than a hundred kilometres from Vienna. The open-air swimming pool and the milking machine for the forty cows were among Austria's first, the horses could be exercised on fine meadows, but Karl kept his gelding in Vienna as he hoped to be spared the pleasures of the countryside.

According to her best friend, Herta returned from her Sicilian honeymoon like one of Queen Victoria's daughters 'She is as she was'. Whether Max had diverted some of the funds intended for the journey to his Hungarian mistress was so openly gossiped about that Herta over-reacted as Lady of the Manor the Altenhof was not.

MERCILESS MORNING

1

Karl soothed the jealousy over his triumph with the Spider by honest descriptions of the flabby flesh. Otto's response was 'Nobody could accuse the butcher's boy of that. Nor us, come to think of it. Let's go to the Diana Bad this afternoon, we'll take a cubicle.'

Erotic fantasies had long weakened boyish shyness; a handsome partner was vastly preferable to solitary practices; and so was the passionate embrace accompanying the orgasm to the chaste kisses with the dancing class girls. Fulfilled, without any feeling of guilt, they raced each other in the pool, rode the artificial waves and before dressing lust was again gratified. Otto's good sense hedged the enjoyment. 'We shouldn't be seen too much together or your friend Franz might kick up another virtuous stink.'

'That toad is no friend of mine. We aren't molesting and importuning, or whatever that peculiar expression is.'

'The very opposite, you show too much sentiment. No romantic claptrap of Achilles and Patroclus, you started it with your talk about the White Russian bitch. Girls aren't haveable, whores are too expensive or have clap if not worse. The buffet advertisement "Clean, No Frills" puts it admirably for our kind of fun.' Otto was older and called the tune.

In pursuit of camouflage, Otto introduced his friend to a distant cousin described as 'Quite a girl!' A just appraisal of Lis von Granera, blond, chubby, her excellent complexion emphasised by a sensual mouth. It was friendship at first sight in their readiness to laugh at themselves as quickly as at others. Lis found it hilarious to be intended as a blind, and made pointed remarks about a relationship which she soon divined and approved.

Lis's father was reputedly the illegitimate son of a prince and, though possessed of several university degrees, had lost his wife's money in unnecessarily shady deals. An occasional cinema was the limit of the Graneras' entertainment, so that visits to the opera and theatres were an expected bonus for Lis. She and Dolly were frequent guests in the Fechtner box at the Landtheater with Otto making up the foursome.

Karl enjoyed playing host to his friends, but the box was also a reward for a classmate, Paul Zabeh, who increasingly covered up his shortcomings in Greek and Maths. The Classics Master was slightly deaf while the Maths Master felt obliged to inspect the back of the class when Karl struggled with an equation on the blackboard. Paul's promptings were worthy of a professional and staved off the worst. No such assistance was available to Ernst. Despite this, the boy remained stoically amiable, aware that Krainer gift baskets were beyond the Häussermann means. He even prevailed on his father to extemporise from the stage, 'The letters from Fechtner and Barovsky have arrived' and thus overwhelmed his friends by their being named in the Burgtheater, a signal tribute that swept aside all Otto's caution.

Fechtner involvement with actors varied in form and substance. Early one morning Karl surprised Father saying goodbye to the Burgtheater's *jeune premier* and two remarkably handsome ladies whose stage experience told in their immediate '*Qu'est qu'il est mignon*' and similar endearments. No less prompt, Karl praised the elegance of their *evening* dresses and as it was such a nasty *morning* would they ask Father to let him stay home? The request was granted by a silent nod and Karl went back to bed. Satisfaction with exploiting Father's embarrassment turned into self-reproach for a betrayal of Mother, who would no longer want him in her arms. He was not sure whether 'unfaithful' could be applied to a widower, but certainly to a conniving son. He had bargained away the required tacit disapproval for the comfort of the warm bed. He rather than Father had to feel ashamed.

———

Herta often came up from the Altenhof and stayed in her rooms at the Liechti. She was mixing a cocktail and offered a glass to her surprised brother. 'To soften the shock. Father will probably marry that Burgtheater actress who has been much in evidence lately.'

Karl refrained from flaunting the strong evidence of the two French actresses. 'She has been suspiciously nice to me, but isn't she married?'

'So what? It's a Protestant marriage like mine. Her husband is an excellent producer but older than Father and, after getting her into the Burgtheater, has outlived his usefulness. She is convincing in stage drawing rooms and we could do worse in the Liechti.'

Karl shared the favourable opinion of the actress but not of a prospective stepmother. He changed the subject. 'Why wasn't Max's sister asked to your wedding?'

'Henriette lives in Berlin. She isn't on the best of terms with her family.'

Karl remembered having been sent out of the house on Henriette's only visit. 'The plot thickens. She must play a particularly gruesome part in the Tarburg saga.'

'My mistake for giving you a drink. Behave at least to our not improbable stepmother.'

Good manners were all the easier to a lady so patently anxious to please, almost like Mother's Nordics. After her very regal Mary Stuart in Schiller's drama, Karl's objections weakened less because of her much-admired performance but because the unfortunate Queen had been married to a Valois and that would somehow 'fit in'. But then 'A new star outshone the old,' according to Granny. Professor Neumann recommended his niece, a student at the Reinhardt Seminar, for an audition at the Landtheater. Tania Reichenbach was also preparing her thesis on Botany, Father's subject, while it did no harm that she was a tall dark beauty, half a year younger than Herta. Anton Bluhm recognised an interest deeper than university studies and cast Tania maliciously as Mary Stuart in a Sunday afternoon performance for schoolchildren. Karl ignored so lowly a theatrical event and despite the only review dwelling on Tania's stunning looks, he would have judged her a poor second for a leading Fechtner role. Even when Mitzi informed him that there had been an overnight guest Karl smiled tolerantly; glamorous French actresses had spent a night and disappeared.

— — — —

After Hitler became German Chancellor in January 1933, the militias of the extreme right and left found an easy recruiting ground among the vast number of unemployed. In the worst peacetime winter Vienna had ever suffered, General Director Fechtner persuaded fellow industrialists to set up an Emergency Relief Fund, heading the list of contributors. The conservative and liberal press praised this truly Christian generosity, while the Socialists attacked any private initiative on principle. The Nazis thrived on hunger and poverty; thus the full fury of party propaganda turned against 'The Christian generosity of non-Aryan outsiders', insinuating ludicrously sinister motives. Race not religion designated the Jew, and the initiator of the Fund was the main target.

The Schotten Gymnasium was not immune to racial fanaticism, which provided an outlet for the virtuous inferiority of Franz

Schmidt. His hostile allusions to Karl were laughed away in the Upper Chamber where marriage to a Jewish heiress was accepted as the natural solution to financial problems. The poorer pupils, envious of Fechtner wealth, were more amenable to a display of Nazi fervour. When Otto was absent because of a cold, Schmidt organised a few boys into shouting 'Jew, Jew' below the meeting place of the Chamber whose members slunk away unmolested. Karl remained behind, alone, deserted by all his friends, stunned by the unsuspected hatred. Snowballs were aimed at him but the bell rang and the band dispersed.

Karl's later return to class passed apparently unnoticed by the Classics Master, yet it was he who prevented the boy from locking himself in the lavatory during the ten o'clock break the following day. The rescuer refrained from any comment on the way to the Abbot, who asked Karl to sit down, an unprecedented favour at an exceptional private interview. Without referring to the incident, the Abbot discoursed on the regrettable violence of youth, how he had been pelted with snowballs during an anti-clerical riot at the university which in retrospect seemed almost funny. Not to his listener, raw with the shame and agony of being called a Jew, a monstrously wrong insult. Realising the insufficiency of discreet compassion, the Abbot provided practical support; he led Karl back to the class where he stated that the Cardinal Archbishop had praised Dr Fechtner's initiative as truly Christian charity.

Far from accepting defeat, Schmidt flaunted a swastika in his buttonhole, amidst eager anticipation of dramatic developments. The German Master was too diffident to raise the issue, but the Headmaster wrenched out the emblem and threatened expulsion if Schmidt disgraced himself again. Unanimous satisfaction hailed this retribution, no other Nazi belonged to the Upper Chamber which made for a certain solidarity with the equally excluded butcher's boy when the erstwhile persecutor came close to a similar fate. Karl was handed a moral victory, the classmates were unnaturally considerate, but the shock of the terrible isolation left behind an unconscious distrust which stopped further meetings of the Chamber. Otto did not mention the incident but his unusual tenderness on their next visit to the Diana Bad was a better proof of sympathy than words.

———— ————

Enlightenment came unexpectedly from Herta. 'Roebucks under century-old trees' she read from a paper. 'Poor old Toki under a rosebush, anyone can look through the fence, the wretches must be blind. The Nazi idiocies are not quite so easily disproved, even though only our paternal grandfather was . . . Jewish.'

The unpalatable clarification had to be comprehensive. 'And Grandmother? I know she came to Vienna before I was born, but did she wear her baptismal certificate round her neck instead of pearls?'

'You are dumber than your age warrants. This concerns you too.' She ascribed her brother's blush to shame for his thoughtlessness. 'Her maiden name was Ochsenstern, which sounds rather . . . off-putting. But the Regent for Queen Christina was called Oxenstjerna.'

'Where does the old Swede come in? Our beloved Grandmother lived several generations and countries removed.'

'The Oxenstjernas were among the greatest Swedish families and one of them might have accompanied Charles XII to the Balkans.'

'And you had the nerve to say that *I* was schizophrenic! I didn't credit you with so much historic ingenuity.'

———————

Perhaps the incident had been reported to Father, as the Abbot and later the Cardinal were asked to the regular Thursday Luncheons, which continued Mother's mix of artists, writers and politicians. These luncheons became famous for the quality of the conversation, food, drink and the hand-made cigars, while the inclusion of the two clerics among the rotating dozen did Karl no harm at school.

Lis provided a more personal morale booster by introduction to what she called 'the legitimates'. Voltain paternity of a Granera could be no more than surmised, but lack of precision only spiced the friendship between a possible and a probable granddaughter. Princess Marie Louise had not finished her novitiate when her vocation crumbled in the austerity of the Cloistered Carmelites, but she preserved her faith as well as the looks and humour resembling that of her cousin presumptive. Lis rightly judged that a princess of his own would please Karl whose casualness when referring to Max's princely mother and sister-in-law had been overdone.

———————

Aristocratic connections held the balance against non-Aryan relatives. 'My sister has resigned from the Luther Society and Uncle Siegfried from the Chemical Works. They've moved to a very pleasant district in Berlin. Kurt is studying Chemistry in Zurich, so when this Nazi madness is over he can take his father's position.' Father paused, but this was somehow not the moment to ask after the two older cousins. 'How did you get on with Max's brother last summer?'

'Oh Eugen is all right, but two months at Pörtschach is too long with anyone. Mother also preferred the sea.'

'It's natural that you are still influenced by Mother's preferences,

but you must begin making your own choices, Karl. I've no objection
to a beach with Ohli in July.'

'Rimini, please. The Malatestas were a marvellously gruesome
family. There are many books and even an opera about them.'

'Trust you to choose a holiday because of gruesome rulers. Can't
you do better?'

'I've got a folder from the Italian Tourist Office, kilometres of
golden sand, an ideal centre for excursions.'

'I'm glad to hear of some practical reasons behind your historical
obsessions. Ohli enjoys travelling about, Granny doesn't and neither
do I really.' A stern look commanded the son not to bring up past
journeys. 'I'm quite content to spend a few weeks on the Altenhof.
Eugen will keep an eye on you at Pörtschach and bring you back to
Vienna. I'll try him out as private secretary.' An exchange of glances
doubted the wisdom of this appointment. 'He'll have your rooms.'

'And I'll sleep with the roebucks under century-old trees.'

A quick smile acknowledged the reference to the Socialist description. 'I suggest you move into Herta's quarters. She won't be coming
up so often, Max needs her.' Again a look that forbade the obvious
'What for?' The dialogue was as remarkable for the spoken as for the
unspoken.

———————

Rimini's fine beach resembled the photo in the folder. In his smart
two-tone bathing costume and white bathing cap Karl was swimming
far out when two older boys cavorted and dived ever closer. They
tried Italian but followed him into French – insufficient, however, to
express their admiration of the latest in beachwear, two round openings on the sides. In the plunging their fingers strayed wilfully to the
exposed flesh while they gabbled an invitation to *Romeo and Juliet* at
the cinema. Their 'Ah, so much love' sounded more purposeful than
the two older schoolmates' 'A film will do you good' and he accepted
on reaching land. Despite their gooseflesh, the Italians were promi-
nently excited, and Karl's sex was likewise unmistakable in the
tightly fitting suit. The two gasped and scuttled away, thereby
arousing Ohli's curiosity. 'Trying to make a date, hm. In this silly
bathing cap you look like Mother at your age. The poor boys must
have got a nasty shock on realising . . .'

Karl had no intention of giving up the cap and not solely because
he disliked the salt water in his hair. During the siesta he indulged
in the restricted practice of 'So much love' to hand. The open-air
cinema in a medieval courtyard, more genuine than the film set,
would have offered the right opportunities had those silly Italians not

been so single-minded. Feeling perhaps that he was a poor substitute, Ohli entertained his grandson with memories on the way to the hotel. 'At high school we played *Romeo and Julius* in an ingenious translation, all references to love eliminated. Brother Lawrence's dotty schemes remained incomprehensible till the only pupil who knew sufficient English interpreted from a Shakespeare in the school library. Poor Julius never lived it down.' Did he really add an almost inaudible 'Perhaps he didn't want to'?

Art and history should ideally have complemented sex, but now had to fill the void. The mosaics of Ravenna inspired Karl's second literary attempt, in which the Empress Theodora sent a black rose to guardsmen that caught her fancy and had them stabbed on completion of their task. Ohli recommended changes in the purple prose but his grandson was too proud of expressions like 'nymphomaniac', unjustly extended in conversation to certain actresses.

A long-distance call from Father delighted the Rimini pair with the proposal of a week in Rome. They shared a contempt for organised tours and planned their itineraries according to architectural and historic criteria. The visual impressions then confirmed Ohli's knowledge and inflamed Karl's imagination. As the last Roman Emperor, a boy his own age, he tried not to resist but to seduce the Barbarian chief, for the good of the country, of course. Cesare Borgia had murdered his brother and raped his sister when not much older, but incest was marvellously resistible. Best of all, Ohli listened interestedly to the daring fancies, provided dates and setting were respected. Facts came first, followed closely in the family tradition by food and drink, over which the age gap was bridged by sympathetic understanding. 'I told your mother not to worry about your fantasies, but don't overdo them. I never objected to mental acrobacy, unlike most teachers – as for instance the one floating in the wine-dark sea just now.'

'That's a Homeric epithet, so you must mean the Classics Master, but I didn't know he could afford a trip to Greece.'

'Only by courtesy of your father.' Ohli cleared his throat. 'I wasn't aware he hadn't told you, more discreet than I. He consulted me about another invitation to Pörtschach but Greece seemed preferable. You can look after yourself, but a Benedictine monk and Eugen . . . Would you like to stop in Venice on the way back?'

'No, please. Mother loved it and Paris was so sad without her. I chose Rimini which she didn't know; Father understood, as Rome is also *terra incognita*.'

——— ———

During the brief stop at Pörtschach, Ohli handed the boy not to

Eugen but to Herta, whose childhood lisp had ominously returned.
'I want to give Ohli a kiss and to thank him for putting up with that
extra week at Rome. Max is waiting at the car. You have your old
room, wash and change. Then we'll have a little chat.

'Gloom and doom, like in a Greek tragedy. Not that washing and
changing featured.' Unconcerned with incomprehensible father talk,
Max drove them to the hotel.

'So you have Mother's suite. Ohli was wonderful but I missed her
terribly.'

Herta's unexpectedly compassionate 'That doesn't make it any
easier. I'm not much good at this' ended lamely in 'I've been asked
to tell you . . . Father got married.'

The shock was made all the more shattering by the realisation that
he had been bought off with the week in Rome and the Master's
Greek holiday. 'The actress?'

'The wrong one. Tania Reichenbach, of all the unlikely . . . She
is half a year younger than I, and you are to call her Tania.'

'I won't call her anything, at least not to her face. I won't talk to her.'

The apprehensions that such a resolution was futile reversed
recent patterns. In Italy Karl had shunned places connected with
Mother, now he sought them out. Pörtschach lacked the memorable
closeness of that wonderful month in the Tyrol, but that was too far
away. Second to the memory of having Mother all to himself was
Mother as the centre of the whole family. Karl took the lake steamer
to Maria Wörth, lit a candle in the Church often visited with Mother,
but established no spiritual communication. A lookalike of Toki
might be a sign, especially when accompanied by Aunt Charlotte.
'Your mother recommended Maria Wörth for a quiet holiday and
I'm not disappointed. But then she never disappointed anyone . . .
Everything we possessed went on my husband's illness and, apart
from breeding Pekinese, I was only good at needlework. Few could
afford pedigree dogs during the Depression, so your mother paid for
a course in tapestry renovation. I repaired your lovely Louis XV
chairs, I wish though I hadn't.' She smiled at Karl's obvious bewilderment, 'I haven't done such a bad job but . . . perhaps I shouldn't
tell you, I tried to warn Adele, it's an unlucky house. Let's hope her
death broke the run of back luck.' She had obviously restrained a
stronger expression. 'You have all my best wishes and blessings. Here
is my card, if you ever need me . . . It's unlikely but I would be so
very glad to repay your mother.'

——— —— ——

Mother had responded immediately by sending Aunt Charlotte, but this was not the assistance desired by Herta. 'Pekinese and tapestry are not much use against Tania. Too many spurious aunts and uncles.' She wiped away the rebuke. 'I'm playing tennis with the Infanta tomorrow. Would you like to be introduced?'

The next day Herta's perceptible headshake ordered his refusal of the proposed set. 'How very kind of Your Royal Highness, but I don't play as well as my sister' gratified Herta by an understatement. Austria's Davis Cup Champion coached those who gilded his racket, yet gladly stopped his training after a week, unaware that his pupil's clumsiness was due to defective sight.

Eugen never insisted. 'Your papa asked me to keep an eye on you and that hardly includes tennis. He was, however, quite specific about Greek and Maths of which I know less than you, so . . .' Comprehension was less perfect on the next topic. 'No loss the Spider hasn't turned up. But that good-looker Yvonne, what about an evening out?'

'How good are you on German philosophers? Your title won't get you anywhere with Yvonne, but talk learnedly on Schopenhauer . . .' Eugen could not talk learnedly on anything, let alone someone he had never heard of. Accounts of his failed intellectual and sexual attempts reached Karl from both sides, as Yvonne was more relaxed than previously. She and Karl were 'The prettiest couple on the floor', rare praise from the manager of the hotel bar, a former Hussar Major notorious for his outspoken appraisals. After this accolade they were asked to Herta's table, drank a little more and tumbled into bed together. The protagonists enjoyed the once-only fling, but Mrs Venteser planned hopefully for the following summer.

——— ———

Back in Vienna Father's jocularity thinly overlaid his embarrassment. 'I trust you've outgrown the fairytales about wicked stepmothers. Not a part for Tania, she'll be more like a sister. She realises the difficulty of adjustment and won't interfere.'

Tania's intelligent interest in Rome helped over the awkwardness of the first family meals, but her ignorance of Fechtner *mores* occasionally upset even her husband. She entered, however, into her stepson's ingenious avoidance tactics but, inevitably, one day he almost collided with her on leaving the music room. He muttered an excuse for nothing he had done and she responded with 'Your Father tells me you are very musical.'

'If you heard me play, you wouldn't think so' was unfortunately true, but her amazing 'Then your piano lessons are a waste of money' had to be put straight immediately. 'If anything, a waste of time.'

Bewildered by the rebuke she switched to 'Why is *Burmah House* written in English under the street number of the Liechti?' The question afforded Karl an opportunity to assert a proprietary attitude. 'The town hall has no idea. They even sent a man to verify, as if we had made up the name. Changing the plaque requires so much red tape that Father gave up, though Burmah is the last country with which he was likely to be connected.'

Tania did not interfere. A strangely unsure Father suggested concentration on the school subjects by 'release' from the other private lessons. Karl relinquished the piano without much regret but retained English and French; less by enumerating the literary studies than by one pointed reference to the two lovely actresses: '*I* don't get enough practice in French.'

Tania's absurd penny-pinching contrasted disturbingly with Mother's generosity. 'Typical of Mother not to mention that she paid for Charlotte's training. God only know how many lame ducks she helped out.' Granny was pleased when Karl offered to make Charlotte Schupp another regular for the Landtheater box.

——— ———

Otto's 'What whoring about this summer?' was less a question than an introduction to his own exploits. 'I no longer qualify as *virgo intacta*, though there were doubts after you so shamelessly seduced me. But we won't go into that. I followed your lead into the Third Reich, not a White Russian like yours but a genuine member of the German Maidens Organisation. The beloved Führer has ordered them to produce babies so no precautions are required. No wonder the Nazis are popular with young males, including my brother. The pater nearly threw him out and my mama, cautious lady, thought the SS connection might be useful one day. I feel quite randy remembering my Valkyrie. The Diana Bad this afternoon?'

'No longer necessary.' Karl enjoyed the effect of the apparent refusal. 'Bed is more comfortable, I've moved into Herta's room. We won't even have to lock the door, Father is a great respecter of privacy. Everybody has to be announced by house phone.'

The twelve telephones were much talked about by Vienna, but not the comfort of the large bed; or so at least Otto hoped.

——— ———

The changes in the Liechti's guest list were so gradual as to justify Karl's 'All Quiet On The Home Front' paraphrase. The famous playwrights had died, Felix Salten was the outstanding author. Some of Mother's intimates were dropped but not replaced by Tania's. Apparently she possessed none or they were perhaps not drawing-room-broken. Sheathed in gold lamé that ostentatiously emphasised her dark beauty, she was a feast for the eyes and tongues of ever fewer friends and more acquaintances. The step-grandfather, a discreetly humorous physician, and his vivacious wife would have been gladly accepted among the nominal uncles and aunts had they not been Tania's parents. The poisonous politeness between real and step-mother while their husbands chatted amiably would have inspired Schnitzler, but Karl never became reconciled to the intruders.

Great German actors, mostly exiled, starred at the Landtheater and the Liechti. A Berlin cabaret idol brought the house down with a song about 'Countess X, the tall blond beauty . . .'

> 'Then she has a big game hunter
> While favouring a negro punter
> It's rumoured that her sexuality
> Comprises Lesbian immorality.'

In the interval the Director reported at the box of the principal shareholder, who expressed disapproval of 'That silly song'. Anton Bluhm smiled maliciously, 'It's more interesting to those who know that Countess X is no other than Henriette Neunhaus.' This explained a lot, but the precautions against Max's sister still seemed excessive.

Yet Father imposed another mysterious exile in so impatient a voice as to discourage all questions. 'You just have time to dress for *The Land of Smiles*. The driver will take you to the grandparents, with whom you are spending the night, so prepare some clothes for school.' Father rang off.

The grandparents had no clue to the improvised enjoyment of a typical Léhar unhappy end. The performance, especially the marvellous tenor, dominated the conversation at supper. 'Tauber's voice holds up remarkably well but his hands are crippled with arthritis. In this part he can at least hide them in the sleeves of his Chinese robe. The wear and tear of age are not as easily cured as Max's rheumatic punishment for duck shooting. They took the cure at the same spa to the utter disgrace of Herta.'

'Surely he can do better,' was the brother's uncharitable comment.

Granny tutted while Ohli looked agreement. 'Max was sitting in the mud, not with Herta, you are getting too fresh, she was keeping him company. Someone was singing in the next cubicle and, as she can't tell Verdi from Wagner, she asked the bath attendant to stop it. He returned Tauber's visiting card with "Compliments to a connoisseur".'

——— ———

'The Head suggested or rather insisted that I should not come back after the Christmas break. No, nothing like the butcher's boy, just Greek and Maths. You are kept afloat by History.'

Decent of Ernst not to mention the substantial lifebelts of gift baskets and journeys. 'What now? The Jesuits are stricter.'

'A good Lutheran might look beyond monastic schools. The Reinhardt Seminar, where for a change I have some pull through my father. What bliss to do Greek tragedies in German. Let's go skating.' He climbed into the bus that stopped in front of them. This was not Karl's first venture on public transport but he had never paid. Offering a ten Schilling note for a fare that amounted to less than one, he told the conductor to keep the change; the sensible man did so, after a hard look at the boy who had no idea of the sensation he had caused.

'The conductor was ready to throw his coin tray into Karl's face as the passengers anticipated.' Ernst's account showed him a promising actor. 'The obvious ignorance of the common ways restrained him to muttering something very ungrateful and be gone.' Fechtner lore had received a popular addition.

——— ———

In February 1934 the Socialist militia rose in armed revolt and surrendered to the Army and Prince Starhemberg's Home Defence Corps only after days of bitter fighting. The Republic expired in blood and was replaced by a Corporate state that outlawed political parties. This cut a link with the parliamentary tradition of the Empire and might impede a Habsburg restoration, the only alternative to Hitler's expansionism. Dr Fechtner had always opposed Socialism and was closely associated with the small centre party whose leader resigned from the government. Starhemberg, Max's cousin, took his position as Vice Chancellor, but political influence through in-laws was unpalatable.

Like most of his classmates Karl admired Starhemberg, 'The worthy descendent of Vienna's defender against the Turks' as quoted ad nauseam by the press. If some Tarburgs were notorious, they were also related to the famous; Starhemberg was definitely a name to be dropped, all the more as the Prince's liaison with a Burgtheater actress was in the Imperial as well as in the Fechtner tradition.

Disentangling the Tarburg financial imbroglio, Father reinstated the old Count in his ancestral home now owned jointly with Max and the German branch of the family. Eugen obtained valuable agricultural property for which he departed unlamented.

As Granny refused to release Ohli for another summer, nobody would 'keep an eye' on Karl who opted for Dalmatia. Otto or Lis would have been ideal company but lacked the means; inviting them, like Ernst in Mother's day, was opposed by Tania as extravagant; Yvonne was a pleasant last resort with Mrs Venteser lending respectability, a term rarely applied to that lady.

The hotel on the coast had once been an Imperial villa, which acted like a magnet on Yugoslav politicians. A ministerial offspring taught Karl a thing or two, including poker, in which the apprentice's bad luck was so persistent that Mrs Venteser began keeping an eye. She quickly stopped the cheating apparent to anyone but a well-brought-up boy, who broke with the culprit; regrettably, as this ended more games than one.

Mere cheating by the son of a Succession State Minister paled into insignificance before a particularly brutal murder in the Austrian heartland. A gang of Nazis occupied the building from which the Empire had been ruled; they refused the severely wounded Chancellor medical assistance so that he slowly bled to death. Starhemberg played again a decisive part in defeating this second upheaval and preventing the Anschluss. Though the very existence of their country had been threatened, Father advised by phone against a premature return and the three Austrians went on the planned cruise of the Dalmatian islands. Nostalgic comparisons with the Norwegian fjords eased under the difference of companions and setting, but most by the additional four years that had witnessed such fundamental changes. The Ventesers were a convenience, Karl was a social asset in an unsentimental exchange.

—— —— —— ——

The revulsion against Nazi brutality isolated Franz whose *rapprochement* attempt was, however, rebuffed. In the last year at school Paul extended oral prompting to cribs, to complement the increased cramming by private tutors. Yet the basic necessities of reading, riding and the theatre were irreducible and even encouraged when Father took Karl to Ibsen's *Ghosts* and afterwards to supper. 'I chose the play to help you understand the misfortune of the two older Auer children. Both were exceptionally gifted, musical talent is sometimes allied to hereditary . . . insanity.' Beethoven's syphilitic deafness provided connection with genius. 'As in the play, the symptoms increased with maturity and both are now in an institution.'

'And Kurt?'

'You are old enough to know the truth though only parents can understand the tragedy of incurable children, especially when they feel responsible. Both longed for a healthy heir and sensibly decided that Aunt Rosa should have a child by another man, a difficult choice.'

'Some royal dynasties should have been equally sensible. Did they choose an Olympic champion?'

Father understood the allusion to the champion bull recently employed on the Altenhof. 'It might be put more elegantly, but the choice was much odder. Do you remember the Catholic priest with the Auers in Switzerland?'

'Well . . . and Aunt Rosa President of the Luther Society!'

'As a priest he was unlikely to claim paternity and the Auers wanted the child to be theirs without any fear. Kurt had to be told, so that he shouldn't be afraid of sharing the fate of the older pair.'

The frankness seemed promising for a clean sweep of family mysteries. An exchange of glances asked and refused the answer. Uncle Karl was not to be brought up.

He was brought up by Granny among a subject of more immediate interest. 'Perhaps it was to pay off the debt he owed his brother that Father repaired the organ.' To avoid misinterpretation, Ohli elaborated. 'The organ of the Schotten Church required extensive repairs. You were not to be told, as it might impede your last-minute zeal in Greek.'

'Decent of Father and it all helps. But I'm still scared stiff of the *Matura*.'

The dreaded examination confirmed the uneven performance at high school. The thesis in Geography, written by the Krainer research department, received high credit; Paul conveyed the minimal Greek and Maths acceptable; Karl contributed an excellent German composition and astounded the examiners by his knowledge in History.

The passing of the ordeal relaxed the 'No Frills' rules prior to the *Matura* dinner. 'Why do we have to celebrate with chaps we have hardly spoken to at school? The enjoyment is about equal to the Science exam I nearly flunked. I'd rather stay in bed . . . By the way, I tried once more for our grand tour but there isn't enough spare cash.'

'Bloody shame, Otto. I've been looking forward to confounding the natives with our oh-so-fluent Greek. It won't be the same with Yvonne.'

'Rather her than the morons I'll be travelling with. The pater will cough up enough for Greece on the cheap, so we can meet in Athens. Let's sit in that divine tub of yours before facing said morons.'

44

Otto had misjudged the reluctance to end an association of so many years. The dinner's awkward jolliness saddened into the realisation that the promises of keeping in touch simply meant the annual reunion, at least between the dinner jackets of the Upper Chamber and the dark suits of the majority. All, however, ate and drank too much, rejected adjournment to a brothel not on moral but financial grounds, and maudlinly delayed the final goodbye.

No taxis at this late hour and after parting from Otto Karl felt first dizzy and then sick. Perhaps it was the punishment for rebuffing Franz again at the dinner; even the Toad would have been welcome in the misery of vomiting as on the day of the appendicitis. Why should anyone want to get drunk? So nauseating an experience would not be repeated nor even related to the family.

2

Mothers, or rather the absence of, coloured the grand tour. Yvonne doubly enjoyed the journey without hers, Karl missed his especially amidst the decaying grandeur of Istanbul, recalling the eighteenth-century engravings they had looked at together. She had admired the superb skyline of oriental dreamland and a voice from the past used her very expression on the ship pulling away from the harbour. Willi Hollthal explained that he had replaced a legation secretary at Ankara and was returning 'to equally humble duty in Athens. Why didn't you let me know . . . a singularly stupid question even for a diplomat. The Consular Academy will be doing the same to you, Karl.'

'No, we haven't enough money' provoked a hilarity rare when the *meltemi* is blowing.

'The Tarburgs can't have ruined you that quickly!'

'I couldn't keep up the Liechti on the salary of a Minister. Father decreed Law and when I dared mention History he blanched with rage.'

'And you are turning an interesting shade of green. Herta told me of your prayers for the ship to sink on the crossing to Algiers, kindly refrain from similar exhortations. Try these pills against seasickness and in an emergency you are close enough to the railing. Yvonne and I will withdraw discreetly.'

Willi drove the pair from dingy Piraeus to the hotel in the centre of Athens and called for them in the evening. 'The Minister gave me the Legation car for an excursion to Delphi and asks you to dinner.

He isn't a career diplomat but was a deputy of the centre party your father supported. Hence . . .'

'Delphi is fine but please, Willi, get me out of the dinner. Couldn't you say I have B.O. or something equally off-putting?'

'The poor man will be vastly relieved that one of his countrymen is not after a free meal. Talking of food, my favourite taverna is right below the Acropolis.'

Local colour was enjoyable in the setting, acceptable in the mandolin orchestra and food, regrettable in the retsina. 'Ambrosia of the Gods this resinated muck? Isn't there some drinkable wine?' Over it, Willi's attention to Yvonne became sufficiently pronounced for him not to mind a twosome with her on the arrival of Otto.

———— ————

'Am I glad to see you, after weeks with the morons. They are waiting round the corner, out of sight as one possesses no garment but *lederhosen*.' At the nearest café the five schoolmates devoured the cakes as if they hadn't eaten for days, and Karl ordered a second helping but did not reciprocate the enthusiasm over the meeting. Lederhosen had a go at 'These bloody Greeks, can't even pronounce their own language. I had top marks at school and nobody understands a word. Best thing in the country is Austrian, Elisabeth's palace on Corfu.'

'As preposterous as her villa near Vienna. We are all good monarchists, but being an Empress is no excuse for bad taste.' Otto needed a break from Austrian parochialism. 'Paul come along. I'm interested in what Karl has been up to. He hadn't much chance to get in a word.' Plain enough even for the morons to realise that the meeting had outlasted its doubtful welcome.

At Willi's taverna pompous generalities were abandoned for personal preoccupations. 'Pity you are set on theology, you'd have made a marvellous prompter at the Landtheater' was a grateful reference Paul understood, others were beyond his comprehension and he soon excused himself. Regrettably there was nothing to relate that would have shocked even a budding priest; and, worse, there was neither time nor place to break a chastity that had lasted longer than either considered healthy. Otto's youth hostel closed early, they separated most reluctantly, the few hours together had been wonderful and frustrating.

Karl joined the crowd taking the air in the Garden; mainly families with screaming children that should have been in bed, but also predatory young males appraising the blond foreigner. The open-air cinema was showing *Sissy* and after that talk about the

46

Empress it seemed a curious coincidence. This second viewing soon became boring, apparently also to two youngish chaps who followed him out. The first approached with a stream of incomprehensible Greek and sadly shook his attractive head to any other language. The second possessed lesser features but English. 'Excuse me, you are so sensitive' was sufficiently original for Karl to inquire on what this judgement was based. 'You wiped away a tear with a very elegant handkerchief.' Karl could not but agree, and conversation never flagged on the walk back to the hotel. 'Will you come swimming with me tomorrow? It's my day off and there mightn't be another chance. I'll ask a friend to drive us to the beach, he's the son of an admiral.'

Descent from high naval rank weighed lightly against the Delphic oracle, but it might be fun to know the people and leave the country to Yvonne. She would certainly prefer to be alone with Willi; not that she had a legitimate chance, Willi was too sensible to compromise his career by an impecunious Jewish marriage.

Fat Mimis, the naval scion, drove his small Fiat to the nearest beach, where he seemed to know everyone but introduced only Angelos. That dark character hardly needed his limited French to make his intentions clear; the warmth of the sea encouraged the transition from straight diving to games that excluded the error of Rimini. The cinema acquaintance lost the competition both in the water and out; Angelos would see that nothing was missing from his new friend's hotel room.

The Greek's looks had promised passion, but his tenderness was a welcome bonus. They parted most reluctantly, but if the siesta were to last through the night, Yvonne might catch them *in flagrante*.

Enthusiastic about Delphi and Willi, she accepted stoically Karl's almost frank explanation of his priorities for the remaining week in Athens. 'Willi is looking after me in the evening, but the days might drag a bit. I might go to a beach, not yours, no competition. My mother would be horrified.' Unlikely though that seemed, an argument about Mrs Venteser's shockability might spoil the enchantment of emotional and physical achievement.

Mimis nearly spoilt it by allusion to Angelos's protector; the intended malice prepared a tolerant acceptance. 'I have to work tomorrow afternoon, for a politician. I'm lucky to earn some money what with all the unemployment, but I only go there when it's absolutely necessary.' The matter-of-fact presentation of financial necessity excluded jealousy, and in the evening they went as usual to the open-air taverna in Angelos's neighbourhood. Far from trying to hide their relationship, Angelos proudly showed off his blond foreign friend in the age-old tradition. Greece was wonderful, without the hypocrisy of Austrian society that affected even Otto.

Yet Angelos was not introduced to Willi at the Piraeus leave-taking, partly to spare the diplomat embarrassment at the friends' final embrace; 'The give-away of the century' according to Yvonne in a summing up of Athenian experiences on board ship. At Corfu they drove in a horse carriage to the Empress's villa, as preposterous as described by Otto, especially the motley statuary. Only Elisabeth's beauty overcame the handicap of modern dress in marble, not in the Imperial manner but in the youthful simplicity of *Sissy*.

— — — —

At the Liechti the porter had been dismissed and the NCO pensioned off in an economy drive combining both positions. A Vauxhall replaced the Mercedes, partly as an anti-German gesture, but also because Father was learning to drive, little short of eccentric for a prominent industrialist. Worse, the State Theatre subscriptions, kept up through hard times, were not renewed. Tania was, of course, responsible; she did not care for opera and since obtaining her Doctorate concentrated on her career in the Landtheater; she had never understood the Fechtner way of life she was slowly destroying.

The Law studies occupied little time in the first year; riding filled most mornings, but the gelding was getting long in the tooth and tired quickly. Unaccustomed idleness increased the longing for the Athenian excitement, satisfied most gratifyingly by Mistinguett's *Casino de Paris* show. Vienna had a first taste of a grand Parisian review in which twenty heavily made-up young men performed daring *danses apaches* with Mistinguett despite her venerable age. Karl was present at the stage box every evening and soon rewarded with smiles from *Les Boys* and even Mis herself. When Lis and Otto rebelled against a surfeit of *apaches* seduction, Karl took his customary seat alone till an enterprising *Boy* indicated that the faithful spectator was expected at the stage door. He shared the meal with the cast and the bed with one of them. French conversation and techniques benefited in the remaining fortnight of the season, even sentiment was pretended, but except for the basic ingredient the theatrical artificiality contrasted amazingly with Greek naturalness. Mis hinted at a Viennese *apache* being decorative, but Karl never contemplated jumping the footlights, one actress in the family sufficed. *Le Boy* promised to write, Angelos did instead, asking about the possibility of a reunion in Vienna. How could he be explained to Father and who would pay his fare?

––– ––– –––

The afternoon banishment from the Liechti had been explained by the song about Henriette; the overnight exile had a less ludicrous reason. The dismissed porter-cum-switchboard-operator had eavesdropped on a warning that the large contributions to charity were goading the tax office into sending two inspectors the following morning: another team would check the Krainer residence. The caller had to support her family on her meagre civil service salary, and reinstatement of her husband at a Krainer shop would help. The porter's dormant Nazi conscience wakened on dismissal and he denounced the non-Aryan fraud. The tax employee had violated an official secret but the General Director had committed nothing illegal; he had, however, displeased the government's radical faction by his connection with the centre party. A retroactive decree extended the actual violation to 'Intellectual Assistance' for not denouncing the informant. The quality press mocked the belated enforcement of an unreal morality; the gutter papers jumped on a scandal that never was.

General Director Fechtner resigned, to dissociate the Krainers from the information they had undoubtedly received. The Dean of Innsbruck's Catholic University undertook the defence, rallied legal support, but could not stop the political progress of injustice.

Overemphasis of sympathy was a bore worse than the Altenhof; in Otto's company the country might even be enjoyable over Christmas. The family occupied all guestrooms, real and step grandparents shared a bathroom, and the words 'intellectual' or 'assistance' were taboo. Presents were on the decline but the boys received identical ski outfits, immediately tried out on a gentle slope where Karl bumped into more trees than justifiable by defective sight.

Birthday brought no increase in the allowance but a 'Hoard of the Niebelungen' with the Ring provided by Father. 'Your initials are the same, so you might like my brother's signet ring. Topaz is *his* stone, but the setting is very original . . . Renaissance.' He had stopped short of 'Valois', but Father's awareness of the Zodiac's significance was as unexpected as an heirloom from Uncle Karl. The grandparents contributed pearl studs, Yvonne an Imperial Eagle on a gold neckchain which accommodated also Marie Louise's medallion of *Notre Dame de Lourdes* and Lis's St Christopher 'in anticipation of a car'.

––– ––– –––

To counteract Nazi propaganda, first-year students had to pass an examination on Austrian history. After a final revision, Otto spent the night in Karl's bed and shared the breakfast served by a stony-faced Mitzi. With equal bravado Karl handled at the exam Austria's participation in the Crusades by condemning Richard the Lionheart's behaviour in the Holy Land and justifying the King's imprisonment in Austria. Patriotic fervour suited the spirit of the exam classified as 'Excellent'.

Academia aspired to the Thursday luncheons and informed Father who was openly pleased. 'You created quite a stir, but a well-founded courage of conviction deserves a reward. Say, a couple of months in Paris?' This was the generosity of pre-Tania days while the monthly stipend bore her niggardly mark. 'But, Father, I can't possibly live on that . . .' 'Pittance' might have offended at this first disagreeable demand for funds.

'Why not? I had much less at your age.'

'Because we are now *the* Fechtners' remained unanswered.

'You'll have to make your own booking.' Father extracted a thick wad of hundred-Schilling notes from the desk drawer and handed over a few. 'No need for a sleeper at your age.'

That his age was chosen for toughening up had little to do with educational principles but all with Tania. Better to avoid a confrontation and pay the supplement from his rapidly dwindling capital.

———

'I'll have to live like those characters in *La Bohème*.'

'Write how your Puccini season is shaping up.' Otto settled Karl into the sleeper, and Lis met him in Paris where she was working as an exchange student. She had suggested several hotels at the right price and Karl had opted for the *Acropole* in a confused hope to find an Athenian atmosphere on the Seine. The fat porter, eyeing him lustfully and the elegant luggage greedily, parodied Greek directness; the badly-heated room lay a cruel halfway between the hotels of previous stays and *La Bohème*. Karl asked for the entire capital deposited with Ohli and received one half with a stern admonition to live within his means. The petty economies at the Liechti had not interfered with food and service, but now every meal had to be priced, theatre and opera were unattainable luxuries because cheap seats did not connect with entertainment. Films were a welcome substitute but at *David Copperfield*, another lonely boy, he sobbed so unrestrainedly that the seats around emptied precipitously. His friend at the Casino de Paris escaped for a few inconsequential sessions from the clutches of a wealthy protector, but the shabbiness behind the theatrical glitter prevented any joining *Les Boys* as was again suggested. Visits to the Louvre failed to rekindle the *déjà vu* of childhood, walks through the town he loved were embittered by his changed circumstances and self-consciousness undermined the former self-confidence in the cold rainy spring.

Paris was not gay but grey. The one bright spot, Lis, had been enjoyed in Vienna more comfortably but less adventurously. Fellow students had mentioned an amusing spot, and on one of her rare free evenings she ventured with Karl to the disreputable nightclub. Lis was expressing her apprehension at the couples of real-life *apaches* valseing and tangoing when an unmistakably Viennese voice assured her 'Looking wicked is part of the trade.' Heinz imparted to his compatriots the lore of low life so entertainingly that a meeting was arranged *Chez Smith*.

The Tea Room of the English Library was favoured by the sophisticated homosexuals and elderly spinsters with a sprinkling of clergymen providing an occasional link. The two handsome Viennese aroused discreet interest, Heinz's comments on professional procedures were fascinating, but his proposal of introduction to a customer was just laughable. However, furthering Heinz's business by dancing with him in the nightspot was all the more fun when terminated by not just playing hard but impossible to get. Before virtuous refusal became frustrating, Ohli's instalment ran out and Karl returned.

Had Father known of these additional funds he would have been even more displeased that his son 'had not stuck it out', unaware that loneliness as much as stringency had shortened the Paris stay. The sad experience had, however, taught Karl that Otto could and should be accommodated on the summer travel allowance maintained in full. Established generous norms were respected, but new contingencies suffered from Tania's hateful 'no extravagance'.

Paternal benevolence was boosted by acquittal. The defence wisely disregarded the doubtful legality of a retroactive charge, pleading instead the moral dilemma raised by denunciation. Though no benefit from the information was proved, a large supplementary tax was assessed and secured on the *Palais* as well as on the Altenhof. The civil servant was given a suspended sentence as she was 'motivated by love for her husband' and dismissed without pension. Dr Fechtner was praised for self-resignation and equally unemployed.

———— ————

Axel Munthe's *Story of San Michele* depicted an idyllic Capri, enjoyed more economically from the old-fashioned *pensione* on the Marina Grande than from the main village. The *padrona* mothered the polite boys who attempted Italian when most foreigners shouted in incomprehensible tongues. The two deserved the best and cheapest food, wine, boats and donkeys, though naturally they must also visit the great sites on the mainland, Pompei, Vesuvius and the splendid coast from Sorrento to Ravello. Mother's preference for horse carriages was imposed in the Italy of sanctions and petrol rationing; horse and coach were old but well-kept, the coachman young and even better-kept. He overcharged the foreigners but in the end refused the generous tip which evened out the price; they should have haggled but his contempt for the stupid boys changed into liking because they were so obviously in love with his country and each other.

Reckoning was delayed till the goodbyes at Naples. 'It was a marvellous holiday, but here it ends.'

'Of course, you aren't supposed to come to Athens. Are you dotty?'

'Remember the pretty girl that showed us round the Roman Villa at Ravello? She seemed not unwilling, but unfortunately partial to your blondness. You always steal the limelight. That's perhaps why I'm getting engaged to Dolly. She and even more her mother prefer you, but realise that with a princess in the running . . . despite Marie Louise's bulldog face. The Voltains are centuries older than the Tarburgs but the Freyers haven't completely given up; I'm to wed Dolly only after graduation, probably after installing mod. comfs. in our dreary castle.'

———— ————

Even temporary separation would have been hard to bear after this month of perfect round-the-clock intimacy; but definite loss . . . ! Divine balancing of accounts, a debit commensurate to the credit, seemed plausible to Karl's fanciful yet orderly mind. That he had never been alone on a ship made it worse by memories of happier voyages. Memories were for the old and he was only eighteen so he would flirt with that slightly overweight girl who had pulled up her deckchair.

Angelos and Mimis were waiting at the quayside and the resumption of the enjoyable routine was hardly interrupted by General Metaxas' bloodless coup; so quiet and efficient compared to the bloody revolts in Vienna. Angelos's politician jumped on the bandwagon and needed his 'secretary' perhaps really for some paperwork. This left time to attend a cocktail party at the Austrian Legation, where Willi introduced his friend to a compatriot, Christl Kourdatis, who knew the Tarburgs, had danced with Max's older brother and invited Karl to her villa on an island. A month was, however, too short to waste even a few days on social rather than sexual intercourse. Karl preferred sharing a bed with Angelos to sharing a table with Athenian hostesses, yet the bloom had gone out of the summer. The leavetaking was outwardly passionate, inwardly dispassionate.

———— ———

'Parisian cold showers under the Mediterranean sun, poor Karl. You too need a seachange.' Lis enjoyed mocking Otto's illusions of a secret relationship with hints incomprehensible to the fourth in the Landtheater box. Studies had prevented her from looking after Karl in Paris but now she had handpicked a fellow student, pretty Gusti, conveniently engaged to a consul in a distant land. The unromantically wholesome girl fitted neatly into the intensive preparation for the first Law examination. In a return in time Karl and Otto spent every afternoon on the same benches which they had occupied for so many mornings, since the crammer course was held in the Schotten classrooms.

Gusti was all right between Roman and German law, but Lis cheered more lastingly on Sunday afternoons. Her father was performing some unspecified tasks for the owner of a rest home, which did not prevent ridiculing the provider of ephemeral prosperity. 'Don't expect much panache from old Erdöpany. Hungarian titles came cheaper than Austrian, only a hospital wing not an entire hospital, besides disguising the Jewish name.' The information was imparted in French while being driven in their derided host's limousine.

'If my dear Papa aids and abets Erdö by making wills, they'd better hurry up. Some of the inmates seem unlikely to outlast the hour. Karl, you aren't going again to the loo?'

Karl excused himself ever more frequently and a burning sensation made urinating increasingly painful. Undressing at home he noticed a slight discharge and after a very uncomfortable night he hurried to Uncle Doctor. 'Gonorrhea, nothing to worry about. I'll send you to a specialist.'

'How much will it cost? My allowance . . .'

'I'll talk to your father though I haven't seen much of him since his marriage.'

Father was surprisingly sympathetic. He did not ask for the girl's name but insisted on her seeing the specialist at his expense. Gusti consented reluctantly and claimed to have been found free of infection. Professional ethics protected the only possible source. The treatment was unpleasant, the tests excruciating, libido at zero.

Eros's loss was Emperor Otto's gain. Restoration of the Monarchy seemed possible till a Western veto prevented the only alternative to the Anschluss. Forbidding Austria to decide its destiny made clandestine National Socialism respectable and vindicated Hitler's attack on the peace treaties. For most, however, it did not dim the nostalgia for the Imperial past; Marie Louise, Yvonne and Karl joined the Monarchist Youth Movement.

Politics receded before an exam which required solid knowledge, not bravado. Yet questions could be deflected, not deceiving experienced professors by mental acrobatics but lightening their labour by coherent if slightly off-point answers. This was the art of successful lawyers and the amused examiners connived with the candidate at the display of historical background over the legal substance. Distinction in two of the three subjects resulted in a highly creditable pass and allowed full enjoyment of the last ball in the Carnival.

———— ————

'You enjoy balls, don't you?' Father watched his son descend the staircase. 'Strange how you remind me of . . . he was dark. I saw him only once in tails, hired of course. Pity I didn't think of his ring for your portrait.' The reference to Uncle Karl was not justified by 'The *Salonblatt* wants to publish your picture as you are opening the ball with Marie Louise. They also asked Tania, but she prefers to be photographed as an actress, not as a socialite.'

The Ball in Schönbrünn was opened by twenty carefully chosen couples, which did not include Erwein Erdöpany, though he looked more Hungarian than his sire. He was waltzing with Lis, Marie Louise had disappeared with some cousins, while Karl was unexpectedly alone in the Chinese Room of the Palace. The young man sitting opposite reminded him of . . . the Emperor Franz. Not quite so superbly degenerate, still strikingly Habsburg.

'You aren't the first to be intrigued by the likeness' sounded far from offended, and a pleasant conversation about the Emperor's famous portrait was interrupted by Erwein's 'You two were bound to meet'. He introduced Clemens Meister, a fellow medical student, with whom Karl made a date for the following Sunday.

Clemens was reputedly the son of an Archduke and a ballerina. For the semi-Imperial visitor complaisant Mitzi lit the open fire in the library, Karl scattered cushions in front and donned silk pyjamas and dressing gown. When he opened the garden gate a whiff of eau de cologne indicated Clemens's equal keenness but the fashionable Kniže 10 would cling to the cushions for days. The olfactory overdose spoiled an otherwise impeccable act and further dates were left vague.

The host hurried ahead to unlock the garden gate and then found to his horror that Clemens had pulled the housedoor shut. The massive portal did not budge, the street was deserted in the icy February night, the garage hardly less cold. Shivering an eternity in his silks, he dashed to the gate at the sound of footsteps; Providence had sent a policeman who refused, however, to pass the gate. The heated argument whether this was an extra-territorial legation failed to warm Karl, when he lost to 'Then why is Burmah House written in that foreign spelling on the street sign?' Why indeed?

Taking pity on the bundle of misery, the constable offered the hospitality of the police station. 'I shouldn't by rights. You aren't homeless.' As true as handtooled Italian slippers being the worst footwear in the dirty snow. Defeated by the duty officer's rules and regulations against entering Burmah House, Karl phoned a bewildered Otto to fetch him from the police station to the more congenial Barovsky flat.

Father refrained from elucidating the unconvincing tale of the nocturnal lock-out and wrote a cheque for police charities. Paternal goodwill engendered by the examination result continued beyond the full-page photo of a haughty Karl in tails; the *Salonblatt* liked the photogenic as much as additional subscriptions.

'Are you sufficiently brave to drive with me to Zurich?' Some weeks earlier the Vauxhall had skidded on slippery ice into a parked car. This made Father nervous on his first long self-drive and after several enforced stops he consulted a chemist about a binding drug. Karl had read that Chinese opium smokers were not only emaciated but also constipated; his imaginative deduction was proved correct by the indicating accompanying the pills. 'Opiate Likely to Induce Somnolence'.

'That chemist is either an assassin or an idiot, probably both. He must have seen the car. We'll have to stop at the next hotel.' At the next Fechtner-standard establishment he showed his appreciation of filial watchfulness by discussing the reason for the trip. The Swiss concern was offering a contract on more favourable terms than eleven years before, because of the successful Krainer reorganisation. 'Tania fears it might interfere with her career. Your mother also opposed the move, naturally on different grounds, strange . . . she liked the banker who now urges me to accept the offer as he is very pessimistic about Austria's future. Moreover, with that enormous tax mortgage on the Liechti I wonder how to keep it up.'

The suite at the Zurich hotel was a delightful rebuttal of Tania's 'no extravagance' nonsense. It was bliss but also disquieting to be jerked like a yo-yo from the lean month in Paris to the splendid dining room overlooking the Lake. Zurich wasn't a bad place, but abandoning the Liechti, Mother's memorial, would be a terrible wrench. While Father lunched with the Swiss tempters, Karl played host to Kurt Auer, who hoped that the Fechtners would move to Zurich. University experiences and living on insufficient allowances formed a bond, though one cousin was at present enjoying a luxury of which the Nazis had deprived the other. At the end of the stay Father seemed inclined to be 'gilded by all that chocolate', as put picturesquely in the banker's Jewish accent.

———— —— ————

Great Uncle Ferdinand's accent stressed precise German, deliberately distinct from softer Austrian intonation. 'I haven't asked you for elevenses to annoy your father, though he'd certainly disapprove of beer with a breakfast gulyash, but then he disapproves of my politics even more. I've always been anti-Semitic and now it's through him that my family continues, ironical. Except for us two, there has been no male issue since my great grandmother, and not many girls either in six generations. No record where our eye defect originated. I don't want you to suffer in the Anschluss, your father is on the Nazi blacklist, a non-Aryan Monarchist. This tax business could be warmed up for a show trial. He'd better be out of the country.'

'Shouldn't you warn him yourself, Uncle?'

'I tried, but he was so . . . let's say distant. Probably thought I wanted money, the eternal phobia of the rich. He won't suspect you of that.'

Father was given no opportunity to suspect as he was asked openly for an increase in the allowance. 'It started far too generously when you were a boy, now is hardly the time as your Pan-Germanic uncle would be the first to admit. Rather ominous that he gives me the same advice as my Jewish banker. He means well and I'll phone him, but the Nazi scare is exaggerated, I've refused the Swiss offer.'

———— —— ————

Karl blamed Tania's wiles less for the rejection of the Swiss chocolate pots than his dire financial straits during the post-exam leisure period. The gelding was not replaced, a horse was hired only twice a week. Accompanying Lis and Erwein to the Splendid, Karl was impressively welcomed by the manager who appreciated Fechtner patronage from his summer employment at Pörtschach. The bandleader came from the same past and gratifyingly inquired after the favourite dance tunes. His sibylline 'You are too pretty for your own good' was imparted to Dolly and Otto at one of many pleasant evenings hosted by Karl at Vienna's leading nightclub.

The unique Austrian stamp collection was kept up to date with the grandparents' assistance, but sets from other countries were returned to the dealer for less than the purchase price. Not much, because the Fechtner heir obviously hated parting with his philatelic treasure and lack of funds was unlikely to last.

A cousin of Otto gave a party on his first leave from the reopened Military Academy which provided once again an acceptable career. The cadet looked suitably dashing in the uniform of the Empire, but his father was more interesting, pleased by Karl's comment on the Biedermeier furniture and startled by his knowledge of cut glass. The stimulation was reciprocated, and on return to the Liechti Karl opened the period cupboard that contained the lesser pieces. They were his, as recently confirmed again by Granny. The blue-and-white Renaissance cup was rather ugly, but the old Baron possessed nothing so original.

The Baron did not ask for the name of Karl's 'Uncle' who was obliged to sell his collection. 'This is a museum piece, fifteenth-century German. I don't think I can afford it.' He could, at the price fixed by himself, a considerable sum which temporarily relieved Karl's needs.

———————

At a Landtheater first night the adjoining box was occupied by an exiled Balkan King, to whom Dr Fechtner presented his wife during the interval. Alone with Anton Bluhm, Karl voiced his resentment, 'Why did Father present Tania and not me?'

'Because the King prefers unambiguously ambiguous looks like yours.' His smile emphasised the resemblance with a satyr. 'Further enlightenment dispensed at my flat Sunday mornings. By the way, your father told me how much you admire Tauber. I got you two tickets for *Don Giovanni*. In future ask me directly.'

———————

Under the eyes of a suspicious father the King would hardly have made an appointment, yet one was arranged with an equally notorious actor in Berlin. Looking at a rising star for the Landtheater was coincidental to using accumulating Krainer fees that could not be exported because of the Draconian exchange regulations. Kniže, whose Number 10 had impeded the Habsburg liaison, was the leading tailor in Vienna as well as in Berlin, which facilitated the transmission of measurements for Father's shirts and the authorisation for a complete wardrobe for his son.

At the Bristol, next to the Adlon where Karl had stayed with his parents but now reserved for Nazi officials, he was handed a ticket for the stage box in the Schiller Theatre and a note from the actor. Karl rang the Auers to invite them to the performance, but they refused. Aunt Rosa would explain at lunch the following day.

A huge bottle of Kniže 10 was Europe's most prestigious tailor's solitary window display. The only customer, Gustav Gründgens, was ordering a showy purple flannel with silver stripes. The taste of Germany's greatest actor was very special, and the sales manager assisted in the choice of impeccably discreet clothes.

The play was as anodine as the would-be matinée idol whose looks had to compensate for too much. He stared at the box and remained incredulous in his dressing room that the representative of the renowned Landtheater was little more than a child. Karl was insufferably gracious, a mixture of an Archduke and a Hollywood impresario. 'An interesting performance, but the play doesn't do justice to your talent.' The actor relied more heavily on charm which he had intended to deploy at a smart restaurant but not with so young a companion. He dared play to the box where Karl was enthroned in solitary splendour but would not join him afterwards.

———— ————

Coming away from the theatre Karl looked at the window displays of shoe shops and so did a nice young man; no doubt remained when both switched their attention to umbrellas. The Berliner's 'Unnecessary this spring' was so nervous that Karl reassured him with a foreign, Austrian accent. On parting they made a date for the following Sunday at Potsdam.

In the taxi to the garden suburb Karl remembered Aunt Rosa's 'To be expected in Berlin' seven years earlier. Her worldly amusement then contrasted poignantly with her present diffidence. 'We moved here because the presence of embassies provides a certain protection. The cowardice of supposed friends at Wittenberg was an eye opener.' Even in the capital the Auers avoided appearing in public, let alone in a stage box, much though they would have enjoyed a theatre outing. 'I'm glad you got on well with Kurt in Zurich. With Father you were, of course, staying at the best hotel. But here on your own? Times have changed since the Adlon days, waste seems sinful.' She remained unconvinced that her nephew had been living more meanly in Paris than her son in Zurich. 'You could go back to the luxury of the Liechti, but Kurt has to stick it out, he is barred from German universities because of his race.' She looked at Karl and understood that he knew of the tragic Auer heredity. 'The two children in the institution are a great expense but seem safe for the present. The rumours of what happens in public asylums are terrible.'

The old aunt had been as frightened in her quiet flat as the young Berliner among the crowd at Potsdam when Karl suggested a carriage drive through the park. 'Such showing off stopped when Röhm and the boys were massacred on The Night Of The Long Knives.'

'The Austrian Minister will get me out of any trouble.'

'You, not me. I'll get beaten up and sent to a labour camp. Even the young Krupp is in a camp for being too flamboyant, though his father gave millions to the Nazis.' Yet the excuse that this drive was in memoriam of an earlier one with his mother might pacify an interfering SA lout and a coach was engaged. Surely the Berliner's fears were unreasonable but sufficiently strong to kill desire; they parted at the U Bahn station.

——— ———

Vienna's best-dressed young man took Lis to a performance by the worst-dressed woman. A Jewish heiress had married a Count of the Empire, the equal of sovereigns. She lost her husband in the war, her money in the inflation, her looks and voice to time. Remembering past flatteries at her musical evenings, she sang and played to some acquaintances. An unscrupulous impresario saw possibilities in her very impossibility and trusted the nastiness of the public. Twice a year the Countess, draped in old curtains and hung with beads, croaked at a piano in the Concert Hall usually reserved for the greatest musicians. She insulted the booing and jeering audience in a pathetic slinging match that appalled Karl more than Lis, whose poverty had destroyed her belief in human kindness.

——— ———

Exploring a new country seemed more promising than yet another Mediterranean summer, besides the educational benefits impressed by Margarete on Father. A paying guest in Cambridge, Karl was accorded the favours of his host's pretty daughter in a punt, too uncomfortable for romance and so obviously routine as perhaps included in the fees. Neither the seduction nor the pimply brother's cricket mania impeded the appreciation of an academic atmosphere which made college life almost desirable.

The dread of communal life dissolved among the multinational students at Exeter University. A single room allowed privacy essential even among well-mannered and well-educated fellow boarders, who responded well to the teachers' relaxed endeavours. The young lecturer on Drama invited her more intelligent charges to an evening cup of tea where she impressed by appropriately dramatic utterances, delivered by a studiously melancholic blond 'My heart died many years ago', stunned Karl into envious admiration. He longed for experiences to justify so moving a statement, but felt unsure of his heart. Neither the girls nor Otto or Angelos qualified, but he would keep trying. One great sad love seemed so much harder to attain than the course's parchment diploma with the highest marks.

———— ————

'We were thrown out, definitely *persona non grata* when we asked Father to transfer the Altenhof to us.' Herta was driving her brother from the Tarburg railway station to the huge medieval castle.

'Hardly surprising. And it is *personae*.'

'I passed Latin without a bribe, you exasperating prick. The Lechfurts warned us to secure the Altenhof before the Anschluss.' They stopped in the courtyard and a liveried footman carried Karl's luggage to a vast room with washing facilities behind a disguised door to the daring innovation of a bathtub. He then called on Herta's in-laws and was invited for lunch.

'We have two households. Papa is a dear, in small doses. Mama can be very trying. Now the Lechfurts are a charming couple. They are dining with us tonight.'

Max had not defended his parents but was obviously happier explaining remoter relatives. 'Hildegard Lechfurt is a German Tarburg, the branch that remained in Silesia when the Prussians annexed the province. We haven't been closely connected since her grandfather was made prince by Bismarck.' This disapproval was understandable to all Austrians except Pan-Germans like Uncle Ferdinand. 'Her husband Norbert is a passionate hunter and no better game than in the forests that no longer belong to us.'

Too German to qualify for charming, the Lechfurts were pleasant, but Karl preferred the lunch with the old couple that came within the all-embracing uncle category. Uncle Rudi's encyclopaedic knowledge extended over subjects useless for practical purposes; Aunt Valerie's regal comportment was hardly marred by an opaque right eye. She tactfully alluded to previous misalliances by joking about her lack of the thirty-two quarters required for a lady-in- waiting. Over coffee in the neglected garden she expressed her pleasure that Karl had been educated by Benedictines, and had remained influenced by his mother's Catholicism. Herta, cutting flowers, listened with mixed feelings to 'Talking to your brother is a pleasure. Usually I sit here all alone, waiting for the Grim Reaper.'

'You do have strange callers, Mama' caused an exchange of incredulous glances which confirmed the mutual liking.

Max was jealous of his brother-in-law. 'Another lunch? We are bidden at most once a month! Mama has obviously fallen for you. Did she try to convert you?'

'We talked about religion and horses. Did she hurt her eye in a riding accident?'

'That's the official version, but . . . Mama was very friendly with an equerry. Dear Papa looks deceptively peaceful but flies into violent rages. He struck her and his signet ring damaged the eye.'

Herta's idea of a Children's United Front was dropped as Karl could not risk paternal wrath by suggesting a transfer of the Liechti to his name. He agreed, however, to convey the Lechfurt warning about an imminent German move.

———

The crammer course for the more demanding second law exam lasted the whole academic year. Back in the old classroom Karl once again attempted distasteful subjects, but without supervision his attendance became increasingly irregular and eventually ceased. 'Catching up later' was silly self-deceit, yet he faced the inevitable disaster with the unfounded conviction that it would not happen. Occasional bouts of conscience were quietened at the Splendid, which required substantial funds.

In his illicit leisure Karl called on Mother's schoolfriend. Aunt Charlotte was profoundly grateful for the Landtheater box, which she could not have afforded, since she was saving for a second-hand car. He would probably want a sports car for his twenty-first birthday.

He'd be lucky to get a Fiat. What a bore! Everyone thought he was made of money. The bad eye would cut short her gushings.

'Don't worry, my brother is a police officer and he will arrange the eye test. I usually ask him to the box and he'll be only too pleased to help.'

Supply and demand dried up simultaneously. Cups and goblets could no longer fill the gaps and the Baron demurred. 'The collection is richer than I. Such lovely pieces are hard to resist and I considered bringing in my Swiss emergency fund. But that would be madness in these uncertain times.'

The same afternoon Father peeled off some hundred Schilling notes from the wad in the desk. 'I can't wait for the plumber, we have guests on the Altenhof and Mitzi is coming with us. You'll have to pay him, Karl.' He closed the drawer and put the key somewhere below. Nothing more natural than looking for the hiding place, not particularly secret as a slight twist of the baroque carving opened a small panel. It would be absurd not to try the key; the wad had never appeared bigger. Father did not jot down the sums abstracted, and there was nothing wrong with an 'on account' of Mother's gold pieces locked away in the wallsafe. This was no more thieving than disposing of stamps and cups. It really was Father's fault for withholding the rightful inheritance and not increasing a schoolboy's pocket money to a student's allowance. 'Righting the wrong' was made more convincing by putting the blame for the niggardliness on Tania.

Anton Bluhm was ready to provide opera tickets which Karl could fetch on Sunday morning. Remembering the Director's 'Further enlightenment', the nakedness of three drama students was a shock easily born. The large bed accommodated a fascinating free-for-all, except that Bluhm – now Toni – wisely refrained from touching his Maecenas' son. After these tumultuous happenings it was fun to sympathise with Granny's moral outrage over poor Frau Hofrat's son having an affair with the maid, corrected by Ohli to chauffeur.

Addressing Toni in public as 'Herr Direktor' was titillating considering the 'Sunday Mornings' with a frequently changing cast. 'The Secret of the Baroque Desk' was a popular supporting feature, the helpings so modest that they passed unnoticed among the many payments from the wad. Familiarity with the self-service roused curiosity about a folder marked HOROSCOPE. The front page was headed by Karl's hour and date of birth; the printed Circle of the Zodiac was filled in with symbols explained below. Several pages stressed the instability caused by the rare constellation of Sun, Moon and Venus in Capricorn, partly relieved by the benign Sagittarius Ascendant. *The Week by the Stars* bored with unvaried generalities, but outstanding astrologers had made remarkable predictions, especially Nostradamus about the Valois, more obscure but hardly less discouraging than his own 'Constant struggle, violent social and financial changes'. 'Help from unexpected quarters' would continue through a threatened late calamity. 'Wide-ranging journeys' seemed the only desirable aspect in all this threatening 'Instability', which was the main element. Capricorn's persistency would prevail, but the potentiality for love would disintegrate into mere sensuality.

It fitted. 'Instability' he had called yo-yo, the Baron was 'Help from unexpected quarters', Toni's mornings 'sensuality', but disintegration apparently preceded love. It was certainly Mother who had the horoscope cast, but why did Father keep it so handy?

———— ———— ———— ————

'Now why should Hans Wilner be staring at us so intently?' Lis and Karl were skating. 'He is in German Lit. and supposedly in the SS. He certainly looks more Germanic than any of the big Nazis, but don't do anything rash. It's pretty clear he's after you, but what for is *not* clear any more in these beastly times.'

The large blue eyes followed Karl round the rink after Lis's departure. Was this the 'Potentiality for love' or merely a potentiality for scandal? Throughout the winter those blue eyes looked straight into Karl's whenever he was skating, without a wink or smile, Nordic directness or dumbness. However regrettable, Lis's warning could not be disregarded.

The Nazi danger was brought home by the appointment of von Papen as Minister, since Hitler was unlikely to waste so subtle a politician on a secondary target. The upper classes opposed the Anschluss, the people largely Slav and Hungarian welcomed the inclusion into German Superiority. The political drama was momentarily forgotten at the first night of *Giuditta*; no operetta by a living composer had ever been performed at the Opera, but at this unprecedented homage the Nazis would not jeer Jewish Tauber because he sang too well but also because Léhar was the Führer's favourite composer.

Vienna's most brilliant Carnival since the fall of the Empire began at Schönbrünn, where Marie Louise and Karl danced a minuet in Rococo costumes before Princess Fugger as the Empress Maria Theresa. In a very Austrian way this was an assertion of independence, as the great Empress had resisted a treacherous Prussian attack against heavy odds with the support of her people. Princess Fugger was closely linked with the Chancellor who courageously resisted Hitler's demands, which gave political significance to a social event.

Karl and Otto wore tails to *Giuditta* in case they attended the ball in the town hall to which invitations were too readily available. In a first Carnival even a lesser ball is not easily missed and they decided on a brief appearance in the huge neo-Gothic hall. They were hailed by Ralph Caldwell, an English paying guest at one of Otto's numerous cousins. 'What good luck! Our fourth didn't show up and Irene wanted to leave.' The striking oval-faced brunette in a sophisticated green dress did not look a meek third. 'Rather strong-willed, daughter of a colonial governor. The Redhead is less determined. Neither understands much German.' Ralph had switched into that language.

No need for a gubernatorial parent to make Irene an attractive dancing partner. That he had not intended to come and she had been on the point of walking out started talk and laughter. Irene Wynn Roberts was staying as PG with some distant Voltain relations; in

Vienna everyone was related. Naturally he escorted her home and made an appointment for the following day.

Dragged between Karl and Otto round the skating rink, Irene made fun of her ineptitude, matched by her partners with tales of their clumsiness at other sports. Confronted by the hilarious enjoyment, Hans Wilner's enigmatic stare became openly annoyed and after a showy shrug of his massive shoulders he stamped off.

The Austrian Chancellor was 'invited' by Hitler and without any support from the Western Democracies had to appoint a National Socialist lawyer as Minister of the Interior. While crowds worshipped an enormous photograph of the Führer in the window of the German Travel Agency, the Young Monarchists were too civilised for public displays of political fanaticism, but stickers OUR MOTTO EMPEROR OTTO in the Habsburg black and yellow affirmed their will to resist. Weak on organising screaming mobs, the Monarchists excelled in social functions, admittedly not the most effective defence in the rapidly deteriorating situation. After a gloomy pep talk by the Chairman, Karl startled the Committee with 'Don't you think I should open our Ball with the daughter of a British Governor as a proof of outside interest?' The only non-titled member's dialectic was worth a try.

Archduke Anton and his wife Ileana, sister of King Carol of Rumania, were the patrons of the Ball, but the attendance of the late Emperor's eldest daughter and a younger son was for Monarchists more significant. Marie Louise had not only ceded her place but also lent her elbow-length gloves to Irene who wore an inappropriate *décolleté* dark dress, but gallantly struggled through the left-turn waltz following Karl's advice to keep her eyes fixed on his shoulders. His ambition to partner Archduchess Adelheid was disappointed as she had vowed to dance only after the restoration of her brother; so Karl danced mainly with Irene to the annoyance of many a marriageable girl and their mothers. A few conceded that the couple were attractive, slim, of middle height, moving gracefully; the envious majority denigrated 'graceful' into 'haughty' and for want of a better condemnation discovered that the girl should not be darker than the boy. Marie Louise's 'Odd that Monarchists should be so critical of our last Emperors. Both Franz Joseph and Karl were much fairer than their wives and deeply in love with them' effectively ended that line of attack.

———— ———— ————

Mother had brought out Herta at private dances; Tania would certainly find a dance band at the Liechti extravagant. Father abhorred cocktail parties but, if the young wanted barbarous concoctions, a well-stocked drink cabinet was at their disposal while he and Tania withdrew to the Altenhof. Carpets were removed, dancing was to records, and the piano was played by several guests. Lis led a first raid on the kitchen, when the usual party food ran out after double the usual party time. In the early morning Karl took Irene down the back stairs to the large frigidair emptied of readily consumable nourishment though not of provisions requiring cooking. This seemed somehow hilarious, they fell into each other's arms, laughter turned into kisses till Irene drew abruptly away. 'A man . . . He's gone.'

'Decent of Father to disappear so discreetly, but he doesn't know yet we've eaten his breakfast.'

The only reference to the kitchen episode was Father's 'I hope you've kept your appetite' when Irene was asked to a family lunch. She parried with mishaps at parties in Africa and held her own better than Max at his trial-by-lunch. An invitation to the Altenhof sealed the approval.

3

All-important one day, the approval became meaningless the next. Mounting German threats forced the Chancellor into the gamble of a plebiscite on Austria's independence, perhaps relying on the popular joke 'Church, Jews and Homosexuals united in the Patriotic Front are unbeatable.' On the eleventh of March Karl asked Lis and Erwein to an operetta with a famous Jewish singer recently deserted by her Aryan actor husband. British nationals had been advised to stay at home as did most theatre-loving Viennese, but even after Bluhm's announcement of the German invasion the cast played on gallantly to an almost empty house. The delirious mob sporting Swastikas had stopped all traffic and the two young men escorted Lis on foot before parting. The district was quiet round the Liechti, where a light shone through the curtains of the study. 'Father you must leave immediately. The Germans will be here in a few hours.'

'They can't put all Monarchists into concentration camps.' Reluctantly he agreed not to hazard a Nazi respect for the law; in that unlikely case nothing would prevent his return. Tania wavered throughout the argument, then packed a suitcase while Karl was put in charge of the Liechti and given the keys to the wallsafe. Father would drive Tania to her parents before attempting the Hungarian frontier a mere 90 kilometres away.

Apprehension kept Karl awake till his sitting room door was opened. Not even Mitzi bringing breakfast entered without knocking, so the two nondescript men had to be the Gestapo. German efficiency, as only six hours earlier the Chancellor had broadcast that the Federal President refused to order resistance, ending his dramatic announcement with 'God save Austria'. Too late for that, but Father might still be saved through the Secret Police preceding the invading army. 'My father is on our estate, the Altenhof.' He gave the correct phone number, country exchanges operated only during post office hours, time was gained. The men had apparently orders for only the one arrest though the Emperor Otto stickers might have provoked another.

Exhaustion allowed sleep till an early phone call. Aunt Charlotte knew that the previous porter had reported a warning and she applied the technique of spy thrillers after gushing about the joy of seeing the Führer. 'My brother says to continue the driving lessons and not to worry about the test. The chairs I can store as long as you wish.' But she must have laboured over the ingenious indication that her brother was willing to help and that she offered hospitality.

In the next cryptic call the Young Monarchists' Deputy Chairman urgently requested funds to rent a house at the skiing resort in the Tyrol. Another opportunity to balk the Gestapo of an obvious prey by immediately transmitting a sufficient sum for escape into Switzerland, the first priority on a very busy morning. Funny to have been officially initiated into what had long ceased to be 'The Secret of the Desk'. Father had pocketed the familiar wad of banknotes, but there were plenty more in the wallsafe together with Mother's gold coins, some of her jewellery, a thick bundle of bonds as well as a dozen savings banks books in the names of Kurt and Karl with the single password Adele. The anonymity of bank deposits was usual, less so the exclusion of the living wife for the dead.

No talk, hardly a greeting in the long queues before the banks to give the SA guards no pretext 'to Restore order'. The novels' 'tangible fear' became real in the silent advance to withdraw an amount that would not arouse suspicion. At the second bank Karl abandoned this absurd precaution as any withdrawal was a declaration of no confidence in the Nazis. By midday his pockets were bulging with the largest denominations which he deposited with the grandparents.

The porter remained in his lodge and Mitzi served a particularly tasty meal, her and cook's expression of support. Back at the safe the vital decision what to salvage and what to sacrifice was likely to prove wrong. Jewellery, coins, some cash and the lesser pass books should convince the Gestapo that nothing had been removed as a search of the Liechti was likely when Father was not found on the Altenhof. The choice between the risk of alerting the Gestapo and eventually remaining without visible means of support was excruciating. He laughed at the expression, wondering whether invisible means would come to the rescue. The bundle of Bonds was all too visible and, moreover, the quarter of a million schilling issue was registered in Father's name. Prudence as well as ignorance of how to deal with such an enormous amount counselled leaving one half behind. Perhaps he exaggerated the danger and the rest might be retrieved when disposal had been arranged.

No more could be stuffed into the briefcase without arousing suspicion, the keyword to his present circumstances. Aunt Charlotte's Cops and Robbers had soured into a deadly Hide and Seek. He might be known at the next taxi rank, so he hailed a passing car and got out a block before the grandparents. Ohli failed as a bond broker, nor could he indicate a trustworthy friend of Father. It would be easy for the Krainers, but was there still any connection? The doubtful reputation of Lis's father should enable him to handle a deal which was probably perfectly simple. Frau von Granera was half-Jewish so their phone might be tapped. The Voltains could prove impeccable Aryan ancestry centuries longer than any Nazi, and the approach was safest through Marie Louise.

She and Karl passed a small crowd round the Dowager Princess Starhemberg on her knees scrubbing away the Patriotic Front's slogans outside her magnificent *Palais*. Without hesitation Karl bent down and took the brush from Max's aunt, but was spared street cleaning by a furious SS thug. 'You are helping an enemy of the Reich' subsided in Franz Schmidt's stunned recognition to the normal tones of schoolmates, 'You really shouldn't.' Reasserting authority he ordered resumption of the scrubbing, became confused by the onlookers' catcalls and marched the new enemy of the Reich to the nearby SS barracks installed a few hours previously.

Hans Wilner, resplendent in the black uniform with the silver insignia, cut short the incoherent report. 'Helping an old lady, even a Monarchist, doesn't make an enemy of the Reich. Prince Voltain rang to complain about this absurd arrest. Mr Fechtner is, of course, free to leave.' He added almost inaudibly 'I'd imagined a different meeting.'

No time for relief, let alone disappointment. A vengeful Toad might instigate a Gestapo raid and the Monarchist stickers would make the absurd charge stick. Too bulky to be flushed down the toilet, burning in the central heating furnace might be observed by the porter, so Karl carried the thick bundle through the dark streets to a telephone booth. He thanked Marie Louise's father for his prompt intervention and then, in a boyish revolt against the adult reasoning required all day, he plastered the stickers over the booth. The useless bravado for which no Wilner could afford protection facilitated sleep.

——— ———

The next morning Karl reversed previous proceedings by putting some hundred Schilling notes into the desk drawer to enhance the realism of unpreparedness. He hesitated over the Horoscope, but though 'Violent changes' had been followed by 'Help from unexpected quarters', the folder took up too much space. He tried to stuff the stamp collection, cups, and watches into Mitzi's shopping bag which contrasted so conspicuously with his Kniže suit that he had to revert to the inadequate briefcase. Two trips instead of one to save the easily transportable fraction of the Liechti's treasures. The grandparents had discussed suitable businessmen among the Thursday Luncheon guests, but they were all prominent opponents of the Nazis; the intellectual majority was equally implicated besides knowing as little about bonds as Uncle Ferdinand. In despair even the Cardinal was considered, but finally one-third of the Bonds were entrusted for sale to Granera after Lis's assurance that he was too Catholic and cowardly for outright crookery.

——— ———

Monarchists did not attend Hitler's triumphal progress to the Burg where barely a week earlier the Imperial Family had impressed Irene. She was staying at home like all Karl's friends, but alone in the Liechti? Reading for once failed and walking through the deserted streets Karl passed a cinema that dared to open on this 'Joyful Day', probably because the owner was too compromised to care. Certainly, because *Sissy* was the civilised Habsburg opposite of brutal Nazi reality, even at a third viewing.

Lights were blazing at the Liechti and cars with Swastika standards were parked outside. From the booth still partly adorned with his stickers, Karl phoned the Liechti and was answered by Security Battalion Five. The Führer's astrologer could envy the accuracy of the 'Violent changes'; a year earlier the police refused his entreaties to enter the Liechti and hesitated over his 'not being homeless'. That he certainly was now, but help was more likely from expected than from unexpected quarters. The grandparents must not be involved in case he was wanted, the Reichenbachs had never qualified as relations, but dear Aunt Charlotte had offered hospitality in her chair enigma.

Mrs Schupp smothered the child she had not borne and the respectful familiarity of her old maid was not unlike Mitzi's, which started worries about the Liechti's servants. Surely not even the Nazis would fling them out into the street without some compensation, yet perhaps he should have made some provision.

Tucked into bed as in his childhood, his thoughts turned to Mother. Was it not better she had been spared the loss of the house she had chosen and arranged with so much love? She would have stood bravely by her husband throughout all political and racial upheavals, but would he still have been her husband, given his taste for females less than half his age? 'Whom the gods love die young' Ohli had quoted. Sissy proved the truth of the proverb, the fairytale princess loved by a young Emperor, the most handsome couple that ever ruled. She miraculously survived TB, he escaped assassination; benevolence or malevolence of the gods? Emperor Franz Joseph's love never ceased, but Sissy failed in her duties as Empress and sought refuge at Corfu; she had been granted so much and had, therefore, to pay dearer than most. Her son murdered his mistress and then committed suicide, the Empress died at the hands of an anarchist, slowly bleeding to death in uncomplaining dignity. Karl had no intention to murder Gusti, though she had given him clap, nor to commit suicide. Mother would not have been assassinated by the Nazis, but she had undoubtedly been spared a lot. Reasoning induced dreams and sleep, nightmares belonged to the waking hours.

———

'Our dear Emperor prided himself on being the first servant of his people while this Nazi rabble tramples on their betters.' Granny vacillated between lacrimose and bellicose. 'The family lawyer will get the Liechti back quickly enough.' Realising that no Jewish lawyer would be so suicidal as to tackle the SS Security Battalion, she lowered her sights. 'You've nothing to wear. Ohli will get your clothes out.'

Even the purest Aryan required courage against legitimised law-breakers. 'There aren't enough gaols if they arrest people like me. I'll pack the suitcases you had at Rimini and call for you here on the way to Charlotte. Granny can't be left alone.' He was more concerned about his wife's nerves than his safety.

Nerves revealed a dormant resentment. 'I never approved of Kurt, I shouldn't have allowed Adele to marry a . . .' Granny lurched from one impasse to another. 'Especially after the suicide of his brother, mixed up in a naval scandal. Not spying, that would have been better, almost.' Before she was forced into elucidating Uncle Karl's heinous crime, Herta rang. 'I've just returned from Italy where I met your Hungarian nephew.' Granny was innocent of Hungarian relations but given no time to remonstrate. 'Max and I are driving to Vienna tomorrow, tell Karl to call at the Empress Elisabeth in the afternoon.' Having explained that Father must have escaped to Italy was preferable to explaining why his brother had shot himself.

The taxi driver assisted Ohli in bringing up the luggage. 'The guard at the Liechti first refused me entry, but an officer eventually received me in your room, seated at the desk. Thank God you got rid of those stickers, otherwise he'd have been less . . . friendly. It sounds crazy, but he somehow conveyed he was sorry you hadn't come yourself. Even crazier, as when the SS moved in they had orders to detain any occupant, but you were luckily out, the brute actually said "luckily", so at present they aren't after you. He encouraged me to pack not just the two Rimini cases but also that sharkskin trunk from Berlin. To top it all he helped me to squeeze in your tails and skisuit. His name is Hans Wilner.'

——— ——— ———

With one 'Potentiality for love' lost by hesitations, Karl quickly made a date with the other. Without any danger to Irene he could meet her at a large café, yet precautions were justified on the way. In a grim parody of the Berlin pick-up, a lout shared Karl's fascination with ORTHOPEDIC APPLIANCES and then sat at an adjoining table. Irene remained admirably unfussed, abandoning the expected romance for practical needs. Karl would pay her and Ralph's expenses in Vienna and be refunded abroad. She would take the stamp collection, the Redhead other valuables, girls were probably less suspect. For the benefit of the lout they flirted ostentatiously, then Irene made his life difficult by leaving first and Karl jumped into a passing taxi.

Entering and leaving hotels by different doors, dashing round corners, stopping suddenly in the spy film practice were approved by the Baron. 'Our cup transactions were sensibly kept quiet, this business would land us in a concentration camp. With war likely I need extra funds but can't risk a bank transfer from Switzerland, you ditto the other way, the ideal deal for enemies of the Reich. I doubt whether postal censorship is yet working effectively, but I won't mention your name. I'll tell you the code when I get confirmation from Zurich. We settle then, naturally at black market rates.'

At these rates Karl faced a Spartan future abroad, while in Vienna he temporarily disposed of more money than he could have expected without permanent ruin. He therefore anticipated the worst by entertaining at the most expensive restaurants and nightclubs as if he had been a Nazi victor and not a victim.

He led his three guests to the usual table at the Splendid, opposite an unmistakably German party, the Gauleiter and his staff. They danced stiffly with ample-bosomed blondes which provoked Karl from a gentle cheek-to-cheek with Irene into unsuitably fanciful steps. For once the orchestra did not sustain the best customer; the bandleader's grimace varied the 'too pretty' into 'You are too foolish for your own good' and this did not require years to work out.

——— ——— ———

'You are now the owner of the Liechti, signed, sealed but not delivered' was Herta's welcome. 'If father had taken Norbert Lechfurt's advice . . .'

'Is he all right?'

'Thanks to Max and me. On the invasion night the Austrian border guards were more humane than the Hungarians. Cars were piling up in no-man's land, Father was in excellent company. Archduchess Adelheid and her brother were driven by the Belgian Minister into their Hungarian Kingdom, from which the Regent wanted to exclude them for fear of German reprisals. All the others had to return to their country that existed no more. Father arrived pretty exhausted at the Tarburg, but immediately assigned the Altenhof to me, the Liechti to you and had you declared, not insane as you should be, merely of age. Border control had by then been tightened, but the guards know me as I often shop in Italy and there was no hitch in driving Father over. By now he should be in Zurich where Tania is to join him. Not you, he doesn't know yet that you are homeless. But I doubt that he'll take her to Burmah.'

'Why there of all places? Surely not because of that mysterious Burmah House on the Liechti?'

'I'd forgotten about that, very odd indeed. A former agent of the Tarburgs now manages a tea plantation in Burmah and was home on leave. He's sure he can obtain a visa for Father. You and I must get along with the Nazis, we have too much to lose. I've made a date with our new lawyer, a party member recommended by Norbert.'

The lawyer had little hope of dislodging the SS from the Liechti, but the transfer of the Altenhof might be recognised, the Tarburgs had some influence in Berlin. The new owners should resume their former administration as speedily as possible.

Max put in an appearance the following day, accompanied by his brother-in-law who waited in the forest so as not to compromise the mission. The peace and quiet of a sunny spring day provided a blessed relief from the recent upheavals. He suddenly understood Father's preference for his own land to travelling. Pity Irene would not see the Altenhof to which she had been invited. So much for making plans, yet that was an essential enjoyment when in love. Max had been gone a long time. If it was another swoop by the SS, Wilner would not be in command. What a missed opportunity, but how could it be squared with Irene? Problems seemed worse on an empty stomach. At last a car was heard, better hide till the agreed two blasts.

'Cook insisted on preparing a meal while I was talking to the agent. It would have been unkind to disappoint her.'

With due consideration for a neither old nor faithful servant wasn't it less charitable to let a brother-in-law starve? Max drove as though on a race track and not on narrow country lanes, an assertion that the game had passed to the Tarburgs.

——— ———

'I've annoyed you more than once with the good old Jewish saying "Your worries and the money of the Rothschilds". Now Louis Rothschild has been arrested – and so might you be, unless you become an Albanian.'

'That was already very unfunny in *Così fan Tutte*, dear Otto. Queen Geraldine is distantly related the Voltains, but that's hardly a reason to adopt me.'

'Adoption it is, not quite as regal but connected with that upstart kingship. The son of the Court Minister boasted at the crammer course of making compromised Austrians into Albanians. They are supposedly Aryans, nobody knows, cares or can write, except the Imam who registers births and deaths, perhaps also your marriage with Irene. It's worthwhile following up.'

'When I know the name of my prospective father, old Voltain might ask Geraldine to check him out. I'd hate to be circumcised pointlessly. As a consolation I'll buy myself some more gold cigarette cases.'

'Not the most economical way for a non-smoker to export funds. Lis's father might hand over.'

——— ———

Granera did hand over the proceeds of the bond sales after deducting 20 percent 'because of the risk'. Lis was furious but Karl was in no position to argue and brought the second third of the bonds to be sold likewise. Leaving so much in the safe might have been wise or foolish, he would never know; subsequent decisions would soon prove right or wrong, which made them all the harder. A compatriot of Ralph, a journalist, exchanged a small sum at the black market rate and introduced a Dutchman interested in a fairly large amount. That elderly gentleman seemed trustworthy, but would total strangers 'remember' to repay abroad when even Austrian 'friends' were doubtful? Irene and Ralph were reliable, but the stamps and gold cigarette cases might be confiscated by the customs. Perhaps a total loss, perhaps enough to start . . . what?

The plebiscite that had been Austria's last hope was transformed into a tragic farce of voting 'For or Against the Anschluss' after the event. SA and SS guards watched with German thoroughness that no voter drew the curtain of the ballot booth and Karl cast his vote openly in favour to receive a card certifying that he had done his duty. Göbbels' Propaganda Ministry declared an improbable 98 per-cent of 'Joyful Acceptance', probably based on a real majority as an advantageous exchange rate of schillings into marks swayed many a patriotic Austrian.

Karl was called up, not to defend Austrian independence but to serve the power that had put an end to it. Had the order been readdressed from the Liechti to Mrs Schupp by Wilner to prevent trouble or a party stalwart to provide canon fodder? In either case the SS was aware of his hideout.

The medical officer referred dubious cases to civilian specialists. Karl herded the maximum of 'Lucky cripples' into a taxi and was thanked in accents amusing under less critical circumstances. Once the Eye Clinic had been located in the vast old General Hospital, a cursory test confirmed that the defective right eye could not be corrected. Karl took the report back to the barracks and received his exemption on medical grounds. The military certificate together with the voting card were required for the recently imposed exit visa, in case the Albanian adoption was too long delayed. Emigration passed from the 'if' to 'when' after the Altenhof was declared forfeited; the transfer from an enemy of the Reich was not recognised. Tania's claim to the Landtheater was similarly rejected, but she had secured an engagement at a Zürich Theatre. Eventually she would join her husband, who must be given time to establish himself in Burmah. There was no message for her stepson at a brief meeting. She was absorbed in her own worries and failed to see the comic exoticism of an Albanian/Burmese relation. Leaving Austria was her first priority as for so many others.

——— ———

Ernst's priority was artistic. 'No *jeune premier* has ever directed the Burgtheater, he isn't even a Nazi but no Aryan German was at hand.'

Karl remembered the young actor almost as embarrassed as Father when caught with the two French ladies. He had always been friendly, but not even a Burgtheater Director could help with the Liechti. 'Why not your father?'

'The Master Race doesn't like to be represented by a comic actor. Moreover, he is too compromised by my accompanying the Lothars to the States. I'm marrying Hansi.'

'Congratulations. Very brave to marry into "the accursed race" at this juncture, but Lothar's plays have been performed abroad, so he must have the right connections. Would you like introductions from Bluhm?'

Ernst expressed shocked surprise beyond any Reinhardt Seminar training. 'Don't you even know what's happening in your Land-theater? Some SA bandits abducted him, beat him up, gouged out his eyes and dumped him in his flat. He opened the gas . . .'

Several outstanding intellectuals had preferred suicide to arrest, one had jumped from the window when the SA battered down his door, but these had been merely famous names. Now a friend, seducer, an intimate had met a horrible end. The SA thugs had almost certainly played in Sunday Morning as a start to their thea-trical career. A common practice, and Bluhm was no worse than most directors. In his agony he made the right choice, better dead than blind.

––––––

Too many new faces might stir the Schupp porter into reporting 'suspicious movements', but the meeting with Irene at a café had probably been filed under a similar heading. To mistake Paul for anything but a theology student seemed unlikely, but that too had become suspect. 'The Faculty is in a shambles. Most profs oppose the Nazis and risk concentration camp, a minority advocates co-oper-ation. I want neither. Not only the Israelites are leaving, but many a good Christian, like the Young Monarchist whom you helped so generously. The Chairman waited too long and is now in custody, whatever that means. The lecturer in Hebrew, not a very popular subject just now, has found me a place at Notre Dame in the States. You'll probably get away before me, let's keep in touch.'

Aunt Charlotte approved of Paul – 'He has his heart in the right place.' Her diagnosis broadened into incorporeal analysis. 'Your mother's death did not stop the run of misfortunes attached to Burmah House, alack, alack.'

Splendid gothic novel stuff, to which it was not hard to respond with 'Woe be me.'

'It is time you consulted a fortuneteller. No cards, none of the romance with the King and Queen of Hearts, a plain crystal ball.'

An amatory dimension was not essential. The horoscope had proved all too accurate. He had nothing to lose but a few marks and an entertaining tale to gain.

The crystal gazer was middle-class, middle-aged and businesslike. 'You have to co-operate. Look straight at the ball and open up. A free flow of thoughts but not a word to interrupt my trance.' Both concentrated energetically on the ball. 'You are facing problems for which you are ill-prepared' was probable for all clients at present. 'You contemplate a change, the others were imposed on you, but this is your choice. A change of . . . status, nationality. Don't, it's useless even when successful, futile. You are in love with love, not with anyone in particular. That raises many problems. Studies too are oddly diverse, against the grain.' She sighed and sank back into her chair. 'You are walking a tightrope, but the safety net is open, at least at present. I can only respond to what's in your mind. That'll be 100 marks.' Expensive for a depressingly negative session.

—— —— —— ——

'Futile indeed! What's the alternative to Albania?' Otto was scornful. 'La Schupp must have overheard you on the phone and instructed the oracle. Her Poor Boy Syndrome is becoming dangerous.'

'On the contrary, her PBS is highly constructive. Her superintendent brother is probing the Gestapo for an exit visa.'

'Let's hope the ball woman will be proved as psychic as you about the exam. You seemed to know that studying was futile.'

—— —— —— ——

Irene and Karl were invited to the Tarburg. The girl was lodged next to the castle's pride, a sunken bath in which she soaked away her apprehension as Herta decreed evening dress even at dinners *en famille*. Regrets that they were not meeting on the Altenhof quickly disappeared in Irene's German and Max's worse English. 'Karl will show you to your room, guests have wandered off to Papa's wing. The switch is so far from the bed that you'd better take this candle, it's more reliable than a flashlight.'

'My sister is positively ante-diluvial, but if she isn't afraid of the pile burning down . . .' The candle flickered in the vaguely menacing dark, but even without the romantic trappings they were sufficiently in love. Less poetic than Romeo, Karl did not discourse on nightingale or lark, but hated equally to depart at dawn for the sake of appearances.

After breakfast they went for a walk in the park, more in love in the bright sunshine than in the darkness. Alone with her brother before lunch, Herta sympathised. 'The poor girl tried hard to wash out the stain but the maid had to change the sheet.' No other reference and she probably did not tell Max.

The old couple fussed charmingly over Irene, especially the Countess who had hunted in England, where life had changed less than in poor Austria. No wonder Karl wanted to leave, she was sorry but understood.

Herta did not. 'Your giving up the Liechti will make the return of the Altenhof all the more difficult. The German Tarburgs have promised to intervene at the highest level in Berlin.'

'They couldn't do much for Max's cousin.'

'You aren't a political figure even after opening the Monarchist Ball. However, if you marry Irene and join her father in Tanganyika or wherever he is governor . . . The former colonies are bound to be returned to Germany and you come back with them.'

'For wishful thinking you have no equal. I hand back the colonies to Hitler and am enfeoffed with all the castles the Führer has stolen from Starhemberg. End of fairy tale and back to earth. Granera is demanding more than his pound of flesh and his legitimate half-brother kindly consented to dispose of the remaining bonds. Old Voltain knows no more about such sales than Ohli, but he has contacts and Marie Louise or Otto will eventually bring out the proceeds.'

'He has been engaged an awfully long time.'

To point out that the delay was Dolly's choice might have anticipated Irene's similar common sense. 'I'd love to fall into your arms, Karl darling, and will do so in any case. You have a wonderful talent for choosing irresistible settings, this lovely forest with the castle in the background. But don't you think I should tell my parents when your future becomes more settled?'

Had it not occurred to her that they might contribute to that? Father had paid Max's debts and straightened out the whole Tarburg mess, but a title had been part of the bargain. Love was rarely decisive in his circle, Karl had no illusions why he had been so eminently eligible, though there was nothing wrong with his looks. Girls had angled for him as openly as once the suitors for Herta. English practicality brought home his changed standing in the marriage market. Stupidly old-fashioned to feel obliged to make a proposal. He had overestimated the importance of virginity, waiting was sensible. She was right but had dealt his self-esteem a very nasty blow.

76

Aunt Valerie rose above a mere Poor Boy Syndrome, so her 'I am delighted you are marrying that charming English girl' was answered truthfully. She embraced him and consoled intelligently, lovingly, like Mother. 'So many marriages turn out wrong . . .', 'my own, Max's' remained unspoken. 'You and Irene stand a good chance. Sorry Karl, tactless to speak of chance after what you've been through the last month. It is not final . . . my cousin Dora had to be asked three times.' Again an unspoken 'I know you won't.' 'As long as you can still be unhappy you haven't experienced real misery, the end of all feelings. You wonder why you once cared so much.'

———————

Jealous of Hitler's 'Walk into Austria', Mussolini invaded Albania on Good Friday. The King and Queen fled over the snow-covered mountains into Greece, their country was annexed by Italy. The crystal gazer was proved so stunningly correct over the Albanian naturalisation that little hope was left for love, despite appearances and feelings.

Hitler claimed parts of Czechoslovakia, and British subjects were advised to return to their country. Irene and Ralph departed with Karl's most valuable possessions and he could not even wish them farewell at the station for fear of compromising their mission. Letters to a Fechtner might interest the censor and the agreed code was forwarded to Marie Louise. That 'The Flying Dutchman sang beautifully' was an enormous relief, but a minor Wagnerian character was missing. The English journalist added arrogant insult to fraudulent injury, 'This is a very small commission for introducing you to my Dutch friend. However, if you insist, next time I'm in London . . .'

Confidence remained shaky on payment to the Baron against a simple note from Zurich. 'Your friend will receive all consideration due to him.' Neither name nor amount, yet when the Baron suggested an increase, the opportunity could not be missed as no other was available. The exit visa would soon be granted against 3,000 marks, an exorbitant sum for a legitimate permit. Was bribing the Gestapo really necessary? The nerve-racking dilemma altered form but not substance. But money mattered little against the pervading fear of arrest by the Toad or SA partners at Toni, to be sent to a concentration camp, to be blinded.

Decisions were not helped by Ohli's request 'Can you afford it?' He handed Mitzi one year's wages after her account of the Liechti's occupation, when the servants had been thrown out because they had 'worked for an enemy of the Reich'. Served coffee instead of serving, she talked about the ruin of her family in the Inflation and refused the money till persuaded by the magic formula 'Mother would have wanted it.' Mitzi cried for herself, the Fechtners and Karl in particular, she would send Cook along.

'At this rate . . .' Ohli was deeply worried. 'I feel hopelessly inadequate. I advised my students, not too badly judging by their careers, yet I can't advise my only grandson except to finish his studies. That's why Father didn't take you to Burmah.'

———————

'Paris it shall be. You'll enter the Hautes Etudes Commerciales without exam. The HEC is one of the three Great Schools, that should please your father.' Pleasure was not the feeling of Marie Louise, Lis and Karl seated among the lilac bushes facing the Burg that held so many memories. 'It is good luck that my aunt is working for the League of Nations. She wonders whether you can afford staying at the St Honoré.'

'If I hear that phrase once more I'll scream. The beauty of being ruined is that you can afford not even a third class hotel like the Acropole. Thank Lis for booking me into something less suicidal.'

'All our lives have been ruined by that damned housepainter. Erwein left last week, now you, Karl.'

Goodbyes might be final despite all plans and promises. With the grandparents there were not even those, only worries about Karl's survival in exile. The Auers' wedding present, the ruby-and-gold cups that started Mother's collection was a suitable expression of gratitude to Aunt Charlotte who refused any payment.

Reciprocal grief consoled, the solitary farewell from Mother hurt. Karl decorated her grave with masses of mimosa, her favourite flower. He knelt to pray, for her continuing intercession after communion became harder far from the familiar white marble that stood out among tombs as the Liechti among houses. It was childish to fear that Mother cared for him less elsewhere.

———————

Otto watched for him at the airport. In the taxi he confirmed the limited choices available in a mixture of English and French spiced with Greek and Latin incomprehensible to the driver. Nervous hilarity insufficiently masked the sense of loss as the separation might be much longer than planned. Otto would bring out the remaining funds providing that . . . The three suitcases were registered unopened, but the astounding laxity of the customs only emphasised the severity of the passport control. No sooner had Fechtner been checked against a list than he was ordered out of the queue into a floodlit room where he had to strip. Clothes as well as the naked body were searched methodically, meticulously by practised fingers. Gold watch and bracelet, signet ring and medals were scrutinised in silence, only the Imperial Eagle provoked a grunt of disapproval. After a last embarrassing probe the passport was stamped. He passed through the gate, not daring to wave a farewell. Thank God he had observed the Draconian currency restrictions, though it was maddening that he might have stuffed the luggage with banknotes. Better poor than in a concentration camp. He was free, free to choose his future, it was terrifying.

4

Self-exile sounded grander than refugee but added nothing to the miserly ten marks that just paid the taxi to the modest pension where Tania had visited Father. What a contrast with previous stays as guest to be 'gilded with chocolate'. Chocolate would be fine, he was hungry, Kurt would reciprocate at least modestly that luscious lunch.

The cousin suggested a wine cellar where the small carafe was accompanied by one portion of cheese. Meanness was aggravated by insensitivity as Kurt showed interest in Tania's theatrical career but none in Karl's pressing problems. An empty stomach tempted phoning that nice Jewish banker who had coined the chocolate phrase, but Karl had turned to none of Father's friends in Vienna. False pride or dignified reticence?

The ample breakfast was luckily included in the room price. A prayer for Mother's intercession at the Baron's bank was substantially but not entirely answered. The note was honoured, but the client – no name, of course – had given no further instructions. No doubt another order was *en route*. That Karl doubted, even the most circuitous route would not take so long. Phoning was dangerous, writing meant costly waiting, better to cut one's losses. But the Baron's forgetfulness hurt more than the journalist's crookery.

—— —— ——

Crookery was irremediable, exploitation was stoppable. Heinz, delighted, welcomed his compatriot *Chez Smith* to swap tales about the decline and fall of Austria as well as of themselves till 'Duty calls, I have to meet a client'. Karl was left with the bill, perhaps because of the gigolo's hurried departure, perhaps from habit. His annoyance was noted by the Tea Room's most heavily made-up young exquisite who stopped feeding his clipped poodle with cake. 'You should be used to Heinz's sudden exit from two years ago. I remember, because you are such an unlikely pair. No more than Georges and I. Won't you join us?' Slightly older Georges Arnault was indeed reassuringly inconspicuous and persuaded Karl to have a drink at a piano bar. Soft music and light facilitated closer acquaintance, strengthened by Georges' explanation that the discreet crown in his lapel was the emblem of the French Royalists. Monarchist fellowship continued at a small restaurant where Georges and Raimond were as well known as at the Bœuf sur le Toit, Paris's most sophisticated nightclub. An evening to be repeated besides auguring well for the visit to the Palais Royal.

The widowed Princess Voltain belonged to the white-and-gold elegance of the League of Nations Cultural Department. She was immediately afflicted by the Poor Boy Syndrome, offering to act as postbox for correspondence from Austria. She then rang the registrar of the HEC and explained persuasively that Mr Fechtner needed forthwith a paper certifying his acceptance as a boarder for the autumn. 'That should suffice for a residence permit, difficult as officially you are not a refugee. Socialists and Communists are assisted by their parties but a Monarchist is the pariah among Austrian exiles.'

Without political sponsors the HEC registration sufficed only for a temporary permit, 'until further consideration'. Hopes of joining Irene were dashed at the British Consulate; HM Government no longer recognised Austrian passports, visa applications had to be submitted for valid German travel documents. Karl had no intention of following this preposterous advice, though it would stop the disadvantage of not being enough of a refugee in France, and too much in England, neither fish nor fowl.

————

Fowl proved disastrous at the lunch with a former secretary of Father at a Hungarian restaurant. Burmah's approval of the HEC had just been conveyed by a small amount barely covering the registration fee when a handsome quadragenarian was placed at their table in the crowded room. The Secretary's awed whisper 'Marlene Dietrich's ex-husband' made his guest cut so energetically into his paprika chicken that it slithered from the abundant sauce onto the chest of the distinguished vis-à-vis. Shamefaced apologies failed, and the uncouth guest was not given a second chance.

A lasting chance was Georges' frequent invitations; but Ohli's 'There is no such thing as a free meal' proved correct. Payment was exacted with the determination that made Georges a promising flight lieutenant and an unpromising lover. The joylessness of sex came uncomfortably close to Heinz's professionalism to be deplored at the dive of their first meeting. Karl danced as recklessly as with Irene at the Splendid and against all probability the young tough, who nearly started a row when asked to remove the cigarette from the corner of his mouth, was called Irenée. The similarity of names for such glaring opposites appealed to Karl's sense of humour, especially when Irenée claimed to have done his duty as Basque and Communist in the Spanish Civil War. A novel specimen on both accounts and a potent antidote to the Royalist flight lieutenant.

Where the League of Nations Princess had failed, the Communist of unspecified employment succeeded. A comrade at the *préfecture* would issue a two-year residence permit, yet ironically the desired document removed the beneficiary from the hold of the no-longer-desired benefactor. 'Help from unexpected quarters' was rewarded with excusable ingratitude.

Violent changes flavoured the Voltain drawing room where the 'gallant boy' became a hero because of his assistance to Princess Starhemberg as described by Marie Louise. The refusal to apply for a German passport was heartily approved, less so his intention of spending the summer at Cannes even without mentioning that Raimond was waiting there. The familiar 'can you afford it?' of parsimonious aristocrats was countered by the elderly Imbert de Brillac with the merits of a holiday after the horrors of the Anschluss and before the rigours of the HEC.

———

Brillac's short stay at Cannes pleasantly eased the strain of conforming to a costly routine on the cheap. Raimond's set could and occasionally did talk intelligently, but not on Brillac's level about the worsening Czech crisis. Political opinions naturally coincided over excellent meals, despite bills concocted with more artistry than accuracy. The congenially disparate pair provided Cannes with a scandal that never was. Imbert resembled Father of pre-Tania days and this affinity would be continued at Brillac Castle. In the meantime Karl was left to the care of Prince Osman.

Not particularly tender, as the Prince had been trained at the German Military Academy, but courtly as he was the nephew of the last Caliph. Karl eagerly succumbed to a genuine Imperial Highness, not the wrong side of the blanket like perfumed Clemens. The outcome was more grandly disastrous. Driving back from his flat the Prince emphasised his multilingual disregard of grammar so energetically that he smashed the Citroën's window and cut his wrist.

Blue blood indistinguishable from red stained Karl's white suit and discouraged the dynastic liaison.

———— ———— ————

When not exhausted or privately engaged, Raimond's set finished the night at the *Chat Noir*. Dancing again triggered Karl's recklessness, though the heat provided an excuse for shedding shirt and tie to display the bronzed torso under the white mess jacket for a solo to Ravel's *Bolero*. A fair Englishman applauded as tolerantly as the nightclub's other late customers, but subsequently showed greater interest. He was a jeweller, sharing with friends a villa where Karl spent a fortnight made all the more enjoyable by the promise of assistance with the gold cigarette cases smuggled to London.

———— ———— ————

The Czech crisis had not yet reached its mobilisation climax when the Flight Lieutenant embarked with Karl for Corsica. They hired a car, unfortunately equipped with a radio which ordered officers to report immediately for duty. A forest inn devoid of such newfangled inventions was sufficiently remote to ignore the recall for one night. The creaking of the bed was romanticised by the rustling of the trees as was Georges' lovemaking by patriotic fervour. Military priority secured a cabin for the return to the mainland where Georges insisted that Brillac Castle was preferable to Paris, especially for foreigners of ambiguous status. Karl was alone on a journey through a country gripped by war panic.

The lovely Louis XIII château belonged to another century not only architecturally but also in manners and thoughts. The similarly-attuned neighbours sympathised with a fellow monarchist and condemned French politicians for not defending the remnants of the Austrian Empire they had so wantonly destroyed. The 'Peace in our Time' of the Munich surrender was deplored by families who had governed too long to be deceived by demagogues or dictators.

'Thanks to you and your friends I begin to understand Marx; class is more significant than nationality.' Karl stunned his host. 'I had nothing in common with the Viennese mob the night of the Anschluss, but you have all made me feel at home.'

———— ———— ————

Not so the eager beavers apparently chosen for their total lack of humour and segregated in monastic cells on the top floor of the HEC. Inadequate bathrooms and cupboards compared dismally with the recent *ancien régime* splendour; food and drink competed only in quantity. Rough red wine at lunch was consoling but fatal to the incomprehensible jargon of the afternoon lectures which finished just in time to meet Georges at the piano bar. Karl had to return for the absurd 10 p.m. closing. A deadly earnest Icelander in the adjoining cell desired elucidation on some obscure points; lucky chap that only points and not the entire proceedings were obscure.

Several cups of coffee awakened a sense of duty for the morning lectures; sobriety made bearable the long post-prandial ordeal before the short evening relaxation with patient Georges.

A particularly obtuse morning started a classic chain of consolations: the rough red slept off in an illicit siesta followed by self-reproach appeased at a night out. Relief at the Bœuf climaxed into oblivion at Les Mignons where a sprinkling of respectable male whores was allowed for the sake of variety and foreigners. Raimond provided a virtuous couch for the few hours before re-entering the HEC with the day students. Without the breakfast coffee, drowsiness increased during an endless morning, requiring no wine before rushing to bed. The chain linked into a vicious circle.

Entertainment had smothered bad conscience in Vienna; but, despite a terrible row with Father, failing an exam was not irretrievable; moreover, subconsciously he knew that there would be no exam. Karl was honest enough to ascribe a similar feeling to wishful thinking, yet a war seemed more likely now than the Anschluss then. Studies were familiarly tiresome, yet outside an academic degree lay the hand-to-mouth existence of *Les Boys* or even the misery of Heinz. Psychoanalytical excuses might seem plausible but led nowhere. Better join forces with the Icelander to whose questions Karl had no clue.

———————

Princess Voltain warmly supported the good resolutions and undermined them fatally by handing over letters in a code so primitive as to avoid detection. Marie Louise was 'in fine fettle' despite her tubercular knee, which required long immobilisation to be endured in France. Otto was bringing out more funds after the final exams. Irene confirmed the impossibility of admittance to the UK on an Austrian passport, and urged application for a German. Father stated his interest in Buddhism and preference for an English degree more useful in Burma, for which the final *h* was dropped. Renewed ties with the Austrian past and prospects of a British future legitimised doubts about salvation by the French present.

Yvonne left Vienna after the dreadful November night when persecution turned into pogrom. She suggested sharing a flat, two bedrooms divided by a sitting room, at an astoundingly low rent. Considering her tolerant understanding this seemed an ideal opportunity to continue at the HEC as a day student, freed from the hateful 10 p.m. restriction. No sooner had he changed his status than he reproached himself for abandoning the essential disciplinary restraint. Cohabitation with a member of the Jewish Relief Organisation held disadvantages as uncomfortable as the academic straitjacket. He paid Yvonne the half-share of the rent for two months and returned to the St Honoré. His managerial studies resulted in singular mismanagement, money thrown away on the HEC board and the rent to be saddled with the higher hotel bill.

———————

Compensatory economies were easiest on food, maximum calories at minimum cost. The experience of the childhood slimming craze indicated a diet of cakes and sweets to preserve physical and financial resources. The enchantment of chocolate waned while stomach pains waxed till diagnosed as gastritis. Despite abstention from now nauseating pastries, Karl turned a yellow lividly proclaiming jaundice. Food vanished from the expense account as two heterogeneous consortia of caterers competed in providing the prescribed boiled vegetables and stewed fruit. The physician, formerly of the Austrian legation, understood a Fechtner's dislike of a public ward as well as the financial strain of a private room; he agreed to the shifts of amateurish attendants at the hotel. Hepatitis-by-patisserie required split-second timing to divide the Voltain/Brillac charity volunteers from the Georges/Raimond set.

The set was enlarged by Daniel Weil on his return from Argentina, where his family owned a chain of stores. He was cherubic, chubby, Jewish and lazy, dumped by his divorced parents on a grandmother whose meanness kept pace with the severity of exchange controls. An Austrian refugee had psychoanalysed but not cured Daniel of his proclivity for rough trade. Hilarity and commiseration established a bond of cynicism; however, Daniel had dual nationality and Karl none.

Marie Louise passed through Paris, expressing the need for Christmas sympathy at Berck Plage where plaster was the essential part of her wardrobe. Though less handicapped, Karl shared the longing for a familiar from a happier past and against medical advice he opted for convalescence on the Channel coast. Grey waves battered the windswept beach where the revolting heartiness of masochistic bathers competed with the raucous squawks of seagulls; a poignant contrast to the quiet sufferers on wheeled beds through which Karl zigzagged into the girl's arms. Discarding her convent reticence she removed by a good cry the emotional obstacles to an enjoyable Christmas dinner under a disgraceful artificial tree with vulgar electric candles. Karl clasped over her thin wrist a bracelet chosen from the jewellery she had smuggled out of Austria, and received a silk shirt made by the Fechtner outfitter before the shop was smashed in the November pogroms.

During a break in the depressing drizzle they ventured on a picnic excursion; the portable bed was heaved onto a cart drawn by a mare which proved on the home stretch more spirited than she looked. Jolting over rough lanes, the patient, relatively secure in her carapace, retained her good humour, but the nervous coachman regained his only with the first post-jaundice champagne on New Year's Eve. All those immobilised in plaster casts were united in a cynical optimism: things could hardly get much worse.

——— ———

They could, by the suicide attempt of Yvonne's mother. Losing her job after the pogrom, Mrs Venteser jumped out of a window of her flat, suffered multiple fractures and was severely ill at the Jewish Community Hospital. Yvonne forced a small sum on Karl despite his objections to involving Ohli. Karl was anxious to make a contribution himself, but as the daughter's offering apparently relieved her guilt he reluctantly accepted and forwarded the request to Vienna. Ohli, contemptuous of 'the pseudo-scientific anti-Semitic idiocy', confronted the Hospital's SA guard with his headmaster authority only to learn from the Jewish clerk that Mrs Venteser had died.

Literally broken in body and spirit, what an end for that humorous easygoing woman whose sacrifice made possible the daughter's survival abroad. How to break such news gently, silly facile expression! Hospitals had experience in informing next of kin, heartfelt condolences needed no diplomacy. Yvonne reproached herself bitterly for abandoning her mother, but when she met Karl her excitement over an affidavit for the States rivalled her mourning. Anxieties and hopes for the future pushed aside the past and the insignificant amount was forgotten. That the sum was smaller than the contribution to Yvonne's rent was no excuse, nor that this forgetting was unintentional not deliberate like the Baron's or the journalist's. Bad conscience or perhaps the subconscious wish to sever the link with the only Jewish refugee postponed a reply to Yvonne's letter from New York.

——— ———

Complex feelings and practical problems could at last be discussed with Otto. 'No Freud needed to explain the forgetfulness, you are frightened and quite rightly. Tomorrow you gird yourself with your birth certificate and Austrian passport for battle at the German Consulate as Irene has sensibly advised. You can't sit any longer on a non-existent Austrian high horse.'

Otto's realistic appraisal decided the long-delayed ordeal. 'A forbidding Germania wondered why I resisted so long the appeal of the Reich. I answered her embarrassing questions as dishonestly as I dared. Just when I thought she would tear up my Austrian passport and refuse a German, she remarked with Gestapo cunning that the whites of my eyes were yellow. Luckily I refrained from telling the old cow that it was none of her business as apparently she too had just recovered her Aryan whiteness. We swapped nauseating experiences and in a jiffy I became a German Resident Abroad, a subtle distinction from the ordinary Swastika passports. Jaundiced of the world unite.'

'Off to Irene in GB where they live happily ever after.'

'No, to St Moritz, my delicate health requires fresh air.'

'That you had at Berck, which pleased Marie Louise, Heaven knows why. St Moritz is a silly waste of that lovely lolly my brother helped me to bring out. In full SS regalia he swept me through the controls as if I was to organise a fifth column in Paris.'

Skiing in the thin mountain air tired a still convalescent Karl, so that Otto went on longer runs on his own. Returning in a heavy snowfall he became increasingly worried by Karl's absence from the usual and even unusual places till a snowman lurched into sight.

'Sorry, I should have left a note; I just wandered into the forest, in a kind of make-believe.'

'The Altenhof?'

'I never liked it but it was ours. The loss of everything . . . I'm ungrateful, how many people have a friend who understands immediately? But in a few days I'll be alone again.'

'Hence with admirable logic you totter into the solitude of the wild woods. Russian roulette according to Fechtner rules, what will finish you off, cold, exhaustion or pneumonia? And why this lack of enthusiasm for a reunion with your stepmum and cousin Kurt?'

'Near but hardly dear. Kind Germania warned me that emotional upset might revive that becoming yellow tinge.'

'So you try a physical shock. A bottle of wine might do the trick less painfully.' Otto sat on, then got into Karl's bed and drew his friend's head onto his shoulder in the protective attitude of the older and stronger boy. 'The loss of innocence' turned from an embarrassing into a cherished memory. 'My panicky severance of sexual relations was somewhat premature. As the Barovsky fortune is second even to the Freyer dowry, Dolly is in no hurry . . .'

'Then we have time for a bachelor reunion after your finals before we both settle down as respectable husbands. If you can extract the last of the bond proceeds from Ohli we can spend the summer in Greece.'

'If I pass the exams, if I'm not forthwith drafted, if war hasn't broken out, if you must waste your last pennies on journeys you can't afford.'

'Same old song about the sledge I've hired for tomorrow. No miserly one-horse contraption, a sinfully expensive two. Mother enjoyed carriage rides at Maloja and that's where we are going. A wintry version of that lovely excursion to Ravello.'

Nostalgia miraculously intensified the joy of driving with tinkling bells through the fairytale forest. A novel experience cemented an old understanding during that blissful Swiss interlude.

———————

Father had been right, sleeping cars were a luxury. In the dimmed light of the second-class compartment, Karl folded into the bench ready for sleep. Not so the young Frenchman opposite, who gradually progressed from salacious words to deeds. Discovering what was inside the deceptive skisuit, he momentarily withdrew but returned for another fumbling assault. Rimini updated for comedy. The seducer disappeared into the dawn of a Paris suburb for which he almost certainly was not bound.

Otto would have savoured the farce to the full. Daniel dared not laugh at sex which he enjoyed vicariously. Yet he was a pleasant companion in the strenuous entertainment routine, temporarily ennobled by the scion of an officially extinct royal line. The young pretender looked the part even without his haemophiliac credentials, which were a bore when sharing his bed. Prosaic precautions against haemorrhages dampened passion and another royal blood flowing-too-freely might be more appreciated by Daniel. Appreciation of dead ancestors insufficiently compensated for the frailty of the living dynast who, in turn, considered the intended partner too Jewish. The pretender departed for his estates in unspecified regions.

Non-consummation by the incompatible, over-consummation by the partly satiated. Jaundice had conveniently downgraded relations with Georges till one evening he pulled a folded piece of paper from an envelope. 'Careful, it's not all that easy to get!'

'It wouldn't be a love philtre?'

'Next best thing. Cocaine can be a potent aphrodisiac. You said you'll try everything once.'

The effects of the snuff exceeded the most sanguine expectations, but did not weaken Karl's determined 'once only' for Georges as well as the coke.

They still went out together in a lopsided friendship, and Karl would have preferred the Lambeth Walk with him rather than Heinz. 'My client wants you, not me. I've told him no go, but he offered me my full fee if you join us for one drink. Please do, Karl, I need every franc. The police are clamping down on aliens and with my Austrian passport . . .'

Lingering guilt over the German document decided the introduction to middle-aged Philip, who conversed in English to exclude Heinz from the conversation and the dinner invitation.

———— ————

The wine waiter remembered Karl's preference for *champagne mature* even with caviar. From a nearby table Daniel and his grandmother nodded recognition, explaining that this was not another commercially matched couple would have overtaxed Karl's liver in conjunction with the forbidden food. Mistaken indications encouraged Philip MacLachlan's fairly honourable proposal. The mining company he managed was relocating to Australia far from the coming war but also from congenial companionship. 'After this delightful evening I think I found the solution and according to Heinz you need a protector. I can get your immigration papers processed before Hitler starts anything fatally nasty.'

Karl wondered at his family's embroilment in the remote corners of the British Empire and his silence was taken for acquiescence.

'I trust you don't mind my being . . . practical, it's only fair to you. Don't you think a try-out might be a good idea? If against expectations . . . there will, of course, be an appropriate compensation.'

The lily was neatly gilded but Karl was not a fortune hunter, though Irene's father might well think so. A personal appearance must verify the pre-Anschluss background she had no doubt stressed. To be mistaken for a gigolo changed from amusing into sordid and might even become tempting. He longed for Irene and a vague normality.

Les Mignons pointed in the opposite direction, but Daniel was the sole confidant. It was late and only a dejected Heinz was standing at the bar. He had been declared an undesirable alien and been given forty-eight hours to leave France. Where to? A client had promised to obtain refugee status, but such promises were easily made. He felt desperate, suicidal.

Never mind that the poor chap had painted a distorted picture to Philip, he needed the reward and now sympathy in a grimly familiar loneliness. Words were useless, but Otto had demonstrated the effectiveness of a friendly shoulder in the privacy of a bed.

Heinz's livelihood depended on hardness of character and sex so that the limp sexlessness of the head-on-shoulder was a wonderful luxury with an amusing side; a notorious gigolo filled virtuously the place Philip had wanted to occupy passionately that very night. To share was to halve the fear of the future which held no hope for one, little for the other.

5

Quite a lot when the British visa was at last granted. Ralph was waiting at Victoria Station. 'I've come up for the day to quarter you on mother. She is looking forward to romanticising with you about Vienna, where her old man was *en poste*, and that's why I had to do PG duty there. She was thrilled with your stamps and cigarette cases, probably suspects them to be part of the Imperial treasure. I won't be back before the tripos, so you have my den to yourself.'

Mrs Caldwell hovered loquaciously in the wings of the stage dominated by the ebullient Wynn Roberts. Irene was staying with her older brother Richard who picked up the bills for the dinners and dances she realised Karl could not afford. She was driving him to Sunningdale for a long weekend with her parents when her Jaguar ran out of petrol. Father would have condemned such inefficiency but the formidable Sir Arthur seemed amused.

Lady Wynn Roberts belonged to the world of Aunt Valerie, even of Mother, and conveying this flattering comparison aroused a protective attitude closely akin to the PBS. Over the port the Fechtners' Monarchist creed was delineated to the full satisfaction of the Baronet. Parental approval soothed through the annoyingly early morning tea and the liverish bacon-and-eggs to the enjoyment of a first ride with Irene. Both loved horses and handled them well in the grounds of the Royal Military College, open to the Wynn Roberts. Sport formed another link in her confident and his precarious enjoyment of the present, rounded off nightly by dances as in Vienna.

Margarete Horbitzer, now teaching German, resuscitated an earlier Vienna. With the authority of Mother's educational adviser, she wrote to the registrar of Exeter University where Karl had received a diploma, albeit only of the Summer School. She would obtain

Father's agreement to Arts, more congenial than Economics and less likely to end in failure. She was critical, decisive and eminently practical.

——— ———

Practical considerations enlisted the jeweller for the disposal of the 'crown jewels'. Memories of the past summer and prospects of another Cannes idyll excused London elusiveness and yielded roughly half the purchase price. The buyer of the most expensive cigarette case expressed interest in the Austrian stamp collection and, as Karl had been entrusted with the album for perusal, it was only right to give the jeweller's friend a similar opportunity.

The greenery festooning the Pimm's at the Royal Automobile Club was sufficiently intriguing as foundation for a pleasant meal and when the neatly wrapped album was handed back the absurdly low offer passed unnoticed in the rosy glow.

Pastel shades tend to darken on the mornings-after but rarely to the blackness of Karl on discovering that the most valuable misprints were missing. The jeweller was outraged at this breach of trust, theft by any other name, but not being a collector he had glanced too perfunctorily through the pages to testify. Without a witness, a German had no redress against a respected member of Clubland, quite apart from awkward questions as to how the collection had entered the country. Mother's most precious gift, saved from the Nazis and smuggled from Austria at considerable cost, had been so irreparably pilfered that the derisory offer had to be accepted.

——— ———

The lavish hospitality of deception at the RAC damaged finances and self-confidence; tea at the Carlton restored the latter. Sir Arthur's invitation conceded eligibility, confirmed by introductions to several members who discussed Hitler's latest demands with languid concern. Reasoned arguments learned at the Liechti's Thursdays earned a fortnight in Sunningdale, where mutual appreciation ranged from the political to the personal. Private and public entertainment displayed the young couple's closeness which received a semi-official accolade at a Primrose League meeting. Marriage, though not mentioned since Irene's practical objections at the Tarburg, seemed a foregone conclusion.

Certainly to Richard as he connived at his sister's progress to sites educational and musical. She drove Karl to Exeter where Devonshire cream inspired the right answers at the interview with the registrar, so that Karl was admitted for the Michaelmas term. The academically legitimised foray continued to Glyndebourne at Tania's invitation. After a season at the Zürich Theatre she was staying with Fritz Busch, the conductor, and proved more gracious a hostess at *Così fan tutte* than she had been at the Liechti. From an ill-suited stepmother, she changed into a pleasant acquaintance; mellowed by the superb setting and singing, the two Fechtners found an understanding based on the unmentioned grudge against Father. In a tactful aside to Karl, Tania apologised for having secured only one room for her guests because of limited accommodation.

Irene and Karl joined Ralph for May Week at Cambridge. They savoured the undergraduates' sophisticated antics at the *Footlights*, though an impersonator of Marlene Dietrich hardly deserved Ralph's rapturous stare. The college dances differed tumultuously from the stately Viennese balls but were equally appreciated by the young couple.

Young they undoubtedly were, but whether a couple remained doubtful on the drive back. 'My parents wanted to meet you and they like you, darling. But Germans are not exactly popular just now.'

'Considering that I acquired that popular nationality . . .'

'I'm sorry, darling. We couldn't miss the opportunity of their coming home to present me. You won't even stay for my coming out ball. I know, Ralph needs his room but surely some arrangements could be made. Daddy is going back to his colony, but Mummy is staying here over the summer, I'll work on her. When you come back from your jaunt with Otto we'll tackle her jointly before you withdraw to Exeter. We can deal with Daddy by phone.' Sweet reason left the future in the old suspense.

———— ———— ————

Suspense persisted worryingly through the reasoning of Marie Louise and her aunt to the now-or-never frenzy of the Cannes set. The prospect of war whipped even placid Daniel into action. 'Had grandmother died a little earlier the pretender might have departed a little later. The inheritance is handy all the same, as Heinz is again on the block and I want you to put in a bid for me.'

'Quite a climb-down from the princely intrigue. What happened to that client who got Heinz's expulsion rescinded?'

'His wife became too curious for her and his good. You feel sorry for Heinz, I feel sorry for myself, I'm no good at chasing, nobody chases after me, so . . .'

Cynical reasoning left no suspense. Relieved from anxiety about his daily bread, Heinz proved himself superior in sex and wit to the jeweller still contrite over his friend's depredations. Consoling him in the same villa as the previous year combined noble forgiving with forgetting the war fever before meeting Otto at Belgrade.

———— ————

'Your grandmother would do well in Greek tragedy. She sobbed most awesomely, while Ohli counted the lolly. He wasn't wildly enthusiastic over our meeting here, but he grew alarmingly red in the face on learning about the Sarajevo expedition. Why indeed retrace the First World War at great expense when the Second is coming free of charge any moment now?'

Laying flowers furtively at dawn on the spot where Archduke Franz Ferdinand and his wife had been murdered exasperated Otto. 'As idiotic as the Emperor Otto stickers in Vienna. If any Serb chauvinists had seen you, we'd be in a fine mess, gaol probably. You've learned nothing and forgotten nothing.'

'Far from crushed, I'm rather flattered to be raised to Stuart and Bourbon errors. Had Franz Ferdinand reigned, Father would have been in the government not just as a lowly under-secretary. I'd be a count instead of . . .'

Slow trains swaying through the torrid heat to the Greek border worsened Otto's apprehensions. 'Impalement with these hideously crisp 100-mark notes is not my idea of fun, but the Yugs are not likely to probe as deeply as the Nazi exchange control. French letters are such a useful little article.' Delicate arguments were interrupted by a resplendent uniform indicating his determination to guard the travellers. Guard for or against what? An exchange of glances decided deployment of the useful little article. The guard was voluble in a language much his own, trumped by Karl at random with express-ions remembered from Dalmatian holidays. Judiciously dropping the names of the poker robbers, omitting their deed, distracted attention from Otto's pained shifting about while sweat, excessive even in the midday heat, was pouring down his face. When Otto waddled back to the toilet, sympathy for haemorrhoids was added to respect for acquaintance with Serb politicians. The guard prevented the customs officials from entering the compartment, and himself stamped the passports of his protégés lost all too soon.

6

The train was hours late, but Mimis was waiting at the dingy Athens station and drove them to the hotel facing the sea at Old Phaleron. They briefly recaptured the carefree atmosphere of earlier summers, though Angelos rarely joined them on the beach and at

tavernas as he had added secretarial to sexual duties. The Hitler–
Stalin Pact shattered the deceptive sense of security, briefly for the
Greeks, permanently for the Austrians to whom Poland was not
remote but the part of the Empire in which their fathers had fought.
Enforced awareness of their opposition to the spread of Nazism made
them call on a like-minded compatriot.

'We thought we were in a crisis when dear Willi Hollthal brought
you along. No Austrians were taken over by the German Legation
and I only bow to the Minister at Mass, though we are distantly
related. I had the British Minister to a few dinners, but to arrange
an interview just now will rather strain the hospitality.' Christl
Kourdatis sympathised with the boys whose parents would have been
received by hers.

The British Consul impatiently passed his two unclassifiable callers to the Military Attaché, who doubted whether enemy aliens
could travel to Cyprus to volunteer for the armed services. He would
refer the request to London but held out no hope for an early reply.

In despair they tried to join the Foreign Legion, but French
officialdom invoked 'Respect for Greek neuturality, though the good
intentions will be referred to Paris'. 'The Nazis would have cut
through this bureaucratic claptrap. Even if we don't look exactly like
Hollywood legionnaires, it's crazy to be forced by the Allies to fight
against them.'

'They might yet realise that we are indispensable to win the war.
Give them time.'

'At your expense, Karl. I can't get anything out of the Reich, even
if the Barovskys had spare cash. Heaven knows whether you can use
your account with the Wynn Roberts. You need every penny you
have here.'

'Smuggled out at the risk of your life and bum, dear Otto!'

'It's always your money. All right when you had plenty but now
you simply can't afford me.'

'Makes one wonder who had Jewish grandparents. Let's wait till
the end of the Polish campaign.'

——— ———

During 'Wailing Wall Teas' at the Kourdatis villa, the Austrians
bemoaned the Polish cavalry charges that belonged to the war their
fathers had fought to preserve the towns now bombed into ruins.
Poland fell, the Allied bureaucracy prevaricated, Dolly and Irene
joined the Nursing Corps of their countries and Otto insisted on
returning. 'Quite apart from eating up your money, my idling in the
sun might be interpreted correctly, heaven forbid, and get my family

into serious trouble. I can't escape the loving attention of the fifth column indefinitely and will have to fight for the Nazis against you instead of them with you. Odd war, when all sympathies lie with the enemy.'

——— ———

The inevitable separation ended the brief spell of facing a hostile world with the closest friend. Otto was forced into more immediate danger but could rely on the support of Dolly, his family, connections. Karl lacked such natural assistance in dealing with less dramatic but still vital problems, of which accommodation was the most urgent. An acquaintance of Mimis offered hospitality at Kolonaki, Athens's elegant central district. Son of a Greek consul in Shanghai, he was aptly nicknamed Chinese Laundryman because of his slit eyes; he initiated his guest into Modern Greek, surprisingly easy after the nightmarish Ancient, and hashish, the first smoke since childhood. Unpleasant inhaling provoked coughing, a pleasant dream of a blue swan graped by its graceful neck and used as a powder puff ended in the decidedly unpleasant embrace of the Laundryman. A change of abode became imperative.

The search for a room revealed oriental Victoriana and matching landladies till an impeccably anti-Nazi German photographer revealed the guesthouse of Madame Aphrodite Mascot. Under this stage name the daughter of a Bulgarian diplomat and a Rumanian actress – both professions almost certainly upgraded – had sung and danced across the Balkans before too many chins drooped under her still pretty face. She mixed several languages into her Levantine French, kept her establishment clean, and slept in a cubby hole on the ground floor, where three rooms were occupied by her 'gentlemen', while above two nightclub artists were allowed regulars. The price was equally reasonable, especially in Kolonaki.

Inaccessible to her on the Levantine social ladder, Artemis Nuttall kept an eye on her Greek lover, her Italian son from internment and her British son Robert in line. Their manners and money gained them admission to Christl's parties, but Robert also shone among the lesser members of the international set who considered the War an inconvenience in the pursuit of sex. Their pathetic boasts contrasted too violently with Christl's civilised prudery to break the loneliness of a cold rainy winter.

——— ———

Madame Mascot announced a Rumanian attaché who handed Karl two letters. 'By diplomatic bag, a little irregular but we all like to play these tricks on the Nazis. Prince Bib . . . better not to mention names, yes? The Prince stayed with the Countess and conveyed the letters to Bucharest.' He paused, in admiration of such aristocratic deceit.

Herta's distinctive hand kept to essentials.

'. . . The loathsome females of Tarburg are all working or whoring for the Party and you can imagine the pressure on the Castle. The Nursing Corps does not require Party membership, only proof of Aryan descent absurdly called Ancestor Pass. I had our maternal forebears traced back to the sixteenth century, almost as far as the Tarburgs. No need to do the same on Father's side, but the misunderstanding about his mother must be cleared up urgently, that unfortunate misspelling of her Swedish maiden name, Oxenstjerna. The necessary papers can be obtained at her birthplace in Rumania for a modest £500. The kind intermediary who is forwarding this note has found an absolutely trustworthy lawyer but payment must be in a hard currency not available here. Surely you too will wish to have this regrettable error rectified, so please ask Father to transfer the amount to the address below.

'I have asked Otto here to learn how you are getting on. I strongly disapprove of your intentions and believe it best you return. Once we have the Rumanian papers, we can see the Gauleiter about the Altenhof and even the Liechti. Make Father understand . . .'

Whether Herta had convinced herself of the 'misspelling' should become apparent by Otto's letter

'. . . With the daring of the demented my gracious hostess drives about Tarburg in Norbert Lechfurt's SS car with the Swastika standard flying. That shuts up the nastily envious locals, but her playing Tosca to the Gauleiter's Scarpia shows that she has guts if nothing else. Ludwig has hinted at an appeal to Göring after the minimal requirement of three Aryan grandparents has been acquired. Whitewashed grandmothers are all the rage in Bucharest and I hope the Rumanian John the Baptist can deliver the goods before the beloved Führer gets nasty with people of mixed blood.

'The field of honour employs most of the eligible goodlookers so that Dolly became keen on the warbride racket and we were granted three months to produce canonfodder for the next war. *That* a certain useful little article will prevent, but while I am collecting Iron Crosses Dolly can look after my parents all the better with the prestige of a war widow. The fifth column did report dallying in the sun and the Toad, of all the incompetent SS officers, interrogated me about the morale of the Greeks. I told virtuous Franz some shockers about their morals but refrained from revealing your contributions to either. Good luck with the bureaucrats . . .'

——— ———

A wish answered poorly and in part. Not at all by the British or French authorities, while the monthly renewal of Karl's residence permit provided the Greek policemen with the illusion of power to compensate for their miserable pay. Christl pulled strings less expertly than Irenée's Comrade's in a bizarre reversion of the difficulties in Paris. Now he held a valid passport, so why did he not return to his country? The High Commissioner for Refugees refused assistance beyond his competence till a recommendation by Princess Voltain, a League of Nations colleague, made him intervene unofficially with the Chief of the Aliens Police. 'German Resident Abroad' offered a loophole and the one-month provisional permit was extended to a three-month temporary. Saved by jaundice!

Father's stern homily lacked goodwill in a very unfestive season. '. . . Herta is even more to blame; she is older than you and should not be taken in by that Rumanian nonsense. I trust that you will soon join the British army, thus ending your temporary problems. A good war record will facilitate your coming to Burma and, hopefully, in reclaiming the Liechti. I have spent several weeks in a Buddhist monastery, an interesting experience I shall probably repeat . . .'

Father contemplating his navel and grinding away at a prayer mill showed a wickedly sublimated detachment from the plight of his children. He was the wrong sex for an umbilical cord, but had severed the cord of paternal love.

——— ———

Love for Irene withstood her letter announcing her transfer to the WRENs and her regrets that her brother had failed in advancing Karl's enlistment application. Her lukewarm affection was conveyed by Ralph, whose appointment to the Cultural Organisation of the United Kingdom in Athens apparently benefited the war effort more than his military service. His protruding eyes lent some probability to an exemption for hyperthyroidism. His stay in Vienna endeared him to Christl, his Cambridge degree impressed Robert who had been sent down, but Ralph's disapproval of Mimis was reciprocated. Though not intimates, these four were dearer to Karl than a minor diplomat's wife who had been a beauty too long to justify her husband's jealousy.

Mimis' one-track purpose discovered strange places of divertissement. 'A genuine Greek dancing school. Three females too old and ugly for anything but being trodden on by some forty lusty males. A few rather awful queens leave no doubt that it is not for the tango that we allow ourselves to be pushed around. You'll love it.'

Improbable, but an amusing contrast to the childhood dancing classes teaching social graces. Here a rusty exterior staircase spiralled from a dark alley to a grubby table where a grubbier man levied the fittingly low admission. A few eager disciples purchased tickets for the service of the instructresses who looked as described, but most of the youths were paired in earnest silence broken by the shrill gaiety of two badly made-up queens. 'Try anything once' was trampled down by the contingent converging on the supposedly English foreigner, now known as Charles. The partners ranged from boyishly shy to assertively masculine, all bowed politely, took no for an answer and congratulated Charles on mastering their language. An undeserved exaggeration as the old Professor of Ancient Greek had not pointed out the manifold uses of irregular verbs. Despite Mimis' protests Charles declined invitations to tavernas or an escort home, but promised to return. Dancing schools were not usually addictive.

Mildly addictive nonetheless, judging by the influx of the international set, led by Robert Nuttall, to verify Karl's amusing account. He remained centre of the bare hall, despite the new rich pickings; only with him had dances to be reserved two or three ahead and Karl remembered ball cards Mother had laughed about. Only Ralph could appreciate this incredible reversal from Vienna dances where the prettiest girls had hoped to be asked by the young Fechtner. Telepathy brought Ralph to the ticket table but he fled on seeing Karl. A give-away in conjunction with his interest in the star of the Footlights. A straight talk reduced the phobia and hypocrisy to manageable proportions; Ralph soon ventured on to the dance floor, seeking rather than being sought after. He gained a new personality under his old name, his friend kept his old as Charles. Christl's parties provided a welcome counterweight, especially when in the crowded bus to the villa an airman offered his seat to Charles in preference to the strap-hanging women. Such gallantry would have gratified many of Christl's guests who maintained pretences Ralph had finally dropped.

———————

No pretence from Mimis but dancing as usual, preferably with partners not heavily booted. The blond sailor hardly looked like a toe crusher, but he remained seated, his bluegreen eyes following Charles as intently as Hans Wilner's on the skating rink. He clapped enthusiastically when Charles's rumba with the gallant airman from the bus terminated in a solo little connected with the West Indies. The applause was less deserved than after the *Bolero* at Cannes, yet more sincere; certainly coming from the sailor who covered his mouth when later talking to his insignificant companion.

They followed Charles and Mimis to a Plaka taverna where the sailor sent from a nearby table a jug of *retsina*, the polite way of striking up an acquaintance. 'They are dying to join us, so raise your glass, much as you hate that turpentine. I'll sacrifice myself, for the sake of the Greek navy I once disgraced. Odd, he resembles you in more robust shape, same blond hair, dark eyebrows and lashes in Mediterranean shades. Never mind that a tooth is missing, everything else is apparently in the right place.'

Panagiotis was quieter than the dancing school aspirants, without self-conscious awkwardness. He was the same age as Charles whose country he had visited as a merchant seaman, but he knew only a few words of English. He lived in Pireus and had to return as no serviceman was allowed out after 11 p.m. He was not sure of his next leave. Could he phone?

Madame Mascot did not raise her thinly pencilled eyebrows over the Karl into Charles metamorphosis and she listened approvingly to his first telephone conversation in Greek. 'When he has a longer leave have him come up here. He was very polite, you should hear some of the calls for my gentlemen! Why do you take Mr Mimis along?'

To overcome linguistic barriers which, however, fell in the pleasure of togetherness. Panagiotis' joy at the electric train station persisted through the couple of hours at a taverna; his destroyer was participating in manoeuvres, only returning at Easter which he was spending with his uncle on Aegina. The Englishman would be most welcome and a bed could be found for Mimis at a neighbour's. It was not possible to ring from the naval base, so the appointment was made for the afternoon boat to the island on Maundy Thursday. Restricted comprehension had achieved unrestricted rapport.

'A fine mess if the England-loving uncle finds out.'

'He won't ask for your papers. Think of what I let myself in for, sleeping with a neighbour, probably a snoring monstrosity! In the meantime you have ruined Panagiotis, in his part of town he had to offer to pay for the meal but that he insisted is unprecedented. It cost nothing but it is a month's pay.'

———— ———— ———— ————

Panagiotis was not on the quay. 'The destroyer might have been delayed but overflow of family in the Aegina hutch is more likely. Manoeuvres provide an unbeatable excuse and He'll resurrect after the Resurrection.' Mimis' tasteless pun was lost in the pleasure of the photographer travelling to the same island. He needed pictures of the Easter procession, had rung the hotel, there were plenty of rooms.

Panagiotis' disappearance added personal to the general sorrow of Orthodox Holy Week. Fasting and the constant tolling of bells imposed the suitable gloom till the midnight Resurrection and the endeavour to carry the lighted candles home. Charles's candle flickered and failed while Mimis brought his back to the hotel. The light symbolised hope, no wonder it had gone out.

Charles's morosity vanished before Madame Mascot's version of the habanera, *L'amour est enfant des marins*, explained by 'No less than three sailors phoned. Panagiotis' leave was stopped, he hadn't cleaned the canon, naughty boy. He asked all his friends to let you know why he didn't show up.'

——— ———

He did not show up for some weeks in the terrible spring of 1940 when north and west Europe fell to Hitler and concern about Marie Louise and the French set aggravated the anxieties about Otto and the Austrian friends. Fighting for the Führer they loathed was grim, but the enforced idleness in despondent anticipation of the Nazis marching into the Balkans was hard to bear. Ralph was very busy without visible results, Robert lacked the cultural cover for his mysterious absences, even Mimis had been recalled to active service in which he spent the few hours required of an admiral's son. Christl and her library had to fill the void.

Panagiotis rang; he had a few hour's leave, just enough to rush home for a change of uniform, his was in a mess, he was no good at washing. Could Charles meet him at the Piraeus Station? The next train, it was asking a lot, but he had to explain personally. So please . . .

Lingering doubts were swept aside when the blue-green eyes lit up and the face was pressed against his own in a spontaneous embrace amidst the crowd spilling out of the train. They walked hand in hand, which in Greece meant nothing and to them a lot. 'An NCO bastard blamed me for his sloppiness and I copped a month. You spent a miserable Easter on Aegina, so please let me show you my island. I'm off next Sunday, we'll catch the early boat and come back on the last. We'll eat at my uncle's and I'll introduce you to my mother.'

The neat woman served two 'submarines', a mastic in a glass of water; the girl brought tiny cups of coffee and her brother's clean underwear. The brevity of the leave cut short the stereotyped exchanges. 'Do you know why mother called me back? I should impress on you what a good wife my sister will make despite her small dowry! She didn't ask if you had any money, you are English so you must be rich.'

———— ————

The sunny morning contributed to making this crossing incomparably more enjoyable. In civvies, forbidden but less conspicuous, Panagiotis' resemblance to his friend was striking. 'Mother insisted on preparing some food. She doesn't want me to take you to uncle for a meal, he has three daughters. She thinks of nothing but matchmaking, but she has had a hard life bringing up Ariadne and me after father went down with his ship. I had to leave school and earn some money, luckily another uncle is a captain.'

Real uncles seemed more useful than the by-courtesy lot in Vienna. Charles delved into the Austro/German intricacies below the English veneer to the confusion and disappointment of the Greek. 'You'd better stay English Charles, Piraeus is solidly pro-British though there is little dislike of the Germans. It's the Italians we are worried about.'

The island's only bus stopped at an inland village where Panagiotis hired mules to ride up to the Temple of Aphaea. 'She was a nymph like Aegina, both were raped by a god, must be in the air.'

Not on the ground where the loving union of two young bodies rekindled passion till the return could be delayed no longer. The mules trotted through the pine-scented tranquillity into a knot of villagers shouting and gesticulating in half-hearted menace, like in a badly acted play. Panagiotis laughingly, then angrily remonstrated till the boys were bundled onto a bus. 'As we remained away so long we must be spies. They didn't really mind, it's the accepted reason for wanting to see the Temple, but they tried to get more money for the mules. I didn't fall for that!' The comic finale added a common sense of humour and practicality to love.

Panagiotis was first critically and soon amiably welcomed by Madame Mascot who personally served breakfast with indiscreetly approving glances.

———— ————

Despite the threat of war a vast crowd of pilgrims thronged Tinos to celebrate the Virgin's Assumption. Panagiotis was detailed to the naval guard of honour that passed the miraculous icon over the prostrate invalids. Charles disliked mobs, pious or otherwise, and retreated to Christl's summer house where even the heavily censored news spread alarm. On the fifteenth of August three torpedos struck the gaily-decked cruiser *Elli* anchored off Tinos; the cruiser sank, one sailor was killed, twenty-six wounded besides casualties among the pilgrims on the quay. This seemed the first shots of yet another aggression and the Kourdatis returned to Athens.

Charles's anxiety mounted till he heard the sailor's outraged account. 'The Italians *would* desecrate the Feast of the Virgin, just like invading Albania on Good Friday.' He contemptuously brushed aside the official 'unknown nationality of the submarine'; he had seen the Italian marking on the torpedo fragments. Panagiotis was the toast of the taverna, the personification of a fighting spirit, whatever the price.

————

If the price of appeasement came as cheap as the handing over of German nationals it would not offend Greek chauvinism, distrustful of anyone shirking military service. That the League's High Commissioner had so far prevented this human sacrifice did not safeguard the future; yet Charles was not granted British enlistment despite Ralph's intervention with the Military Attaché. The danger of Charles's inactivity was greater but less comprehended than Panagiotis' exposure to another treacherous attack.

The sailor's destroyer remained at sea for weeks and the Cultural Organiser trusted in restoring morale at the dancing school. The gallant airman relied on an attempted handlebar moustache to overcome Charles's lack of interest but instead aroused Ralph's admiration. Asked to a taverna the hirsuit beau was left in no doubt as to feelings and finance, yet despite the paucity of military pay voiced his disappointment before resigned acceptance. The hurt in his eyes ruined Charles's satisfaction with the selfless pimping.

Retribution came from the uninjured party. 'Why did you go back to the dancing school? I am your friend, so why look for other soldiers?'

'Charles wasn't looking for anyone. He very kindly helped me with the airman as I've been trying to explain to you. You are very unreasonable, Panagiotis!' Ralph intervened.

Hard to answer, harder to refute, so Panagiotis stomped out.

Mimis expertly expounded local foibles. 'Who does what and with what and to whom is all-important but not that obvious in your case. Uniforms enjoy the benefit of the doubt, a moustache and handlebar at that clinches the argument. You danced together, so . . .'

'So Panagiotis' reputation is assured.'

'Dear Charles, we invented logic several thousand years ago to give it up immediately as unrealistic. He has to consider your reputation too, because he loves you. He is Greek, so he wants it both ways. Sorry, no allusion intended. Moreover, his ship might be blown up any moment and personalised dramatics provide an excellent diversion. On his next leave he'll be a lamb, having realised how stupidly he spoilt this one. How about a little revenge at the dancing school?'

Not revenge but resentment of Greek complexities and fear of Nazi intrigues occupied life and conversation. Hitler's entry into Vienna had been momentarily forgotten in the cinema, and *The Magic Bullet* offered a fascinating escape into medical discoveries. Outside the cinema Charles and Panagiotis almost bumped into each other; their eyes expressing the longing for which they could find no words. Both had imagined a private reunion and were unable to adjust quickly amidst the crowd that pushed them apart. So close to Kolonaki, Panagiotis was obviously heading for the Mascotry, yet inexplicably Charles did not follow him but bought a ticket and began sobbing uncontrollably in the dark. When he wiped away his tears, a new reason for them emerged. Dr Ehrlich diagnosed syphilis in a skinny youth, played by Ernst Häussermann, who promptly committed suicide. A very inauspicious start of a Hollywood career. The magic bullet was discovered too late and it was too late for an explanation with Panagiotis.

Ernst's death removed any justification for remaining in the cinema Charles should not have entered. Passing the Catholic Cathedral he remembered the consoling sunbeam on the sublime sculpture at St Stephen's, but the plaster statue of Our Lady evoked no response. Over a side altar hung a large picture of the Assumption, the Feast when Panagiotis had been preserved from mortal danger. This gave hope, quickly shattered by Madame Mascot: the sailor had waited for an hour, visibly agitated, had left no message; what had Charles been up to? Unanswerable, whether it was immature, slow on the uptake or just plain stupid. There was no telephone in the Piraeus house and Mimis, summoned urgently, consented merely to an exasperatingly dry 'Please ring' as the letter was bound to be opened by the mother.

Personal and political calamities converged ironically; the one favourable explanation of the sailor's silence was the absence of his ship as Greece's neutrality would not be respected much longer. In a tragic replay of the weeks before the Anschluss, rumours worsened throughout October and at 3 a.m. on the 28th the Italian ultimatum was rejected. Air-raid sirens wailed shortly afterwards, but the target was Larissa, where an earthquake had put the ack-ack out of action. Despite the cowardly aggression, the first Italian prisoners were treated with contemptuous pity, in contrast to the Viennese rabble's spiteful cruelty to their compatriots who preferred civilised independence. Driving the numerically superior enemy back into the snow of the Albanian mountains inspired unanimous participation in the war effort; Christl and her ladies volunteered for the Red Cross, Mimis took his naval duties more seriously, even Ralph and Robert admitted to some military liaison. The photographer, forced back to Germany, envied Charles, yet the official refusal of any contribution became intolerable. At last a call. 'Panagiotis has leave tomorrow. Can he come straight to Athens?'

———   ———

Trite endearments were a wonderful balm for mutual self-accusations. Childish misunderstandings dissolved in laughter and love; happiness kept no secrets. 'I've been praying for you, for us.'

'We need it, Charles. Will you come to a monastery with me?'

This went far beyond Charles's religiosity, though at least he was not sent off alone like poor Ophelia, but it was still bewildering.

'I didn't say "enter". A brother of my grandfather is a monk at Meteora and mother wants me to get his blessing before we sail again. The old tub is going into dock, it's a miracle she keeps afloat, and I have leave over Christmas.'

The train was overcrowded with soldiers and peasants accompanied by a representative portion of the country's livestock, but in the icy gail of an open rail junction Charles regretted the animal warmth so eagerly abandoned. Eventually a toy-train puffed to an unearthly forest of gigantic rocks. Though pilgrims were no longer hoisted in nets to the seemingly inaccessible pinnacle of the Great Meteoron, the ascent of staircases hollowed into the perpendicular cliff was awesome in the dusk. A gallery opened on to derelict churches and cells; a light flickered in the far corner where three gnarled monks, their robes green with age, were huddled over a smoking brazier, showing neither surprise nor joy at the intrusion. Father Philaretos looked a mere seventy and bore scant resemblance to his Austrian counterpart, Great Uncle Ferdinand. 'I've been to Brooklyn twenty years, I speak American. The Abbot don't, he is a peasant, but you, Panagiotis, kiss his hand or he'll give you hell.' The trembling hand belied such vigorous action, but when Charles bent over it he was pulled back. 'Not you, English no Christians.'

Charles renounced theological controversy for a glass of herb-flavoured liquor. 'You hungry?' Panagiotis' emphatic nod caused uproarious mirth. 'Today we fast. You boys,' he relented, 'eat if it don't cross.'

Not having clamoured for any such thing, Charles felt like Alice in a monastic Wonderland. A tin of squid from Panagiotis' knapsack started a heated discussion beyond Charles's comprehension. Curiouser and curiouser. 'You too smart for me, go to sleep. We monks will be in church at midnight, but you no Christian.' Philaretos looked almost envious when he led the visitors to a room bare but for several iron bedsteads. He pulled some coarse blankets from a heap, 'Better sleep together, it's too cold alone. God bless you, my children.' His heavy boots sounded the retreat on the stone flags.

'Philaretos, Friend of Virtue, not a very suitable name with his insistence that I'm no Christian.'

'He tremendously enjoyed teasing you, playing the ignorant peasant confounding Christian and Orthodox. It certainly is cold, but snuggling up together we might survive.'

Wakened by the dull beat of the *semantron* they followed the sound of the wooden gong to the Church of the Transfiguration and an earthly transfiguration. Robed in gold brocade, the Abbot presided from an elevated throne over the immutable splendour of Orthodoxy officiated by monks unrecognisable in their rich vestments. Charles drifted into Byzantine fantasies attuned to the exhausting vigil that sent Panagiotis to sleep till the rays of the sun gilded the icons. The high priests changed back into old men in stained and patched garb, silently devouring their meagre repast. 'They haven't eaten for days and shared their provisions with us. They are terribly poor.' Philaretos refused the small donation from Panagiotis' mother. 'She needs it more than we, God takes care of us. The Abbot will bless you, he is holier than I. Then you go, we want to sleep.'

Stumbling through the false floor of low clouds, the surfeit of quaint customs made Charles petulant. 'What's this mystery about not crossing?'

Panagiotis' laughter overcame his empty stomach. 'You no Christian. During fast animals with a backbone that could form a cross are forbidden. No fish but squid is OK.'

Dawn and dusk achieved a dismal junction in the thin rain during the journey. The strenuous effort made the blessing more valuable, certainly in the warmth of the Mascotry when the shivering fully-dressed hugging receded in a more rewarding embrace.

———————

General Metaxas' death in January 1941 united the nation in mourning and the resolve to fight to the bitter end. That it would be bitter was little doubted by the vast crowd filing past the Prime Minister's bier in a last homage and lining the route of the funeral procession in the icy sleet. In the pattern of classical tragedy, the death of the protagonist symbolised the transition from heroic enthusiasm to fatalistic resignation. The ferocity of winter stalled the Greek offensive in Albania, frostbite casualties filled the insufficient hospitals, while Germany tightened its grip on the Balkans. The Hungarian Prime Minister's suicide strengthened rumours about Metaxas' timely death, and Hitler imposed a Fascist government on Rumania.

Madame Mascot's 'A gentleman from a certain legation' was, therefore, quite unexpected. Lack of financial support had left the grandmother unregenerated and the Rumanian kept silent on the scheme he had advocated. He tiptoed to the door which he thrust open on Madame Mascot without embarrassing so experienced an eavesdropper. Would coffee be required or perhaps tea? 'Women never change, but times have and so has my king.' The Rumanian chuckled at his finesse – and remained unabashed when reminded of his previous anti-Nazi stance. 'Ah, then Carol was King and now it is Michael. We Monarchists must do our duty, you too. You could be useful to your Fatherland, you have English friends, Mr Caldwell. The German Legation can make life difficult for nationals who refuse to co-operate. When I call again in a few days I trust you'll have some interesting information.'

After spying on him the Nazis were now blackmailing him into spying for them. The Germans could make life difficult not only for him but also for Herta, while the Rumanian's proposal might help her in regaining the Altenhof, perhaps even his own return to the Liechti . . . to belong again, no longer an importunate outcast. The British had rejected all his offers.

———— ————

The Military Attaché just laughed at the Rumanian's childishness. 'You are of no use to Jerry nor unfortunately to us. As for interrogating German prisoners of war there won't be any, prisoners that is, Germans there'll soon be plenty. A provincial governor in Burma advised me that your father might play an important part after the liberation of Austria. Fucking fool had better worry about Jerry occupying Greece. At least the letter made you a political responsibility and I passed your file to the Consul.'

The new Consul was an Anglo-Levantine and thus more sympathetic to wrong passports and more receptive to political considerations. After humming and hawing he made some encouraging noise and scribbled some hieroglyphs on Charles's dossier.

———— ————

German armies invaded Yugoslavia and Greece at dawn on 6 April. A few hours later a policeman ordered Charles to pack some essentials and to accompany him to the University where the German colony was crowded into the main lecture hall. By midday the cheerful throng had been removed to accommodation prepared by their Legation for this emergency. All ill-assorted handful refused the benefit of German organisation, to the chagrin of Greek officialdom perplexed by these foreseeable but unforeseen cases. No food was provided for the non-conformists till a policeman bought some pies at their expense, to which Charles contributed the share of a penny-less family of circus artists. In the dark they were driven to a small suburban hotel assigned to wealthy Sephardic Jews whose parents had obtained Italian nationality in the declining Ottoman Empire. Greek muddle supplied no additional beds for the racially and religiously alien strays who were squeezed in with the indignant occupants. The excitement of the day drained the excitement of a night with a handsome unknown youth.

The arbitrarily imposed hospitality transferred to the Austrian Archaeological School, where straw mattresses provided more space but less comfort on the floor; washing facilities and toilets dated the venerable building. The board did not include meals, which became expensive as the circus family continued to rely on Charles without giving reasons or thanks. For a consideration, the guards also purchased other necessities but refused to inform anyone, even the British Consulate, of this strange place of internment, apparently forgotten by their superiors. The afternoon guard was almost friendly; Charles's endeavour to communicate with the British allies was laudable but prohibited. Gloomy speculations dominated the conversations with the fellow inmates, except with an Austrian musical comedy actress, who sensibly refrained from singing.

Panagiotis' appearance in uniform and with a parcel of eggs and cheese electrified the grim limbo. The friends embraced and were accorded a private room by the surprised guard. 'We have no orders about visitors, probably not allowed but I give you half an hour. Don't do anything silly, boys.' The sailor joked about his fight with bureaucracy to trace an 'irregular enemy internee' though courage had obviously been required to overcome inefficiency and suspicion. The war news was catastrophic: the Germans had overrun Yugoslavia and northern Greece, they would soon enter Athens as a last British line of defence was unlikely to hold. Ralph must be informed immediately, so that the British would get Charles out in time. Hope seemed unrealistic, they might never meet again even if they survived. The guard gave them another five minutes to cling together in their only consolation, each other. Charles was permitted as far as the gate and then the privacy of the room in recognition of so faithful a friendship.

On Good Friday the guards shared with their equally alarmed prisoners the wild rumours quickly exceeded by wilder facts. The King complained about unauthorised demobilisation orders to the Prime Minister, who shot himself. No politician was sufficiently patriotic to undertake the perilous office which was added to the King's responsibilities. Defences were crumbling, air attacks increased as the dive bombers now operated from captured Greek airfields. Morosity thrived on the avalanche of calamities and fasting, kept as a matter of course by the guards, reluctantly or under protest by the internees. Hungry and despondent, they sought the doubtful comfort of the straw mattresses.

Unprecedently, the friendly guard entered the darkened room and beckoned to Charles. He was free, only he, special orders. He was not to alert the others. Sincere good wishes, a handshake and Charles was in the Street full of British and Anzac soldiers. No taxis and in the overcrowded trams his blondness and overnight bag might arouse suspicion. Some soldiers appeared rather drunk and quarrelsome, the mililtary police might ask for identification and he had just the right papers. In the improvised internment he had to hand in the Greek residence permit but neither money nor other documents. He must be unique, carrying a German passport in an Allied capital, yet throwing the wretched thing away left him unidentifiable in document-obsessed Greece. Were deserted backstreets less precarious than crowded avenues? Worse than the walk from the Landtheater the night of the Anschluss when home had been the Liechti.

The Mascotry was the obvious refuge but Madame's welcome lacked warmth. He hadn't escaped? Ralph might clarify the position but couldn't be reached by phone. She let Charles stay for the night but the following morning . . .

———   ———

The following morning Ralph pushed his friend to the head of a motley queue at the British Consulate. 'Panagiotis phoned just in time. The High Commissioner and I have been trying for days to locate you, no trace, typical. The Consul was less obstructive and luckily your enlistment application included photos he could use for an emergency passport. In the present emergency he has a free hand and I leant a bit on him.' Ralph must have leant fairly heavily because after signing on several dotted lines he was handed the precious document and told to put his friend on the military shuttle to Piraeus. One suitcase only.

'Pack two. Your childish obedience to authority is misplaced and I can bring one back if they really insist.' Nobody did on the lorry or at Piraeus where cabin trunks and even furniture were hoisted into the holds of the *Warsawa*, old, dirty and overloaded. Ralph recommended his friend to a harrassed British official, who allocated one of six bunks in a two-berth cabin to the envy of evacuees guarding their mattresses in the most unlikely places. The privileged cabin mates were Levantines, polite but excitable when some Stukas dived out of the sinking sun. Apparently they only verified the damage caused by the blowing up of a munition supply ship, yet all the diverse passengers wished that the convoy would be formed at nightfall.

For almost 2,000 years the light of Resurrection had symbolised hope, but at Easter 1941 the churches emptied into a blackout. Charles's candle had failed on Aegina and the ensuing year had confirmed the ill omen; now no light shone throughout Greece and under the cover of this darkness the convoy of seventeen ships crept out of the harbour.

MIDDAY MEDLEY

1

Except for the British, assigned a bigger and better ship, the evacuees represented all Europe and America, divided by class rather than nationality into loose groupings. The *New York Times* correspondent talked to all, the richest Greek industrialist to none. Charles was introduced by his cabin mates to their families, sat at their table and played bridge through the Stuka raids. When a direct hit set a ship ablaze and it was left behind in accordance with convoy procedure, Charles felt no fear, toughened by three years of varied if less spectacular dangers. Deadly action was an exciting change from deadening inactivity; moreover, he was advantaged where he had suffered most, he alone held a German passport which might be useful to British Intelligence on his enlistment. The diabolical noise and flames of dive-bombing activated his bellicose determination.

Lifeboat drill revealed that only half the women and children could be squeezed into the boats whose one attempted lowering depressed all deeply. The loudspeaker system then harangued everyone in Anglo-Polish to jump into the sea when the *Warsawa* started lifting or perhaps listing. Men and the robuster ladies were issued with lifebelts so narrow as to be fit only for children, who received none. The escorting destroyers would pick up survivors after dealing with the dive-bombers. The dealing seemed rather one-sided, as four ships lit the nights while only one Stuka went down in flames to the rapturous applause of the prospective targets. The destroyers also dropped depth charges and, after an impressive spout rumours claimed a direct hit on a submarine. Less cheering was the rumour on the approach to Alexandria that drachmas were worthless; whereupon the Greek industrialist endowed every passenger with a $5 bill from a bottomless shoebox.

Egyptian officials had nothing to learn from their Greek counterparts, but something from the glib gibberish of a British inspector. 'Emergency papers aren't always recognised outside the Empire. Better continue to Palestine, British mandate. No violation of national sovereignty for enlisting. Really much more sensible.' As if Charles had any choice but to join the other rejects, nearly all Jews longing for the Homeland. So much for his brief passport triumphalism;

considering the new destination Charles tore up the German brand
– psychologically and physically damned hard – and flushed it down
the toilet.

— — — —

Another rush decision as the British officer at Haifa was little interested in this new bunch of immigrants. Kicked about so long by so
many, they found freedom of choice exhilarating even on $5, which
diminished further in Palestine pounds. To emphasise that this was
not his homeland, Charles staggered with his two suitcases to the
next Arab hotel where he paid for the three beds in the smallest
room. One night of privacy between internment, evacuation and
soldiering was more essential than food, though the breakfast on
board had been early and meagre.

The Recruiting Officer asked a rare customer only the minimum
questions. 'Why didn't your father take you along to Burma?'

Why indeed? 'He first wanted to build a new life' sounded
sufficiently pompous for the rumbling protest in Charles's stomach,
more likely it was lack of food. Body noises are discreditable, apologies doubtfully remedial; points are lost either way.

'With your brother-in-law probably a Jerry officer, I can't recommend you for a commission and with your eye no shooting outfit.
Your languages should be handy with the RASC at Sarafand. The
orderly will give you a chit for the bus.' On seeing the recruit's relief,
he guffawed, 'Ha, no money, what?'

'Plenty of drachmas but I was told that's no good.'

'The Yids buy anything at the right price. They'll change it back
at enormous profit to our lot on Crete. The King, plucky chap, has
formed a government there.'

The Jewish orderly displayed his military know-how. 'At the
outbreak many Central European refugees volunteered, hardly any
native Jews, no Moslems, they prefer Hitler. After the MO had
declared half of the Christian Arabs unfit, mostly VD, he was
transferred to Sarafand to declare everyone fit for the Western
Desert. The RO would accept a corpse, he must justify his cushy job.
One eye is a bit much, but he's a spiteful bastard and it'll make
plenty of trouble at the Royal Army Service Corp, that's what those
bloody initials stand for. Here is your pass to Sarafand, you change
at Tel Aviv.'

'I've seen on the map that it's a little longer, but would via
Jerusalem be possible . . . for a prayer?'

'In this country innumerable sects pray without bothering to
enlist. Any more original ideas? It means a night in Jerusalem and to

keep body and soul together I'll give you the address of a hotel, not too expensive.' After listening sympathetically to Charles's financial predicament, the orderly rattled some Hebrew into the phone.

The money changer acted Shylock convincingly. 'I accept these worthless drachmas because you are a soldier. I, too, wanted to join up but my health is not good.' Rooked in yet another currency, what should have sufficed for a year in Greece here barely provided for a week.

Dinner on Mount Carmel was the first decent meal since the German invasion, which seemed more like three months than three weeks ago. No blackout at Haifa or at distant St Jean d'Acre where Richard the Lionheart tore down the bloodstained shirt of the Austrian Duke. The site of the examination bravado was revealed thanks to the beastliness of the Egyptian immigration authorities. The Crusaders had to fight for it; had they been cheated by native money changers? Grand historical fantasies faded in the dingy hotel room. After sharing a bed with a strange Italian, then sleeping on the floor, on improvised bunks, now two beds to spare . . .

The hotel owner knocked and entered. 'You must like us Arabs' was not a political but a sexual gambit and thus easier to handle, though the *jellabah* and headcloth were attractively exotic.

The owner and most guests of the Jewish hotel in Jerusalem, in bigoted exoticism, wore black kaftans and fur-trimmed hats. Christian identification intensified at the Stations of the Cross along the Via Dolorosa. Above the Court of Flagellation rose a chapel where two Brides of Christ lay prostrate before the altar in their final renunciation of the world. In Charles's personalised Faith this was a sign that he, too, had to renounce and, afterwards he handed half his meagre funds to the French nun in charge and entered into the Mass book 'For Panagiotis from Charles'. In instant recompense the withdrawn Dame de Sion became Mother and allowed his tears to dampen the starched whiteness of her wimple. Her 'God bless you' could not fail.

Religious euphoria continued at the Holy Sepulchre, where the Greek monk guarding the minute shrine insisted on introducing the devotee to his brothers at the adjoining monastery. They greatly appreciated the first eyewitness account of the fall of their country and retained the Greek-speaking English friend for dinner where the warmth of welcome compensated for the lukewarm food. As a special favour he was invited to the night service when the Sepulchre closed to outsiders, but they agreed that before joining up he needed sleep. On his first leave, then . . . He must be fit to fight the common enemy.

Enemy Hitler was, but the refusal of Orthodox Jewry to take up arms dowsed the fighting spirit. The hotel staff consented to store his suitcases, even the pigskin, with an unspoken hostile 'You Christian' far from Philaretos's teasing 'You no Christian'.

———— ————

The Regimental Sergeant Major was true to novels and films. 'Not enough that you are practically blind, you are also a Lutheran. Fucking Buddhists next. I'll make it C of E for your funeral.'

'Better make it RC.'

The bastard looked sober but obviously thought he was in a pub. Irony might just prevent a stroke. 'Coming up, same as the blood Irish and Wogs. You are useless for real RASC duty, but one eye should do for pen pushing at HQ. Corporal, find a bed for Private Feschner.'

The deliberate mispronunciation was routine, but raw recruits were dumped on straw mattresses for basic training till attached to a unit. The NCO knew better than to argue with the RSM and he would accommodate his charge in the drivers' barracks.

The RSM had despaired of fitting him in, like everyone in the last three year. A truthful bluff was worth the try. As if complaining to hotel management Charles dared, 'I can't sleep with fifteen men in the same room.'

The Cockney Corporal appreciated the matter-of-fact impudence. One of the four beds in the NCO partition was vacant, the allocation of a bed was irregular in any case, the chap looked clean, an unlikely snorer and might be writing out the leave passes. Charles had won his first battle with the Army.

The next was unwinnable because his languages were of no use to the RASC. The fellow pen-pushers maintained a friendly distance from the oddly polite irregularity, who was tried and found wanting over meals and tea at the NAAFI. Tentative feelers from Tommies as well as Yids only stressed the difference as the twain never associated except at Bingo which Charles abhorred. Some Austrians remained on speaking rather than mere nodding terms as they considered the exemption of the 'Young Fechtner' from the normal drill with less resentment. Charles's self-taught salute sufficed at the Regimental Office but not on pay parade where the RSM nearly had a fit at this lack of savvy. Too late to send Private Fechtner on basic drill, have him paid off parade by special permission.

One morning a lieutenant rushed in to the office. 'No driver at the pool. You there, don't seem to be busy.' The fact was undeniable and Charles headed for the passenger seat. 'What are you doing in the

RASC if you can't drive?' The pertinent question led to further enquiries and by the time they arrived at the shopping centre names of London's most prestigious nightspots had been dropped so casually that the bewildered lieutenant himself carried his purchases back to the car. News of the singular driver percolated upwards and he was never again required to fetch and carry.

———— ————

Letters conveyed feelings more emaciated than censorship required. Father took credit for the governor's intervention, approved of the enlistment despite the faulty eye, but kept silent about the dive-bombing during the evacuation. He had been an officer in a crack regiment on truly active service, not pen-pushing. He ignored any mockery of the RASC duties, as he seemed preoccupied with the possibility of moving to Australia, perhaps lecturing at a university.

Irene's dashing photo in WREN uniform illustrated her 'Well done, darling. At last we've both made it.' At last indeed, but made what? Her outfit was glamorous, his . . . Had she been less practical, they might have got married and his position would have been very different. Panagiotis's feelings were not hedged with mundane considerations; he had shown courage and determination in tracing the lost internees, but how could they learn of their respective escapes even if the old tub made it to Egypt? So many ships had sunk in the Battle of Crete and in convoys, was it possible to find a needle that might not be in the haystack? The sailor rose above the WREN in idealised feelings.

Those called base were not eliminated by the bromide in the NAAFI tea. Though the nights changed from balmy to hot, the Tommies remained glued to their beers in the smoky canteen while Charles, like some Palestinians, opted for a shower before turning in. The tall Arab in the next cubicle possessed the experience of the Foreign Legion, offered to scrub his neighbour's back and used the soapsuds effectively. A pleasantly inconsequential 'no frills'.

———— ————

Leave meant home to those who lived within travelling distance; the Tommies went to nearby Tel Aviv, well-provided for their wants. Irregularly attached to the Regimental Office, Charles obtained a pass irregularly early and was passing the 'Spit and Polish Inspection' when a strapping military police corporal asked 'You wouldn't have a sister, would you?'

'What's wrong with me?' rocked the guard house unaware of the semi-official 'keep off that one'. Cheeky but not chargeable, and the Corporal's 'Fuck you' was amusingly ambiguous.

At the Jerusalem hotel Charles caused an uglier scene by asking for cheese. Milk products with meat were a sin as incomprehensible as beating the head against the Wailing Wall was an atonement. Herta rightly disclaimed any Mosaic connection; despite their accidental Lutheranism they belonged to the familiar Catholicism of the maternal line, so wonderfully comforting at the French Convent. Emotionally and financially it was, however, just as well that a less motherly Dame de Sion was on duty.

Having exhausted his war stories, Charles gave the Greek monks an account of his visit to the Meteoron. 'Philaretos is a terrible tease,' chuckled a greybeard. 'He made us all laugh, God forgive us, at the consecration of his brother as abbot. Now *there* is a holy man but he hasn't been to America.' The deleterious influence of America was incontrovertible, the Abbot's holiness was not. 'The Abbot of Zoodochou Pigis on Samos upholds a great tradition, fighting for centuries against the Turks and now the Germans, helping Greek patriots to escape. Samos is less than a kilometre from the Turkish coast. Come again on your next leave, we'll pray for you, Charles Fenton.'

————

Prayers and the Anglicised form of his mumbled name must be deserved. The request for an interview with the Adjutant passed through the RSM who anticipated Private Fechtner by stating that the Syrian Campaign was going well without his bloody French.

'I also know Greek, Sir. I learned from the monks of the Holy Sepulchre that a monastery on Samos assists prisoners to escape to Turkey. I've met the Abbot's brother and liaison might be established.' Charles had laboured on military parlance and stretched facts no further than most intelligence.

The correct jargon of the report overcame the RSM's visceral distrust. The pushy meddler could no longer be swept under the office carpet and the monumental irregularity would be exposed.

The next morning the MP Corporal dispensed with an implied 'You had it coming' by a curt 'Fechtner, you are wanted'. Omission of authority and charge was all the more sinister in the stony silence during the drive to a house near Jerusalem. A Captain asked the Private to sit down and the opening remark was no less astounding. 'An unusual ring. Your lucky stone?'

'No, my uncle's' had to be enlarged by a curriculum vitae.

'Tallies with the labels in your suitcases, but Jerry is thorough. Haven't you any relatives in Palestine to identify you?'

'My family had no reason to choose the Jewish Homeland! Why not send photos to my father and the Wynn Roberts?'

'Takes time and pictures are unreliable. Jerry would produce a convincing semblance. No one out here?'

'I suppose Ralph Caldwell was evacuated to Egypt. He knows me from Vienna and helped me in Athens. The Cultural Organisation here closes over the weekends so I couldn't find out.'

'You'll be returned to your unit.'

'That will make them deliriously happy.'

Orders must have forbidden comments at the office, but a Viennese driver informed Charles at the NAAFI that his locker had been searched.

———— ————

The conspiracy of silence continued for a week till Ralph's 'Keeping you out of gaol has become a full-time occupation. But first, Panagiotis's tub made it to Alexandria. I risked my soiled reputation with a Greek sailor who only wanted news from you. I stupidly concentrated on the Interpreter Corps, I should have known you'd be put where you are of least use. Luckily you gave me as reference when you got yourself into a spot of bother over the Monastery of Zoodochou Pigis.'

'Now why should the Monastery of the Virgin Lifegiving Source get me into trouble?'

'Because our Brass thought you had got wind of a little scheme of ours. Not escaping Greeks, but a Jerry contact, terribly hush hush till you blubber about it to your RSM who hates your guts. Very different from that parachutist on Crete.'

'Would you mind cutting out the breathtaking suspense.'

'Impossible to spoil this story. One of the few Jerry prisoners had broken his ankle when dropped on a tree and was furiously eager to talk. Austrian, in the Monarchist Youth. When I mentioned your name he grew lyrical, how you had saved his life sending him money to escape although you hardly knew him. The Youth Chairman disappeared in a concentration camp and our Deputy went to an aunt in Belgium. Unfortunately he also had parents in Vienna and they were used by the Gestapo to force him into the Fifth Column. Before invading the Balkans, Jerry crammed some elementary Modern Greek into a few "volunteers" who had learned the ancient version. A pretty disaffected bunch, according to Broken Ankle. The most noteworthy is neglecting his duties on Samos and has established his *bona fides* by forcing a confession on the Abbot of Zoodochou Pigis, who is convinced that the Lieutenant is genuine. You haven't come across a Paul Zobel in the Monarchist Youth?'

'Not among the Monarchists but I went to school with him. He was studying theology in America.'

'So is he the real Zobel or a bait allowing Greeks to escape to win our confidence? He hinted at an Austrian Resistance but though the stakes are higher he is as suspect as you before I identified you.'

'My turn to identify Paul.'

'I had hoped you'd offer that, but I'm afraid you'll have to go in alone to establish how genuine this Lieutenant in such a strategic command is. The Abbot risks his neck helping his countrymen to escape, but will he trust you? Outgoing Greeks are risky enough, but an incoming foreigner . . .'

'Needs to be vouchsafed by the Abbot's nephew, Panagiotis.'

———

Panagiotis was 'One of our brave lads' to the monks of the Holy Sepulchre and his interest in the uncle on Samos showed his esteem for clerical relations. God had reunited the English soldier and the Greek sailor and the continuation of His Grace was implored by blessings and the promise of prayers. Blessed they were indeed in one perfect night when the serene happiness of reunion abolished past and future. The next day they flew with Ralph to Cyprus and hence, attached to a trade mission, sailed to Mersin. The passports of the three dried-fruit merchants bore the stamps of previous visits to Turkey and they proceeded to the main trading centre, Izmir.

The delight of shared adventure lasted through the sampling of figs and raisins to a lonely farm above a creek on Cape Mykale within a kilometre of Samos. Robert Nuttall, the local British agent, maintained that the Turkish authorities did not object to this escape route from Greece, which they considered the responsibility of the German coast guard; to be implicated with return passengers violated Turkish neutrality too openly. 'So it's hush-hush on both sides, a familiar routine as the Samians have been smuggling along this coast for thousands of years. The *caique* is convincingly smelly, the crew reliable as each trip with ten refugees nets the equivalent of a year's fishing. Nikos, the deckhand, hates Jerry because they killed his brother. He'll guide you up to the Monastery as you'll land some distance away. There won't be many pilgrims this Assumption Day but it's good cover for the Lieutenant, even though the great feast here is of the Virgin Lifegiving Source. Let's hope he is all he pretends to be, this cloak-and-dagger business is full of nasty surprises. Best of luck.'

The fisherman grunted, his son greeted and Nikos welcomed. The spluttering engine was shut off when the wind filled the sail in the narrow straits. In the darkest hour of the night they rounded the island's eastern headland, from which Nikos led the emissaries up to the Monastery. The entrance was not guarded, as the porter was chanting in the church, where the German uniform stood out from the black of the peasants.

The Lieutenant must have sensed the stare. He turned, recognised incredulously and wisely kept his place, but the liturgy seemed interminable before explanations could be exchanged in the quiet of the guest room. 'My mother had cancer and wished to see me for a last time. Of course it was madness to return, but how could a future priest refuse such an appeal? Mother was buried the day Poland was invaded and I wasn't allowed to leave. The Gestapo apparently thought I wanted to become a rabbi in America and sent me as a private to Poland, a part where most people remembered Austrian rule. They were utterly unprepared for the beastliness of the Waffen SS, much worse than anything I had seen in Vienna. Some Nazi fool believed that Ancient Greek could be quickly adapted to modern use and the locals are laughing themselves silly at the result. They have little else to laugh about, so there is quite an exodus. I naturally looked the other way when I was put in charge here, but I'd like to do something more positive.'

Charles explained his lowly mission of identification before Panagiotis led them to the Abbot who disapproved of his brother's humour. 'Philaretos was spoilt in America. The monks here are graver, but a German officer meeting a stranger brought by a notorious smuggler will set their tongues wagging. At the meal you'll sit apart, talk can wait till the brothers are asleep. We are tired after the long vigil.'

The sensible advice was followed throughout the meal and back to the guest room, till the door was thrown open by a captain of the Waffen SS. Disbelief imposed a brief silence. 'Reports about escapes from Samos have made you suspect, Paul, and helping refugees guarantees the firing squad. Pity the Army objects to concentration camps for officers. But you, Karl, have a fine holiday coming up after I have settled a little account with you. I haven't forgotten that Otto wanted to exclude me from the Upper Chamber till you had the nerve to say that the Schmidts were quite a decent family.'

'I have my doubts now' was answered by a violent blow in the face just as the Abbot entered. 'Show my men where these traitors can be locked up.'

'I'll instruct a novice where to place *that* German officer.' The Abbot's irony was lost but his dignity impressed the Captain who lowered his voice. 'Have the monks lined up for interrogation. I suspected you'd have the road watched, that's why I came by boat.'

Franz's ignorance of the reason for the meeting of his prisoners provided some solace in the disused store room under a canopy of cobwebs. He obviously thought that Charles had never left Greece, but how to establish a credible hideout that would stand up to Gestapo questioning. Panagiotis would certainly try a rescue, perhaps with Nikos, but unarmed against three soldiers and probably more down at the anchorage?

The two young Greeks, awakened by the Captain's shouting, crept along the first-floor balcony to the Abbot's study. 'The Captain is interrogating the brothers, but they have no idea that this meeting was not accidental and he can't really understand their Greek. He is very angry and struck your friend with his fist.'

'The son of a bitch, he'll pay for it!'

A permissible swear-word for the Abbot's 'Yes, but not in the Monastery of the Virgin. He probably has a crew of three like you, seven Greeks in all. These stairs lead to the cellar. Go with God.'

Strong arms clawed up the woodchute and the two sailors raced under the cover of gnarled olive trees to their *caique*. Support was refused with unanswerable arguments. 'We risk our lives smuggling people in and out. But killing Germans, there is no other way, means reprisals on our families.'

'That never stopped us from killing Turks,' Nikos invoked Greek chauvinism and sentiment. 'We don't abandon friends, Panagiotis loves the Englishman, we have to help him.'

'We must, of course!' the son agreed enthusiastically.

Surrender was simpler than paternal assertion of authority. Cursing and grumbling, the fisherman led his party to the jetty below the Monastery.

The soldier in the requisitioned *caique* hated the war, the Nazis and, above all, Schmidt. No sooner had that demented bastard learnt that the Kommandant of Samos was spending Assumption Day at Her Monastery than the maniac commandeered a *caique* at Ikaria. German charts were all too precise and they chug-chugged to this God-forsaken spot. The landscape was romantic enough, but instead of Brahms or Liszt the grubby crew indulged in an oriental dirge. Schmidt would have shut them up, but a student of the Vienna Musical Academy respected the local wailing. It stopped when a young peasant began rattling away in the incomprehensible lingo, perhaps a message from the Monastery. The frustrated singers were gibbering and gesticulating wildly, the peasant jumped on board, that was going too far but his blue eyes looked so indefinitely sad.

— — — —

The *semantron* was calling to Vespers when Schmidt took a frosty leave from the Abbot, who extended greater warmth to the prisoners. 'Do not despair my children, Our Lady will not forsake you' irritated Schmidt into urging his party away from compassionate inflections. A sharp turn in the path revealed one of his boat-crew waving a blue-and-white rag. Schmidt ordered the prisoners back round the bend and, revolver at the ready, advanced towards the fisherman.

Whatever Panagiotis's shirt in those hands indicated, it might be wise to reduce exposure. 'May I take my shoes off, they are full of stones.' Charles pulled Paul down with him before a burst of shots toppled the soldiers. Panagiotis emerged from the cover of the trees and handed the gun to Nikos who fired as the Captain rushed up the bend and took aim at Charles. The bullet hit the sailor jumping onto the path to shield his friend; he crumpled into the outstretched arms, his blood staining the blue-and-white shirt pressed against his wound. Carrying him back to the Monastery would quicken the flow and he was eased onto the dead Captain's coat.

Nikos quickly returned with a monk carrying a small wooden box. 'I'm the apothecary. When the Abbot heard the shots he interrupted the liturgy. Unprecedented, but we serve the Virgin better by helping our fellow men than asking for Her help.' He disinfected and bandaged the wound with his thick peasant fingers, shaking his head. 'I spoke foolishly, only the Virgin can help. Impossible to extract the bullet, he'd bleed to death.'

The Abbot retained his dignity even running down the hill in flapping robes. 'The apothecary, the Lieutenant and Nikos, no new faces, will fetch a stretcher. The fishermen must dispose of the three bodies, they can't be buried. Nikos will bring back sacks and ropes, use rocks not pebbles. The blood must be washed off the trees and the earth turned. Your fathers knew how to deal with inquisitive Turks. No traces left, all our lives depend on it, and they did violate the Feast of the Virgin. A strong wind is blowing up, that will help with a convincing story. God be with you.'

Panagiotis was lifted on to the bed from which he had fled at the German intrusion. The apothecary vainly tried to staunch the blood by changing the soaked bandage. 'The brothers are still in church, for once we'll pray for his body, not only for his soul. He offered his life for you.'

Charles watched in despair life ebb away. Paul whispered a farewell, he had made arrangements with the Abbot and Nikos. Panagiotis's face turned from white to grey, still preserving an expression of exhilaration. He groaned and opened his eyes which lit up, 'Charles, you are safe.' He enfolded the hand that held his, 'It is best like this. The Virgin . . .' A slight spasm and he lay still.

The Abbot was kindly practical. 'One life has been given for you, no others must be endangered, Charles. I shall conduct the Funeral Service tonight, but you must leave in time for the *caique* to sail when the moon sets. In the meantime the brothers are digging up an old grave to transfer the bones to the charnal house. Panagiotis is the first layman in the Monastery's hallowed grounds, a privilege refused the Imperial governors of Samos. The Virgin will approve of this honour. You must slip away when Nikos calls, so I bless you now, my son.'

As at the Meteoron, a life and friendship away, a patriarch in splendid brocades celebrated the perennial rites while Charles knelt and rose with the chanters. Numbed, he followed Nikos, hardly noticing that one Ikarian had embarked in the wrong *caique*. The sweat of incipient seasickness mixed with the saltspray as the wind rose to near gale force; no German patrol boat would be out, neither should theirs, as the fishermen cursed unendingly while making straight for the lee of Cape Mykale.

The nearer trees were still black but the foliage round the farm assumed the silvergreen of dawn when Nikos presented his report. The Abbot and the Lieutenant had elaborated a plan that might save the Ikarians: the youngest must escape to freedom as his supposed drowning would make the similar fate of the Germans more credible. His two brothers would overturn their boat in a current that would sweep the hull with them clinging to it towards Ikaria. They had tried to warn the Captain that their faulty engine could not make Samos and after repairing the inevitable breakdown they were returning when shipwrecked in the storm. The loss of a brother added a convincing touch to that of the four Germans whose bodies were dumped by the Samians in Turkish waters while the young Ikarian was to join the Free Greek Forces.

Others had dealt with the emergency, yet Charles had accomplished his mission. 'Zobel is certainly genuine and while we were locked up he explained that the Führer makes a great show of admiring the classical education he never received. Military administrators are not required to be humane but humanistic, so when his major fell ill, lowly Zobel was put in charge but not promoted because of his American clerical background.' Charles concentrated on the hurried farewell. 'He still wants to meet our agent, but to allay SS suspicion he will have to catch a boatload of refugees. Nikos wants to join the Free Greeks, he behaved splendidly.'

'He deserves a bonus, the Greeks appreciate a little extra cash. But his disappearance would be highly suspect, so let's first see how Jerry digests that Homeric shipwreck at Ikaria.'

Ralph readily admired Panagiotis's resourcefulness and sacrifice, but shied away from linking the death on this Assumption Day to the escape from the Italian attack on the Virgin's feast the previous year and the Assumption Altar in Athens that had heard so many prayers. He was equally reluctant to discuss the sailor's last words which only the Abbot might have interpreted. Compassion without spirituality joined 'It is best this way' to Mother's outstretched arms in latent self-reproach.

———————

Charles had served his limited purpose and was returned to the RASC for lack of a suitable military slot. His absence had made no heart grow fonder and the trembling of his hands aroused no sympathy. Unverifiable symptoms featured large on sick parade but the MO conceded 'Shellshock, probably. Been recently under fire?'

'A minor shoot-out and some massive dive-bombing during the evacuation from Greece.'

'Classical, the minor danger triggering reactions to the major. A fortnight with your family . . . none here, I see. Sick bay hasn't got the right facilities. I'll give you some drops and put you on Light Duty.'

'Light Duty,' the RSM pretended amusement. 'As you've never been on anything else I'll make it Excused Duty. Don't get into everybody's way.' Easier said than done. Charles had to 'rise and shine' with the NCOs in his quarters; sitting fully clothed in the barracks was as unpopular with the MP as strolling about the camp while the few books in the reading room of the garrison church were unreadable. Father was given a censor-proof version of 'Shell-shock on active service' coupled with an urgent appeal for funds for a possible sick leave.

In the NAAFI the Medical Orderly dispensed a mixture of the morbid and sordid. 'That deserter from the Foreign Legion looked the healthiest of the Arabs but had a curious chancre, refused a blood test and was dishonourably discharged. The MO raved about spreading syphilis, as if anyone wanted to have sex with the Wog.'

'Little you know. I can only hope I didn't catch a dose' wiped the smugness from the face of the Orderly.

He probably bore tales to the MO, quite likely also primed by the RSM that Private Fechtner was expendable. 'Your trembling is worse, you should never have been accepted with this weak eye and

I'll recommend discharge on medical grounds, honourable of course. For a soldier with less than six months' service easy enough.'

———— ———— ———— ————

Not so, as the RASC for unfathomable reasons appeared unwilling to dispense with a soldier excused duty. Just as well, as Father needed several weeks to respond to the changed circumstances. The discharge coincided with a transfer from Sydney to a bank in Jerusalem, accompanied by an Application for Entry into Australia.

Whether the transfer was generous or even adequate depended on Australian red tape, surely more favourable to an ex-serviceman than the Burmese to an enemy alien. Re-establishment of family ties steadied the trembling hands but to everyone's relief the discharge could not be rescinded. Perhaps God had forgiven Charles for making fun of two fat Jews shaking like jelly during the Stuka attacks.

Ralph managed a few days' leave from Cairo and assisted in finding reasonable accommodation at a reasonable rent in the modern quarter near the Jaffa Gate. A passport remained, however, the main concern as it had been since the Anschluss; four absurdly contrasting documents had identified Charles, sometimes simultaneously but at present none. 'Don't you think the variations on the passport theme have been somewhat overplayed?'

'Poor Charles, two more are coming up. Another British travel document good for one journey and then eventually an Australian passport, unless you want to go back to square one after the war.'

'The regular British passport I used in Turkey was only cover but also a precedent for a new name. For a fresh start in Australia Fechtner sounds too Germanic, as rubbed in by that bloody RSM. Charles I've long been, Fenton was contributed by no less an ecclesiastical authority than the Abbot of the Holy Sepulchre. You have already done so much . . .'

'On the practical level, so have you on the equally if not more important emotional. A handlebar moustache weighs more heavily than papers. Dangerous secret mission requiring change of name is too blatantly inappropriate, but we'll wangle a deed poll.'

Ralph's departure was eased by Artemis Nuttall's arrival from Alexandria, where she had quarrelled with her Egyptian cousins. In Jerusalem the most eminent member of her numerous clan, the Patriarch of an obscure sect, introduced her to even obscurer rites; the exploration of the Old town soon extended to the monasteries and churches on the Mount of Olives. Artemis was, however, excluded from visits to the Greek Monks, with whom Charles indulged in discreet but poignant memories, and the Dames de Sion. The motherly nun wondered 'Your generous donation is now "For the Soul of Panagiotis", was there perhaps an omission in the previous entry?'

'No mother, my friend was killed in the meantime.'

Compassion increased on learning that Charles was a Protestant. 'All the more reason to see a priest of the Church in which you have shown such faith. God has granted you the Grace to see your error.'

——— —— ——

Additional Grace was needed to abandon the errors. Apparently granted, as sins of the flesh ceased to tempt in an inexplicable lassitude. Artemis had taken offence when an Arab boy eager to practise his English mistook her for Charles's grandmother, but she forgave where nothing was to be forgiven, put Charles to bed and a thermometer in his mouth. When a slight temperature was accompanied by a rash on the belly, she made an appointment with a GP, thoughtfully choosing a refugee from Vienna. As the physician's English was rudimentary, Mr Fenton's faultless Austrian had to be explained.

'It needed Hitler to get a Fechtner into my surgery! Typhus, I'm afraid, though you were inoculated in the Army. That keeps the temperature down and we might wait till tomorrow before sending you to an isolation ward.'

Next day's 'How right I was not to isolate you' claimed for science the unethical consideration shown to a Fechtner. The rash had spread over most of the body, together with swollen glands now diagnosed as secondary syphilis, all the symptoms but to be confirmed by a blood test.

The picture of Ernst Häussermann shooting himself haunted a troubled night, but the film showed the difference made by Dr Ehrlich's Magic Bullet. The brief pleasure with the legionnaire was dearly paid for, not the first time Charles had been overcharged.

Three consecutive blood tests remained completely negative and the nonplussed GP consulted the leading dermatologist. The great Berlin specialist agreed with his colleague. 'The symptoms are clear, but so are the contradictory tests. Three misreadings by the university laboratory are as good as impossible, yet there is nothing else than another test at a private microbiologist.'

——— —— ——

'After the fourth negative result, the Berlin vampire wanted to parade me before the Dermatological Society. Starkers for those dirty old men to poke their fingers into my tender flesh,' Charles complained to Ralph on a farewell visit to Jerusalem. 'I refused, stupidly missing a free consultation by eminent medics. Not that I have much confidence in the breed, ever since one of the most illustrious, my stepmother's uncle, nearly killed me removing my tonsils. And that typhus diagnosis! The Berliner graciously conceded it was the dermatologists' loss as well as mine; they might have found one of those rare Middle East bugs. My blood is still drained once a week as the Berliner holds forth mightily about medical ethics forbidding treatment of mere symptoms.'

'You look rather pale, but at least no rash on hands and face. To change the subject, though not exactly pleasant table talk either, the storm dramatised the Abbot's clever scheme and overturned the boat without the Ikarians clinging to the hull. The two bodies were washed ashore, leaving no doubt about the drowning of their brother and the four Germans. A corpse, let alone two, is superbly convincing. Back on Samos Zobel captured a boatload of womenfolk joining their husbands, whereupon he was at last promoted. The minimal cost of his whitewashing so impressed my masters that contact has been established, so your mission did serve its purpose. Nikos escaped and is now serving . . .'

'On Panagiotis's Old tub. Ties it up quite neatly.'

Ralph tied up the travel document, ticket and letter of credit but had to leave before the farewell party given by Artemis. She invited a genuine Druse princess, a popular Arab film star, who charmingly drove a frustrated brigadier to drink. Conveying top brass untenderly to bed neatly tied up the recent private's military experience.

2

The bus to Baghdad was crammed with Arabs. Rubber tubes dangling from the roof dispensed water straight into the mouths of the passengers who plied Charles with grey lumps of goat cheese and stale bread as the stops at filling stations only produced tiny cups of coffee. If not the misdiagnosed typhus, typhoid became no less probable than the still unverified syphilis. Medical speculations failed to cheer in the monotony of the Transjordan desert and the cold of a sleepless December night. Loneliness in a crowd was familiar but aggravated by the lack of a common language and the uniform snoring. Uncomfortable thoughts in an uncomfortable seat.

Cramped in body and mind, Charles resisted the enticing hotel bed on seeing the newspaper headlines. The sinking of the American fleet at Pearl Harbour made sailing schedules unreliable, but the travel agent disposed of one cabin the very next day, perhaps the last ship for weeks. Charles paid for the hotel room he had not occupied, renounced looking for the *Arabian Nights*, yet the comfort of the sleeping car contrasted as violently with the misery of the bus as the ups and downs of Sinbad the Sailor.

'Unforeseen circumstances' delayed the ship's departure. The King occupied Basra's only proper hotel, but on the waterfront accommodation was available above a large cabaret. The creaking of the stairs, giggles and groans testified to continuing action after the gruesome mixture of waltzes and bellydances had ceased. Sleep was incidental, but the handful of intended passengers were obliged to stay on the quay, ready to embark at short notice.

Sailing through limitless palm forests into the balmy warmth of the Persian Gulf and calling at ports little changed since Sinbad evoked the *Arabian Nights* despite the very British life on board. The social and national enigma of Charles varied the dreary discussions of the weather and the War over endless drinks. He kept to one sundowner with the freckled third mate whose shyness needed little discouragement. Age and inclination favoured an intimacy, precluded by Charles's scruples despite the negative tests.

———————

A novel from the ship's library brought Charles to India's most prestigious hotel, the *Taj Mahal* in Bombay. Even without the customary bearer the room was very costly, as the police officer emphasised. The CID was curious about the holder of an emergency passport intruding on the preserve of senior administrators and officers; the rapid Japanese advance might delay his departure for Australia. A cheaper hotel might be advisable, it was up to Mr Fenton, but would he mind reporting once a week, a mere formality. As an ex-serviceman he was entitled to use the swimming pool and sporting facilities at Malabar, that should occupy him while waiting.

Swimming was hardly a full-time occupation but between visits to the CID the Berliner's report might be presented. The dermatologist muttered the obligatory 'Interesting case, very odd' but, as he had been even more eminent back in Berlin, he was also more enterprising. 'We'll begin with a blood test, you haven't had one for three weeks. If again negative I'll cut out a lymph gland behind your ear to confirm the clinical picture.'

'That remains to be seen' was the opening shot in a fight to be resumed when the test result was at hand.

No need after the quacks satisfied 'Four-cross positive, those tests in Jerusalem didn't make sense'. Tested and tester apparently shared the blame. 'I'll write up the case in the medical journal, full discretion but full particulars, ha ha. Too much time has been lost in this secondary stage and I'll stabilise with four mercury shots before the salvarsan routine. Turn round, as you haven't much flesh it's a bit painful.'

Sitting hurt as much as walking, but perhaps swimming . . . The large pool provided some relief and Charles picked his way on the soft lawn without a limp. Slightly apart from the hearty memsahibs and children, a pretty brunette in beach clothes more suited to Cannes was reading a French paperback. Switching French from the Dame de Sion encased in a wimple to a liberally-exposed sunbather appealed to Charles's sense of humour and the book provided an acceptable line of approach. Mariette was delighted to talk to a compatriot, made a show of not believing that he had only studied in Paris where she had attended a dramatic school and played some minor parts. Nothing more natural than an appointment for the following day.

The painful buttock engendered sombre reflections. Hadn't Cesare Borgia lost his hair and teeth after mercury injections? The treatment was, moreover, ineffective, according to the *Magic Bullet* film. But there was no other European specialist to consult, as in refugee-haunted Jerusalem. Tommies drowned their anxieties in beer, he would try an Indian film.

——— ———

'The costumes were gorgeous but the plot was so primitive that the subtitles weren't really necessary. Who would want to produce such trash?'

'My husband,' Mariette laughed. 'He was trained in Paris but doesn't mind selling his artistic conscience for the right sum of money. Next week he'll go on location for another epic in Kashmir.'

A hint? 'Does he never come to the pool?'

'Indians are not admitted. He is a Parsee, a small sect, often married to Europeans, I didn't imagine in Paris how lonely an existence it would be.'

Existence became less lonely after the husband's departure, and the termination of the mercury agony. Less painful pricking of veins and buttocks was attuned to sex on a bed from which the vultures encircling the Towers of Silence were all too visible. Christmas occasioned a spurt of sentiment, Mariette's memories overflowed, Charles kept his bottled up. She was exasperated by his impatience to be off, his daily visits to the shipping agent; he was grateful for a fleeting companionship in an alien world, but once again the present had no future.

The past was resuscitated when Panagiotis was struggling out of his shirt behind the low partition of a cabin in the pool's locker room. Charles hurled himself through the swing door and the resemblance remained startling even at close quarters. The English sailor was startled but indicated that there was sufficient room. Their eyes met, they become tongue-tied, shy yet unmistakably excited while undressing in slow motion. The bathing trunks were reluctantly adjusted, Charles joined Mariette, the sailor his mates.

———— ———

The shipping agent finally secured a passage to Australia, but from Calcutta. It never occurred to Charles that it was not obligatory to cross India in a private compartment, which almost exhausted the letter of credit, and his only regret was the impossibility of visiting the famous sites en route. Action made leavetaking from Mariette easy, but she deserved a pretence of grief which she reciprocated more honestly.

Returning to fetch his luggage, Charles noticed the English sailor; they stopped and smiled without awkwardness. 'Let's have a drink over there.'

'I'm afraid there isn't time. I have to catch a train to Calcutta in half an hour.' Their eyes locked in the pleasure of meeting turned sad, acknowledging the loss. They did not exchange names, yet would never forget the briefest of encounters.

Whether because of the resemblance to Panagiotis or because here was an affection in its own right, the missed opportunity saddened the isolation of the spacious compartment till overlaid by the exoticism of the landscape.

The ample breakfast at Calcutta's leading hotel provided adequate nourishment for the whole day and the main sights were in walking distance. Dispensing with the customary carriage delivered Charles into the hands and stumps of the leprous beggars whose pursuit on hooves replacing their rotted knees had to be bought off by a handful of coins. The ravages of leprosy recalled the repellent exhibits in Vienna's VD Museum; syphilis was curable but his had evolved so strangely that a third stage became a justified nightmare on the voyage down the Bay of Bengal.

Secrecy of ship movements poorly justified the wasted thousands of miles and rupees as under the Japanese threat Colombo was the obvious port of embarcation for Australia. Warships of all Allied nations dominated the harbour where the picturesque stayed in hygienic bounds. At sunset women and children withdrew from the sporting facilities, kept open for servicemen till midnight; the young sailors remained remarkably quiet in the large pool of Babel where the British mixed with the Dutch, French, Greeks and Norwegians. The moon was late but the stars illuminated the tropical night sufficiently for an orgy Imperial Rome might have envied; the free-for-all respected rules, no imposition nor inhibition. The fine bodies moved with the grace of an ancient ritual till the celebrants were exhausted and the water was laced with spunk.

The ship enforced the salutory once-only by sailing the next evening, but frustration galled the boredom during the detour south outside the range of Japanese submarines. Mariette's parting gift, *War and Peace*, was of considerably greater interest than the survivors of torpedoed freighters embarked at Colombo. But a Greek seaman urgently required a translator. The doctor, roused from his practice on a repatriated barmaid, worried 'No wonder the fool is moaning so fearfully. Why didn't he see me earlier? I only hope the appendix hasn't burst. I have to operate immediately, but first a few questions. The chap is terrified and so am I.' Pain and hardening of the swollen abdomen had been described and the operating table rigged up before the final 'When did he have his last bowel movement?'

'About a month ago' hurried an incredulous doctor into shoving an enema up and a laxative down. 'Both sufficiently potent to abort an elephant'.

In gratitude for the prevention of manslaughter the Greek insisted on displaying his sensational tattoos, the doctor his family at Free-mantle; neither aroused enthusiasm.

——— ———

Like Captain Cook Charles disembarked at Botany Bay as the anti-submarine boom closed Sydney Harbour. At the Kurrabi Point flat Father's embrace was more surprising than his absence from the shipping office, as he was given neither to waiting nor emotional gestures. 'Yours is the front room, really two with the glassed-in veranda. A maid comes twice a week, a rarity here. They are called char ladies, idiotic euphemism. There isn't enough hanging space and I left some suits in your wardrobe. On the other side of the hall and bathroom is my room, the eating recess and the kitchen, accessible from the backstairs, convenient for Helen.' He paused before the reluctant explanation. 'Helen Hastings attended my lectures on Austria. Keen student, like . . . Herta before she got married.'

Charles drew attention to a ferry leaving for town and his tactful Tania cover-up was rewarded by oblique frankness. 'Helen keeps some of her things here. Trains stop fairly early to the northern suburb where she lives. By the way, she is a few months younger than you, so call her Helen.'

'And I'll be Charles.' English had come naturally as neither had spoken much German for years. Now Father baulked. 'Fechtner should have been good enough for you and Karl was the name of the Emperor. I've always called you Karl to Helen, but ask her yourself.'

Repudiation of monarchist loyalty had never entered the complex emotional and practical reasons for the name change, hard to present and harder to understand in the remoteness of Australia. If here was indeed journey's end, Father's resentment of integration as Fenton was misplaced. No more sticking out like a sore thumb, of belonging nowhere except to a non-existing Austria. Father's long neglect rankled but it was generous to share these two rooms. Was there no money for a decent flat? Father looked no older than at his marriage to Tania but the age gap had widened and Helen might well have drained the remaining funds.

—— —— —— ——

That was ruled out at the first encounter. Father certainly maintained a high standard in variety; after Mother's blonde and Tania's dark beauty, brunette Helen was less striking. A weak chin detracted from the prettiness of her oval face, there was a beauty spot on her left cheekbone, while her eyes were almost as blue as Mother's. In her pleasant, hardly accented voice she addressed Father as 'Sir', decidedly odd, but her 'Charles' was a touching paternal concession gratefully acknowledged by a glance. Another recaptured the long-disused father-and-son empathy; a comparison between Helen's interest in Greece and Palestine with Tania's no less intelligent questions on Rome at the first meeting with her stepson in the panelled dining room of the Liechti.

The Liechti loomed also as background to the Gestapo visit, but Father expressed no gratitude for escaping just in time due to his son's insistence. On a stroll through the Kurraba garden suburb he was slightly reticent about his wife. 'Tania was doing well in Zurich, but since the Germans occupied the South of France all correspondence stopped. Helen was very interested in your War stories, I'm glad you got on so well.' Father passed lightly over the HEC débâcle for which the jaundice provided a carefully-edited excuse, but he insisted on Economics against his son's preference. 'History would not have earned enough for the upkeep of the Liechti, now the needs are more pressing.'

'Hadn't I better take a job?'

'No reason why you shouldn't be doing both, as evening student. A bit hard, perhaps, but you haven't overworked yourself for the last five years.'

Six was truer, but Father would luckily never know. That Charles had perfected his languages in those years appeared of no more use to the Ex-Servicemen Employment Office than to the RASC, but Father knew a string-puller at the Public Library. The elderly archivist disclaimed descent from deportees but claimed resistance to a rape attempt in the Library basement. Father prudently kept to the reading room and to the safety of supper parties in her large villa where she dispensed instant motherliness to 'One who was already like a son'. She promised Charles an appointment to the New South Wales public service, but bureaucracy would not be hurried even by an influential member.

The Employment Office placed Charles as pay clerk in a repair garage where deductions for lateness and absence did not endear him to the tough workforce. The manager introduced him as a Middle East veteran, but he was obviously a Limey which provoked a 'You are just a cheap imitation of Noël Coward' who had recently come to the attention of the antipodes by his film *In Which We Serve*. Charles's 'Except for the cheap, you couldn't be more right' activated the general dislike.

——— ———

Appointment to the Master's Office was sidetracked by the archivist from function to location. 'Sydney's finest old building, the former Hyde Park Barracks.' The elegant Georgian exterior was indeed fine, the interior just old. Atop the worn wooden staircase a Dickensian cashier presented the Attendance Book, after the punchcards in the garage as outdated as the personnel. A pipe-smoking septuagenarian performed the introduction to fellow pensioners replacing the soldier generation, three young moderately pretty typists and two middle-aged females clattering away on equipment actually connected to electricity. Charles was assigned a desk overlooking Hyde Park, then taken to the Chief Clerk, who put Mr Fenton at ease by questions about his war experiences before handing him to the Deputy Master, remarkable for his pre-retirement age and non-Irish name. He commented favourably on the continuation of university studies and hoped the RASC training would prove useful. Less sanguine, the pipe-smoking Chief Accountant elaborated his duties, preparing receipts and statements, taking money to the bank and the pay sheet.

With the garage chore fresh in mind Charles thought of an appeal to the highest authority. 'When will I see the Master?'

'You won't. He sits in the Courts, in Equity. His Lunacy title is a legalistic quirk, the Deputy is the boss here. Relations object to the term, so it is generally omitted though we administer the estates of all certified insane.'

———————

Masterly discretion threw Helen into laughing fits reminiscent of Lis and Otto. Father seemed disproportionately put out till Charles remembered the two Auer cousins in an asylum and rumours that the Nazis had exterminated the insane as part of the war effort.

Though disappointed by his employment, Charles was not shy about it and he teased the archivist for her Lunacy connection when she gave a party to celebrate his elevation to the public service. On this occasion he was exempted from the washing-up performed by distinguished guests, an amazing novelty to Charles used to servants even in wartime Greece. His 'continental manners' attracted the youngish wife of an eminent lawyer: Eve Warren asserted her congenial European frivolity by liberally scattering her little French and entertained a kindred soul while her husband was pleading at court.

The follow-up treatment presented no obstacle; the specialist recommended by the Bombay quack re-enacted the headshaking and grunts expressing astonishment, but administered the injections more gently as the veins had become brittle under the puncturing assaults. The fees were commensurate but, though Father had not been squeamish over the clap in Vienna, strains on delicate relations were better avoided; strict economies all round were preferable to an acceptable confession. The wages of the garage cured the wages of sin.

———————

The age factor increased tardiness at the Master's, where the venerable elders 'entrusted' some of their tasks to Charles, who had long finished his. He took to retiring to the WC with the *Sydney Herald*'s reports from all the war fronts; a snack was easily accommodated within the banking hour and while the others were munching during the midday break Charles ate his fruit over a book afterwards inserted into files deserving scant attention. Perhaps the typists were flirtatious merely because he was their sole contemporary, but they competed in making him unattractive sweets and attractive bathing sarongs, which pleasantly shocked the old fogies.

He signed out in time for a drink at a nearby hotel bar closing at an unreasonable 6.00 p.m. when the non-mobilised or demobilised queer set swept him along to a 'special' restaurant. They were more amusing than the typists, interested in a rare stranger whose exclusive reliance on Helen's cooking was diplomatically as well as gastronomically not advisable. One of them, an improbably wavy-haired digger, had shed his khaki for unspecified reasons to resume a more suitable pink at the leading hairdresser. Figaro liked musicals, especially the perennial *The Maid of the Mountains*, with the durable Maid who had created the role in Australia; he also liked harbour pubs on Saturday afternoons, but Charles withdrew before the fights became generalised and the Black Maria collected the drunks lying in the gutter.

The constipated seaman Charles had saved from dismemberment offered the safety of the Greek Club at brawling time. Many Aussies had fought in their country but none had learned their language and the very Greek enthusiasm found practical expression in a ration book on the cheap and petrol coupons greatly desired by Eve. A dark, muscular merchant marine officer showed personalised appreciation and sense of humour; he had transliterated Panagiotis into Peter as the literal All Saintly was impossible outside Greece where Apollo, Socrates, Christ and Rose are popular for males. The sudden awareness that All Saintly had been justified by the sacrifice on Samos gave a romantic twist to casual sex at first sight.

In the flat Peter smelled the smoke of cigars and from his next voyage brought a box of this unobtainable luxury to a grateful but embarrassed Father. The kind donor called between convoys and provided a change from more conventional bedding.

'I now have the wherewithal to elope with you' was more than Eve had bargained for, but she was delighted with the coupon bounty. 'Don't worry, it won't harm the war effort as the coupons were on the Black Market anyway. Whither does my lord and master command?' 'Lord and master' was unfortunate as Helen had added the former to her unhealthy ways of addressing Father while the latter smacked of the professional Lunacy. Eve's husband often spent weekends with clients in the Outback, leaving behind the car now put to good use. She was an excellent driver, slightly older and plumper than Mariette, more piquant with an upturned nose, and more fun.

Fun was worse than work at the office. The awful plonk at the Christmas party inspired the girls to simpered insinuations and the elders to a display of senile masculinity. Australian conviviality must not be judged from typists and public servants; Eve and Helen equalled their European counterparts. His 'Class is more important than nationality' at Brillac was, however, only partly vindicated as drinking to get blotto was classless in Australia.

Father opened a bottle of hock to wash down the turkey prepared by Helen before joining her shadowy parents. Without her, Fechtner lore coloured discussions of the War and the political sequels. One disastrous peace treaty had opened the way for National Socialism; misguided politicians might do the same for Communism. Having lost everything by the first evil, Father dreaded the second. The strong silent paterfamilias excluded the agonising indecision the night of the Anschluss and Herta's Rumanian scheme, yet acknowledged that the personal shaped the political. 'Let's drink to Herta. I hope Max behaves' showed his anxiety about the Tarburgs under the murderous twilight of the Nazis. He raised the last glass – 'Good luck for your studies.'

— — — — —

Third time round was less demanding intellectually and more physically after the long office hours; rushing to the Neo Gothic University – shades of Cambridge and Exeter – queuing for NAAFI tastealike meals, three lectures and the tram ride through deserted streets to the ferry home. Economic History was superior to pub crawling, Public Administration equal, Economic Theory inferior.

On weekend picnics with Eve, Charles rode the enormous rollers till the shark bell drove him back into her arms. Figaro asserted that his one over-developed breast was more appreciated in bed than on the beach; he preferred riding and bounced along in a gallant parody of Irene's splendid horsemanship.

She had been appointed to Mountbatten's staff in Ceylon and had come down with jaundice, since she was 'burning the candle at both ends'. This was medically less original than his creamcake-induced bout. However strenuous her work, her play would not have included the Colombo pool, Heaven forbid. It was unlikely that she was pampered by as many friends at the military hospital as he during his illness in Paris. A prayer would not come amiss, the Catholic cathedral opposite the office was dedicated to the Virgin, but, as he knelt before a picture of Her Assumption, the artistic comparison with the altar in Athens prevented concentration on the girl's plight. She would be horribly depressed, but so was he in his emotional mix-up, which the ugly emptiness of the Cathedral did nothing to alleviate. His intentions had been good, so they might not pave the way to hell.

— — — — —

Medical mix-up paralleled the emotional. The half-yearly blood test was four-cross positive and the dermatologist went through the routine from dreary disbelief to the Middle East bug theory. 'Or perhaps you really are the one-in-a-million case contradicting all text

133

books. An astounding reverse, no symptoms yet definitely infected. A recurrence is less likely than in new infection, but in either case it's another three courses of treatment.

The dermatologist was wrong, as doctors had been all along. Peter had been away too long and Eve was a respectable married woman. Whatever the cause, the pincushion effect was deeply resented by veins and behind.

The head provided the counterirritant. The results of the first-year exams creditably reflected Charles's preferences, but compared to second-year Statistics the HEC lectures appeared easily comprehensible. Charles tried, failed and told Father, 'I never was any good at Maths. I haven't a clue to these beastly numbers, it's impossible.'

'Had your mother not lavished gift baskets on your teachers, you'd be better off now. But for an average intelligence nothing is impossible.' Even at his most pompous, Father was practical; he hired a tutor who successfully pounded figures into a dully receptive pupil to pass into the calmer third year. Father was proved right; he usually was.

——— ———

The irritants shifted back to the medical and political sphere. Charles performed the acceptable minimum of work not at the public service pace but rapidly to gain time for reading and studying beyond the office files. This had not passed unnoticed and, when the regular clerks were demobilised, he was relieved of the banking and 'entrusted' with the most tiresome chores. He blamed the dust in the archives for a running nose restricted to office hours but finally consulted a GP. 'An allergy, exceedingly difficult to trace. Occasionally just nerves, intense dislike of the environment.'

Anglo-American armies were approaching Berlin and Vienna when stopped by the Yalta Agreement which delivered half of civilised Europe to a totalitarianism as evil as the Nazis. Preoccupied with the Japanese menace and brainwashed into admiring Stalin as liberator, Australian friends and acquaintances paid scant attention to the fighting in Vienna that replaced German with Russian tyranny. The destruction of the town's symbols, the Opera and Schönbrunn, aggravated personal anxieties, for the Grandparents, Herta and so many others.

News arrived predictably from an 'Unexpected quarter', Kurt Auer.

'. . . I got your address from your wife who laughed a lot when I called her Aunt Tania and we are now on Christian name terms.

She is successful on the stage and will write soon herself, now that the mail is functioning again. In case I'm first, Herta and Max are on the Tarburg, he has been wounded. The Grandparents are safe but hungry in a Vienna convent. I graduated before the tragic death of my parents and was granted a work permit because of the shortage of chemical engineers. My employers used the threat of expulsion, which meant the gas chamber in Germany, to pay me a salary no qualified Swiss would accept. I would like to escape the unhappy memories here and very much count on your help to start a new life in Australia. My degree is as good as expected in a nephew of yours. I'll find a job quickly and won't be a burden . . .'

Kurt was less urgent a worry than the closer family. 'He might have been more explicit, I hope Max is not seriously wounded. And that tragic death of my sister and brother-in-law . . . I expected that much about their elder children, but why would Kurt have been sent to the gas chamber?' The full extent of the Holocaust had not yet been revealed to an incredulous world.

'Not obeying the call up, I had that hanging over me during the last year in Greece. I'm glad the Grandparents retired to a convent, they couldn't have managed on their own.'

'I'll inquire about food parcels to Austria, perhaps through the Red Cross.'

Food for the family diverted attention from Kurt's request, which later kept Charles awake. Kurt's fears were the same as his, officially neither refugee nor stateless, in practice both, at the mercy of unsympathetic bureaucrats. But with the end to the expulsion threat, Kurt could demand an adequate salary or return to Germany. There must be an inheritance, the Auers had still been well-off when he visited them in Berlin. They had seemed exaggeratedly frightened of the Nazis but kind. Kurt had been mean at their brief meeting in Zurich, one portion of cheese for both when Charles was worried about money for the next meal. He was an only cousin, but they had never clicked. His Swiss degree would probably not be recognised, and Father would have to pay for further studies. Australia wasn't all that wonderful when working and studying simultaneously. Absurd to bring him out when Charles might have to return for a salvage operation.

'Tania has written and the char gave notice.' The servant problem took precedence. 'When I came back from my walk the char was still slurping her tea. When I refused a cup she said she wouldn't come again. I offered more money and she burst into tears. I had offended her, by not sitting down to tea with her. No more entertaining for her than for me, but you can't argue with inferiority complexes. I won't be blackmailed, though it's unlikely I'll find a replacement. Herta has a daughter, the only good news in Tania's letter. Max was shot up by drunken Russians who pillaged the Altenhof. Herta did something heroic to save him.' The same probability occurred to father and brother. 'Kurt's parents committed suicide when threatened with deportation to an extermination camp. Those Nazi fiends would not spare even a President of the Luther Society. I would like to help Kurt, but it was difficult enough to bring you out, a son and ex-serviceman. If I went to Canberra . . . What do you think?'

'Can you afford it, Father?' was above all an attempt to get rid of an expression that had haunted his youth. Past frustration was, however, more persistent than present selfishness, soon forgotten together with Kurt. Tania joined him in limbo after the opening of communications with the Tarburg, not too long delayed as Carinthia was part of the British Zone.

———————

The carving up of Austria was a fitting background to the cutting of family ties. The Tarburg changed from German Convalescent Home to the mess of a British regiment; luckily the officers were flattered to be asked to the private wing for meals for which they supplied food and drink. Tania's food parcels from Switzerland were forwarded to the Grandparents who badly needed them. Though Truman seemed less enamoured with the Russian liberators, civilian letters were still censored and the story of the Altenhof's occupation had better wait.

Looking up from Herta's letter, Charles's eyes met Father's in an unspoken 'Perhaps just as well'.

Despite Russian obstacles, the Allies eventually allowed correspondence with Vienna. Lis had married Erwein's best friend, 'Grandson of the doctor who killed Franz Joseph', which in their parlance meant nothing more alarming than the Emperor's court physician. Her father had insisted on the wedding in the Maltese Church, he had to show off his Knight's mantle. An invalid was selling shoelaces on the church steps, 'No paper, no straw. Anything similar is not the same', slightly ominous. After the Western Allies had stopped the Russian outrages, it seemed safe to have a child, whereupon her husband came down with TB and now had a pneumothorax.

Ohli wrote cheerfully, Granny tearfully, both fairly content among the retired civil servants and judges in the convent except for the prevalence of widows. They blessed Tania for the food parcels as the good sisters had little to eat.

All suffered and reacted predictably, none truer to character than Otto though his mockery was no longer based on self-assurance but despair.

'. . . My famous looks, second to yours only according to my loving spouse, were sacrificed on the altar of a fatherland that wasn't mine. My left side from face to foot is mangled, ripped and cut. You've managed on one eye, I am also one-armed, one-legged and castrated, with the compliments of a shell fired by the British to whom we offered services at the Outbreak.

'My brother used his pull as a Waffen SS colonel to have Dolly nursing me at the hospital where I was stitched together. The poor girl won't hear of an annulment, which in any case is too expensive. She doesn't stand much chance among the desperate non-virgins chasing the few surviving males of marriageable age. Money is the one consolation I might offer one day, rather original since the Barovskys gave up as robber barons. Willi Hollthal suggested the FO before he saw me, but Frankenstein is out of place in diplomacy. You'd be a different catch, just the right background, educational and nationality mix for present-day Austria. It's the job that would suit you best. For me it's Company Law, the most lucrative. A lopsided snarl and waving my stump should be effective. I offered Herta my services to retrieve the Liechti, but she preferred one of Henriette's lovers. The Liechti is in the American Sector, the Landtheater in the French, slightly the worse for a bomb, better supervise the restitution yourself . . .'

Austria called in an idiom incomprehensible in Australia. Family and friends make fun of disfigurement, wounds, bombs, hunger, no plea for help, for his return except to safeguard his property. The diplomatic career should sweep aside the Wynn Roberts's practical objections, while marriage to the daughter of a colonial governor would greatly assist promotion. Double-barrelled Fechtner-Fenton was appropriate for the London Legation where Irene would make a splendid hostess. Their correspondence had languished during the War, but their special relationship persisted, judging by the innumerable 'darlings' in her irregular letters. European preoccupations might be lightened by Figaro's Australian variations.

——— ———

Variations most unfortunate. Figaro's brittle brightness was pathetically wasted on the toughs who were tiresome before and quarrelsome after getting drunk. When blood mixed with vomit in the pubs, the licensed restaurant popular with the navy seemed almost decorous and the two British sailors almost sober. They were at a loss where to spend the night till the kind Australian offered hospitality, since his parents were spending the weekend in the country. Not virtue but boredom with the arduous pick-up technique made Charles refuse the suggested foursome. He was used to being the hunted not the hunter, at the tavernas in Athens, the nightclubs in Paris, the balls in Vienna. Was he only turned on when his nastily inflated ego was satisfied? Curse Freud! Figaro had done the hard work, so why play hard to get?

Providentially, a sailor complained in a thick Australian accent that he had been stood up by his mate and wouldn't mind a drink before returning to his ship. It was Navy Day after all, what a laugh with Figaro. Perhaps not; on the jetty the Australian seemed much bigger than in the darkness of the ferry's open deck, and his accent was not thick but slurred. No chance of giving him the slip, his legs were longer, and one glass of plonk couldn't do much harm and the last ferry was due in half an hour. Better go through with the social part after warning the hunk not to wake the family across the hall. While Charles was half-filling two glasses from the drink cabinet on the verandah, he heard the front door slam; the wardrobe was open, most suits were gone and so was the sailor. To be chased by this hunk had been risky, to chase him even more so; the sharks preferred human flesh to suits.

Father was luckily alone and on hearing the facts acted with admirable speed; the Great Organiser phoned the naval police and informed them that a drunken sailor had just robbed the flat and would most likely disembark with his booty on Circular Quay. Father asked no questions, no plausible explanation of the stranger's presence was possible, and Charles laboured the pointlessness of stealing clothes several sizes too small and unsaleable as Australians did not wear second-hand suits. He was running out of steam about ingrained habits not being changed by rationing when the call came: the thief had been arrested and the clothes could be collected the next morning.

Over breakfast Father assumed full charge. 'As the . . . chap has been caught redhanded there is no need for identification. A confrontation is better avoided. I'll take a large suitcase, otherwise I'd look suspect myself. Everything should be back in place before Helen comes. No reason why you shouldn't go riding with a friend you do know.' Coolly and clearly to the various points; Father considered further discussion unprofitable and chose a later ferry though he was apparently ready.

Post mortems were not in Father's nature but very much in Figaro's. 'I indicated that my parents' matrimonial double would do nicely, but if three was a crowd one of the boys could retire to my room. Whereupon the fiends declared it seemed simpler, that's the word they used, if I kept to my bed and they would make do with the other, thank you ever so much. Whether impotent or innocent, hardly my most rewarding pick-up.'

'More than mine!' Laughing at oneself invited reciprocity but Charles considered his listener nearly falling off the horse decidedly overdone. 'Beginner's luck that he didn't smash up the flat looking for cash. Even luckier that your father has taken it so well.'

That was indeed astounding. 'The thief is in naval custody but will be taken to a Magistrate's Court. As I have signed the charge, your presence is not required, and you had better go to the office.'

Father was equally laconic about the trial where the sailor blamed drunkenness for the pointless theft. This apparently stopped questions about his presence in the flat, his motives were of no interest, Father's were. His look when Charles expressed his gratitude conveyed the family's vulnerability in miraculous empathy: a naval scandal, according to Granny, had driven Uncle Karl to kill himself at Charles's age; the Auers' dreadful end made suicide appear akin to hereditary syphilis. The naval factor emphasised the semblance and no scandal must be allowed to develop.

———— ————

Developments abroad were broached with characteristic directness. 'I've been asked to reorganise a large chain store in Calcutta. Any advice about clothes?'

'Tropical outfits best on the spot. I suppose the provincial governor who intervened at the Athens Consulate now wants to gild you in chocolate. You mentioned he directed the Burmese resistance from Calcutta.'

'Not bad, two and two put together quite neatly.' Father was obviously pleased that so much was recalled in so few words. 'Pity I can't take you along but you are too close to the finals. As your memory is so good, you might remember that first Swiss offer when you were a little boy. Your mother disliked Zurich but I don't shift my responsibility. We are often given a second and even third chance . . . The present agreement is for six months, so I should be back before the monsoons. By then you'll be a B.Ec. and if the business is sufficiently interesting we'll move East.'

'We' apparently included Helen, who brought detailed news from Calcutta in exchange for terrifying accounts about the lepers. She

proposed accompanying Charles to the graduation but his own paramour had a stronger claim than Father's and, officially at least, the
two ignored each other's existence. Concluding eleven years of academic peregrinations, the new Bachelor looked, according to Eve,
'Not a day older than in that photo with Irene. Opinion seems
divided whether I'm your mother or a cradle snatcher.'

——— ———

Irene could not be thought either; except for clappy Gusti, she alone
was of matching age in the procession of married matrons started by
the White Russian mother of a boyhood playmate. Irene had remained on Mountbatten's staff when he became Viceroy, so when
Charles returned with Father to India the wedding might take place
there. It would do a diplomatic career in Austria no end of good if
the Viceroy gave the bride away.

He did not, but he attended Irene's wedding to a staff officer. She
explained in the clichés used on such occasions, including the standard consolation 'In many ways he resembles you'. Better if not in too
many ways, but women seemed content with second-best. Even Lis
had settled for less than the genuine article and Irene was exposed to
dashing temptations. The invalid at the Maltese Church touted 'No
paper, no straw' and this was the last straw. Not love but pride was
hurt; separation had maintained a romantic illusion long stripped of
real feeling, yet no other marriage partner had ever seemed possible.
Irene had been approved by the highest matrimonial authority, Aunt
Valerie.

——— ———

Aunt Valerie died soon after Eugen's wedding – according to Herta,
'heartbroken at her son's union with a baker's daughter'. The Liechti
had been restituted, after having been pillaged and ransacked by the
Nazis as well as the Russians. Herta ventured to Vienna and succeeded in letting it to the Swiss Red Cross for a nominal rent, better
than mouldering away unoccupied. That was probably happening on
the Altenhof, Max would not go near it, no wonder as he was still
hobbling on crutches. A visit to the Russian zone was out of the
question, even driving through was dangerous enough but all ac-
cesses to the capital had 'idiotically been handed over to the Eastern
barbarians'. The wording indicated the end of censorship or a more
realistic evaluation by the Western Allies. Herta believed in the magic
of a British passport, but Charles would obtain the genuine article
only after naturalisation the following year. Austria remained out of
bounds till then.

India was eliminated by Father's dislike of its climate and politics.

'The break-up of one empire suffices for a lifetime. Communal riots will become much worse once the British leave.' He talked more about background than business, profitable though business must have been, since he was able to resume the country life he preferred. Australia prospered on sheep and so would he, despite 'lack of familiarity' with these animals. Encouraged by Helen's adulation he departed for a farm on Tasmania's north coast after introducing his stockbroker for the investment of a belated graduation present: £1,000.

——— ——— ———

After selling collections and jewellery to live on constantly diminishing funds, the man-of-property satisfaction compensated for the hurt finer feelings. In taking delivery of the share certificates, an astounded Philip MacLachlan added further balm. 'So you have made these blessed shores on your own! You must tell me how at dinner tonight.'

Dinner at Sydney's leading restaurant equalled the previous meal in Paris only in the deference shown to Mr MacLachlan. He had recently returned from a purchasing mission in America and listened sympathetically to Charles's unedited tale. 'I have sometimes regretted your refusal, but you are so damned independent. Do you aspire to the Chief Lunacy? With your B.Ec. I might recommend you for a decent job provided you stop your precious originality.'

'In my loony bin they actually understand most of my pearls. I now sing opera with a young Italian recently engaged; we hide in the archives and laugh ourselves silly. It won't do his career much good, mine is blighted beyond repair. Kind of you to propose business from which my father seems to keep me away deliberately. He could have placed me with those Calcutta tycoons had he stayed a little longer, not such a sacrifice. I'd better concentrate on the Liechti, but if I stay in Australia you might yet regret your offer.'

——— ——— ———

Unlike for the Liechti, there were numerous prospective lodgers eager to share the flat. Lacking a suitable friend, Charles chose the devil-he-knew after Figaro swore solemnly not to drag home high-risk partners. His parents were retiring to the country and he claimed to 'have succumbed to the glamour of the female upper end at the expense of less colourful male parts'. Reassuringly he tinted his hair various shades of orange.

Not reassuring in the flatmate of a future diplomat. To make up for Lunacy, the archivist signed Charles's application to the newly-established Australian Foreign Service. The Austrian remained a possibility and two irons in the fire were a welcome change from none. Charles had been brought up on the topics of the written exams and his historical comparisons were as daring as at the Vienna University. A week of analysing familiar political problems evoked a pro-Australian FO enthusiasm that vanished with Herta's letter.

'. . . There is now enough nasty food in Vienna and most medicines, even penicillin, can be found on the Black Market, but many of the syphilitic women that haven't committed suicide have died. The Austrian Red Cross now copes and the Swiss will relinquish the Liechti. Their rent does not pay my expenses in chasing foreign buyers with whom our lawyer has no contacts. My friends in Vienna have been bombed out or have moved five to a room, I don't fancy sleeping on the floor of the Liechti and the few hotels are hideously expensive. Either Father or you, better both, must come over. With your British passports you are entitled to payment in foreign currency and inflation is still a real danger. Max limps about on a stick and Lis's husband died of pneumonia because of his pneumothorax . . .'

Herta's interest in Lis was natural, but why those mysterious syphilitic women? There could be no possible connection with his own case. At his last check-up he had learned that a new wonder drug replaced painful magic bullets, so why those suicides?

Father's first phone call from Tasmania was to enquire about the exams and to shift responsibility for the Liechti to his son. 'There is the possibility of German compensation, so the lawyer needs a complete inventory of all valuables. You've inherited your mother's interest in the collections, send him a detailed list.'

A crackling line made it difficult to clarify that he had not merely inherited the interest but the collections themselves. It proved, however, unnecessary.

'I'm not happy about Herta dealing with lawyers and I can't go over, as farmhands in Tasmania are as rare as chars in Sydney. The Consular Academy is the seat of the US Administration and the Liechti might interest them as Residence. You as Australian would be well placed to negotiate with an Allied Mission. The Liechti is yours, the Altenhof Herta's. You have to pay off the mortgage and the lawyer, not all that much considering the possibilities with legations or international organisations. If you pass your exams as well as I expect, you'll probably obtain a few months before starting in Canberra. Perhaps the Austrian diplomatic service is, after all, more promising. It's up to you.'

Father had always disposed, now he merely proposed the crucial point. Leaving Austria had been hateful but unavoidable, returning would be wonderful and his own decision. The choice between the dull safety of Australia and the exciting uncertainty of Europe could no longer be postponed. He would consult Philip.

Figaro got in first, as he could not help hearing the conversation from his room. 'Providential, my dear. A client, I did wonders for her, oh, no, I won't go into that, promised me an introduction to the Psychopathic Society. Just what you need.'

'As I'm already into Lunacy rather a retrograde step.' Psycho entanglements unravelled into a spiritualist meeting. With the crystal gazer proved so astoundingly right, this was a case for the 'Try everything once'.

Except for wide green eyes the Guide seemed as ordinary as the half-dozen elderly women. He hoped that the newcomers would join the group, gave an introduction to Spiritualism and switched off the light. Signals were received but the knocking was hard to locate while the baleful sighs might have been a ghost or disappointment over his non-appearance. Not to waste the 'contribution', Charles consented to be hypnotised, anything once.

Leaning back comfortably, concentrating on those green eyes required no effort; they calmed, relaxed, liberated. Did the touch of the hand induce or end a dimly remembered feeling? Why this alarming chorus of rapt expression bending over him? He felt drained, infinitely more than when the mere interplay of light had taken him equally 'Far away' till the touch by an uncomprehending Nanny brought him back to the reality of the garden. 'Far away' remained as mysterious as in childhood but was it the same? Not spontaneous and beautiful but induced and vaguely disturbing.

'An unusually coherent response but you should have told me that you are French. Freed from restraint, the subconscious reverts to the mother tongue, the deepest layer of memory. Luckily this lady understands French but she couldn't make out why you changed your opinion of the Duke of Anjou so violently.'

'Because there were two, the younger brother assuming the title when the older became king.' The Guide deserved a brief sketch of Valois intrigues.

'Remarkable, you revealed not your present but a past life. You are an ideal medium, sliding back effortlessly through the centuries is extremely rare, especially at a first session. We must get a French-speaker next time.'

——— ——— ———

'There won't be another, tempted though I am to listen to your royal past. Pity you didn't utter at your first "Far away", children remember a previous incarnation more easily, when one believes in that sort of thing. The Valois obsession links up with your portrait, all fascinatingly unhealthy. But no help in deciding who shall benefit by your diplomatic gifts. Here it's sure you'll get a legation, in Austria just a possibility. As a foreign diplomat it'll be easier to sell the Liechti internationally, perhaps even as a future Australian legation.'

'Eminently sensible as always. Five passports and one name later it does seem a waste to go back to an exceedingly shaky square one. I've been hanging about in worse places than Canberra and now that Father and Helen are gone I've no one to talk to except, of course, you dear Philip. Eve is accompanying her husband on a business trip to London. Figaro might yet tint my hair while I'm asleep.'

'I'm interested in him. You did express bewilderment very creditably and I don't want a blue rinse. I intend exchanging my executive directorships here for the less strenuous boardrooms in London, but not with my Indonesian halfcast. Fortunately he rarely lets on that he speaks English, he is a joy to look at and in bed, but in between . . . He is constantly restyling his hair, parted left, right, middle, swept backward, forward, upward and in a rare moment of comprehensible speech expressed interest in crimping at large. Hence Figaro with *salon de coiffure* as dowry for my Susanna. I'd like to ask them along for dinner after your Orals, I know a quiet fashionable joint.'

'Why this discretion they won't enjoy. We . . .'

'Fairly obvious. To Australian businessmen you look and sound like not-so-little Lord Fauntleroy, probably owning shares in their companies. You are moreover a diplomat, that at least is settled.'

———

It was not because Ralph introduced a third choice.

'. . . Cloak and Dagger are out of fashion. Not for cover but as Admin. Officer I'm doing what might pass as honest work in the Cultural Organisation. Our Man in Izmir has become Functional Officer, a position comprising everything and mainly nothing. His last scoop in the Fraternity was the surrender and prompt release of good Zobel still capturing women and children on Samos. Robert visited the Monastery where the sole marble cross will bear Panagiotis's name with the inscription 'He died for his country'. Not quite true, but next to you he loved his country best. Aussies are popular in Greece, the CO would find a niche for you to perform some useless job at the Brit. taxpayers' expense. You had a rotten time in Athens, make up for it now . . .'

Mimis played on the same strings in the enclosed note.

'. . . The civil war had one positive result, uniforms galore. Another Panagiotis will not be easy to find, but for you not impossible. Can you afford wasting the years when you are not loved
solely for your cash? . . .'

Transferred from finance to emotions, the hated phrase hit where
it hurt. Money had seemed replaceable, youth and looks not. Love
and even desire must be reciprocal; the desperately poor boys in the
Dancing School had preferred him to rich pickings. And Panagiotis!
Where else . . . ?

Christl rounded off the temptations.

'. . . During the German occupation I sold my jewellery not for a
pound of flesh but for some miserable vegetables. Then the
Communists took many of my friends as hostages and marched
them barefoot with thousands of the élite to the snows of Mt.
Parnis and to their death. Churchill and Eden risked their lives at
the height of the civil war to save Greece from Communism, but
your old protector, the Refugee Commissioner, had to be sent as
Minister to London to explain the position of the King, Greece's
only hope for stability. Willi Hollthal came here for the reopening
of the Austrian Legation and mentioned you might join the
Service. It would be wonderful if you were appointed to Athens,
but officially or not I hope to see you soon . . .'

———————

Charles's answers on Current Affairs could not be faulted, though
expressed a little forcefully. The rare candidate having studied
Ancient Greek shocked more by his opinion on classical tragedies, 'I
hated all this ranting and raving at high school. I only passed with
the help of a fellow student who commanded the German garrison
on Samos during the war.' The examiner was pained at this undiplomatic frankness, but Homer might evoke a better response. 'I rewrote
the Trojan War when I was five years old' was offensively pretentious, but failure must be made absolute. The deterioration of the
initial precise language was emphasised by slight trembling. The
discharge for shell shock was noted on the application and a recurrence would not do for a diplomat.

'The diplomat no doubt shook the examiners with his brilliant
replies.'

'Shaking did play a part and I got what I deserved.'

'Which means you did something uniquely daft and ruined your
future.'

'Right again, Philip. I'm sick and tired of being a fraud, beginning
with my name. Officially I am a Protestant, Australian and was more

or less engaged to Irene; practically I am a Catholic, European and was in love with Panagiotis. At thirty I have to be myself at last, whatever the cost.'

'It'll cost you plenty. Being yourself is an expensive luxury. May you never regret it.'

'I will. Deep down . . . I'll tell my father I sacrificed my career for the family or something equally wet to give him the illusion the decision was his. As a good, if short-term, Aussie I voted in the election last week; a blessed change from the frightened queues shuffling past the SS guards at Hitler's sham plebiscite for the Anschluss.'

'Whereupon Contrary Mary hastens back to Austria under the Russians. These two are less self-destructive. The orange barber seduces the mysterious oriental not just into speech but hysterical giggles. More than I ever achieved, thank God. And they crimped happily ever after.'

————

The colleagues considered resignation from the security of the public service lunacy and wished a frigid good luck, though Charles's typist actually shed a tear. The Deputy Master expressed understanding and surprise that Mr Fenton had not made the FO for which he seemed uniquely suited.

Doubts about the wisdom of this failure spoiled the plane journey and increased in the cold and rain of the Tasmanian winter, all too reminiscent of Europe. As usual, Father hardly mentioned business which now, unfortunately, meant those bedraggled creatures bleating in the fields. Instructions for Austria were equally woolly, except the injunction not to touch the Landtheater, obviously intended for Tania as a divorce settlement.

Helen's perennial salads suited the heat of Sydney but not the cold drizzle. The open fire recalled the Altenhof, but without servants to clear away the ashes . . . More warmth was generated by agreement on the tragic absurdity of dividing Germany 'permanently' and carving up tiny Austria among four quarrelling powers. 'I bought this encyclopaedia to help a first draft on *The Notion of Justice in International Relations*, but eventually I'll need original sources.'

'Your experiences in the last Imperial government should do for a start. If you had taught me as much about business as about history I'd be more confident of the future.'

Instead of the expected rebuke came an unprecedented confidence. 'Your *Trojan War* when you could hardly write indicated your interest in history which was opened up to me by my brother Karl.

Your inclinations are similar in many respects . . . music.' The pause indicated something less reputable than opera. 'In that Buddhist monastery in Burma reincarnation is a fact, happening after a few years or centuries. I remembered your *déjà vu* experience as a child at the Valois wing of the Louvre and that my brother wrote a Ph.D. thesis on that dynasty, the reason for my permitting your portrait in a costume apparently pretentious. Now this spiritualist session in Sydney . . . Perhaps I should have stopped your preoccupation with the past, but I appreciated your comments on the Liechti luncheons and your journeys. As a counterbalance I insisted on your studying Economics. The sale of the Liechti will start you off on a career of your own choosing. The Austrian diplomatic service after all?' A cheque for £1,000 sweetened the farewell.

3

The £1,000 were invested, as the money still held by Irene's father and the jewellery with Marie Louse's aunt should suffice till the sale of the Liechti. Transfer of the flat to Figaro paid for a first-class cabin shared with a sheep farmer who did not snore despite his appearance. On the lowest deck and less comfortable than some second-class single berths, but the passengers were so strictly segregated that Charles was glad to have chosen status at the start of yet another new life or, better, a return to the original.

He was asked to most parties in the luxury cabins, despite his refusal to participate in the games so desperately organised by the purser; diving into the pool proved that no physical handicap but sheer eccentricity made him prefer books to quoits. A letter to Countess Herta Tarburg in the ship's post box provided a gossip of last resort and, together with dancing well and widely, established Charles in his pre-war position as leader of the younger set. On a reduced scale, yet a remarkable change not only from previous sea voyages but from the entire Austrian experience. The allergy stopped and the ship's doctor examined Charles's facial cavities with an impressive collection of instruments. 'No trace of an irritation except in the tearducts. The sea air worked wonders. Or else – since you were sneezing the whole year round, it was psychosomatic, dissatisfaction with your work or the environment in general.'

At Colombo Charles led his set to the pool of orgiastic memories, now as regrettably respectable as the horse-carriage ride to the crater at Aden; a hearty Australian girl was sweatily holding hands but she was prevented from further harm as she shared a state cabin with even heftier parents. At Alexandria a frustration had to be wiped out; seven years after one Egyptian official had refused to let him land, another proved most eager to display his person and town to best advantage. The readiness of Mediterranean sex compared favourably with the alcoholic preliminaries in Australia.

The delightfully warm weeks between the Australian and European winters ended with the disagreeable need of using new acquaintances for old companions. After Charles had won the argument on generous end-of-journey tipping, a businessman expressed interest in the degree and languages of the polite young man; an encouraging first European opportunity, although located in Leeds, was not rejected out of hand. More immediately, the hearty Aussie family hoped for the polyglot guide's experience in Gay Paris; they would hire a car, the trip would be extended, time explicitly and money implicitly were of little concern.

———— ————

Concerned about accommodation in London as his mother had moved to the country, Ralph had arranged for a stay at Robert Nuttall's small flat. Our Man in Izmir had resigned from the CO and was following a course of Oriental Studies and gladly provided a safe house in London. He talked amusingly about Athens, sadly about Panagiotis, but it was alarming to wake opposite an empty bed at sunrise. Outstretched arms rose and fell, no response to a 'Good Morning', while enquiries about breakfast were shushed. As gymnastics it was excessive, as religion it had to be endured. Robert had embraced Islam and been circumcised at the Great Mosque in Cairo. There was no outward sign of eccentricity, yet Charles had better not waste time.

Lunch with Irene's parents at Sunningdale was less strained than expected. Government House tact eased the awkwardness. Agreement on the criminal folly of abandoning Central Europe to the Russians helped over the regrets that Irene had not been able to come up from Devon, where the young couple were farming. Sir Arthur felt sure that his son's business connections would be useful, but 'Let us know how you are getting on in Vienna' politely severed ties that had probably never existed.

No ambiguity about the tie to Margarete Horbitzer, still teaching German, now in greater demand than during the War. She would write to her sister who had survived the horrors of a concentration camp because of her medical qualifications. She had testified before several international organisations, including the Red Cross in the

Liechti; she lived nearby but was too frail to offer hospitality, yet whatever was within her power . . .

Though unlikely to yield tangible results it was heartening to possess reliable friends. His own reliability was less steadfast: the jeweller had been fun in Cannes and not responsible for the stamp collection disaster, but for lack of desire and time a phone call sufficed. The tie to Eve was more resilient as she was ready to drive Charles as much in Europe as in Australia. A useful second string.

———

The first proceeded to Paris in a Bentley, the hefty parents in front, the hearty daughter holding hands and rubbing knees in the back. Charles extracted himself from the booking at the Aussies' grand hotel on the pretext, luckily true, that his winter clothes had been kept all these years in the St Honoré. The conscientious guide was crushed by an ignorance that was not bliss and he ended the strenuous tour of duty at the Bœuf. The Aussies appreciated a wicked nightclub more than the Louvre, were duly impressed at Charles being greeted as an old friend by the owner and insisted on inviting a guest waving greetings from the bar. They were delighted by Georges Arnault's Frenchy English and extracted relevant information with graceless directness: yes, he had been in England, during the War, as a pilot, in the Battle for Britain. The parents, at least, understood that the boys would have some secrets to get off their chests.

Georges had escaped the Germans into a fairly hostile Spain but succeeded in joining de Gaulle in London to become one of the first officers in the Free French air force. He had been shot down over the Channel, but rescued, and was now a wing commander. Recovering in hospital he had taken to poetry, first reading then writing, continuing now that he was a wing commander. Raimond was a successful dress designer, Daniel and Heinz had disappeared at the outbreak. War experiences divided, dissolving the memories of intimacy, but they would keep in touch.

Experiences need not divide when deeper bonds united as with Marie Louise. 'While you disported yourself disgracefully, I got married. Lionel came to Berck shortly before the Germans requisitioned the installations. He was a worse case, TB of the spine. No outsider can understand the misery of the plaster community, it turns one either to or against religion. Lionel took the right turn and we decided to limp together through life, but not while my aunt was alive. She dragged the flowers of France's widowed and unmarried chivalry to look me over. In all other respects she was highly intelligent, or she would not have survived in the Resistance. She left me this flat but not her friends, who can't stomach my descent from the enchanted circle.'

'All the more reason to make his acquaintance over some decent food. My Australians can't wait to sit next to a real princess. The Russian Restaurant?'

The meal ranked with Versailles and the Casino de Paris in the sightseeing imposed on the Australians by Charles, till he invented an urgent call from his sister. Free transport and meals were insufficient reward for sustained heartiness and hand holding, which stripped even the Louvre of its Valois magic. Austria loomed with a surfeit of home-grown disenchantments.

———— ————

Disenchantment left remnants of magic at the Tarburg when Charles occupied his old quarters. The German branch, driven from their Silesian estates by the Russians, had found refuge in what had recently been the British officers' mess. Prince Ludwig had been cleared by a denazification court of employing slave labour – a ridiculous accusation since he had been ordered to work his coal mines with prisoners of war after the call-up of the German miners. He admired Father for saving the Austrian Tarburgs from bankruptcy, was trying to do the same for his own family, was equally authoritarian with his wife and son Friedrich but more tolerant with his daughter, the widowed Countess Hildegard Lechfurt. Charles liked her dry humour and the good manners of his small niece. 'Hildegard Sophie is quite a mouthful. Wouldn't Adele or Valerie have been more natural than the name of her godmother?'

'My first daughter was named after her two grandmothers, but she died during the war and there was no point in telling Father years later. Hildegard is reserved for the merry widow, the child is simply Soph and you are Karl; luckily I can introduce you as my brother to avoid this Fenton nonsense. Poor Max got quite confused. Sorry to disappoint you, I did not suffer a fate worse than death to stop those Russians using him for target practice on the Altenhof. Drink was more fun than shooting up an aristo who had already collapsed. The peasant women hid him in the forest till he was taken to hospital outside the Russian zone. The Ruskies got so drunk they forgot him and me. As they were real Russians I wouldn't have been too thin for them.'

'Unlikely, though your charms might have been less plumpish at war's end.'

'Don't be beastly. The Mongolian troops who first entered Vienna

helped themselves to what took their Asiatic fancy. Wristwatches
were popular but quickly thrown away, since winding up presented
a mystery. Fat women lasted a little longer, but few had maintained
an attractive obesity in those hungry years. Some old crones satisfied
the weight requirements and were raped by entire companies. Many
committed suicide, more died within a year of that dreadful Asiatic
syphilis for which no cure was known.'

Too gruesome for personal syphilitic confidences, even of the
lesser Middle East variety. Essential Australian data ended with
'Helen is definitely an improvement on Tania'.

'Tania was very kind to the Grandparents, sending them parcels
from Switzerland after we left the Altenhof and couldn't get any
more food in Vienna. She is playing at the Landtheater, quite
successful.'

'I'd like to see her on the stage, in *our* theatre.'

'I'll arrange a meeting. We have little enough family left. Great
Uncle Ferdinand and Aunt Marcelline were killed by a bomb, rather
hard punishment for his woolly pan-Germanism. If only it had
happened to the Auers! When Ludwig was trying to get back the
Altenhof, Max and I went to Berlin to convince no less than Goering
that we'd squeeze more milk out of the cows than the Party hack in
charge. It will appeal to your weird sense of humour that the selfsame
butcher, now a stout Communist, is again "administering", supposedly on our behalf but, of course, lining his own pockets. Well,
in Berlin we visited Aunt Rosa and Uncle Siegfried in their lovely
flat. They were more aristo than all the Tarburgs put together,
almost *ancien régime*; they didn't wait for the tumbril but preferred a
pill to the extermination camp. They were superbly dignified, only
sorry they couldn't do more for their son. Any idea what happened
to Kurt?'

Herta's image of the French Revolution strangely linked with the
last daydream in the flat of childhood. Not he but the Auers were the
victims, guilt about Kurt flared briefly but inadmissibly. 'He wanted
to come to Australia but it couldn't be arranged. Why wasn't Eugen's
wife asked for lunch?'

'Because she has run away with a British major, more useful than
a Count whose title she is not allowed in this abominable Republic.
But with her first grab she killed Mama.'

——— ———

'Valerie was inordinately fond of you, Karl. Why? You are a charming boy, charming, know more about the Valois than even old
Ottavio Voltain, ADC to the Emperor. We had quite a row, not with

the Emperor, of course. Daughter is a friend of yours? Interesting, interesting, but didn't you bring an English girl, Valerie, thought you'd marry her. Have you? I'm never told anything. Now there is the Voltain girl. She left you a book. Who? Valerie, of course, the Voltain girl hasn't died, has she? Illuminated, gold and blue, Minnie, where is that book?' The housekeeper remembered that the book had been lent. 'Absolute nonsense, my visitors don't borrow missals, have enough at home. She hoped you'd become Catholic and, after the death of Max's first child, made them marry.'

'Forgive me, Uncle Rudi, but if "them" means Herta and Max, they'd been married about ten years.'

'Certainly, certainly, excellent luncheon, but Valerie considered that Protestant pastor the next worst thing to the mayor of Tarburg. She arranged a proper wedding in the chapel here, family only, amazing number of cousins one collects over the centuries. Reminded Max of his duties. My sons . . . the eldest took me to court. That German boy has better manners, though the great uncle accepted a title from a Prussian, Prince for the junior branch! Tell me more about Australia. Capital chap that Captain Cook, I wanted to join the Navy but it had always been the Hussars for the Tarburgs. Nearly got myself killed in that first war. Come again whenever you feel like it. Monday, there aren't any decent newspapers. I enjoyed talking to you.'

——— ——— ———

'Has Uncle Rudi been talking at you? You look wan, Karl, but his monologues are for favourites only. Mostly it's just "certainly, certainly" without his taking in a word and then complaining that nobody tells him anything.' Hildegard Lechfurt had come for coffee, but Herta was preparing the party and Max was supposedly exercising his leg but really taking a nap.

'I learned some interesting lore, not least that remarriage.'

'Aunt Valerie considered her granddaughter's death a retribution for that Protestant wedding. My papa also wanted an unbreakable tie, probably to ensure against a future where a non-Aryan connection might turn from a liability into an asset. It isn't gallantry that keeps our Tarburg branch on top. Even an amiable fool like Max realised he might have to give up the Altenhof if he divorced Herta, easy enough under Nazi laws. She provoked him with her absurd *vivere pericolosamente*, smoking forty cigarettes a day while she was pregnant despite all the doctor's warnings. Of cocktails and wines she knew more and consumed as much as her officer friends. Nothing serious, but in her precarious position she liked to be seen with the second power in the Reich. In between, Herta tried her very unsuitable hands at the Altenhof cows, which promptly dried up; and when her very delicate child died within a year, Max muttered darkly about racial disparity. Herta became pregnant again at the strategic moment, abstained ostentatiously from smoking and drinking. Max was dragged by his mama and cousin to a second matrimonial blessing which resulted in our robust Soph. And now I must help Herta with the preparations for the party.'

By entertaining the Colonel, Herta obtained considerable compensation for breakage while the Tarburg housed the regimental mess. The compensation was ably negotiated and foolishly returned to the British Commissariat through the intermediary of her officer friends for her father-in-law's eightieth birthday party. The Americans threw their money and drink about in their zone, but this was the grandest feast paid for by an Austrian since the rebirth of the country. Among the sixty guests, titles from count upwards plus two bishops greatly outnumbered the commoners led by the mayor of Tarburg; his wife made herself objectionable on the armchair reserved by the carved double eagle for Archdukes. The post-war dignitaries got lost in the pre-war lavishness that the Tarburgs could certainly not afford, as Charles wrote to Father. A report had been requested and even a watered-down account might make Father knock some sense into his wayward daughter. Herta's management triumphed socially and ruined financially.

———————

High among her triumphs ranked friendship with Duke Conrad XXXIV of Anholt, who drove her and Charles to Vienna. Entering the Russian zone was less hazardous than leaving, and the wartime Volkswagen was sufficiently common to be waved through the checkpoint. The head of Germany's oldest dynasty associating with the holder of an Allied pass would probably have aroused the manic Russian suspicion, but even without that fear the cold lowered the spirits in the open car to shivers fitting Vienna's ruins and rubble. Herta's regular patronage of the small hotel near the burnt Opera secured well-heated rooms.

It was wonderful to hear familiar voices confirming appointments, but uncanny to sleep in strange beds in a town where Charles once again owned a *palais*.

He was taken there by the lawyer, whose glib boast of the prompt restitution was countered by reference to the Republic's Basic Law ordering the return of all confiscated property. Equally demolished was his claim to have obtained an extension of the lease, as the Red

Cross was indispensable in the prevailing misery. The mysterious Burmah House street sign had outlasted the Nazi occupation, but the garage had been pulled down to make a drive to an incongruous marble portal in the Führer style. The Swiss Representative expressed his appreciation of the lovely *palais* in so strong a French accent that Charles switched into that language to deflate the cocky lawyer. The conducted tour of his own house was embittered all the more by the ugliness of the office furniture framed by the miraculously undamaged panelling and silk hangings. Charles's room still contained the bookcase, empty of course, and an ugly brass bed for an employee on night duty. Except for some armchairs all furniture had disappeared together with the pictures and collections. Legations should be keen on such a desirable residence, all the more as the Swedes had opened up again next door and the Americans' garden adjoined his own.

Lawyer and Liechti lay halfway to the convent, where the Grandparents seemed little changed among the well-remembered furniture of their large room. Tears wetted the French cheese and chocolates forgotten in the happy reunion of which they had so often despaired. Embraces eased from painfully emotional into peacefully reassuring in this untarnished time regained.

Reassuring illusions were shattered by the sight of Otto. In the obscene destruction, one brown eye appealed and the soft voice mocked, 'Don't force yourself into an embrace, Karli. Poor Dolly occasionally feels obliged, but you . . .' They were holding each other, desperate, overwhelmed. 'Not what we had dreamt up as children.'

'When you stop monopolising Karl, may I apply for a kiss? We've known each other almost as long though, unfortunately, not as intimately' revealed Dolly's lasting jealousy. An uncomfortable triangle, yet she was a considerate hostess, patiently cut up her husband's food, and valiantly produced stories about dead and surviving friends.

Her outburst of frankness was, however, not forgiven. 'You'll give us an expurgated account of your doings, Karli, and when we meet alone you tell me all the juicy bits.'

—— —— ——

'You must tell me all the juicy bits while I make coffee, Karli. I haven't got a maid, like Dolly, but I wouldn't change with her. Better no husband than such a cripple.'

'Isn't sentimentality worn any more, dearest Lis?'

'That luxury went out with the Anschluss. Otto has become

absurdly touchy, he can't bear to look at himself. Haven't you noticed there are no mirrors, not even in the bathroom. Dolly keeps one hidden in a drawer. On his own he would have done away with himself, but he feels he has a duty to leave her comfortably off. Dolly is apparently faithful or at least discreet. I've stopped seeing them, I've enough troubles of my own.' Lis was teaching English at a high school, where her colleagues outdid the pupils in vulgarity. 'You were never much good with your hands, Karli, so watch carefully what I am doing to the poor child. She calls herself Titi, short for Brigitte after her grandmother. She doesn't cry much, Titi of course, only when I stick safety pins into her. The two grandmothers can't stand one another and take turns in spoiling her. My papa hasn't mended his murky ways and at his next windfall he'll have to pay back the money he kept so shabbily from the sale of your bonds.'

'Delightfully incoherent as ever, dearest Lis, but I'm glad you brought that up. I'll leave him double the usual commission, but he really went a bit Shylocky and I can do with some cash till I sell the Liechti. Why have you all reverted to Karli? I haven't been called that since I was a little boy.'

'Because compared to us you are! You only saw the beginning of the nightmare, the delirious reception of the Führer, but the same beastly mob smashed up all the Jewish shops in the Krystall Nacht. We never knew when a kind neighbour would want to maintain racial purity by denouncing my Jewish grandmother for deportation. Otto's brother was sufficiently high up in the SS to get me into the Nursing Corps by a very Austrian back door, but I hated all that blood. So I married a doctor, Erwein's best friend. A dear, but only the best friend and he was aware of it. Would a stronger psychological girder have helped him through his last illness? The bombing was dreadful, the shelling worse, and then the Russian liberators . . . I wasn't raped, I was too young and thin. No nasty cracks, Erwein now sends food parcels. Before that I was hungry and alone with the child. Since Otto's misfortune I haven't talked to anyone as we used to. Now I'm going to cry on your shoulder, but Titi mustn't see me or she'll join in. Let's go to the bathroom, I'll need a towel.'

— — — —

Tania's leading-lady voice sounded overjoyed at the call and modulated into deeply regretful that a very demanding part left not a moment between rehearsals. Would Karl like to attend the dress rehearsals? They could meet after the first night, there was so much to tell.

That was exactly what the stepson dreaded, though he credibly simulated joy at the prospect of seeing her on and off stage. The length of his stay depended on the lawyer, the hotel was too expensive simply for happy reunions, but he'd be back. By then Father must give instructions for the unwelcome encounter.

No instructions were needed to face Otto at the Candle Inn where the semi-obscurity favoured lovers as well as the disfigured. 'Somewhat different from pre-war, but it's lovely to have you back, however. I'm not so wickedly selfish as to hope for your return to this sad town. You can't run the Liechti as a guesthouse, nor as a brothel – it wasn't built for that. Happy memories only embitter, I could sing a little song about that. Different if Willi Hollthal got you into a nice legation . . . he'll be happy to see you. And why are you crying?'

'For the obvious as well as a medical reason. Australia I abandoned, in England I was abandoned, and now you want me to abandon Austria and all those I love.'

'Do! You'll save yourself a lot of disappointments. And the medical justification for this disgraceful display?' He listened to an outline of the allergy and its sequel to take charge, as in their boyhood. 'I'll make an appointment at the eye clinic, with the same professor who declared you unfit. Lederhosen is his assistant. Strange how the proles survived while most of the Upper Chamber were killed, lucky chaps. Ernst Häussermann who didn't make it to the *Matura* is lording it over culture for the Americans. He'll be delighted to ask you for dinner at his HQ. I have tickets for *Tannhäuser* – just we two. Dolly isn't very keen on appearing with me in public, nor in private either, poor girl. Now out with the misdoings you couldn't admit in front of her.'

———————

Opera had returned to its Viennese cradle, in which Mozart had first been performed but which for almost a hundred years had been the preserve of operetta. Here Charles had enjoyed Léhar with the Grandparents, but watching Mother's favourite Wagner in the one theatre they had never visited together sadly impressed the general unsubtle shift. 'I'll cry only in the third act, but no wonder I look puffy. Lederhosen watched with sadistic glee his master pierce my miserable tearducts with long needles, the most terrifying in my life as a pincushion. My screams were suitable for the Burg not the Landtheater and drove the milling crowd from the waiting room, so perhaps the Prof. deserved his fee. "Special" as a friend of his assistant which most decidedly I am not.'

Orchestra and singers almost matched the performance seen with Mother, but the shabbiness of the audience was aggravated by the uniforms of the Allied officers with their overdressed females. The babble of voices was as pronouncedly Austrian as the loden suits and dirndls, unthinkable before the War. 'Haven't you noticed that even your lawyer and doctor speak with an accent the proles at school would have been ashamed of? Distancing themselves from the German brothers whose spittle they were licking. Great realists our Viennese, all were in the Resistance. Paul made no silly claims about Samos. He was ordained last year and is preaching in English in the American zone. You can't decide on Vienna because of one opera performance, you can't even afford the hotel till you sell the Liechti.'

'True and drearily familiar. Aunt Charlotte is happy to have me back. Yet except for the Grandparents nobody seems particularly keen on my staying.'

'Babysitting for Lis isn't your line, and I'm too busy making money. You need sentiment and sex, all I can provide is the local version of that Colombo pool. The Römerbad was opened by Franz Joseph, his brother was blackmailed there by a baker's boy and had to leave Austria, but now the trade is well regulated, perhaps because it is in the Russian District. I haven't played the Phantom of the Steam, but it is in all respects the hottest place in this beastly cold town.'

— — — —

Brother and sister braved the cold at the Central Cemetery, while Konrad Anholt waited for Herta in a café to drive her back to the Tarburg. The solitary flower stall displayed a bunch of tired mimosa, pathetically small for the snow-covered whiteness of the slab. The marble urns looked clean, the gold lettering hardly faded. They placed a more durable pot of cyclamen on the grave of Great Grandmother, who had never been joined by her son, cremated with his wife in the wreckage of his home. Thoughts turned to the Auer aunt and uncle, likewise denied a resting place on which a floral remembrance might express grief. The possibility that the Auers like so many concentration camp victims had been melted down into soap remained unspoken on the way back to Konrad's car.

No flowers graced any of the graves; as much a tribute to the Auers as to Mother, Charles bought the stall's last cyclamen. The snow had apparently revived the mimosa, or perhaps they looked fresher through the tears. Mother heard the prayer in the unearthly silence of whirling snowflakes, no longer stinging but caressing. Nowhere else had she come so close and brought a relief which might justify a return to Vienna even if the living were too preoccupied with their own sorrows. The grey sky and solitude threatened no more. Frozen but serene, Charles swayed in the antiquated tram back to the hotel.

Mother interceded promptly. The lawyer requested assistance in showing the Liechti to a South American delegation whose chief was undiplomatically forthright. 'On my visit to the Swedes next door I realised how suitable the dimensions are for a small legation. We'd rent when the Red Cross vacates the premises, with a buy option till funds become available. The fabric is unusually well-preserved, no chipped marble, graffiti on the panelling, slashed silk hangings. The SS were rarely so considerate.'

True, with an envious lout like Franz Schmidt typical of those super-barbarians. Yet some higher officers acted more humanely than the mob outside the Party, Norbert Lechfurt, Otto's brother and in this very house Hans Wilner.

——— ———

The blue eyes unmistakably identified the lined face in the improbable place 'Opened By His Apostolic Imperial And Royal Majesty' as inscribed on a marble tablet. Stairs ascended to four floors of cabins with unhygienic plush couches to which the couples retired from the steam and rest rooms. Seated on the steps encircling the warm pool, Charles contrasted the lusty young equals at Colombo with the distinction between aged buyers and often ageing sellers in the artificial dimness smelling of chloride. A bordercase waved, 'so Nefertiti is making up for lost opportunities' – words which identified the older schoolmate rejected by an enigmatic smile. 'No ambiguity about your present interest, fine Germanic proportions running to seed but still one of the best. Cleared by a denazification court but as an SS officer barred from all professions except the oldest. The irony that these brutes now live by the favours of "deviates" they wanted to exterminate. Not Hans. I withdraw with the discretion you so stupidly left untried at school.'

An even discreeter nod indicated an empty bench. 'So you don't mind talking to an officer of the Battalion that occupied your *palais*!

'On the contrary, I want to thank you for helping my grandfather with my clothes and putting that evil Franz Schmidt in his place.'

'Thanking the SS is not fashionable' was followed by an awkward pause. 'But our acquaintance dates from the ice rink though we never talked.'

'I'd been warned that you were a fanatical Nazi and was afraid.'

'Serves me right. But all those girls you were dragging about!'

'The Römerbad isn't very suitable for sorting out misunderstandings. Come and have dinner with me, Hans.'

'I've often wished for that, Karl. It's a bit late . . .' The pause was longer. 'Saturday is the big evening here. No doubt your friend has told you . . .'

'Can you make it tomorrow? Good, eight o'clock at the Candle Inn.'

Hans's careful walk on the slippery floor drew attention to his missing toes. Frostbite, the badge of the Russian front.

—— —— —— ——

Otto commented analytically on the meeting. 'An instructive tale of our enlightened twentieth century. Two students of a famous university afraid of talking to one another; you forbidden to finish your studies, he to use his academic qualifications. He releases you from arrest but participates in the occupation of your house, where he doles out some of your clothes. Second act: you bribe your way into a penniless exile and join the enemy army, to be nearly killed by a school fellow. The other party loses his ideals and several toes, is found innocent of any crime, yet included in the élite of scapegoats for the sins of a nation; he is reduced to shovelling snow or selling what's left of his body. Grand finale in a whorehouse: the two protagonists arrange to wallow most unhealthily in "what could have been". Beware of pity, potentially more dangerous than self-pity. I know your revulsion to physical defects, the effort you have to make to bear my sight. It's only toes with Hans but nebulous romanticism needs at your age four unimpaired feet to stand on.'

—— —— —— ——

Early arrival proved their mutual eagerness besides providing a joke about Aryan exactness versus Austrian punctuality, the latter implying non-Aryan. Jocularity forced the contrast between the SS uniforms of the barracks and the uniform nakedness of the bath before tying up more loose ends than expected. Hans had indeed forwarded the call-up notice and, within Nazi limitations, prevented wanton destruction at the Liechti. 'Small objects and pictures disappeared quickly but the Prince in Grey Velvet was lifesize and I didn't let on that it was you. The family portraits were slashed and torn from the frames but I saved the face of your grandfather. My father was furious I had not secured the entire picture.'

'Some confusion between dear Ohli and a lesser saint?'

'Not far out, Karl. My father taught at the school of your grandfather and greatly admired his objectivity despite political differences.'

'Pan-Germanism like my own Great Uncle, I suppose?'

'Yes and seemingly justified by the break-up of the Empire. When the Nazis came to power he took his family to Munich to lecture on German literature. Nourished on heroic sagas, I joined the Hitler Youth and automatically graduated to the SA where the leaders preached romantic friendship and practised prosaic orgies. When the Führer shot the SA Chief in bed with his minions, it became expedient to pretend moral outrage; what had been openly encouraged now led to the concentration camp. I transferred to the SS and was sent to Vienna to organise cells at the University. I was better at that than on the ice rink. I could kick myself for my cowardly stupidity.'

Was this a second chance? Had the attraction continued through eleven lost years? Hans's present destitution could not be held against him; they had more in common than Heinz and Daniel who had given it a try. Otto had warned of pity. Was there a deeper feeling?

'You wouldn't have survived in the last years of the Reich when we learned to wipe expressions from our faces. You display thoughts as clearly as if you shouted them. Remember *Giuditta*, Tauber singing "I pardon fate"? I saw you at the Opera from the fourth gallery. This is not a second chance and I'm not psychic, I only had to watch you. Not that we ever had a first chance in the Anschluss, but now I am not a lost opportunity but a dead loss. May I ask you to stay away from the Römerbad till the next big snowfall? I'm permitted to sweep streets. The dinner is on me, as I had always imagined, to make it clear that I was not after Austria's richest young man for his money. Please let at least this part of the dream come true, exactly because I can afford it even less. Don't stay in Vienna, you aren't sufficiently toughened. Please leave now, I'm not sure whether I can trust myself much longer, Karl.'

Bending against the icy wind in the empty streets, Karl was not sure whether to trust his judgement. Following the selfless advice of his well-wishers meant loss of their comprehension, the alternative to shared misery was solitary indifference. Practical considerations imposed . . .

———— ————

. . . a reprieve. Eve rang from Paris, fittings for a Schiaparelli dress. She had not eloped with a millionnaire, she had won it at a charity ball, but she was looking forward to eloping with Charles. She had brought the car, needless to repeat that he was her guest.

Beautifully timed to save hotel expenses till a room became vacant in the flat of Aunt Charlotte, now reduced to taking in lodgers. Was the Austrian solution implicitly abandoned by instructing the lawyer not to let to the South Americans? Only a sale was acceptable. Surely a buyer would have been found when he returned in the spring. This return consoled Granny, while Ohli approved of a journey updating knowledge. Lis's common sense almost concealed her sense of loss; till her father repaid the extortionist 'safeguard' from his next windfall, there was little harm in antipodal sponging. The additional funds not transmitted to Zurich were, however, lost, as the Baron shot himself after drunken Russians had smashed his precious cups that were not filled with alcohol. Odd that friends wished him to depart because they wished him well.

————

Eve wished to show off her Schiaparelli dress before extracting funds for the grand tour from her complacent husband in London. This left Charles free to commiserate with Marie Louise about the death of a city and of a society, while Lionel injected French realism, halfway between Australian insouciance and Austrian despair.

Old habits indicated a nightcap at the Bœuf and, having talked Austria the whole evening, the Viennese accent of 'Three guesses' seemed natural. Delighted by the immediate recognition, Heinz withdrew his hands from Charles's eyes for an embrace that would have shocked before the war. Continents apart for a decade, Daniel resumed with equal pleasure the camaraderie of the strongest negative bond, not to belong anywhere. His dual nationality became uncomfortably ambiguous at the outbreak of war and a Central American passport purchased for Heinz was sufficiently valid for a retreat to Argentina. Daniel's father made both work in his enterprises which their efforts had failed to ruin by the time he died. Daniel was cynical, polished, sure that his money could buy everything; Heinz smoked and drank too much, sure only of his friend's generosity; a complementary divergence in the brotherhood of the uprooted.

Daniel's mother had married a titled diplomat and launched her son, his lover and a slim volume of George Arnault's poems to the malice of Paris society at a reception that surpassed the Tarburg birthday party in everything except taste. Dresses, drink and conversation were certainly more sophisticated, but every nastiness was laboured to appear witty. From inside neither London, certainly not Vienna, nor even Paris resembled the memories idealised during the years of Sydney exile.

4

Not heeding disappointment in three capitals, Charles based his itinerary on pre-war remembrances and completed the depressing picture of Europe's self-destruction. Eve had cunningly lined her tartan skirt with ten-pound notes; exchange control so long after the war had been won simply showed the inefficiency of the government. In the increasing warmth of their progress south, she occasionally retained a comment by the guide/navigator who foolishly tried to trace the past: at Marseilles where he had embarked with Father and Herta, the port had been razed by the Germans; Cannes was a deserted shadow of two hectic summers. Only Monte Carlo, where he had never stayed, maintained a fairly solid winter season. Eve won not sensationally but usefully at the Casino, Charles lost the few chips he hazarded; the inevitable 'unlucky at roulette, lucky in love' applied only in the negative part.

Nostalgic memories of Mother surfaced in the Italian towns scarred by battles and bombs, but untouched Rome was remembered for the arduous exploration with Ohli. He received several fond postcards, but then he was in one piece, while recall of unimpaired youth might upset Otto. Yet his youthful image dominated Naples and even more Capri on the one-day excursion to which Eve was limited. Alone in a carriage the perfect ride to Ravello could have been morbidly yet satisfactorily relived. Skinny decrepitude had saved a few horses for the dilapidated vehicles and to deprive Eve of the famed Sorrento drive seemed unfair; even more unfair to blame her gushing enjoyment of a sacrosanct landscape. She chatted herself out of a lover.

——— ———

Exhaustion concealed the severance. Pictures, weaponry and torture instruments would impress less at parties back in Sydney than when staying in a genuine castle bearing the name of its titled owners, never mind if it *was* the other way round. Warnings about bathrooms tucked away across ill-lit corridors boosted the old-world quaintness, so that driver and navigator were united at least in their anxiety to reach the Tarburg with the minimum delay. This decided them to ignore the car's increasingly unhealthy rattle near the goal which wasn't all that near. Ominous clanking superseded the rattle while coaxing the car up the castle hill into the porch where flames laced the smoke with perfect timing; a bucket of cold water preceded the conventional welcome.

Plain ordinary water would have prevented irreparable damage, but the motorists had lately neglected to check so trivial a requirement, perhaps because of the steady rain. Now the engine was burnt out, there was no replacement, not even an agent for English cars in Carinthia, and the cylinders had to be rebored by hand, costly in time and money. Eve seemed unaware that they might be outstaying their welcome and unconcerned about the expense of the breakdown that need never have happened.

Max chose a 'trustworthy' mechanic: 'My racing experience has familiarised me with axle grease.' No less a fallacy than his farming expertise acquired by squandering a large estate, but Charles had not learned anything in the Sydney garage either. He apologised for the planned days probably extending into as many weeks and the mechanical post mortem was abandoned for a call to the lawyer. His evasive answers barely justified a trip to Vienna promising little beyond a holiday from Eve, who deployed her Schiaparelli dress to the admiration of the German Tarburgs.

Spring improved the ruins of Vienna. No icy winds requiring horrid needles to de-block tearducts. Granny needed no climatic stimulus to a sentimental flood which imposed an immediate visit to Mother's grave at the other end of town. Mimosa, more plentiful now, initiated the proven pattern of prayer and problems. Sunshine and fellow mourners with flowers notched up an emotional plus quickly cancelled by a legalistic minus. The lawyer retained some of the Red Cross rent for intricate Austrian claims not to be offset against possible German compensation. A way might be found, even a buyer for the Liechti, but in the present political uncertainty . . . Glib and glum.

Otto's humour was enshrined in bitterness. 'Admirably tactful not to write from Capri but psychologically wrong, I live on memories and Capri is among . . . no, *is* the best. Perhaps for you too, hale but luckily far from hearty. Not because we'll never be eighteen again – it was Before the Fall.'

'How true, though the Pharisees would object. Still, naughty of Lis to tell you.'

'She told Dolly at a charity bazaar for the blind. They are worse off than I in their entire dependence on others. I couldn't . . . How was the Sorrento drive? After freezing us stiff in that sledge at St Moritz in memory of your mother, nothing would prevent your sentimental wallowing in milder climes. A horse carriage?'

———————

The school mate seemed unreasonably annoyed when met at the

Opera. 'Very naughty of you to leave without ringing me.'

'Is Hans Wilner still about?'

'Nefertiti is no longer enigmatic. According to Römerbad rumours, Hans was recruited to guard a Central American dictator.
The most respectable employment for an ex-SS, but without
toes . . .'

The same despotism that saved Heinz by a passport in Paris had
restored Hans to what he had been trained for. The extraordinary
convergence in the lives of two male prostitutes was too incredible a
story for fiction. False documents to escape the Gestapo were a
stock-in-trade, but guarding a bloodthirsty tyrant in an effort to
escape the caresses of old queens belonged to the myths of the
twentieth century.

——— —— ——

So did concentration camp survivors. Margarete Horbitzer's sister
bore no resemblance to the vaguely-remembered plump Dr Olga
Weiss: frail skin and bones, anxious eyes never at rest, a slight
tremble. She had nursed the victims of inhuman experiments at
Auschwitz, her only brief reference to the extermination camp, and
co-operated with international rehabilitation efforts, like the Red
Cross. 'Margarete often spoke of your mother's exquisite taste. Judging by the few pieces of furniture . . . When I get my compensation
from Germany, I'd like to buy one of those lovely tapestry armchairs.
The *palais* is, of course, most suitable for a legation, not my world,
but I'll spread the word, the Salvation Army . . . I'll notify Margarete if I hear of anything before you come back.' No complaints,
no appeal for sympathy, years in hell had not blunted her readiness
to help, like her sister who had, however, suffered merely the indig-
nities of a refugee.

——— —— ——

Technically a refugee, Ernst Häussermann had fled the Reich not for
politics or race but love. Self-exile was better rewarded than common
exile and he returned to a position he could never have expected. The
Americans' cultural watchdog presided nightly over writers and actors, some remembered from the Liechti though many of the Thursday luncheon literati had been killed or driven to suicide. The host
was obviously pleased at the reunion, praised Father's rescue of poor
Toni Bluhm at the Landtheater, now again a financial mess but
artistically successful largely due to Tania. Ernst overplayed the
reversal of roles by constantly refilling glasses and plates till his
solicitude was halted by an enquiry why his dramatic suicide in *The
Magic Bullet* had not started a Hollywood career. 'Because I'm not

photogenic' was under his guest's silent stare enlarged to 'and can't act'. His patronage extended to tickets for the Varieté to which the Burgtheater company had moved after the destruction of their building. The brilliant enactment of a play about Rommel on the stage where *Les Boys* had thrown about Mistinguet gained further by being viewed from the same box Lis and he had so often occupied in their youth.

Her amusing comments provided a rare continuity in almost total discontinuity. The shock of the first return had subsided, but nothing more had been achieved in the second; icy winds blustered from the Hungarian plain and Herta was getting impatient with Eve.

———— —

'Eve isn't wasting time, the mechanics are. No sooner had Ludwig left for London than she seduced his son, just what poor Friedrich needed. Odd how loss of virginity marks your sojourns.' A sheepish grin seemed the appropriate reply to Herta's sledgehammer allusion and tolerance.

To escape the charged atmosphere and possible confidences from either lover, Charles took Soph and her constant playmate Norbert Lechfurt for long walks into the lovely forest. Mother had enjoyed the woods at Igls, the trusting boy had grown into a trusted uncle who dispensed poems and songs on sylvan beauty sparingly. Irene's ghost also stalked the avuncular idyll in which 'Uncle Karl' lost the connotation of Father's brother. 'Norbert is below the acceptable ten-year limit but Friedrich is too old, though he has the same claim; more than the innumerable uncles and aunts of our childhood. Why didn't Margarete Horbitzer make the grade?'

'Because she was a glorified nanny, the genuine English article wasn't available in Vienna after the First War, same as now. She was rather proud of her courtesy title "Educational Advisor", not that she contributed much to our education. Still better than the Thursday luncheon spongers who never lifted a finger for us after the Anschluss. And the one who would have helped, that fabulously wealthy banker in Zurich, you didn't even try! I don't expect you'll ever grow up though Papa compares you to his old chum Ottavio Voltain, whose granddaughter he occasionally believes you've married. Marie Louise had no dowry and Irene was much better looking. Still, a princess . . . Had the Empire lasted a few months longer, Father would have been ennobled and with a title of my own I might not have switched from a Baron Hollthal to a Count.'

Max's 'Speeding up the hammering, drilling, filing, soldering and what-have-you' ensured that the mechanics dawdled during twice the specified time. The car purred expensively after the embraces of an undramatic departure. Then Herta stepped in front of the waving chorus, her face the Mask of Tragedy, her arms outstretched; she too knew that they would never again meet at the Tarburg.

———— ———— ————

This uncanny knowledge was swamped by Eve's maudlin sighs and meaningful looks which nearly landed them in a ditch, but not in bed. She was persuaded that her 'infidelity' had broken up a beautiful romance but the pretence of jealousy quickly ceased to amuse. Over her protests he rushed her to London – whither he had promised to accompany her, though he had less commitments there than in Vienna.

Bypassing Paris they arrived at Dunkerque in darkness and rain. Too tired to search for a restaurant, they were glad to discover a hotel on the shattered waterfront. At the request for separate rooms, the porter muttered something which was not a demand for passports, unusual in strictly policed Europe. Charles checked the door next to the large bed before falling asleep. Noises were reminiscent of Basra, the blast of a foghorn compounded drowsy confusion. Light shone through a big keyhole close to the pillow; a burly man was busy on a Rubenesque woman whose grunts combined pain with ecstasy. The ring seat focused on the action but whether money passed was beyond the field of vision; the expertise indicated a pimp rather than a customer. Sleep was impossible but Eve was not equal to anything so wildly exciting; a break in the wholesome abstinence of the last month might, moreover, give her the wrong idea.

———— ———— ————

Robert's ideas were equally wrong, from the queer bars to the gang-bashes on the towpath at Putney. But his tastes as culture vulture ranged as wide and he would make a more appreciative travel companion than Eve. Her invitation to a party at influential friends was accepted for the sake of Ludwig; in '49 a German was a social liability but a prince an asset for a lady from the Antipodes. Bringing together the son's seductress with the father smacked of Oscar Wilde, especially as her husband might be useful in Australia where Ludwig had mining interests.

He thanked 'Dear Cousin Charles' – the Anglicised version was particularly tactful as they spoke German – for the introduction and hoped they would soon meet again at the Tarburg to which he had just dispatched the nanny of his own children. 'Probably the first to enter occupied Austria, but Herta's request was most urgent.'

No doubt due to the recent reference to the 'glorified nanny'.

Charles had remained 'her little boy', which was sometimes consoling, at others irritating, and thus afforded an opportunity to behave accordingly. 'May I call you Aunt Margaret?' evoked a look of incredulous happiness confirmed by a few tears and a rather fine German poem in praise of gratitude. She was returning to Vienna as soon as the British pension problem was resolved; in the meantime her sister would watch out for opportunities to sell the Liechti.

——— ——— ———

The rejection of the Wynn Roberts' opportunity amounted to incipient self-destruction. Irene wisely stayed in Devon but her brother asked Charles for lunch with the director of a company with interests in Greece. Whether to use his knowledge of that country or to increase the distance from Irene, any opening had to be considered seriously as the alternatives had narrowed since the deliberate failure in Sydney. On the appointed day Charles went back to bed after breakfast, dallied in the bath, wore a markedly Australian suit, miscalculated the travelling time and arrived half an hour late at the Savoy Grill. The enumeration of an apology astounded, tales from the Master's Office revealed a talent for entertaining and none for business. 'After the break with Irene it was wrong to benefit from the Wynn Roberts' was branded by Robert as pretentious claptrap, an opinion shared by the perpetrator. After sabotaging a golden opportunity it seemed pointless to bother with the shipboard acquaintance from Leeds.

The stay in London had lived down to Charles's worst expectations, entirely his own fault, certainly not Eve's. She had been a God-send in Australia, a good companion on the journey, vastly preferable to the hearty Australians; yet he felt about the same though showed more sorrow than on saying goodbye to Mariette; a promise of keeping in touch, a possibility of meeting again, in Australia, Austria, somewhere . . .

——— ——— ———

. . . wherever that was. A stop in Paris was tempting but unjustifiable luxury, but so was the irresistible sleeper on the Vienna Express. The familiar clanking and swaying ungraded daydreams to introspection; stocktaking was more to the point, with the stock of dubious quality. Had he taken unfair advantage of the Australians? He had given good value though not always of the kind expected. But was the indifference to Robert, his intelligent host, and to Ludwig, the most congenial Tarburg? The money for the sleeper would have paid for a few days in Paris where Daniel and even Heinz had once been close. Had he lost his capacity for friendship, torn between too many people in too many countries? The intimates of childhood had fallen to Disunity of Time, Place and Action, a rather nifty paraphrase of Aristotle! Marie Louise was wrapped up in her husband, Lis in her child, Otto in his disfigurement. The last unencumbered friend, Ralph, was in Greece where one emotional rung higher . . . No one had mattered since Panagiotis, high time to disprove the horoscope, Mimis had warned of middle age. Was Vienna an end or a means?

——— ———

Aunt Charlotte was suitably delighted to house dear Charles again, but her chances to applaud his change of name and everything else were limited by his boredom with another edited version of his collected misdeeds. The other true believer in the Boy-Can-Do-No-Wrong concluded her lacrimose embrace with 'The Mother Superior wants to see you'.

'What have you been up to, Granny?'

'Don't be facetious, Karl. That might be more realistic than South American legations.'

The Reverend Mother was much younger than her charges from whom she had learned that the Fechtner *palais* was for sale. She mentioned it to the CARITAS, the Catholic Relief Organisation looking for larger premises. No less than the Auxiliary Bishop seemed interested as the Cardinal Archbishop remembered the *palais* from a visit before the war.

The excellence of the Thursday luncheons probably speeded the appointment at the Archiespicopal Palace. The Auxiliary Bishop extolled the CARITAS's universal charity despite the paucity of funds which necessitated an appeal to Christian altruism. Dr Fechtner's assistance to the unemployed in the darkest days of the Depression set a splendid example his son would surely like to follow. Christian generosity, the charitable end sanctified the meagre means.

The Bishop had worked on his brief, hence Christian not Catholic like the Abbot of the Schotten had once used to bolster the pupil's standing. Episcopal jocularity missed the point: Father's *richesse oblige* ended with the riches in the Anschluss for which the Cardinal had asked his flock to vote. His later protests against Nazi atrocities when the Gestapo threw his secretary from the window of this very office did not restore the Fechtner fortune. Negotiations halted in an icy blessing.

——— ———

Warmer blessings were bestowed by the Salvation Army, at least in Australia as Charles had never noticed the uniform in Austria. If the tambourines of the Swiss branch earned sufficient francs the Liechti was theirs, less welcome than Mother's Church to which he turned in his hours of need, but the present need required foreign currency. One of the Liechti's remaining chairs seemed poor reward for establishing this contact, all the more as Dr Weiss insisted on payment if the close-fisted Swiss did not make an acceptable offer.

Success from one duty call encouraged another. Willi Hollenthal asked Charles to dinner, his wife pointedly praised Herta and withdrew under the threat of a business discussion. 'I've talked to my Minister who knew your father and is intrigued by the Fechtner/Fenton possibility. Claiming Austrian nationality is a mere formality and after minimal training you'll be released into the very confined diplomatic world. Very confined, Karl! The foreign posting will arouse the jealousy of colleagues and more venomously of their wives. You'd better get yourself one, to vouch for you.'

'I can't afford to get married till I sell the Liechti.'

'Top of our recommendations for legations but none are anxious to buy as long as the Russians occupy parts of Vienna. I'll introduce you to my Minister . . .'

'Many thanks, Willi, but I won't take a vow of chastity for the Austrian foreign service any more than for the Australian.'

One up one down, the third in gratitude for the food parcels to the Grandparents. Without guidelines from Father, Charles repeatedly postponed the call, but Tania sounded genuinely pleased and chose an original meeting place favoured by the warm summer. Linked by their enjoyment of sun and water at the swimming pool in the Vienna Woods, they expressed their sincere surprise at how little the other had changed despite the difficulties of the last ten years. Her father had died, she was sharing a flat with her mother and had helped to clear away the rubble in the Landtheater before performances were resumed. No reference to the ownership nor to Father's private life, though she was interested in his lecturing, Calcutta and the farm in Tasmania. The most handsome woman at the pool left equal grey areas about her movements after Glyndebourne, but wondered why Kurt Auer had not been invited to Australia; the poor boy had been so disappointed and her look clearly expressed that she failed to comprehend why she had been similarly rejected. They shared the horror at the blinding and suicide of Tony Bluhm, the Austrian Nazi hoodlums had been worse than the German, except for one polite SS officer assisting her to recover her clothes from the Liechti. Bar Granny, Tania was the last person to learn about the Hans Wilner complexities, but the Grandparents and Herta could be discussed without restraint. Pleasant though the meeting had been, the next was scheduled for the middle rather than the near future. No invitation to Tania's flat to see her mother, a chilling reminder of Reichenbach indifference after the Anschluss. Now even nominal ties had ceased as Tania had made her career under her maiden name.

———— ————

Tania was an actress Aunt Charlotte loved to hate out of mistaken loyalty to Mother. The meeting at the pool got short shrift. 'You did your duty. Do you remember the crystal gazer?'

'Indeed. She saved me from that Albanian mess. Mightn't be a bad idea to see her again.'

Aunt Charlotte dried an unexpected tear. 'When Hitler's astrologer fell from favour because the stars foretold disaster, all fortune tellers were rounded up and sent to concentration camps. Would you mind giving me the exact hour and date of your birth, for a horoscope? I arranged for one when you were born, Charles, but your mother never showed it to me.'

'You were spared some very depressing reading. What have you now on offer?'

'A marvellous woman from Transylvania. She prefers not to see her clients, so as not to be influenced by personal impressions.'

The neatly-drawn circle of the Zodiac with the position of the planets preceded a shorter typescript than Charles remembered. The generalities were depressingly familiar, as they should be, considering that most had already come true. Specific warnings were added, or had he forgotten them?

'. . . Conflicts dominate the emotional and material imbalance. Do not change continents, the second is a failure, the third an illusion. A strong constitution overcomes disease; disaster from accidents is avoided in the nick of time till a peril threatens near seventy . . .'

'Ingenious! By the time I am seventy, the Dracula girl will have joined the vampires and I can't ask for the money back. You wouldn't have told her about Australia and Calcutta?'

Aunt Charlotte protested indignantly. 'I hope you won't regret your cynicism one day. And I had completely forgotten Calcutta.'

———— ————

Not Asia but Africa vindicated the continental warning. A distant Barovsky relation had recently escaped with his very attractive wife from Hungary; the Communists had taken their estate, so the couple would use their extensive experience in nightlife. The President of the Hungarian Jockey Club was a waiter in Salzburg; they intended to open their own nightclub. Competition was too fierce in Europe, but, contrary to the Bergman/Bogart film, Casablanca was waiting to be enlivened by a gipsy orchestra. The jewellery they had brought out might start them off and Charles could join their venture after the sale of the Liechti. Charmingly and unconvincingly presented, a congenial occupation with congenial partners in an exotic country was tempting, yet the astrological warning was hardly needed.

'The warning is on target, but what's the alternative?' Lis's and Charles's combined onslaught had made her father disgorge most of his extortion and they were celebrating while feeding Titi. Suddenly the child sank her few teeth into Charles's finger and then cried 'Kali-Walli' interpreted by her mother as a derivation from Cannibal.

'All right if the horrid child is not adding to the Karl/Charles confusion, but is referring to herself, though I recommend more conventional food. I'll insist on it if we get married.'

'We might perhaps totter together to the grave after a grand wedding when you are seventy. That's probably Miss Dracula's final disaster. Any earlier we'd have hysterics sleeping together, but we aren't that desperate for a good laugh. Titi and I need money, not yours, Karli. What's happening with the Liechti?'

'Because they'll pay in Switzerland, the Salvation Army wants the Liechti for a song, to quote Otto. Why is he spending the summer in the damp dungeon he so dislikes?'

'To please Dolly who lives on self-delusion: Countess Barovsky commanding her faithful retainers, two toothless hags whose cooking is worse than their cleaning. But Otto has begun to make money. Behind the all-too-visible barrier of his disfigurement, he is even more determined than my father, right or wrong.'

——— ———

Was it right, as the lawyer claimed, to sell the Liechti for an optimal $15,000 or wrong, as Otto believed, for a derisory amount even under Russian occupation? The Salvation Army took over the mortgage, paid the dollars in Switzerland and the reasonable fees of the lawyer in Vienna. An additional $1,000 made the fee less reasonable, but proved the lawyer's distrust in the Austrian currency and trust in Charles who could instruct the Swiss bank only from outside the snooping of the censor. The lawyer would pursue compensation against Germany, at present synonymous with never-never land. Dr Olga Weiss who had conjured up the buyer could hardly be persuaded to accept the two remaining armchairs.

Their tapestry had been artistically repaired by Aunt Charlotte before the move into the Liechti; their removal asserted the shattering finality of the sale on the last solitary visit. Every empty room was crammed with memories, from the Thursday luncheons in the dining room to the Gestapo's pre-dawn call on his quarters which ended what seemed in retrospect a golden youth. Mother's bedroom was purged of Tania by the overwhelming reproach of those out-stretched arms to which he had so cowardly failed to respond. The sadness of the farewell to the childhood flat had dissolved in Mother's understanding and the consolation of an upward move; the next move was inevitably downward. Burmah House, still un-explained, had justified its reputation for bringing ill-luck.

Apple of discord was more appropriate for the proceeds of the sale which, Father decreed, must pay for his divorce. This might extend to alimony, as he had deserted Tania, and the value of the Land-theater, obviously to be hers, was difficult to assess. Charles panicked; he had renounced a career in Australia on the understanding that the entire proceeds were his after paying off the mortgage; half might well have been the share falling to the Altenhof in all fairness. But no further unforeseeable commitments from those miserable $14,000. After the Anschluss, Father had behaved . . . oddly, but now he broke an unambiguous promise.

On Otto's advice Ohli made a statement before a public notary that the same deed transferred the Liechti to Charles and the Alten-hof to Herta, thereby securing Tarburg support *in extremis*. Their litigation had been condemned by Father, yet Otto insisted on removing the proceeds to an account at a different bank in America.

Charles then wrote a letter he regretted the moment he posted it. Bitter indignation pushed him beyond the broken promise; infuriat-ingly, he claimed to have saved Father's life at the Anschluss. Unforgivably, he reproached Father for the Jewishness that had caused so much misery, and even quoted Granny's opposition to her daughter's marriage.

Characteristically, Father ignored the pointless outburst and the reminder of the promise, but rejected the son's part in his escape; future letters would be returned unopened. Charles believed in his so-much-the-better even less than the Grandparents and friends, especially as the desired yet dreaded break spread to the Tarburg.

Herta, an exemplary exponent of pound foolish penny wise, rang charges-reversed to complain about his account of Papa's eightieth birthday. 'Perhaps the party was a bit extravagant but there was no need to report to Father. Now you are cast out or off, what's the difference? Max is coming to Vienna for a refund of my travel expenses. You could save him the trip by celebrating the Liechti sale at the Tarburg. Ludwig thinks you very polished, odd considering how you infuriated Father.'

Father was making trouble between his children. Herta had never raised such an absurd claim and her dispatching Max proved her reluctance.

———— ————

Max's reluctance was apparent when he presented a roughly-drafted expense account. 'Herta did her best. It was quite dangerous to cross the Russian zone. I still don't like it and certainly wouldn't live there. With the mortgage paid off we might be able to sell the Altenhof.' He put the account into his pocket. 'Do you remember our drive there, when I kept you waiting in the forest? I behaved abominably because . . . it was to that same spot that the peasant women carried me after the Ruskies had shot me up. Mama considered it divine justice and, had I not remarried Herta, she couldn't have saved me. I don't have to be a theologian to agree with that. Mama's Catholicism was straightforward and consoling.'

———— ————

'Consoling that one opportunity is left, Otto, though not particularly brilliant. Ralph once wrote that the Cultural Organisation would find a niche for me in Athens.'

'You deliberately sabotaged all others! After the break with your father and probably with Herta, diplomacy is a non-starter. Willi was annoyed with you sitting on the high horse you haven't got. Now that Dolly has left us alone, we can talk seriously. At least she kissed you once more, not the last time, she'll come to Athens . . . For me the memories don't fit. We tried so hard to get away and now you have chosen it of all places. Odd thing, Free Will.'

———— ————

Odd certainly, Free fatefully, Will deplorably lacking. The less pompous Only Myself to Blame became all too real on the Venice Express as Charles had forgotten to sign his Allied Pass. Russian guard and Pass disappeared and the train was immobilised at the checkpoint. Wild guesses sent the culprit to Siberia; the sleeping car attendant conjectured merely a day in the guardhouse to demonstrate Russian vigilance. Fear hardly coloured Charles's annoyance at his stupid negligence, which caused him to miss the boat to Piraeus. The Russian representative in the Inter Allied Commission must have been persuaded by his colleagues that negligence did not necessarily indicate a capitalist spy; the guard handed back the Pass with an incomprehensible rebuke and the train proceeded after a delay of two hours.

Rain occasionally washed away the fog in an appropriate degradation of the sunny Venice Mother had loved. She had known and shown the town's beauty which Charles vainly tried to recapture as he trudged from site to site in the dark November. Allocating only the day to an extension of the farewell at her grave had seemed foolish at the checkpoint but now avoided a more distressing night in a cheap hotel.

The boat's main attraction lay in immediate departure. The few passengers seemed to be embarked on errands of infinite sadness which they eagerly divulged in the stale smoke of the saloon. In brief spurts of energy, they paced the enclosed deck while the rain persisted through the Adriatic and the long detour round the Peloponnese as the Corinth Canal had been blown up by the Germans. What a dismal parody of those joyful summer cruises with Yvonne, perhaps departed not just for the New but the Other World. Or was it simply his slackness in tracing her because of that silly 'misunderstanding' over her mother's wreath? Would he similarly lose touch with the other friends from whom he had so rashly chosen to be parted?

ARID AFTERNOON

1

Not from all. Ralph was waving from the same quay as at the Easter evacuation, while Mimis was as sincerely pleased as at the last pre-war arrival. After the anxieties of the lonely voyage, loyal friends were a 'safe haven'.

'I've never been called anything so respectably unsuitable,' Mimis laughed with the old ease. The sun broke through the clouds and gilded the war scars of Piraeus in a propitious omen. The links were unbroken, not re-established as in Paris and Vienna, probably because of the shared experiences in the war that had marked their lives. Ralph had secured a small flat in Kolonaki, a lucky stroke as Athens was crowded with refugees from the civil war which had just ended in the north. Not exactly the Liechti but with a private entrance an improvement on the mascotry. Madame was living in an outer suburb, probably with her taxi driver but certainly in sin, quite an achievement at her age. She swore that no luggage had been left with her and, since her paramour could not squeeze into Charles's clothes, she must have sold them on the black market. In Sydney the stolen clothes had been recovered by Father, but one suitcase abandoned eight years ago was not allowed to spoil the evening in the old Plaka taverna. The intuition to return to Athens had been sound after all; better a modest niche in the CO than guarding his every step as a diplomat.

— — — —

'You won't have to guard against the carefully-chosen callers. The previous occupant left only last week.'

'Any chance of my succeeding to his job as well as to his flat, Ralph?'

'He was axed to save the British taxpayer the cost of recording the local dirges – euphemistically called folk music. I am sorry, Charles, several niches envisaged for you have been walled up. Too late to let you know, the tidings were brought by the new Director for immediate implementation. The transition from hiring to firing good people with Greek experience has been painfully rapid. After 100 years as the paramount power, handing over to the Americans was traumatic. For initiation into local Byzantine politics call your old protector as League High Commissioner, lately Minister in London to counteract Communist propaganda. He, Christl and Artemis are most anxious to see you, but I owe you at least a teaching job at the CO in the next academic year. In the meantime I'll get you more private lessons than you can handle.'

Strange that Ralph had not foreseen the consequences of the British military and political withdrawal on cultural activities. A hint before the interview with Willi Hollthal, and Charles would by now be a legation secretary. Brilliant intuition had returned him to the dreary private teaching of ten years earlier. But without Panagiotis; his grave might also facilitate contact as Mother's had, but a tram ride to the Central Cemetery was less arduous than a winter voyage in an old boat to Samos. Ralph prevented the necrophilic pilgrimage by sending female pupils, who paid well if irregularly, flirted acceptably and proudly displayed their haughty teacher at cocktails. Some of the callers inherited from the flat's previous occupant were tried and found emotionally though not physically wanting. Old friendships as well as new social and sexual distractions brightened another period of waiting.

Apart and above the classifiable pattern a father figure evolved. To the Mother surrogates was added a Father substitute, an intellectual equal without the authoritarian paternalism. The Minister had distinguished himself at Oxford, been in charge of the resettlement of Greek refugees, served in several Liberal governments and, as the League's High Commissioner, had protected German dissidents like Charles; lately he had persuaded the British government that the return of King George would bring stability to Greece, as proved by an overwhelming majority in the plebiscite. Dinners as the Minister's elegant Kolonaki house – a British regimental mess at the same time as the Tarburg – resembled the Luncheons at the Liechti, but were more cosmopolitan, with conversations in several languages. The diplomats and administrators kept to Western ways, joked about the intrigues for intrigues' sake, and deplored the oriental vagueness in Greek attitudes.

The civil war had destroyed both communications and seaside hotels, so that Charles's lessons continued through the summer. For autumn the CO offered the position of Regional Director in Crete, which sounded like third secretary at a legation, though the salary was exceedingly low even allowing for free accommodation. 'You'll administer British culture under a board of three local notables. A year of comfy exile will get you literature classes in Athens,' Ralph advised. The lease of the flat was up, the Minister was leaving on a

mission to the States, Christl was putting her daughter into school in England, and Charles embarked for Crete.

———————

Chania's richest olive merchant was Treasurer of the English School. Gogo, his younger and slimmer wife, had come along 'to break the ice', which seemed superfluous in the prevailing heat. She informed Charles that his predecessor had been monopolised by the wife of the School's Vice-President, without revealing if the ladies took turns or if the early bird got the Director.

On the ground floor of a neo-classical villa, the Director's desk faced the secretary's in the Registry; the dining room made a possible, the dismantled kitchen an impossible classroom. An open staircase mounted to a large room, where an iron bed and washstand flanked a glass cupboard for Europe's tiniest school library; neither curtain nor rug distracted from the rustic austerity. Charles's appalled 'Worse than Spartan' was corrected to 'Cretan. You have a fine view and the Turkish bath isn't far.' Gogo opened the door to a smaller room with a bare shelf – 'To store food if you like cooking', though where that might be achieved remained obscure. She promised a brazier, 'Olive stones smell nicely but are poisonous. Some people die every winter. I'll send a reading lamp with the maid. Gossip is simply awful' was confirmed by the husband's scowl.

Australian conmen seeded plots with diamonds to swindle gullible investors. No diamonds here and none as gullible as the Regional Director. The CO conning revived the shellshock shakes, barely calmed by a siesta on the lumpy mattress.

At the board meeting President, Vice-President and Treasurer expounded sublime educational theories lacking any relation to reality, except for a new mattress. Generosity combined with grandiloquence into high spirits at the Tennis Club, originally intended for the ball game. To order vegetables grown on the single court was evidently absurd in this huge fertile island, but the Germans could be blamed for anything; sport no longer interfered with backgammon, cards, dancing and meals. Gogo scored with Charles at a first home invitation; her Vice-Presidential rival withdrew ungraciously from the competition, not entered by the President's spouse due to her premature death. Tedious provincial inanities were limited by Charles's plea for solitude, a romantic eccentricity conceded to a countryman of Byron. When it became too cold for swimming, long walks through the olive groves recalled Jerusalem, but without amusing Artemis . . . No company was preferable to bad.

The *Romeo and Julius* of Ohli's school determined the choice of the orthodox version for Charles's literature class, but his castigation of Romeo as wet and Friar Laurence as dotty made the students gasp at such daring. Eyes were lowered in shame at the teacher's 'I don't know nor do I want to', variously ascribed to Christian humility or, even more embarrassing, British frankness. Shocking Chania's intellectuals paled before Hildegard's disconcerting news from the Tarburg.

'. . . Ohli's pleasure at your appointment in Crete was mentioned by Herta so pointedly that she must have wanted me to use the address. Deep down she regrets that absurd expense account, but you have become a non-person since the arrival of your father with Helen. She has created upheaval, the first mistress ever to reside in the Tarburg. Uncle Rudi mutters "charming, charming" and complains that Ottavio Voltain doesn't know if ladies' hands are kissed in Australia. My parents aren't sure if it's insult with or minus injury, as your father is divorcing Tania, whom he met in Vienna. He also met Krainer Junior – extraordinary that both are now British – but any financial arrangements remain as obscure as the German compensation for the contents of the Liechti. He is certainly decisive and sold the Altenhof to that crooked "administrator". He is still attractive, hardly a grey hair, though Helen calling him Lord is all the odder for his being the Castle's only resident not to possess the title. He no doubt would now have one, had Franz Ferdinand become Emperor. Franz Ferdinand's younger son stayed here for a week, partaking with our fathers in fascinating stories of orgies of what could, would and should have been. Your father talks about settling in England, he obviously commands ample funds. Soph and Norbert are thrilled by this secret letter to their beloved uncle . . .'

This 'could, would and should' had often been discussed with Father and even Philip in Australia, but in Crete the link with the past snapped; one-sided Imperial speculations were hard to maintain in an intellectual void. Deprived of human relationship and minimal comfort, Charles once tried Mimis's cure-all, the sailors' tavernas in the port. Not worth the scandal that an ingenious 'Collecting material for a book' would only aggravate; the wrong kind for a regional director. The right kind in the absurd school library could not be lent out from a bedroom better kept hidden from public sight. 'Neither borrower nor lender be' upset only Gogo, who desired access to Shakespeare. She renounced the only author she knew, when reminded that her exclusive use of the staircase would multiply the risk of gossip, but she probably complained to the CO in Athens.

—— —— —— ——

'The Director will be amused by your explanation of the "literary infertility" in that weird anonymous letter. He wants to make up for the appalling accommodation, just as well I've been appointed to Japan.'

'In my Cretan "infertility" I've been dreaming of these Christmas holidays in the bodily and spiritual comfort, of your flat, Ralph. One at least . . . it's bliss to be soaking in a hot bath.'

'I've written some poems, I didn't tell you because you made fun of Georges Arnault in Paris. Now my first novel has been favourably reviewed, the CO has kicked me upwards to a larger country. My reports on the cultural shambles here no doubt contributed to my hasty removal.'

'Shambles is rather apt for living at the mercy of Gogo at the last outpost of civilisation.'

—— —— —— ——

Civilisation had flourished in Crete 4,000 years ago; when sage and thyme scented the air instead of the brazier's carbon monoxide. Minoan ruins became a practical alternative to Gogo. Less approachable, however. Charles asked the driver of the overcrowded old bus to stop below the Phaestos hill. Head-shaking was the local reaction to sightseeing, but the murmur of disapproval was unusual. So were the shouts and gesticulations from a distant field, while Charles climbed through the lush grass. The guard of the site crossed himself – 'The Virgin protected you in a German minefield.'

'Six years after the end of the war? Why isn't there any warning?'

The guard possessed all the right answers. 'The archaeological and the agricultural departments can't decide which is responsible. And why a warning? Some sheep got blown up but they couldn't read anyway. Nor can tourists, foreigners never know Greek.' They had been speaking that language, which failed to persuade in the country which had formulated logic. 'I'll let you in without a ticket and, as the tourist pavilion is still closed, I'll put you up for the night.'

Women in mourning for relatives killed in inherited vendettas served but did not sit at the evening meal, washed down with the local firewater. A bed was prepared on the low table that had held the repast and, despite the hardness, Charles passed out till wakened by a sharp pain in one foot. A huge pig was probing his toes, not playfully like Titi, but in gnawing earnestness. Dracula of the farmyard!

—— —— —— ——

High-risk archaeology was appreciated by the sophisticated gatherings in the Minister's house during the Easter holidays. All too short a break from Chania, where spring was in the air and Gogo on the ground. A *non sequitur* made dinner with her alarming – 'My husband was called away unexpectedly. I am still young. He is impotent' was probably less truthful, but her tears dissolved his resistance. She scorned Charles's prudent 'Anything once', and advertised her triumph by embarrassing inflexions and touches at the Club.

On the last day of the examinations, the Treasurer stormed into the Registry and ordered the secretary out. His menacing bluster softened, 'Here is your ticket for tomorrow's boat. I know it isn't your fault, I've seen Gogo making up to you, but so has the whole of Chania. I gave her a good beating and sent her back to her parents. They had expected me to kill her . . . and you too. I must at least be seen to run you out of Crete. I rely on you to depict me as close to murder.' Husband and lover sympathised with one another more than with the tiresome woman.

The departure was dramatised for the sake of the public, and for that of the complacent revenger who had, nevertheless, shattered his rival's prospects at the CO. By the time the Director received his regional underling, 'unexpected quarters' had come into play. 'Truth is usually relative in Greece. The School Board informs me of your resignation without any comment. One member, however, sent a glowing report – hardworking, popular with the students, the usual clichés plus an original 'drinking much less than his predecessor'. Still no reason for your precipitous departure, a black mark against you. Considering the appalling accommodation, the CO will shut down in Crete, your file goes into Closed Operations, and after seven years you join, not rejoin. If you need a job in the meantime, you seem the right man according to the Treasurer. Oh, I shouldn't have let that out of the bag.' He obviously enjoyed having done so. 'The AEI is expanding throughout Greece. It's neither American nor very Educational, but a commercial Institute. You, as a former regional director, have the suitable title.'

The cuckolded husband had secured Charles's future, the Grandparents now stirred up the past.

'. . . We celebrated our diamond wedding in the town hall, where the Red mayor seemed unduly concerned with getting our vote before we descended into the grave. That, by the way, had to be changed, as cremation would offend the good sisters here. So we can't be placed next to Adele, but she and my mother will understand why we have agreed to burial on the Convent's plot. It's not far, when you bring mimosa to Mother. The sisters think you a heretic for having sold the Liechti to the Salvation Army and pray for your conversion; so do I, but above all I wish Herta had paid half of the mortgage. She and Max have joined Father in England after putting Soph with the Ursulines, Mother's school. Ohli frightened the headmistress with Latin tags, I the sister teaching Domestic Science by telling her that such a pompous name was absurd for a bit of embroidery. Ohli takes the poor child to the theatre on Sunday and occasionally brings her out here. She tires me and now I understand why my mother seemed to care so little for Herta and you. Soph must think me a heartless great-grandmother but we are strangers. You, Karli, I miss very much . . .'

Hildegard's letter filled in the gaps.

'. . . Herta, Max and their chattels followed your father to the estate he bought in England. Abbey Court displays the Tarburgs' coat-of-arms, while the Tarburgs have been dispatched to Ireland in search of a farm they can afford. They sold their share of the Tarburg to my father – together with the proceeds from the Altenhof quite a tidy sum – and they seem happy to obey your father.

'War-widowhood has paled from heroic into merely regrettable, so I am marrying an Austro-Italian. He is intelligent, has money and a lovely house in Trieste, but no title, which bothers Herta more than me . . .'

Herta's and Charles's premonitions about never meeting again at the Tarburg had come true. Max had sold his birthright to become as uprooted as Charles, despite the warning example. Opting for the unknown continued to the grave, since the Grandparents had decided against sharing their daughter's resting place. Would he ever again lay mimosa on the white marble? He had neglected a nearer grave, had not even got in touch with Panagiotis's family. When he did so, an unrecognisable shrill voice recognised his; no, she did not want to see him, he was responsible for her son's death. Panagiotis's sister must have snatched the receiver. 'Mother has become . . . difficult since we went to Samos. The Abbot did not blame you, on the contrary, but she has lost her only son. I'm only a daughter, unmarried. We need no help, but do go to Samos, he expects that.'

Impulses could be wrong or just plain crazy. The 'sacred duty' of lesser romantic novels hardly extended to marrying a sister for love of the brother. That would qualify him for the tender care of the Master in Sydney, besides being unfair to the girl. The affairs of convenience with Mariette and Eve had turned inconvenient with Gogo, but a marriage of pity was lunacy.

——— —— —— ——

This was brought home on Samos which in the hot stillness of July bore little resemblance to that stormy day nine years ago. Driving straight from the boat to the Monastery aroused the taxi driver's curiosity. 'Foreigners aren't often so pious, but perhaps the monks' patriotism has become known. They buried a sailor in their sacred ground. He tried to kidnap the German commander and has the only marble cross, with a photograph.'

The same picture Charles had added to those of his family preserved through all vicissitudes; set according to Greek custom into the white marble, the likeness was suitably unsmiling to hide the gap in the teeth. The visual prop eased cathartic remembrance but not communication as on Mother's grave. Love like the sailor's was improbable, impossible. Yet try, be yourself, don't get caught by another Gogo nor in the trap of pity for the sister. Hope lay with another Panigiotis.

Intense emotion made the tearstained guest appreciate the monks' simple fare. Discussion of the fateful Assumption Day continued privately with the Abbot whose compassion encouraged asking for an explanation of Panagiotis's 'It is better like this'.

The Abbot took Charles's hand. 'Except for your love, everything stood against you, convention, customs, upbringing. The Virgin granted him this insight to ease his death. You might have to learn by bitter experience that it was better.'

No, it was not. Contrary to spiritual and worldly wisdom, love would have prevailed and might yet with a similar friend.

———————

Work prevailed for two years with the opening of branches in several provincial capitals. The shrewd AEI accountant first formed a committee of dignitaries, upgraded from Chania as usually presided over by the local bishop. The most original unveiled his own statue to the gasping envy of his fellow clerics expecting to see the town's patron saint. The most interesting had been the secretary of the late Archbishop–Regent and practised his English over cups of tea ladled out of a huge soup tureen in honour of British habits. His dean drove the car flying the episcopal standard to the sights of the diocese, the bishop blessed the bowing villagers while the teacher assumed an impressively grave expression. Reflected deference did not compensate for lonely evenings; on a first visit Mimis was allowed to ruin his own reputation and to dent his host's. But by then enrolments had been creamed off in that popular town and the Former SO Regional Director was announced in the next, if not with fanfares at least in the local paper.

Before the provincials realised that the eminent educationalist was not theirs for long after payment of the Institute fees, Mimis was not to cause havoc and scandal again. He was propelled on an excursion to Olympia where he comported himself not on an imperial but impressive scale in the ruined House of Nero. In the museum he kissed the irresistible mouth of Antinous, facilitated by the broken-off nose and observed by an American who followed suit. Shared tastes inaugurated a pleasant evening in a taverna where Mimis boasted of his Neronic exploits. Next morning triumphalism was deflated when Mimis had to lock himself in the train WC till departure as some youths claimed payment for services rendered.

———— ———— ———— ————

The opening-enrolment-transfer routine exhausted the dubious attractions of the provinces. Athens beckoned when a group of teachers followed the example of Greek political parties and theatrical companies by breaking away from the American Educational Institute to form the Institute of American Education; the ensuing litigation dragged inconclusively through the years till both dropped the A when American became unpopular. The IAE secured 'The CO Regional Director's Invaluable Experience' at a low valuation after the customary work permit troubles, but then no business operated without a cousin in politics to circumvent regulations.

Eavesdropping procured a flat. Charles was describing unsuccessful hunting to the Minister at a restaurant when a well-dressed lady at the next table claimed without preliminaries, 'I've exactly what you are looking for, freshly done up and central.' The tiny flat was not 'just what a bachelor needs', but quite cosy, the former servants' quarter up two flights of the back stairs in an old Kolonaki house. Privacy was appreciated after its lack in equally modest provincial hotels and Charles settled down to enjoy the last days of summer at the Phaleron beach.

2

A growing awareness of being watched made him look up from his book to meet the eyes of a youth sitting a few yards away. The large eyes conveyed an interest reminiscent of Panagiotis at the dancing school; he was the same age but Charles was now fourteen years older. Sentimental memories are better washed away by the sea. Charles swam long stretches under water and the boy dived all around, playfully, skilfully. He followed Charles out and pulled his beach towel closer for the next move in a slow, soft voice that matched his brown eyes. 'Excuse me, you dive very well. But why do foreigners always read books?' was an amusing *non sequitur* while the later 'Why are you alone?' was not impudent but frankly interested.

Good books over indifferent company was too incomprehensible to offend the tall strong-limbed Greek who seemed a little old to be studying for exams to enter the eighth class. He introduced himself as Stelios and switched from the obviously uncomfortable school topic to a permanent grudge. 'When I was a child I upset a kettle of boiling water. My mother put a mixture of bread and, excuse me, piss on the burn. The priest and the village women prayed, but a cousin who had been to America brought a doctor from the nearest town just in time. Because of my illiterate mother I have this ugly scar.'

'It's hardly noticeable' was true in comparison to Otto's disfigurement and the guilt about revulsion against physical impairments made Charles agree more readily to a meeting the following morning.

At that meeting Stelios abandoned his personal grudge for the worse woes of ancient tragedies which to his surprise were also studied abroad. His effort to shine was moving and deserved recognition.

'Would you enjoy seeing *Hippolytos*?'

The eyes expressed the difference between mere 'enjoy' and sheer 'joy'. 'I've never been to the theatre, I must find the money for the ticket.'

'I have two seats for tonight.' Mimis would be able to get them.

———

Stelios's light-brown mop rose above the crowd at the entrance of the ancient theatre. His eyes lit up with joy. 'I came early and then became afraid you were having me on. The kind of joke my friends would play.' It might have appeared unseemly to mention Charles's concern for his behind on the hard marble, but not even the lack of a back-rest spoilt the excellent performance watched in total absorption by his companion.

Memories at the nearby taverna ranged from Willi to Panagiotis, but on the positive side no strident music aggravated the indifferent food and retsina. These made no dent in the euphoria of Stelios who had never visited the Plaka and was still preoccupied with mythology. 'Didn't Phaedra realise that her stepson was Poseidon's lover?'

'Neither did I though Poseidon had given horses to other favourites. In the orthodox version he was merely the grandfather of Hippolytos who had taken a vow of chastity.'

'Very un-Greek!' Stelios laughed heartily. 'Excuse me for a moment.' He was heading for the WC while Charles was looking for the waiter who reappeared with Stelios. 'The bill is settled, you paid more for the tickets.'

Panagiotis had behaved similarly at their first outing, but a schoolboy did not dispose of even a military pittance. Considering his repeated failures the best assistance was scholastic. 'I'm sorry I won't be able to see you for a few days, some friends are arriving tomorrow. You'll have to study anyway.'

'An hour in the afternoon is enough. If I stay home in the morning my mother insists on my studying, my father on helping him with his carpentry. They quarrel so I go swimming' added a Solomonic touch to making light of exams.

Charles sympathised in thought but in speech admonished Stelios sensibly till the arrival of the last bus. 'The day after the exams on the beach!'

——— ———

Even after four years in Greece Charles avoided 'untruth' whenever possible. Daniel and Heinz indeed arrived the following day and pleasantly monopolised their old friend. A rare thunderstorm rained away the beach appointment, just as well as a telephone was being installed, obtained by the Minister within a week instead of the usual year of waiting. Surely Stelios would try again when the weather improved. Before lunch with the Parisians there was time for the long-postponed visit to the cathedral. Charles prayed briefly every night, but at the Assumption altar he concentrated on family and friends, dead and living, exclusive of the beach encounter.

Yet Stelios stood at the entrance of the house in Kolonaki. 'I looked for you on the main stairs, I said I was a student. As you didn't come to the beach . . .'

'In that downpour? Wouldn't tomorrow have done?'

Stelios pointed accusingly at the telephone. 'Why didn't you give me your number?'

'Because I got the phone only today. Haven't you one at home?'

'At the shop, but my father never remembers a message. Please don't be angry.'

Stelios's anxiety was touching, his disappointment over the backstairs silly though they were rather squalid. 'Would you like to come on an excursion on Sunday? My French friends are driving to Delphi.'

'I've been there with my school, I can show you round. We are doing French but . . .'

'Don't worry! After spending years on the verb *aimer*, Greek schools apparently give up. Could you be here by eight?' He had not accompanied Yvonne to Delphi for one young Greek, now another was to guide him there; the same beach further linked both. But the first had initiated Charles into a pleasant way of life for which the second probably lacked sufficient brightness. The age gap of fifteen years was much smaller than between Father and Tania, let alone Helen, but that was an absurd comparison in this neo-Panagiotic delusion.

———— ————

No delusion, Stelios was ringing the bell shortly after midnight. 'My parents sleep early so I managed the last bus. I've brought along the breakfast mother had prepared.' He displayed goat cheese and olives with boyish shyness which quickly turned into tender sensuality. Afterwards he snuggled up trustingly, like Charles long ago into Otto's embrace. 'I've never made love in bed. With the girls I went to a dark spot, they were willing enough to catch a husband, so I was always afraid. And I've been with whores – not in brothels, that's too expensive. On certain vacant plots you go into the bushes for a few drachmas, but many are ill.' He hesitated, raising his head and looked straight into Charles's eyes. 'A customer of father was waiting in the shop. He wanted to blow me, I needed money for the cinema, so we managed behind some planks.' He laughed in sincere amusement. 'My mother had heard that most foreigners were queer, she probably got it all wrong, though there was a fat German . . . and someone asking me to rub oil on his back. I wanted to prove her wrong so I sat next to you because you were reading as if for an exam. When you dived into the sea I suddenly wanted mother to be right.'

Stelios must be afforded every chance to fulfill what the friendship of Panagiotis had promised. The Samian Abbot's 'Except for your love everything stood against you' must be heeded by making Stelios generally acceptable.

———— ————

'Do you really imagine that Stelios would become acceptable to the Minister or Christl?' Daniel was accompanying Charles home after dinner with the Minister. 'Heinz wasn't invited, quite rightly as he simply isn't capable of any intelligent table talk. With all my money I failed to have him accepted even in broadminded Paris. That's why he started drinking and I brought him here for a change of atmosphere. You inflict the blessings of education when you need a rest from your beastly Institute and he wants one from his school. He is full of good intentions, appreciates yours and hates putting them into

186

practice. Sheer SM, not Marks and Spencer, you idiot, Sado-Masochism.'

'A double life may be thrilling, triple is a strain. Keeping Stelios, friends and the Institute apart . . .'

'I've joined the first two by getting tickets for *Tannhäuser*.'

——— ———

The tenor had been and the soprano might become a great name, the ballet stamped about unseductively, the chorus was garbed in surplus khaki with tiny coats-of-arms like regimental badges. Stelios became increasingly bewildered; to refuse a stepmother like Hippolytos, OK, but the goddess of love! Elisabeth should have been glad of such an experienced husband.

Stelios caught the last bus but his realism lingered and was defended by Heinz over a late supper. 'That he advocates duplicity on the stage does not mean he'll practise it . . . yet. He's bowled over not just by you, Charles, but theatre, opera. He is attractive but a sparkler he is not and the teacher/lover conundrum won't work.'

'If he put the same ingenuity into studying as into finding excuses for his laziness, he'd be speaking English by now.'

'To deliver him unto those greedy queens descending on Athens as the new Sodom? Use the common sense with which you so charitably joined me to Daniel. He has paid a few visits to the Venusberg, very discreet but I'm an old hand at the game. I don't blame him, I've become horribly skinny. Let's face facts. Stelios makes up in intuition what he lacks in intellect. He has a reliable friend he could bring along next Sunday.'

——— ———

Reliable but so plain that Daniel decided against finding out any hidden charms. The friend assisted Stelios with a new camera, a Christmas gift, which revealed an artistic strain. 'Octopus Drying in the Sun' won a prize in a competition, thereby ending awkward questions about the donor of the camera. The potentialities of the octopus proved superior to those of the friend who, nevertheless, was instrumental in the shedding of pretences. At outings and in bed younger companions replaced Heinz who mellowed in the certainty that materially he was as secure as ever.

——— ———

The Tarburgs were miserably insecure, the Grandparents reported.

'. . . Herta and Max returned from that wild goose chase in Ireland, very bitter about your father whom they blame for pulling up their roots in Austria. Now that the Russians have withdrawn the Altenhof has enormously gained in value and as for giving up the Tarburg . . . The furniture will remain at Abbey Court, not what Max expected when he married an heiress. After castle and country house they now live in a small flat in Vienna; the furniture is an odious jumble of donations; the only decent piece is an armchair from the Liechti you gave to the sister of Margarete Horbitzer who is back and visits us regularly. We contributed a rococo clock which looks out of place, but Herta will inherit our remaining furniture. The proceeds of those foolish sales Max invested in the paper factory of a distant cousin and he is now hawking nappies and napkins. Not from door to door, and many Viennese firms are still impressed by his title and also his game leg as the hatred of the Russians is universal.

'Herta particularly loathes the Australian lady of Abbey Court, which will come to Soph who spends her summers there. Your father has become all the fonder of her since he quarrelled with both his children. She is still at the Ursulines and at weekends has to wash up as her parents can't afford a daily maid. Ohli wants me to end with *sic transit* . . .'

─── ── ──

Equally applicable to Count Poldi Berchtram till his marriage to Artemis. He had been born in a *palais* close to the Liechti and was a Hussar in the First World War which his uncle, as Imperial Minister, had helped to start. Neighbourhood, horsemanship, Monarchist tradition and expatriate regrets combined in an Austrian understanding encouraged though incomprehensible to Artemis, busy with forging copper into lumps more appropriate as weaponry than jewellery.

Stelios's delight at attending the wedding in the cathedral evaporated in new failure at his exams. His mother refused consent to a fortnight on Rhodes despite his description of Charles as an excellent teacher. Luckily Maths was not specified but even so the unprepossessing woman made her point about her son's laziness and ingratitude for the financial sacrifice required by his endless studies. Artemis was a born fixer as she had proved on more desperate occasions; she awed by her Levantine Greek made incomprehensible by foreign words, the decorative function of the copper was even harder to appreciate though the clanking was menacing, and a Countess was probably related to the Queen. Artemis held all the trumps.

─── ── ──

Rhodes was more securely enchanting than Stelios. He was fascinated by the medieval fortifications and mosques, since in school Knights and Turks had been dismissed as barbarians. He took the lead in sightseeing, sex and swimming, but turned into an obstinate schoolboy at the stipulated hour of study when he chain-smoked. Minor grew into major rows, diagnosed but not stopped by an unflattering comparison. 'I'm so grateful you helped me escape from my mother and now you behave just like her.' On parting Stelios's eyes confirmed his gratitude for 'the most wonderful fortnight of my life'. One look and they laughed in rare understanding. 'I was a mule but I will pass those bloody exams.'

Charles disembarked at Kos where sentiments varied during the first lonely night. The needed balance of concessions and compromise was probably just as unworkable as the constitutions dreamt up by idealistic experts for ex-colonies. Well-meant involvement ending in bitterly resented entanglement?

Ralph privately resumed disentanglement, while relaxing with his oldest friend, before assuming his official functions as CO Deputy Director, in Greece. He had become a successful author, as eager to hear about the Minister's politics as about Mimis's tavernas, always in search of unlikely topics. 'A trade to be learned like any other. Ever done any writing, Charles?'

'An Athens paper published a romanticised account of my Cretan experience.'

'Maliciously garbled, I'm sure. I've been commissioned to edit a Greek companion to my *Key to Japan*. I have Robert for Athens, he was so impressed by his mother's splendid cathedral wedding that he is moving back here; off his prayer rug he is very knowledgeable. Give me a chapter on Crete and if it's any good you are launched into the lucrative guidebook racket.'

'You seem to have transferred your congenital nastiness to the characters in your novels. I must be getting old to prefer you to stormy love.'

'Better preserve your back-handed compliments for the bitchery on Mykonos.'

The bitchery of the sophisticated Paris seamstress mob made the dazzling white village into a parody of pre-war Cannes. Ralph stood it only a day, Charles a week till reminiscing with Daniel turned into deploring the unwholesome Franco-Hellenic artificiality.

———— ————

Stelios was not waiting at Piraeus; no excuse when he rang, merely an acknowledgement of having received the letter with the return date; after an awkward pause he suggested meeting that evening.

'The papers published pictures of the famous people on Mykonos. You know some, I would have liked to meet them. Instead I had to study.'

That the 'famous' had been the reason for the quick departure met with total incomprehension which, contrary to all advice, strengthened Charles's educational zeal. An IAE colleague would facilitate admission to the Industrial College but whether Stelios really attended the obligatory crammer course remained doubtful.

Charles pondered over this retribution for his own truancies while he laboured over the Cretan chapter for Ralph. 'Gogo interfered surprisingly little with your appreciation of ruins. In your peregrinations for the AEI you must have seen enough of the Peloponnese to do that chapter too. Appearing in print legitimises your return to the CO for which you have as little qualifications as the rest of the staff, except for Christl who is an ideal social secretary.'

Ralph was the arbiter in matters British, Mimis in persons Greek. His constant warnings against forcing Stelios into a way of life for which he was not suited could not possibly include Mount Athos. In the bus Charles's neighbour aired his Greek-American over a heaving sack between his feet. Despite determined refusal 'You want see?' he pulled a string and a hideous reptile raised its head. Stelios manfully took the seat next to the offended snake-charmer, -breeder or whatever, and remained a considerate travel companion in the Holy Mountain's unconventional circumstances. He obtained the best rooms from the guest masters by claiming that his friend was a famous author and joked about the rough food. 'My mother made me promise to keep the fast but she never said anything about sex.' Memories of Meteora, but in the warmth of summer when incredible edifices on inaccessible cliffs inspired writing and photography in a cooperation never achieved under the drudgery of studying. Charles had been wretchedly unhappy in one Samian Monastery, he was now supremely happy in a dozen Athonian. More of a puzzle than a pattern.

———————

The elusive intimacy continued in Athens as the friends had dispersed for the summer. Finishing the article on Athos, which Ralph was to submit to a London periodical, sharpened the holiday enjoyment of beach and tavernas, while most nights were spent together. Luckily not all, as one morning Stelios's mother called, accompanied by an old woman swaddled in black. Gratitude for help with her son's studies was expressed ungraciously, but thus was her nature. Peasant directness wondered why her beloved child missed the last bus so frequently. She worried the whole night, he must come home. Her voice rose stridently till shut up authoritatively. 'Don't pay any attention to my daughter, she is mad. You are paying for Stelios's studies, so two or three nights a week . . . but not every night.' Children were livestock reared for the market and the bargain was satisfactory.

———— ————

So satisfactory that Stelios was to come only early on Assumption Day to fetch his friend to the Orthodox liturgy. He was late, all the more unusual as it concerned Panagiotis about whom he could never hear enough. Irritation grew into worry, the telephone in the shop was not answered on this important holiday; there was no alternative to waiting till confinement within four walls became unbearable in the sweltering heat. Starting later than the interminable Orthodox rite, the Catholic High Mass calmed with the familiar harmony of choir and organ. He had to become a Catholic also in name, and not deprive himself any longer of the Communion; but prayers required no official seal to be heard by the Virgin on Her feast. A delay at the cathedral had made him miss Panagiotis, so Charles rushed home to undesirable thoughts in lieu of equally undesirable food. August fifteenth was his unlucky day, indirectly, through the tragic fate of friends. On holidays buses were infrequent and Stelios had once before cycled up; in the erratic Athenian traffic . . . Fears ballooned into panic.

Next morning Stelios answered the phone at the shop and stammered into a rigmarole about a taxi-driver uncle insisting on a family outing, leaving no time to ring. Pause, a crash, a whispered 'I'll ring back' in English, which was insufficient for the explanation some minutes late. 'Father was listening, so I knocked down his coffee and he went out for another. All this coffee is bad for him' was abandoned as a delaying action with an audible sigh. 'I felt ashamed on the day Panagiotis died for you while I betrayed you. Please let me come tonight.'

Betrayal was bewilderingly pompous for the Industrial College, but Stelios had been thorough; he had not sat for half the exams and flunked most of the others. Charles would have looked no less crestfallen had the *Anschluss* not forestalled his own confession of 'Betrayal' back in Vienna. Father's fury might have put an end to his son's studies; Charles would condone another attempt. This generous intention fell to the crazy justification of 'I could not darken Panagiotis's memory by my failure' misapplied from God-knows-what ancient tragedy. The misery of Assumption Day erupted into increasingly violent denouncements of moral cowardice.

The brown eyes expressed infinite sadness. 'You are right and so was my mother. I'll have to tell her, because I'm of the fifty-four.' He accepted defeat with this mysterious number, leaving Charles trembling with nervous exhaustion.

———————

'Mysterious my foot!' Mimis laughed. 'Stelios belongs to the fifty-four class of recruits. He uses this instead of the year of his birth, which he probably can't tell off-hand, like most Greeks. His deferment for studies is automatically revoked and he'll be called up. I can get him into the navy if he contacts me.'

Stelios did not and the void was filled with professional upsets. The Cyprus crisis enabled the IAE to engage in unsubtle blackmail; a Canadian teacher possessed not only the right diploma but also a Greek wife as bulwark against chauvinistic zeal. Charles's work permit was more problematic and he would surely understand that the fees for his excellent literature classes had to be adjusted to the general level. He understood and wished that the unfair competitor would drop dead. The figure of speech acquired frightening substance when the Canadian's pallor turned deadly and he succumbed to a kidney disease. An exasperated grumble proved frighteningly effective.

———————

The letter from Vienna was not in Granny's Gothic but Ohli's Latin copperplate.

'. . . Your grandmother died in her sleep. To be left behind would have been worse for her than it is for me. She always regretted that you did not marry, Marie Louise remained her favourite. She must have bequeathed her hankering for titles to Herta whose child got her heredity as well as her environment wrong. Herta bullies, Max dotes and poor Soph only respects her grandfather in England. Hildegard came from Trieste for the funeral. She hasn't forgotten Granny's compassion when her husband was hung from a meat hook after Stauffenberg's bungled attempt on the Führer's life. Norbert was not in the plot, but he had a title and was an officer, enough for the Gestapo to execute him summarily. We were at the Tarburg as visible proof of Herta's Aryan ancestry and suddenly Max's clan were in even deeper trouble. Non-Aryan and aristocrat had become equally suspect.

'Charlotte paid her visit of condolence, kind but she does talk. She worries a lot about your horoscopes, especially about "Love disintegrating into sensuality". From my happy marriage I conclude that One is preferable to Many even in classical *mores* . . .'

Ohli had spelled it out so clearly that telepathy sprang into action, employing in a typically Greek twist Stelios's rejected friend. 'Would you or Daniel want any Christmas decorations? I was given a stall because my father was killed by the Communists.' The unsolicited information continued after a whisper almost inaudible over the phone 'Stelios is my partner'.

———— ————

Four rows of stalls glittered with cheap baubles in the light of candles, but instead of the snow appropriate to the Russian Ballet décor thin drizzle impeded the search in the early darkness. Despite his rough clothes Stelios looked an unconvincing street vendor and a shrivelled woman left empty-handed after picking through the tin toys. Charles and Daniel chose from the disarray to the delight of Stelios who tried to refuse payment. 'You are our first customers and Daniel must have an enormous Christmas tree for all this angel's hair. The crowd is just inquiring and comparing, to return for the actual purchase the last day or two. At present they enjoy bargaining.'

'The tank will make the son of my char very happy. You must be frozen, tea is what you need after you pack up.' Their astonished look indicated that the expected herbal brew was needed against indigestion. 'Brandy will warm you quicker.'

The friend gulped down his drink and departed, taking with him the lore on street vending. The Holy Mountain article in a glossy magazine avoided pointless recrimination or spineless reconciliation. Stelios was immensely proud of seeing his name in print but not deceived by the supposed remuneration. 'That's for your writing, not my one picture.'

'There wasn't space for the others. I'll keep them for future use.'

The gold-flecked eyes conveyed the old trust and a new gratitude. 'It'll make all the difference during my basic training at Corinth.'

———— ————

Military censorship passed the routine complaints about loss of liberty and friends. After the forty days of initial confinement, the taxi-driver uncle would bring the family, but perhaps the following Sunday?

His joy marked Stelios among the recruits pouring through the barracks gates. His father and uncle had reminisced about their training and had shown little interest in his. How wonderful to unload petty chicanery before sympathetic listeners. After a gigantic meal Stelios loosened his belt but though a boa constrictor came to mind he did not fall into a digesting stupor but insisted on emotional physical privacy in the orange groves.

Stelios's joy though not his appetite was constrained a fortnight later. 'I won't be sent for officer training though thanks to you I know more about the world than the other chaps. I'm just slow.'

'To be a reserve officer would have helped in whatever you'll be doing. What now?'

'The Artillery at Thebes, I haven't told my family about the twenty-four hour leave' was not a hint but an appeal.

Stelios's unbounded optimism tempered the rigours of discipline. Drivers of army trucks were punished for the engines' as well as their own misdoings, but he would be all the better qualified when they had a car in their future writer/photographer collaboration. Charles's weekend visits to Thebes dealt successfully with the immediate practical problem, spy hysteria. A soldier booking into a hotel was as suspect as sharing the room with a foreigner, but however much the patriotic porter hated the Turks, *baksheesh* featured in his vocabulary. No such accommodation when the artillery man was posted to the Bulgarian border, out-of-bounds to foreigners.

———— ————

Foreigners only, on the luxurious yacht of a shipping tycoon to which Charles was whisked by a skeleton from his worldwide cupboard. Sir Philip MacLachlan introduced Charles as the co-author of a sensational book on Greece, 'Pick his brain when you aren't quite sure whether a temple is Archaic or classical'. Few bothered and round-the-clock gossip demanded more stamina than the Holy Mountain. 'Seeing the Cyclades in such comfort is rather spoilt by that name-dropping mob from whom one can't get away.'

'You, righteous Charles, are the phoniest of all. You dazzle with the society to which you belonged till you cut yourself off, contrary to my wise counsels. You flaunt your languages and learning before monolingual businessmen and their pseudo-sophisticated women folk. Still, forced proximity does become tiresome, so may I contribute to a car for next summer?'

'No thanks, Philip. I'll get the car and you can invite me to the hotels I couldn't afford.'

———— ————

Ralph went to London to 'make the right noises at the CO, confound my publishers and on the way back throw my arthritic mother into the mud at Abano. Would you like to take over the Weekly Cultural Letter for Cyprus Radio? It's particularly important during the Athens Festival, but no Greek dares to work for the British Colonial Administration. With your theatre background it should be fun to review the season's tragedies. Perhaps fun isn't the right word.'

Less with every impeccably staged performance. The enjoyment shared with Stelios at *Hippolytos* vanished under the onslaught of raving and ranting. Charles reverted to his schoolboy belief that 'the imprudence of the protagonists was as much to blame as Fate' and the unorthodox comment was duly broadcast. Politicised like everything in Greece, it made the wicked Persians, Turks and British responsible for all national and most private disasters.

——— ———

Ralph was fingering with distaste the newspaper clippings. 'Linking ancient tragedies to that Cyprus mess! Lucky your name isn't affixed to those highly original Cultural Letters. Go easy on originality in what, I hope, will be your next writing. A heavily Americanised compatriot of yours has asked me to edit *Greece* in his Golden Guides. Not compatible with my official position so I recommended you. He liked your chapters in *Key* and provided you tame your originality . . .'

Roland Gulden found in a Fenton what he expected from a Fechtner. 'Professionals rarely master the GGG formula, of presenting accurate information amusingly. That's why I prefer semi-amateurs, also because they come cheaper. I won't offend your intelligence claiming by that the budget is ample. It's adequate and revision fees provide a steadier income than uncertain royalties. As area editor you can choose the contributors; perhaps a name from the society column, a title Americans feel safe with.'

Count Poldi Berchtram's name was not often linked to safety, but he would sign the chapter written by his stepson. Robert was the expert amongst the team which included the Minister, an ambassador and a woman novelist. Gulden approved at a taverna dinner easy on the expense account, and introduced Charles to the President of the Greek Tourist Organisation.

——— ———

Charles was not keen on driving, he had enjoyed the unhindered observing while travelling with Eve. Now work legitimised Philip's and Stelios's arguments for a car, but the horoscope's 'constant struggle' resumed from the Vienna driving lessons. Cyprus had roused anti-British sentiments in a bureaucracy notorious for delaying and mislaying the irrelevant papers required for a driving licence. Stelios was so enthusiastic on Christmas leave that even the practical obstacles were faced. In lieu of Aunt Charlotte's brother securing 'Unimpeded sight' an envelope was discreetly handed over at the eye test; pathological incapacity to understand engines was overcome by pretended incapacity to understand the language of the exasperated examiner.

The elusive driving licence was signed, sealed and ungraciously delivered just in time to drive Philip in a rented car to Corfu where the Minister procured the best attention and accommodation. The castello retained the country house atmosphere imparted by King George II during the few summers he reigned over his country and the cosmopolitan guests were nearly as distinguished as the setting. At the Achilleion Philip fell under the romantic spell of the Empress Elisabeth and wondered that Charles, the stout Monarchist, could joke about her bad taste as once with Otto and Yvonne. The exchange of historical with financial titbits was stimulating, arrangements had proved satisfactory, and Charles was put in charge of future summer journeys.

'You are admirably parsimonious with my funds, Charles. Luckily you always tip correctly and I like your grading into princely, knightly and bourgeois reward for services. You seem less concerned about your money than mine. All very well not to touch the pittance you got for your house, but the investment is overconservative. I'll introduce you to a more enterprising Greek-American stockbroker in Athens.'

——— ———

Financial gains were possible, the loss of the only remaining family contact was definite. The black-bordered notification of Ohli's death listed Charles among the mourners; conventional, Herta could not have done otherwise but she also forwarded the grandfather's gold pocket watch and chain to the Austrian Embassy, now installed in the former Archaeological School. The misery of the internment unfocused but did not lighten the grief when the Councillor handed over the lovely baroque timepiece. 'By the good offices of Willi Hollthal, I worked under him in Rome. I'm happy to oblige, because I danced with your father at an opera ball.' Father would have coped with less heroic dimensions, but Charles was offered the full weight. 'Will you escort me to a charity ball? A rather special entertainment.'

The inconvenience of steering the tall matron without seeing above her muscular shoulders turned into embarrassment with her announcing in a stage whisper 'We are just passing a dear friend I want to make jealous'. Cheek-to-cheek would have required unseemly contortions and the resolute squeeze to a heaving bosom gained in telling post factum. Heavy thanks for the transmission of an heirloom.

——— ———

Memories weighed heavily on Heinz while he patiently corrected Charles's inexperience in the mud surrounding the town where Stelios was now stationed. 'The roads exist more in the cartographer's mind than on the ground. It seemed such a bright idea to gather material for GGG and visit the gallant soldier. It's only thanks to you that Daniel's car hasn't slithered into a ditch.'

'Belated repayment for letting me cry on your shoulder in Paris that miserable night I had to hide from the police. Your Vienna and mine are worlds apart yet only a fellow Viennese could understand my desperate loneliness. My customers gave money, not sympathy. I still wonder whether I slept with men because they kept me alive or because I didn't care one way or the other. Daniel is generously patient with my smoking, drinking and bickering, but he deserved a holiday from me. Stelios won't be too happy either to see me.'

Stelios was pleased with an additional admirer of his stripe, Charles had never made it to corporal during the war. Not just the NCO but his entire company could have trooped into the Hotel *Vienna* so fascinated was the owner with Heinz's outrageous tales of that city. The accidental name was surely suspicious and nothing spoilt the optimism of the festive season.

Heinz hardly addressed his captive audience on the return journey. In the outskirts of Athens he reverted, however, to his preoccupation. 'Vienna disunites but also unites, in the beginning as much as at the end. That's my claim on you, Karl.'

———— ————

Stelios wrote in basic English about the need for a car in their GGG collaboration. On discharge he insisted on working with his father to contribute to the purchase of a battered Beetle, without gimmicks but also without the prohibitive duties thanks to the connections of the taxi-driver uncle.

The first outings in 'their' car justified the bother and the expense. Stelios remained tactfully at home on Ralph's last weekend dedicated to fairly inaccessible ruins to distract from the regrets of yet another separation, 'Blessedly undramatic compared to previous farewells. Pity I am leaving the CO just when you are rejoining, but to stone for three postings in Greece I was appointed Director in a very cold climate. I don't fancy having my balls frozen off and also dislike the CO restrictions on my writing, so I put in for a leaden handshake. I'll come back to Greece for vacations and as you are co-ordinating your heterogeneous mob so well for GGG some other publishers will be after you and you have to come to London.'

In July Charles drove Philip to the best beach hotels, in August he explored with Stelios lesser establishments off the beaten track for GGG potentialities. Pleasures were shared more readily than work; to even the score Charles would use his standing with the Tourist Organisation to get Stelios into the Guide School.

The pattern was familiar, enthusiastic planning instead of serious studies. Shock treatment might make Stelios realise that a better life required a minimum effort; he was to return temporarily to his family.

——— ———

'No need for my marvellous fortune teller to predict that the temporary will soon become permanent.' Mimis creased questioning eyebrows. 'He also casts spells . . . We'll see him tomorrow.'

The entry of two youngish males silenced the female-dominated waiting room till a gargoyle restarted the coffee grounds versus tea leaves argument. The eggs carried by all were not to be broken in the heated dispute but by this superior soothsayer. He looked remarkably unremarkable when he requested Charles to cut a dirty pack of cards into three piles to be interpreted in a toneless voice. 'Bitterness and more to come. Not the usual love or money, that is rare.' He prodded the uncooperative cards impatiently. 'He is not in love . . . with anyone else' was added after a perceptible hesitation. The reshuffled cards were spread in a different pattern. 'He'll come back, several times, again before a grave accident.' This concluded the man-to-man forecast while the egg would reveal Stelios's future. The white poured from a small hole into a glass of water coalesced into a mushroom that barely changed shape when the glass was turned round and round. 'The young man from your cards was born on an island, a big one. Egypt?' The seer's geography did not equal his divination. 'He is very simple, not like you. He is not serious, he just wants to enjoy himself, but he won't succeed. Whatever feeling he is capable of is now with you.'

Doom and gloom from the stars to the cards, the latter probably involving mind-reading as the accident of the horoscopes was negligently affixed to the main theme of Stelios's returns. The small emotional assurance came immediately under strain. 'When you sent me home I felt terribly angry. I drank an awful mixture of cherry brandy, beer and wine at a party and a woman whose husband had passed out asked me to take her home. In a dark spot . . . it's hard to resist when no precautions are needed. It was your fault . . . a little.'

A little, without significance, less scarring than the endless schoolroom quarrels. Mild jealousy and milder guilty conscience combined in sturdy reconciliation.

——— ———

Reconciliations weakened in repetition. To practise his English and earn pocket money Stelios guided Charles's and Daniel's foreign visitors, not all above snatching one's friend's friend. 'One year in London and I'll be ready for your books. It's impossible to learn English in Greece.'

'You'd better tell the CO, IAE and countless institutes to close down.'

Bested too often in linguistic arguments, Stelios played the financial trump. 'It won't cost you anything, he'll even pay for the ticket.'

A vague offer to justify a 'Try before you buy' had been taken seriously but was too farcical to matter in the bitterness so rightly predicted. Stelios's English was too unconventional for the Guide School, his photos too conventional for GGG.

Gulden was, however, pleased with the editing. 'You've gilded the Golden with extra layers of culture and history. The Schotten education will tell; preferable to the "olive-skinned, apple-cheeked girls" in *Turkey*. Interested in giving it eventually your trade mark? Easy on Neolithic digs, GGG are up-to-earth. You aren't allowed such puns, but I am the publisher.'

———

Besides lecturing at the CO, Charles tutored privately: Economics because of his degree, History because of his inclination. Few Greeks could afford his tuition or British universities, but he held a monopolistic position among the progeny of ship owners, diplomats and politicians. Severity with the grandsons of the Prime Minister in '41 rounded off the internment episode, but also initiated the move to a larger, more attractive flat near the Minister's house. Stelios had abandoned formal studies for the paternal carpentry; he proved his vocation by an ingenious writing-desk–bookshelf which fitted the multiple corners of Greek architecture.

At Christmas pretences were permissible while coaxing the Beetle through the stillness of the mountains. A snowfall at the highest pass transformed them into daring explorers; the white fir forest was a magic discovery for Stelios, for Charles a poignant reminder of the Altenhof; different approaches to fairyland in which they refound one another. The Tourist Organisation had made the reservation and due respect was shown to the 'famous author' especially after the waiter had uncorked the champagne, Daniel's gift. They retired early to be isolated in the warmth of their room, safe from the howling storm. In the brilliant sunshine of Christmas Day they built a snowman and pelted each other with snowballs in the harmony of changing moods.

One-heart-and-almost-one-mind vanished at the film shown by the Austrian Ambassador to the King and Queen. Felix Salten's *Florian* lacked the inspiration of his *Bambi* cartoon, nor did Stelios care that the author had been a regular guest of Charles's father. Yet the boredom of the film was a small price for the prestige conferred by the embossed invitation to a Command Performance.

The Queen of the Hellenes had been born in Austrian exile, the Imperial family was exiled from Austria. The Ambassador of the Republic did not attend the lecture on Pan-Europe by Archduke Otto, but the Ambassadors astounded everyone with a court curtsy from which she rose with the help of Dr Otto Habsburg. As such he had been introduced in the Historical Society for a realistic appraisal of European conditions. Yet Count Berchtram presented Karl Fechtner to His Imperial Highness, who gratifyingly remembered General-direktor Fechtner's part in the pre-war Monarchist movement. Presentation to the Imperial Family at the Ball in der Burg had flattered youthful ambitions, but this was the Emperor Otto of the perilous stickers and countless daydreams: Otto I or V – the numbering depended on succession to the medieval German or the nineteenth-century Austrian Empire – relied on his trusted Baron, Count and soon Prince Karl Fechtner as the Power behind the Throne and eventually Chancellor. No more improbable than the careers of Bismarck or Disraeli, the fantasies had flourished in adversity, stagnated in the routine drudgery to be uprooted by the Heir himself in the suitably depressing lecture hall. Dr Habsburg was addressing a Greek audience, not Austrian loyalists; he was objective and shattered Charles's unquestioning Monarchism.

——— ———

Public and private aspirations collapsed intellectually but lingered emotionally for want of anything better. Stelios obstinately clung to one year in England as a cure-all and had offered his services to Ralph.

'. . . Stelios as cook-housekeeper ruined my digestion, though doing for me is at least morally superior to doing a rich queen. I thought English had given him up, but oddly enough a former CO teacher is looking for an au pair. Though blind from glaucoma he is mentally and physically fit, proposes two hours of teaching in exchange for being walked about and read to. He has shown angelic patience, he'll need it! He won't make a pass at the innocently immoral boy as he is happily married. His wife will be visiting friends in Athens and arrange an inspection. Chance of a life . . .'

So it appeared till Stelios was needled into objections by good friends. Dogs guided the blind in England, he had seen it in a film; two hours for lessons was a lot if he also had to read aloud; was there a cinema in the country?

The wife called punctually to meet the young man Ralph had so warmly recommended but his lateness could not be indefinitely excused by discussions of traffic jams in Athens, London and worldwide. Stelios answered at the shop, urgent work, he had not rung because he disliked being shouted at. Charles rang off, white and trembling, and the lady 'feared he might have a stroke' as Ralph reported. Apoplexy was prevented by the low blood pressure but not the rage over this latest sample of moral cowardice. Au pair was too much like work and running away was easier than an excuse.

Had Charles not answered the phone he would have become guilty of the same despicable cowardice. 'I'm at the newspaper stand below.' Stelios must have raced up the stairs, the lift did not mount so quickly. 'It was wrong not to keep the appointment, it was impolite.' Admission was impersonal, attenuating circumstances not, the 'You take such matters so seriously, much more than anyone I know. We get on so well if you don't make all that fuss. The daughter of a neighbour had a wonderful time in London, arranged by an au pair agency. It will be easy to find something better than helping a blind man to the WC.'

Charles emerged from the grey zone separating the subconscious from the conscious sense of futility. Despair and happiness equally stimulated love making; one knew that nothing else remained while the other believed he had solved everything.

Pruning back to mere sex was not workable, but the moment for a clean break had passed. Slow attrition gave Stelios's groundless optimism a chance to reverse the irreversible. He tried touchingly but inadequately; in films and even an occasional book he joked about the shortcomings of lovers and briefly realised his own. An upsurge in English exercises was abandoned for lack of nagging encouragement or because the neighbour's daughter failed in the au pair attempt. Beyond remedial discussion, incompatibility might be presented dramatically in a novel because it was so universal and yet so personal. The writing bug mutated from guide book to love story in a heterosexual transposition. Retracing the improbable plot, the insider realised what the outsiders had always known, 'that everything was against them'. The correctness of the Samian Abbot's appraisal somewhat exonerated Stelios and permitted the tender resignation of a Léhar operetta during a long summer.

——— ——— ———

'The bitter-sweet of a dying love,' Charles summed up.

'My next act, dying not love.' Heinz's laugh spluttered into a wracking cough. 'Daniel insists on dragging me to Paris after a fanciful diagnosis of rheumatism in my shoulder. The pain gets quite nasty.'

A week later Daniel phoned from Paris. 'Heinz was rushed to a clinic for an operation, but it was found that the cancer had spread from the lung to the liver and he was stitched up again. Too late for surgery, he is on chemotherapy and radiation but it won't do any good. He needs you, but is too proud to ask. I'll pay all expenses and lost fees. Please come, Charles.'

Daniel was a close friend, Heinz was unclassifiable yet in some respects closer. Ohli had made no demand on his deathbed, but he was a teacher himself. Charles was not irreplaceable either at the CO or for the son of another Prime Minister, but for Heinz . . .

Heinz slurred his Viennese early in the morning. 'Forgive my ringing, but once they start on me I become too dopey with all that morphine. I quarrelled with Daniel, he had no right to ask you over. It would have been wonderful to die in the arms of the only person who understood me, as far as that's ever possible. Grand opera is not to be as the blessed day may be tomorrow or in a month. Daniel removes sleeping pills to keep me alive for what? I should have made provisions, then I could have asked you for the appointed hour. Neat Puccini, no endless Wagner. A nurse is hovering. Goodbye, Karli.'

Heinz's unprecedented intimacy was natural, the appeal overwhelming. Yet Heinz himself had warned against endlessly hanging about a dying friend, yes friend. Puccini was wrong, Heinz belonged to Alban Berg's *Wozzeck*. A letter might cheer him up, no anodine clichés, a joke about a compromise composer, Richard Strauss's *Death and Transfiguration*, Heinz was musical. He had attained a superficial sophistication, yet Daniel had not bridged the gap despite his money and patience. Charles possessed neither; or, rather, had exhausted both in the amiable winding down, sealed by Stelios's return to the bosom of his unloveable family. Evenings at tavernas ended in an hour at home, too short for friction, too long for the routine. Yet Daniel's grief after Heinz's death indicated that even routine was preferable to loneliness.

———— ————

Philip wrote from Sydney where he had spent the last summer. He proposed meeting next in Italy for some real luxury. One of his Australian directors would attend the Gallipoli Landing celebrations and if Charles put him up in Athens they could then fly together to Frankfurt where the ANZAC had some business and Charles could get a new car. At least a Beetle, the present museum piece wasn't up to foreign parts. Assistance with the purchase was again offered, all travelling expenses were paid. Charles could pick the itinerary to Venice, whence the ANZAC would wing his way home, leaving Charles to the tender mercy of . . .

Going abroad alone, for the whole summer, was a grief that could not be fudged. At long last Stelios shared despair; he had caught a glimpse of the life from which he was now excluded. The picture of Heinz dragging out a wasted life stopped the impulse to protect a lover who accepted defeat as he accepted everything.

———— ————

The utter despair in those soft brown eyes often haunted Charles on the journey that should have been theirs. They could have shared the novelty of driving in a Europe greatly changed since the winter with Eve. The companion was again an Australian, but he was now the passenger and the ambitious itinerary demanded unwonted concentration. The Beetle was baptised Mitzi, in memoriam of the Liechti housekeeper, though the ANZAC smelled romance. He dutifully scribbled down notes for GGG revisions, tried and failed to please, and was abandoned without regret for Philip in Venice.

Recently knighted, Sir Philip appreciated an introduction to Hildegard who had no need to drop names because she lived with them. 'Naturally I rushed over from Trieste to give you the latest family low-down. Max's leg played up, he fell and broke it; hard pavement is unsuitable and he hates selling nappies. Herta hates even more being poor in Vienna where she once reigned as heiress. They are retreating to Carinthia, not the Tarburg, we won't go into that folly, but a flat in a mini castle above Laudorf. Soph finishes at the Ursulines next year and will then marry my Norbert in the Tarburg chapel. Your father might attend as he dotes on Soph, you'll come, of course, reconciliation all round.'

'Trust my family to spoil your scenario, Hildegard.'

The scenario at the villa-hotel on Lake Garda followed the whims of the English owner who accepted guests only on recommendation and probation. Though probably not imposed on Churchill and other stars in the visitors book, lesser mortals shared a fellowship of pretended intimidation. The genuinely rustic rooms and superbly simple food belonged to the pre-war Fechtner lifestyle beyond Stelios's appreciation.

———— ————

He did appreciate the Italian clothes bought by a gnawing conscience and he fell in love with Mitzi. He drove her on weekend excursions when he refrained from questions about their first summer apart and flirted equally deliberately with girls. The heavy winks were a vulgar bore. 'Your pick-up technique was more subtle when we met.'

'Don't you want to get rid of me?' was unanswerable and they drove home in the silence of distrust. Both felt guilty and found solace in physical closeness. Stelios pointed to a white scar on his arm, 'Good not to ask about the summer, but bad not to care sufficiently. A couple on the beach played their radio full blast and when I asked them to turn it down the man stuck a knife into me. His girl was peeling a peach and he wanted to show off. Noise never bothered me. You have influenced me a lot, Charles, and it is hard to go back to my old way of life.'

The spontaneous 'You don't have to' both knew to be untrue.

Even the ambiguity of a patched-up relationship was less painful than Daniel's determined 'Sentiment is dead, long live sex, the more the merrier'. 'More' was a rapidly changing retinue of sailors and soldiers; 'merrier' was the din of bouzouki orchestras in popular tavernas. Compared to that bunch Stelios seemed an intellectual giant. Daniel's invitation for New Year's Eve was an appeal hard to refuse, but he was restricted to one companion at the taverna promising ALL THE DARLINGS OF ATHENS. It sounded grim, was hellish and united Charles and Stelios in revulsion against the inane cacophony. Understanding was further shored up at Easter when Stelios piloted Mitzi over mountains not intended for cars. He showed equal expertise in negotiating the old guidebook formula 'One sleeps with the inhabitants'. Division of labour masterly applied: Stelios for the by-ways of Greece, Philip for the highways of Italy.

— — — —

Italy as well as Charles's family fulfilled expectations. Soph was staying with her grandfather as she wanted to study Garden Architecture; though she had not expressedly rejected Norbert, his mother abandoned hopes of wedding bells.

The chiming transferred from the Tarburg to Athens. Stelios was obviously preoccupied at the first meeting, at the second he came to the point with the bravado of uncertainty. 'My mother has arranged a marriage for me, a house with a flat above a shop. The girl isn't bad, a bit plump, but I'd rather stay with you. I want only one half of what the house is worth, but I must have some security if you throw me out.' The bartered bridegroom apparently thought the price tag not just reasonable but flattering and on receiving congratulations looked as sad as Charles felt at this preposterous finale.

3

'Not Smetana, Mozart for that preposterous auction; a quartet, you, Stelios, his mother and bride. All right for a libretto but too implausible for a novel. Life stranger than fiction . . . I'd better keep such original observations for my lectures.' Ralph was in Athens for a CO lecture.

'You couldn't have come at a more opportune moment. As a novelist you might be able to tell me whether I am relieved or heartbroken.'

'Both, after thirteen stormy years. *Stelios* is written with your heartblood and turning yourself into an unconvincing spinster aggravates the sentimentality. But the way you used that walk in Jerusalem when Artemis was mistaken for your grandmother for a more realistic end than the cut-price offer.' He read from the manuscript,

'To spare them the awkwardness of goodbyes, Stelios pushed to the front of the crowd only after the gangways had been lowered. He was waving his handkerchief long after the others, reluctant to part from . . . he was unable to say what. Another persistent leave-taker sympathised in a very Greek manner. "That girlfriend looked a little old for you." Stelios hesitated and with his eyes still on the receding ship muttered "She is my mother", and abruptly turned away.'

'Which way are you going to turn, Charles?'

——— ——— ———

Not to Irene. She came with her family and the confident husband's 'Old friends must be left alone' was well-founded. For Charles the affair was dead, for her perhaps only buried by her son and daughter. The reminiscences were pleasantly sentimental, the reunion mercifully uncomplicated.

Uncomplicated was the key to the pleasant companionship of Philip, who rebelled, however, against the paucity of luxury hotels in Turkey. Charles continued gathering material for GGG, for the first time alone with Mitzi and not minding the adventure.

For the following summer the Cypriot Ambassador to Athens, whose son Charles was tutoring, guaranteed luxury. He reserved rooms at the best beach hotel and insisted on an audience with the Archbishop-President in view of a GGG for Cyprus.

An awed hotel manager called Charles to the phone; the Minister of the Interior confirmed the audience for the next morning, annoyed but unsurprised that the official invitation had not arrived. Dressed in bathing shorts, Charles drove in the blistering August heat to the island capital; he changed into a silk suit below the presidential palace to the bewilderment of the guards at the first security check point. Though pleased to be addressed correctly, His Beatitude remained cool about a guide book as he did not wish His Island to be swamped by tourists. Mentioning the hush-hush visit during the war of the Cultural Letter might offend, conversation floundered till Charles asked in Greek how the beach and sea were kept so clean. 'Why did you tire Us with English, my child! We shall consult Our Minister of Public Works. More interesting than the questions at the preceding group audience when it was sometimes difficult to distinguish men from women; alas, all too frequent nowadays.' The President bestowed an archiepiscopal blessing, a rare favour on a heretic foreigner.

———— ———— ————

Sir Philip MacLachlan felt that he had better credentials for a private audience with a Head of State and flew back to London. Mitzi was precariously secured on a boat to Istanbul where she was nearly dropped on the quay next to Mimis. He had kept in contact with the American who had kissed the head of Antinous and now gladly put up kindred souls in his house near an American base. He gave useful hints on local dangers, a gang of belly-dancing females on the roads who stunned in more sense than one to rob drivers foolish enough to stop for closer inspection. 'Step on the gas, especially on hearing a shot.'

Charles followed the well-meant advice on the fifteenth of August. Already driven near top speed, Mitzi went into a spin towards a ditch where she turned over. Expectancy not fear dominated the minute of least control, yet he could not retrace how he had been thrown to the stony ground. Mimis was standing on his head inside the car, unable to open the door on his side or move to the other. The shot had been a puncture, no belly-dancing brigands, but when had they last passed a car in this middle of nowhere? At last a speck appeared on the road stretching limitless in both directions. A Citroën 2CV drew up and two young Frenchmen released Mimis from his trap. Charles resisted the temptation to escape from the grime and dust under the torrid sun to a cool, clean hospital bed, but he just knew he must not be hunched up in the two-seater.

Much later he was rolled into a blanket to be stretched out on the back seat of a large car with his legs sticking out of the window. The blood-stained bundle was dumped in a hospital that was neither cool nor clean. A chorus of witches, surely not nurses, neither disinfected the bruises nor brushed away the flies, but sighed like professional mourners. Piercing screams indicated Mimis's mutilation. A doctor then twisted and tickled Charles's toes; satisfied he gesticulated to him to stand up. Lack of a common language slightly facilitated resisting medical authority; shouts dismissing the witches compensated for the doctor's loss of face. Enter Mimis, drenched in sweat, excessive even in the ghastly heat; his dislocated shoulder had been set with wrenches proving more the strength than the skill of the butcher. 'You can't lie forever in this heavenly establishment. Mitzi is a total wreck, whither now, Charles?'

'Show the recommendation from the Ministry of Tourism and demand an ambulance. The window is not too dirty to distinguish a Red Crescent contraption.'

Mimis's perspiration swelled into rivulets. 'I forgot your documents and money in the glove compartment. The nice French boys will drive me back.'

No bandits needed to strip an abandoned car. The horoscope had predicted disaster at seventy, but a broken back, no money or identification papers fitted nicely on the fatal Assumption Day. Brakes screeched, barked commands and a resplendent officer smelling of cleanliness entered. 'You are a journalist' expressed neither accusation nor admiration in faultless German. Mimis must have used the international word; to insist on the superiority of a travel writer wasted time. 'Writing about Turkey qualifies you for a military hospital.' Intended as a favour, Charles remembered the RASC and softened the grateful refusal with compliments on the mastery of German. Privately pleased, professionally hurt, the officer promised an ambulance and left the patient to more black thoughts. In Turkey the military certainly had the best doctors and hospitals . . .

Mimis's perspiration had subsided. The sinister idlers round Mitzi had not entered her though no breaking would have been required. Money and papers safe, more than one could have hoped for. Ensconced in Asia's hottest and narrowest ambulance, Charles received insufficient air and compassion through a slit opening onto the front seat. One French Samaritan volunteered for the hospital chase, the other drove Mimis to the Ankara hotel and received in recognition for patient assistance the now redundant ample travel provisions.

Perspiration, clotted blood, dust and flies during the two hours of stifling confinement before Charles obtained some air, not fresh but air. A white-clad figure claimed in Levantine French that they had arrived at Ankara's leading hospital. The demand for a private room caused the day's most spectacular loss of face. 'We do not have any. We are only a humble establishment. You must go elsewhere.'

'Go' was irritating and where was 'elsewhere'? The University Hospital, so modern that it was still a building site. The stretcher zigzagged round cement mixers and scaffolding to another battle for a private room. Charles was X-rayed, perfunctorily washed, the wounds painfully sterilised. 'The fifth and seventh vertebrae are cracked. Standing up, even sitting, might have induced a break and you would be paralysed. We'll put you into plaster for a couple of months.'

The struggle in three known languages and one unknown was vindicated but not over. Suspension on metal supports was hard on chin and crutch even before three demons began slapping wet plaster from neck to knee in a suffocation/castration competition. Protests were ignored, pain pushed exhaustion into a faint from which he woke to the compassionate clucking of Mimis. Charles joked at the carapace, swallowed some pills and was brought back from very far by the call to prayer. Saracens chained their prisoners to the wall, but he was completely cocooned. The call was curiously cracked, a record, not the stuff of pirates. A nurse washed his face and hands, but shied away from his feet. Instead of goat cheese and olives he obtained dry biscuits before the head of the orthopaedic section justified his position by ordering extension of the plaster up to the chin. The suffocation was so successful that the wet mess was immediately cut down to pre-expert size.

Construction noises orchestrated the American's repentance for the-shot-that-never-was; he had driven up during the night and would deal with the Turkish insurance company and customs as foreign cars were entered in the owners' passports to ensure re-export. In the struggle with bureaucracy he would liaise with the local CO tracked down by Mimis though only a skeleton staff withstood the Ankara summer. A helpful skeleton offered intervention by the British Consulate as there was as yet no Australian and 'Officialdom will be required. We are in the Orient.' He brought a forbidden bottle of whisky and entrusted the patient to a permissible cheer. A vision of beauty, the dietitian inquired in perfect Bostonian after culinary preferences. 'Something light' resulted in white beans with raw onions. The Turkish taxpayers' money had perhaps been spent in a callisthenic institute and without her intervention the 'heavy' evening meal was digestible. A weight-lifter hauled the plaster on to a bedpan, a nurse administered a painkiller and left sleeping pills. Seemingly unnecessary after the frantic activity in total immobility.

Overstimulation slid from immediate to longer-range worries. The first horoscope had set no date for the disaster and the second might have indicated around 1970 – only two years off – not the age. The physicians had never expressedly excluded paralysis; sleeping pills might yet be the answer, he was tired, very tired of the 'constant struggle'. Calls to prayer further fragmented sleep till the cleaning woman began sweeping dust from one corner to the other. A thump on the plaster attracted her attention, she looked in alarm at Charles's window-washing gestures towards the grimy panes and fled leaving bucket and broom to be fetched, but not used, by a male. Failed pantomime started the discomfort, incomprehension and pain, but also the combined efforts of the American, the skeleton and the British Consul that obtained a miraculously swift insurance payment, albeit in non-convertible lire. Mimis grew restive despite his culture–sex equation; museums were near, 'Poor boys in want of an outlet' even nearer in the adjoining wards. The pun of 'Flight to Athens' was not allowed to grow stale; lire were not accepted for foreign travel and the Anglo-American alliance was revived to convert Mitzi's bloodmoney into six plane seats removed for the stretcher and Mimis's ticket.

At dawn Charles shamed the nurse washing the openings in the carapace by conjuring up Greek derision of Turkish neglect. He then signed papers absolving the staff of responsibility for his escaping their care. Heaved, hauled, pushed and pulled, he was carried from the second plane when one of the porters suggested the easy solution. 'The stretcher is so heavy, it'll bump down the steps on its own.' Certitude that no foreigner understood Greek was demolished by idiomatic curses extending over several generations. The stretcher steadied before Christl and the CO Director who looked horrified and supervised removal by yet another ambulance.

————

Christl had reserved a private room in the leading hospital; all apertures were washed without play on national rivalries. Daily small tips were the Turkish custom, but never any clumsy hints as from the attendant wheeling Charles to the X-ray chamber. At the end of such a day, Greedy did himself out of a princely tip when the patient was forthwith cut out of the frightful encasement. Comments on the medical backwardness in certain countries were followed by stern warnings not to sit up or even lift the head for a month; rolling from side to side was sufficient freedom. Though far from the luxury of the childhood clinic, the removal of the language barrier helped through minor annoyances, dizziness and nausea while he was relearning to walk. Flowers cheered, except the costliest arrangement brought by the stockbroker's private secretary who cursorily mentioned the delay 'Only a day' in executing a sale and reluctantly admitted the considerable loss incurred. The Minister urged action, but in Charles's odd accountancy this was payment – cheap at that – for escaping paralysis. Daniel's splendid gladioli were reminders that beach and bouzoukia were still compensation for three months spent at Heinz's bedside. Christl coloured the convalescence with her Catholicism, practising like Marie Louise, not preaching. She embodied the common background so consolingly that the fifteen-year gap ceased to matter while a similar age difference had emphasised the incompatibility with Stelios. He fitted neither into the realities nor the escapism of a bedridden patient and was not informed of the accident.

A tight corset deflected from sex but assisted the writing of a coffee-table *Greece*. The review in the *Economist* resulted in an invitation to the weekly Bank of Greece luncheon, on Thursday, as at the Liechti, but with twice the number of guests. Charles's conversation with the lady on his left was interrupted by 'I am the Lesbian' boomed by the bishop on his right which stopped idle chatter till the financiers remembered that bishops bore the names of their sees.

—— —— —— ——

Eastern hospitalisation made original table talk during a very Western fortnight with Philip in London. Culture and friends differed little from thirty years earlier, but a car was purchased and business discussed with Gulden. 'Mr Greece, I believe. That's what you are called after your fourth book. Unfair competition, considering you collected the material for GGG. No hard feelings, even an author must live, though sometimes . . . Sorry about your accident, I appreciate you never mentioned hospital expenses, not in the contract. Good job *Turkey*, new subtitle *Famous Places I Never Visited*. Better write about the places you do visit this summer, from France to Yugoslavia.'

Philip enjoyed variations of luxury tourism like Mitzi II's stately progress through the Loire Valley, where he teased Charles about his Valois obsession. The vague familiarity with a region not seen in this life crystallised at Blois Castle into the *déjà vu* certainty felt in childhood at the Louvre. While the guide extolled the ingenuity of fitting doors invisibly into the panelling, Charles made straight for the secret stairway from the last Valois king's bedchamber.

—— —— —— ——

The bedchamber in Vienna was less familiar, as one wing of the

Palais Schwarzenberg had only recently been converted into Austria's grandest hotel. Yet here the connection was obvious, as Charles had been initiated into his favourite sport in the *palais* riding school.

The essential connection had, however, disappeared. The site of Mother's tomb was disfigured by two modernistic monuments. Against memory and reason Charles searched in ever-widening circles, could not locate Great-Grandmother's tomb either, and was informed at the cemetery administration that the fee due every twenty-five years had not been paid and that after the five-year period of grace the monument had been sold to a marble cutter and the urn to an undertaker. The ashes, well, when nobody claims them . . .

He had failed Mother again and ignorance of cemetery finance was no excuse. Strange that the Grandparents had shown no concern, but they had been preoccupied with their burial place near the convent, had been too old for the long drive to the Central Cemetery, had likewise neglected Great-Grandmother's grave. But a bomb had disposed of her children while Charles had never doubted that he would join Mother in her resting place. He left his mimosa where that had been. Father had not cared about the tomb of the first wife when he came to Vienna to divorce the second and was living with the third. Herta might have assumed that sacred ground remained dedicated in perpetuity. Charles did not try to shift the blame but, having lost the miraculous communication only possible from Mother's grave, the only other held no significance. The Grandparents' tomb, certainly well-attended by the sisters, would make pain and loneliness unbearable.

The spiritual link with youth had snapped, the material was better left alone. From the outside the Liechti seemed unchanged since the Nazi 'embellishment' but Charles would not enter the HOME OF THE SALVATION ARMY. Instead he took Philip to the Museum of Modern Art opposite, not visited when still the Liechtenstein Gallery housing Europe's most prestigious private collection; too late for regrets when he rushed through exhibits that gave him the creeps, symbolising unattractively the loss of what had been. Yet on the surface Vienna had miraculously recovered and Philip enjoyed the touristy reflection of the Imperial past, including tea with a princess too poor to go on a vacation. He jokingly commiserated at the farewell dinner that Charles's heart belonged to the Habsburgs, his spirit to the Valois, his religion to Rome, his friends were in London, his finances in America, his work and sex in Athens; too many homes did not make a real home.

Home was almost real at Lis's despite their second and longer separation. 'The couch is rather a come-down from the Schwarzenberg four-poster. Too narrow for Erwein, he isn't as slim as you, and believes if he doesn't sleep here Titi won't know we sleep together. Absurd, she knows we couldn't marry because he was Jewish and now can't leave his American wife because of their children. They think he's old Hungarian nobility, hilarious. Paul Zobel preaches at St Stephen's, he is my confessor and coming to dinner.'

Paul had not talked to anyone about the Samos command. 'A thin line between Resistance and treason. I was, after all, an officer. The boatloads of females I captured kept the SS quiet, though they suspected me. But not having been involved in the disappearance of our bloodthirsty schoolmate, believed drowned. Instant Divine Justice!'

'And Panagiotis?'

'The Virgin's Grace, according to the Abbot.'

——— ———

Though the Austrian and the Greek cleric must have had some revealing discussions, the Stelios imbroglio was reserved for Otto. 'You demand too much, Karli. You give a lot but few are able to reciprocate. Dolly could – marry her. My doctor found some bomb splinters wandering near the heart. She'll be a wealthy widow, even after a decent legacy to you. You won't be able to buy back the Liechti, now worth a hundred times more than what you got. But as tax lawyer I've defrauded the state of millions and this flat is sufficient to entertain on the post-war level.'

Dolly appeared only at dinner, delighted by the sincere congratulations on her looks. 'Otto forces me into the most expensive beauty crazes. He is a very generous . . . husband.'

Otto switched a little too casually to the successes of Ernst. 'He is an excellent Burgtheater Director and Parliament will vote a *Lex Häussermann* to enable him to write a *Matura* thesis. He handles politicians admirably.'

——— ———

Hildegard handled the family adroitly. 'Laudorf is on a scenic route to Yugoslavia, so it's natural for you to drop in. Herta hopes you'll stay a few days, play it by ear.'

Herta threw her arms round Charles's neck; she did not embrace him, she clung to him in the admission of failure. One glance recalled the certainty of never again meeting at the Tarburg where they had last parted. Now she was the tenant of a flat in a castle smaller than one wing of the Tarburg. No more the Lady of the Manor, she cultivated a grace that had been natural to Mother; Max had aged considerably, limping about on a stick. They acted fondness in the stilted manner of old plays, had perhaps even persuaded themselves to make misfortune bearable. Yet they complicated the simple household by every conceivable divergence in taste, food and drink. She cooked one elaborate dish at midday, for dinner it was cold meats and salads, but she dressed in her outmoded evening gowns while her menfolk did not bother with ties. She attended the Lutheran Service, patronised the pastor and invited him to the annoyance of Max. She over-emphasised differences and treated the char woman with a consideration occasionally lacking towards her guests.

Hildegard received no thanks for the reconciliation as outwardly distance alone was responsible for the long separation. She was family and took part in the condemnation of Father's inequities. Max was the most inarticulate and, therefore, most violent. 'Not content with turning Soph against her parents, he prevented her union with your Norbert.'

'Norbert did visit her at Abbey Court but she had lost interest. You are furious because my brother married an Anholt, perhaps to atone for his misconduct with Australian Eve.' No diverting Max from 'Soph's enslavement by a wicked grandfather among the Tarburg silver and furniture'.

Retention of the chattel under whatever agreement was shabby, but Charles protested against 'enslavement'. Father domineered but respected his children's own way to hell. The novelty of defending Father was matched by Herta's praise of Tania who had donated Reichenbach furniture for the tiny guest room. She played in Switzerland as well as at the Landtheater and Karl must call on her on his next visit to Austria.

———————

A weekend at Laudorf, preceded by two with Lis in Vienna, became the norm after the annual summer travels before the final leap back to Athens. Spain, Morocco and Tunisia were explored intensively for GGG, with Philip on the luxury level, more adventurously with Robert or Mimis, who were presented to Lis. She organised highly pleasing cultural and social programmes, but scandalised Dolly's party for the Dancing School survivors, mostly matrons. 'Karl isn't all museums and ruins. When I stayed with him last Christmas he took me to the brothel district in Piraeus. Mitzi got stuck in the throng of customers and a huge female hung her tit through the car window. Playful rather than lustful.' The matrons speculated on Mitzi – such a vulgar name.

Lis's shocker was due to nervousness about a check up. Her

grandmother and an aunt had died of cancer, and she dreaded the gynaecologist's annual examination. Given the all-clear, she celebrated with Charles at a restaurant in the Vienna Woods where she remembered a proposal made twenty years ago. 'I'm well ahead of Dolly as she isn't yet on the market though she would like to be. She has wanted to marry you since you trod on her toes at the Dancing School. She'll be a wealthy widow, but she can't laugh like we do. Erwein pretends senile passion for old times sake but he can't make an honest woman of me. That's up to you when you grow tired of your Moroccans. Some look rather stunning on these coloured photos, I'm almost envious. If they don't do you in before you are seventy, then I'll be your fatal accident.'

—— —— —— ——

The seven candles on the birthday cake flickered and one went out. Max looked much older than his father at the memorable eightieth birthday celebration, copied by the Laudorfs in a minor key on Austrian champagne that imparted no sparkle to parochialism.

No longer able to drive, Max talked about cars, his true love, on the road to a Benedictine Abbey whose school he had briefly disgraced. Leaning heavily on his brother-in-law, he limped up the church steps and both knelt before an altar of the Virgin. The Abbot insisted on giving them coffee, a Tarburg was a Tarburg, though a very different one on the drive home. 'Mama would have been pleased to see us today; perhaps she did. She had little joy from her children, we've been . . . bad Catholics. Yet the prayer today . . . don't wait too long, Karl.' Spiritually he was closer to his brother-in-law than he could ever be to his wife.

Brother and sister managed to heave Max onto his bed when he stumbled over a carpet. The doctor ordered complete rest for a week, but there was no cause for the Countess to miss her bridge party. Keeping the patient company proved oddly awkward after their brief closeness and Charles suggested a book. 'Papa never stopped reading, so I rather took against it. Better tell me what you have written.' His interest lay, however, in what was not written, the handling of Mitzi.

'Before every trip I devour the handbook and the moment I close it I've forgotten all that mechanical crap. Chronological tables are my line, though Father doubted a date in the Pelopennesian War. I sent him my latest book.'

Max was not to be sidetracked into an unknown war. 'I suppose Soph wrote to you, he uses her as secretary. I would like to see Soph once more before I die; I love her, Herta doesn't. Despite the feud with my elder brother, we attended his daughter's wedding to a cousin so she is now a princess. Herta is absurdly envious since Soph is unlikely to find a prince in England. Certainly not through Eugen's wife who is still with her Major while her only son talks like a prole. Herta won't have him in the house, though it isn't the poor lad's fault that his mother ran away. My sister is still man-hunting and resists retirement to a very posh home paid for by Ludwig. It's easier to confess my family's sins than my own.' Max's gloom was understandable and justified.

———————

Justified by a letter from Herta.

'. . . After your departure Max became unmanageable. His leg was X-rayed, another fracture. The White Mafia clamped and nailed it together for a third time, but the Ruskies smashed it up too expertly. Worse, he has lost all desire to live and, though I spend all day in hospital, he longs for Soph. Ludwig has written to her, otherwise Father might suspect a trick to get her here . . .'

No appeal for useless help since she knew that her brother had launched a Literature Course that tickled his fancy as well as his listeners'; society ladies thrilled to the private lives of poets more than to their works. A broken leg was less grave than Heinz's cancer . . . and just as terminal. Herta's next letter started with the improvement after Soph's arrival.

'. . . Max doted on her and had got up despite all the silver-mongery in his leg. She seemed fond of her father, yet after a couple of weeks the horrid girl left and he gave up. He withdrew into himself, probably didn't even notice that I was glued to his bedside. Then his hot water bottle burst and flooded the bathroom in the flat. That was the last straw, and I was hysterical. Max died the same night. He would have liked you to be at the funeral service, he had become attached to you, but communications between Athens and Laudorf are abominable. I cry a lot and Christmas will be very lonely . . .'

The relief that she would not be alone was audible. Herta would love to come for a fortnight; crying at long-distance rates was silly and she hung up.

'That you cry a bit yourself helps enormously. I'll get out of this awful mourning and they'll have to put up with me in black and white at Laudorf. Max wouldn't have been shocked.' His virtues, Soph's vices and the White Mafia dominated the do-you-remember, interrupted by dinners with Christl and the Minister. Herta departed if not consoled at least recovered.

———— ——

Lis needed consolation to recover.

'. . . Herta is right about the White Mafia pronouncing me fit and removing my what–not six months later. Not that you'll miss it when we get married. The operation was supposedly successful, so we might celebrate with better reason next summer. Erwein says in America I could sue. Otto will go before me, he looks awful, though Dolly does her best, she is used to nursing . . .'

By summer Lis's zest for life and amusement had recovered to match her healthy appearance. The usual pleasure round was resumed with Titi and her fiancé 'whose *von* is exactly ten times older than Erwein's.' Canon Zobel added a politico–religious gloss at St Stephen's where he celebrated the Latin Mass before a side altar in conservative opposition to Vatican II. Returning from a shopping expedition into the countryside, Lis dropped a jar and splashed her frock with beetroot pickles in a place and colour hard to laugh away.

Herta laughed away her past contrariness that had long complicated domesticity; the Lutheran pastor, tea and red wine disappeared from the table, but she still smoked two packets of cigarettes per day. After the memorial service on Max's birthday, Charles bit his tongue not to ask the obvious when she insisted that life without her dear husband was a bore. She had nursed him so many years that she was joining the Red Cross; Charles suspected that it was partly a compensation for having been forbidden to serve in the Nursing Corps during the War. They got on as well as in Athens and made plans for a future summer holiday.

———— ——

Charles and Philip favoured Morocco for all that is desirable in a summer journey. They were lunching by the pool of a beach hotel when a worried manager announced that shots had been heard from the adjoining Summer Palace where the King was celebrating his birthday. Ghoulish 'Arab Experts' dwelt on the murder of the Iraqi Monarch and Charles decided on the dash back to the comfort of their rooms at the Rabat Hilton. Philip was so nervous on the wide detour back to the capital that a couple of tranquillisers was all he could swallow for dinner. The French news broadcast kept him within the Hilton grounds for the next days: NCO cadets, supposedly doped, had taken the King and his guests prisoners, killed some at random including the Belgian ambassador, yet on regaining full consciousness threw themselves at the King's feet and begged for mercy. 'Undated *Arabian Nights* rank definitely low. I'll enjoy my seventieth summer in British safety which will bore me to death.'

A relief, as the following summer required Eastern travels which Philip would have disliked even twenty years earlier. Gulden appointed Charles to an unprecedented ninth area editorship which necessitated extensive driving through Turkey and Iran. Herta sprang to it like the lioness in *The Domain of the Silver Lion*, a favourite childhood adventure story set in those very parts. She had recovered most of her spirits, some of her interests and craved adventure. Being locked together in the car might strain brotherly love so she approved of meeting on the Turkish coast only for the outward trek to Tehran where Robert would take her place.

4

Sisterly love might have sprung from nobler motives than quarrels with the remaining family, but Herta had always been brave and no one would be a better companion for the wildest parts of their childhood reading. There was no GGG justification for crossing on his own Mount Olympus; except on a timber cart, no tourist would attempt the ruts of a dirt track interspersed with naked rock. The silence of the rugged mountain was awe-inspiring, all the more when Mitzi III, a souped-up Escort, stopped between two majestic firs. A nimble goat would have outrun first gear; overheating required patience. Twilight was falling, not of the gods but of a long, tiring June day. Wolves were a possibility at this altitude, sheep dogs were just as fierce. After twiddling knobs and wires without conviction, Charles knelt down and prayed. Mitzi purred and ploughed on as befited her one year, but Charles had been shocked into awareness of his fifty-six. If he couldn't outgrow his boyhood, at least wait for an equally retarded sister. 'Saved in the nick of time' must not be tempted wilfully. He had three weeks to relax at a Turkish beach resort before meeting Herta, who was coming by boat from Cyprus to Mersin. If she was adventurous sensible risks might be taken.

———— ————

She was never put to the test as all flights to Cyprus had stopped after the airport had been bombed. The Greek Army had overthrown the Archbishop-President who fled for his life to the British base. The Turks retaliated by invading Northern Cyprus and war seemed imminent. International communications were cut, especially near Mersin, the invasion port. Charles eventually got through to the hotel chosen for meeting Herta, only to be told that it served as Army HQ. He hung on just outside the prohibited zone though most of the news was incomprehensible and the rest alarming. His passport and driving licence showed that he resided in Greece and the leisurely weeks scheduled for the drive to Tehran could not be whittled down to less than one. No silly risks on the longest journey alone.

Military convoys choked the coastal road and forced Charles up a peaceful valley. Deceptively idyllic, as countless warriors had followed the little stream in which the Emperor Frederick Barbarossa drowned during the Third Crusade. Charles was off on historical fantasies that only Otto had shared though Herta might have been interested in the sites and sights towards the Black Sea. Despite the constant drizzle, Charles plunged dutifully into the muddy water from a hotel impervious to his languages.

Along the coastal road the rain grew heavier and the rivers higher. The bridges barely rose above the numerous streams and the widest had swept the iron spans from the stone pylons to a sand bar; only minutes earlier, as Mitzi soon stood at the head of a line of cars at the terrifying torrent. Some remarkably stoic lorry drivers returned to a mountainous junction with the unpaved central axis to Iran. The mountains loomed sinister through the steady rain, Mitzi was low-slung and advice at a police station was contradictory in sign language. The most dramatic 'Saved in the nick of time' must not be hazarded on saving a mere 1,000 kilometres.

Herta would not have laughed at the enormous detour in the torrid heat, but she would have navigated along the line drawn on the map of Tehran. Since he was arriving from the north, the Queen Elizabeth in the northern suburbs had been chosen not only on monarchist grounds; but any slowing down to consult the map provoked a bedlam of hooting and shouting. Driving around in circles lacked the attraction of sightseeing, two cars crashed, nobody hurt, but the shouting! Charles drew up and engaged a taxi to fray the path to the Aoun Elspet as finally comprehended. Robert, punctual on three continents, had not arrived nor did his Athens flat reply to a call from the local CO office. The Archaeological Museum was splendid, the crown jewels were not, caviar was as expensive as elsewhere, the visas for the speediest return to Laudorf were stamped in the passport; Tehran became unnerving in the frustration of waiting and a note left with the receptionist named a hotel in Shiraz.

A surprising number of drivers had likewise wakened at 3 a.m. to avoid the traffic chaos and after crossing the vast town the road south-east was dotted with wrecked cars. In the grey dawn morale fell to nadir with a sharp clatter reminiscent of Eve's car. Sudden silence failed to reassure, as rusty tubing several metres back indicated that Mitzi had lost some of her vitals, hopefully non-vital. Even puns soothed when faced with mechanics that vindicated Max. If it was the exhaust, would poisonous fumes prevent progress to the next garage? After the emptiest stretch of desert a repair shop soldered on the metal at record cost and speed.

The Persian poets must have spent weeks not merely twelve hours in the gruelling desert to find the rose-gardens of Shiraz remarkable. But they had been properly housed, while the recommended hotel was locked and barred. Faced by this slip-up, Robert would surely make for the best hotel like Charles who, nevertheless, tried for hours to ring the Queen Elizabeth, only to verify that he lacked the luck required for long-distance calls in the orient. The switchboard operator was tipped generously and on the second day connected. Mr Nuttall arrived the next morning, Mr Fenton had left. Charles immediately rang the Shiraz hotel that had apparently closed down. The gentleman was very cross, he was told, and had left for Tabriz, yes Tabriz.

Robert must have been in a hysterical rage to ruin every chance of meeting by rushing to the opposite corner of Iran. Travelling by bus through the wilds of Anatolia was worse than alone in Mitzi. The GGG itinerary had to be observed as well as the no-risk intention which had yielded nothing but trouble. No driving on the fatal Assumption Day, though wasting a day in a border village was a heavy concession to superstition. The Turkish roads seemed even more rutted and quickly shook off the exhaust. The mistake of spurning military assistance with the cracked spine was not repeated over Mitzi's loose bowels. A wave of the Ministry of Tourism recommendation at the barracks of Agri procured an NCO keener on airing his German than supervising another soldering though he kicked the behind of the mechanic who pointed his blow-torch towards the front tyre.

Next GGG duty-call: Lake Van on a 'non-stabilised' road, justifying the funny name by loose gravel that imposed a snail's pace. The weakened front tyre gave up with a whimper, not a bang, Mitzi III went into a slow-motion spin and settled on her roof in a neighbouring field. A disgusted 'Not again' was acerbated by the undeserved retribution for the kick in the mechanic's behind. So much for trying to cheat the Assumption Day malediction. Not yet a scratch marred his headstand and, except for her shattered windscreen, Mitzi looked similarly intact.

So close to the border the road was regularly patrolled. An officer put a guard on Mitzi in her unorthodox stance and hailed a civilian lorry to which Charles transferred his considerable luggage before squeezing between two bearded villains who eyed his gold wristwatch with disquieting admiration. The suspicion of highway robbery had caused the first accident and might now round off the second. Mimis's 'Sexual attack is the best defence against Orientals' was unworkable on two fronts even without shock, age, heat, smell and every conceivable impediment. The Ministry recommendation caused headshakes, but official seals and stamps disunited the villains as far as the hotel at Agri, surely a penal settlement. Charles had hardly washed off the dust, miraculously no blood, when no less than a Major proposed to have the car towed to the very garage that had so efficiently fixed the exhaust. Delivery of a windscreen from Ankara required at best three weeks.

'At best' was not a warning but a slip in otherwise correct French, but reliance on the negligent mechanic violated the 'No silly risks' on the thousands of kilometres through Turkey and the Balkans to Herta. He was sound but unlikely to remain sane biting his nails at Agri, he had no all-inclusive insurance to cover the unpredictable expense and Charles donated a second car to the Turkish Republic. The incredulous officer blamed such frivolous waste on shock, the polite word for lunacy, but promised to help with official papers and to secure the best seat on the through bus to Istanbul; thirty-eight hours, no domestic flights, war with Greece seemed still likely.

The prospect of war-time Agri almost justified abandoning a perfectly good car. The luggage had to be adjusted to his reduced circumstances and Charles held a jumble sale of non-essentials that netted just enough for the hotel bill and the bus ticket. He then gladly shook the dust from the pair of sandals he had not sold.

——— ———

How could Robert by his own free will travel by bus? Charles's hellish conveyance broke down to oriental wailing and restarted to martial music; war had probably broken out. The parody of music was aggravated by incomprehensible harangues; the driver refused the appeal to turn down the amplifier by taking both hands off the wheel and putting them under one cheek to mimic sleep all too realistically. Yet sleep enfolded men, women and chickens while Charles longed for the tranquillity of the journey to Baghdad before radios sweetened bus journeys.

On arrival in Istanbul the irritations of two endless nights exploded into an overwhelming desire for the peace of Laudorf. The horoscope's 'constant struggle' was true to form; no external flights and no sleeper on the only express passing through Carinthia. The car donation had not been endorsed by the customs at Agri and the Istanbul office was not competent. On the strength of his recommendation Charles demanded to see the director. Mr Barbarosh was impressed, offered coffee and confirmed that Agri was the place. Not for Charles; no bribe was too expensive to avoid the abominable return journey, yet a shot into the dark broke the deadlock. Beside the Emperor, a ruthless pirate who commanded the Turkish navy had been nicknamed Barbarossa; could Barbarosh be a derivation? 'You descend probably from the glorious victor of the battle of Preveza' left the director momentarily speechless. 'Even in Turkey few know of Barbarosh Pasha – but an Australian!'

The Australian pulled out all the stops till a clerk was ordered to make the required passport endorsement; his refusal proved that Turkey was a democracy of bureaucratic tyranny. A more docile official scribbled half a page, not the suspected order to the firing squad but to the frontier customs. The blood of pirates defeated even bureaucracy.

After a meal in the dining car, Charles stretched himself out in the empty first-class compartment. He awoke when a second passenger was joined by a third on the opposite bench; the instalment of a fourth on Charles's side was foiled by a rage worthy of Ohli which drove the intruder back to the third class. Exhaustion ceded to rows and worries, yet the customs official barely glanced at the passport of the once again solitary first-class traveller. The triumph of history turned into a waste of energy.

Bulgarian functionaries and their wives in the obese Communist mould devoured huge chunks of meat and cheese. Despite the assurance that the dining car would continue all through the Balkans it had remained in Turkey; the Sofia station buffet refused Turkish lire for coffee and a sandwich but would accept a $50 travellers cheque, no change on such suspicious paper. Communist blackmail drove a hungry and especially thirsty Charles back to his compartment where a new overweight lot were munching contentedly. The gorging comrades ignored the starving capitalist who was not yet so thin as to be transparent. After forty hours of dehydration and starvation, a Shylock reincarnation accepted a bundle of lire for bottled water and one sandwich. 'To Each According To His Need' was Marxist doctrine.

———————

After the long ride from the station, the taxi arrived at Laudorf in time for breakfast; when Herta returned from the Red Cross her brother had eaten the larder bare and was willing to interrupt sweet sleep for an hour. 'As we are bidden to the Tarburg, I'll keep the horror stories for Ludwig and Hildegard. You were spared quite a lot!'

'And so were you, though you certainly had a handful. When the planes to Cyprus were cancelled, I returned to Laudorf and a nasty pain became ever nastier. I thought it was appendicitis, lay down and hoped I'd die.'

'As district vice-president of the Red Cross you ought to know of less painful ways.'

'The pain became too much, I called an ambulance and was cut open. Besides the appendix the White Mafia removed a growth, benign but they want a follow-up operation. If it's benign why waste money and I won't have a stinking artificial exit.'

'A brilliant piece of Greek logic. Unless you promise me to have the operation I'll have you certified. Surely Ludwig will co-sign the application and I'm an old hand with loonies.'

'All right, I promise. I'll give you a power of attorney at my bank and have already named you my heir, except for Mother's jewels that are part of Soph's statutory one-third. She'll get some even earlier as she has become engaged. Could be worse, Lord Peter Montaubert. The first Marquess was beheaded in the Civil War' set the seal of approval.

————

Marital expectation animated Lis. 'I'm glad sex had no part in your Anatolian misadventures. You wouldn't hide it from your confidante of forty years. You'll misbehave in Morocco whenever you must, next summer while I have all the latest tests in the States, Erwein pays. I'll retire at sixty and Dolly is a very good reason not to wait much longer if Otto is as ill as he looks. They are driving back specially to see you.'

Dustsheets still covered the furniture and, when Dolly opened the wall-cabinet, bottles and glasses cascaded with sickening crashes to the floor. Otto laughed into the shocked silence. 'Broken waste, superbly symbolical. Only salvage a second-rate sherry to toast those who are about to die.'

Instead of hypocritical remonstrating, Lis allocated the macabre probabilities. 'In the competition of bomb splinters, cancer and two major car accidents, Dolly seems the likely survivor.'

'. . . I proposed, Dolly disposed. Otto died from the splinters as expected, but unexpectedly left millions – of debt. He speculated heavily to leave more to his wife and you, no life insurance considered him a justifiable risk. And we wondered why he kept quiet about you marrying Dolly! Grim irony that his labours were as vain as her wasting youth and womanhood. She couldn't face poverty and washed down the right dose of sleeping pills with the same second-rate sherry. Paul conducted the funeral service at the Barovsky Castle, now to be auctioned after six hundred years in the family. "Accursed generation" is a bit melodramatic but I can't find a more suitable word. We are thinning out alarmingly . . .'

At four score and ten the demise of the Minister surprised less than his last will. The housekeeper shrieked with grief at the funeral of her beloved master and cursed him on learning that most of the fortune was left to the family's place of origin with the proviso of his bust in the municipal garden. Not as much as a memento for Charles whose devoted friendship had not escaped Russian attention; he refused to write about the Minister for the Russian Encyclopaedia, as he was never more anti-Communist than after starvation in Bulgaria. Soviet editors were in any case unlikely to publish the eulogy of a Westernised Greek whose circle of diplomats opposed everything Communism arrived to impose. Death was more natural among his contemporaries than Charles's. Soon only Christl survived from a generation of civilised cosmopolitans.

Philip had contributed to the war effort from a safe distance and had not been toughened in the common European suffering. Perhaps he was just ripe to be pushed by a few faintly heard shots into a greedy, grumpy senility. No more summer journeys; would Charles, therefore, return the balance of the travel expense account? If he ever came to London, a bed would be found.

Philip had always been 'With it' and Alzheimer was fashionable. Cowardice was sad enough an end to an irreplaceable friendship.

Another, less regretted, revived, sort of. Without a car Charles went again to the closer though now polluted beach where Stelios had deployed his pick-up technique. Surely the balding, paunchy quintuagenerian had no such intentions when edging his bath towel closer. He shifted to reveal the scar of the burn, and when he took off his sunglasses the lovely brown eyes lit up with the joy of their best days. Intuitively they re-enacted their first encounter, swimming and diving before speaking. Stelios started with the same words, affirming the impression made on a lazy memory. He had taken over his father's carpenter's shop after the usual family quarrels. He often came for a quick dip on *their* beach, before the meal with his wife and two sons. Would Charles be his guest at *their* taverna one evening?

Stelios enquired eagerly after old friends while never mentioning his own; his family he dismissed cursorily 'What you'd expect'. His great passion was sailing, so he was now building a house far inland. He laughed at the illogicality, realised only thanks to Charles who had influenced him in so many ways. He lingered, till reminded that his wife would resent his missing the last bus even more than his mother had.

The return of the native was providential as Stelios, experienced in the transport of furniture, could organise efficiently the move to a flat. The old was the dowry of the owner's daughter, yet though Charles disliked leaving the Kolonaki quarter that held so many memories, the two rooms next to the ancient stadium were in easy walking distance from the CO; on the third floor, no lift, but grandly termed a penthouse because of the large terrace with a splendid view over the National Gardens and the Acropolis. Stelios donated a couch which he proposed using forthwith.

'The personalised inauguration does not befit our middle age.'

'You've hardly changed, except for your reading glasses. I look older, with this paunch since I stopped smoking. Emphysema, I should have listened to you in Rhodes, not have waited for doctor's orders. Working on the couch I hoped we'll try it out together, but I understand.' He hesitated. 'You have taught me certain things, tastes. Couldn't you introduce me? . . . I know I'll have to pay.'

Pimping for a lover who had preferred a dowry was satisfactorily original.

——— ———

The dilemma posed by Titi's letter was desperately unoriginal.

'. . . The specialist arranged by Erwein gave Mummy only a few months. She wanted to die in Vienna and is now here in hospital. You aren't to see what she looks like and in any case you couldn't do anything useful. She is marvellously cheerful, but wonders occasionally if there isn't a curse on your generation . . .'

Lis and Heinz, divided so completely in life, united by the same illness and thought in death. Charles must disregard the sensible selflessness of the childhood confidante and future wife. He telephoned Titi who reiterated between sobs that his coming would upset Mummy. Nor was he to attend the funeral, she wished for no preference over Otto.

Since Charles had failed Mother's outstretched arms, he had been prevented from assisting those he loved in their last hour. To spare him or to spare themselves a traumatic farewell. He had eased Panagiotis's last moments, but then he had been the cause of the sailor's death.

————————

Herta fatalistically resigned from foreign travels, but Titi had to be helped through her first summer holiday alone and was integrated on the ambitious GGG itinerary which required a car. The previous two had been bought in London but Philip's hospitality had become almost as doubtful as a welcome by Father. As he was in his mid-nineties a polite enquiry about a visit to Abbey Court was ventured but found no more grace that the accompanying book.

'Instead of writing superficially on so many countries, you should concentrate on one theme as I have done in my *Notion of Justice in International Relations*, just finished. It might have been interesting to discuss certain aspects with you, but on second thoughts a meeting is not desirable . . .'

The interesting discussion would be with Herta about first thoughts and whether the notion of justice stopped short of family relations.

The letter to Philip was returned with a note from his executor asking where the legacy of £1,000 should be paid. Less than the refund of the travel account! The Anti-Midas touch was Philip's term for Charles's unprofitable investments and might have inspired the 'joke' of this insultingly shabby inheritance; but not the complete neglect by the Minister. Finances required consultation with the Swiss Bank, so a Fiesta was ordered for delivery in Zurich; the account executive was, however, not available until September. Zurich also held memories of Cousin Kurt, but the only Auer in the telephone directory pleaded ignorance.

Mitzi IV was leaner and meaner as befitted post-Philip travelling, but he was missed more for his witty than his material contributions. In Morocco a car radio was an invitation to thieves; instead fertile imagination intertwined historical and personal fancies on the long lonely drive while collecting new impressions.

The most sensational was unprintable, at least by GGG. Mimis was whisked from Casablanca airport to the least touristy of the Atlantic beaches where a restaurant opened inland by a French woman and her young Moroccan lover was much talked about. Neither location nor food, least of all the five cells sharing one toilet, justified the exquisite guests and their expensive cars. Personnel was, however, plentiful, youths from a tender to a robust age lounging about in the courtyard and garden. 'They are all thieves,' Madame's bedridden mother instructed the newcomers. 'Leave all valuables with me, it's safe under my mattress. I'll give you a receipt. Keep only what you need for the callers, all night is double tariff. The windows are barred and always lock your room. In between come and talk to me. My daughter is besotted.'

Madame pretended that the customers came for her cooking and presided over the meals served by boys recovering from and for their basic functions. Table talk was on finance and politics, but after her withdrawal the merits of the locals were compared. Round-the-clock action was broken by meals but continued into sleep.

The horoscope's 'disintegration into sensuality' soon bored by a surfeit and Charles drove some favourites to the beach, envied by their brothers and cousins; few clients wasted time on an outing which was repaid by a faint human touch to strict professionalism. Mimis remained single-minded, 'Single is hardly the word and at my rate of consumption it's more expensive here than at a luxury hotel. While you were swimming the headman of the village set himself up at the entrance and tried to levy a tax on the boys who all jumped over the terrace railing. Trade halted till the greedy tax-gatherer gave up; his village is anyway inordinately wealthy as the wages of sin are easy money for vigilant parents. I did some social research and as a Greek I almost understand the oriental mind. So I'll stay here for further studies and you get going to Titi in Seville.'

———————

Philip had always stayed in a splendid converted Andalusian mansion; Titi had made bookings at a lesser downtown hotel which proved as elusive as the Queen Elizabeth in Tehran. NO LEFT TURN and one-way streets foiled any attempt at an approach, but the Tourist Organisation recommendation impressed a police car sufficiently to guide the well-known writer. Arrival to the sound of sirens was impressive but not addictive for forays to the airport. Though worried by the plane's delay, Charles went to bed, tired from his long journey. At an unearthly hour he woke in the arms of Titi who cried a little and laughed a lot in a Viennese mixture which lasted through half of Europe.

Criss-crossing Spain became tremendous fun; they occasionally had to stop because of uncontrollable laughter. Fatherless and an only child, Titi was familiar with the friends and circumstances of her mother's youth, they were not aware of an age gap and exchanged opinions in one look. Humour united as much as background: Charles was a child of the first Austrian Republic, the despised remnant of Empire; Titi belonged to the Second, the worse for German and

Russian occupation. Yet to both, Monarchy was, like Catholicism, the natural order. They indulged in Habsburg nostalgia and made the wide detour to remote St Juste, the monastic retreat of Charles V, the first ruler in whose empire the sun never set. That Charles had been the name of the first and last Spanish Habsburg as well as of the last Austrian Emperor fascinated their namesake and interested Titi; visits to museums she, however, abbreviated; 'You go right, I go left, if there is anything I'll call you.' Obviously nothing would warrant her notice on the opposite side.

They took turns at the wheel, except in the mountains where Titi manifested her fear of heights by closing her eyes. They had, however, been opened by her ex-fiancé's tactlessness towards Erwein who was such a help to Mummy. Canon Zobel had consoled – not always effectively – during the protracted suffering; they would meet him at Lourdes to which he led an annual Austrian pilgrimage.

Tarburgs had for centuries been Knights of Malta; Max had been accommodated on the Order's train of pilgrims and though Our Lady did not heal his shattered leg he was as deeply affected by the unique atmosphere of Lourdes as his brother-in-law ten years later. The boys and girls spending their holidays pushing wheelchairs and generally assisting the invalids seemed less selfish than his own generation. Christianity preached and practised rose above the ugliness of ecclesiastical architecture and the souvenir shops. The elation of the nightly torchlight procession climaxed in the vast underground Basilica of Pius X where 300 priests celebrated Sunday Mass in a moving grandeur never achieved by a Hollywood producer. The young volunteers noiselessly removed the emergency cases, most of the congregation was unable to stand, but all transcended their suffering during the multilingual liturgy. 'You are so blatantly Catholic that it's absurd to remain officially a Lutheran.' Titi was right, but so much, official and unofficial, was absurd.

———— —— ————

From the sublime to limericks in three languages and dutiful sightseeing. The owner of a country hotel had mothered Charles twice before and was bewildered at his refusal of the honeymoon-room. Nobody in France had believed the uncle-niece pretence for a hundred years! She should have been astounded by the handsome couple's preoccupation with business in Zurich.

A financial wizard had shown off at Madame's male brothel. 'The chicken-livered should stick with unexciting international trusts, RRR for instance. Those in the know go for high tech.' He named a space-age choice. Charles conveyed his insider's tip to his account executive who reduced yet another get-rich-quick to losable dimensions. The Fenton fees and royalties accumulated over twenty years were hardly worth his while, so he quickly approved RRR and advised buying a small annuity starting at sixty-five.

Titi sympathised with Swiss abhorrence of risks. 'Your Greek-American stockbroker will be happy to invest in science fiction; and you'd better pray for what's left from the sale of the Liechti. Nowhere more appropriate than at the convent to which the Empress Zita had retired and which was on our way. Instead you detour like a thing possessed to Lichtenstein, as if we hadn't seen enough pictures.'

'Those I could almost make out lying in bed, but I never bothered to cross the road for a good look. The Gallery of the Principality is small, so the pictures rotate. Let's hope we get the Dutch.'

Not the hoped-for flowers; tons of flesh by Rubens justified Titi's museum strategy. Charles insisted on spending the last night of his most enjoyable post-war journey at the hotel at Igls where he had stayed with Mother.

———— ————

'The lovely days of Aranjuez are now ended' had been cited to Titi at that Spanish palace and were, therefore, relevant in an excellent performance of Schiller's *Don Carlos* to which Ernst Häussermann sent tickets. Equally relevant off-stage; though not apparently with Tania who was still the leading lady of the Landtheater; she had married a slightly younger physician in whose pretty Biedermaier house they tried to find a name for this relationship through divorce and marriage. On a trip to England the couple had suggested visiting Father and were invited to tea; considering the remoteness of Abbey Court this was insulting, and they naturally refused. With the ghost of the wicked stepmother finally exorcised the pleasant meeting would be repeated in Athens or Vienna.

Placid plump Margarete Horbitzer and her febrile fragile sister had retired to the Israelitic Community Rest Home despite Dr Weiss's paranoical fear of even the most comfortable institution. The dinner bell evoked the summons at the concentration camp, recalled with another former inmate. The horrors of the past overwhelmed the old lady and turned her benevolence into malice; she counselled a visit to the Liechti.

The Salvation Army Major personally conducted the *Herr Baron* – the owner of such a *palais* could be no less. Avoiding Mother's bedroom was futile because the shock came in the big dining room, scene of the Thursday luncheons. A dozen elderly females sprawled on untidy camp beds in the late morning. Dissolute crones stared, one half-heartedly drew back her blanket. Discarded streetwalkers had replaced Austria's intelligentsia under the miraculously intact silk hangings in the white and gold panelling. The outrage was so enormous as to be almost funny.

———

'I am not amused by an announcement outrageous even among the Hatches, Matches and Dispatches. The Austrian gutter press would have reported the break-off free of charge. After rejecting a Count and a Marquess, my daughter can't wait to marry a Mr Travers. At least no newspaper announcement about him. A garden architect like Soph, so I suppose they slept in a greenhouse and planted shrubs on their honeymoon. It's all Father's fault.' Herta's perennial accusation apparently still attributed the evil to garden architecture.

Hildegard put the record straight. 'Your father found out that Peter Montaubert is gay. He wasn't after money, he has plenty. He might even have fulfilled his matrimonial duties occasionally for so suitable a cover-up. Soph was so much in love that she wanted to marry him all the same but her grandfather was adamant. Why is he so anti-gay? After all . . .'

'Exactly! "A gay son is a mishap, a gay grandson-in-law is carelessness" to misquote Wilde. Let's keep to Herta, she looks awful, not just because of the bad news. She alternates between poohpoohing her illness and hinting at the imminence of her demise. Impossible to pin down.'

He made another attempt when, alone together, he and his sister were finishing the wine after dinner. He sat next to her, put her head on his shoulder and coaxed her into some coherence between sobs. 'You have the British passport and I have the stiff upper lip. I'm in constant pain, but I won't allow the White Mafia to cut me up again. If you were staying with me . . . I realise you can't bear the Laudorf provincialism. The Tarburg was different . . . I promise to see my doctor when he comes back from leave. I'll let you know in Athens.'

———

Athens's remaining attractions were purely professional: lecturing at the CC, tutoring children of ever-changing prime ministers, being commissioned for ever new books on Greece, even writing the leaflets of the Tourist Organisation. An ironic reversal from that summer forty-five years ago when love or at least sex were part of the landscape. Now it was organised in gay bars, connected with drink on the Western model, driven into Turkish baths and cinemas showing pornographic films. Charles had always considered the local music part of the background noise, but had joked with expatriate friends about the lack of logic. Now he became exasperated at the stubborn stereotypes; driving Tania and her husband into the country, he had talked Greek to some villagers for ten minutes before being told that it was a pity he couldn't speak Greek.

Civilised table talk persisted only at Christl's but the social back-biting at most dinners increasingly bored Charles. At cocktail parties he became renowned as 'Last in, first out', mainly because he cut his whiskies from three to two for the sake of a better sleep.

Daniel's Jewish good sense awoke to the danger of wasting his capital on hunks of the Armed Forces at bouzouki tavernas. For years he had drowned his innate shyness in noise and retsina, had splashed his money about in a routine few Greeks could maintain financially and sexually. Heinz's death had triggered off the flight into mass consumption which was ended by love for a mongrel. Daniel's masochism bloomed under the canine despotism, more persistent albeit cheaper than the nights with the military. Resumption of the old intimacy with a most willing Charles was prevented by the pernicious dog who growled at foreigners, bit Greeks and ignored his doting master. As compensation or consolation, Freud knows, Daniel became simultaneously obsessed with metaphysics, discussed only over the telephone because of the mongrel's unpleasantness. By practice dreams were better retained, interpretations were fanciful but rarely sexual as desires were not suppressed but enjoyed in the flesh. They disagreed amiably on practically everything except politics which became increasingly murky in Greece.

Herta submerged her illness beneath Father's death.

'. . . His determination almost made the century. We were named as grieving children in a proper *faire part* and specifically disinherited in his will which cited the Altenhof and the Liechti against any claim under Austrian law. Characteristically thorough in cutting us out, yet quite unnecessary under British law. How much of his considerable property was left to Helen, how much was grabbed by my scheming daughter? She makes the best from both worlds: the Austrian statutory share from her parents, a clean sweep from her grandfather. I could disinherit her for neglect of filial duties, but we both condemned the washing of dirty Tarburg linen in public and you'll still get two-thirds. . . . The scattering of his ashes from a helicopter is unexpectedly flamboyant, perhaps guilt over neglecting Mother's tomb . . .'

For which Herta was equally guilty, even Charles . . . He had hoped to be forgiven for that silly panicky letter refusing to pay for

Father's divorce. Financial squabbles dividing a family beyond the grave – manner of speaking. Reconciliation with the survivors, or rather resumption of relation, as there had never been a quarrel. Helen, however, rebuffed Charles's approach unequivocally. '. . . A meeting would be contrary to your father's wishes . . .'

Father was vindictive beyond the . . . scattering, but he had been a remarkable man, occasionally even a remarkable Father as over that theft in Sydney. Unable to share his regrets, Charles became impatient with Daniel's hysteria over the disappearance of the mongrel on a country walk. His master called and whistled late into the night, returned three days running, then put the mongrel's photo with a reward into the *Athens News*. The poorest foreigners paraded unconvincing lookalikes, which goaded Daniel into declaring his present sorrow greater than over the loss of Heinz. Such pathetic perversity shocked Charles into withdrawal till the taboo on the mongrel was guaranteed by a more edifying disappearance.

The futility of worldly success attracted mature men of distinction to the self-abnegation of the strictest French monastery. La Grande Chartreuse kept postulants waiting for years, but Georges Arnault was finally admitted; he renounced a solid reputation in literary circles, but his poems had never been popular, too marked by the experiences of a war pilot. Daniel had sat out the war in Argentina but asserted that the mongrel's loss was sufficiently traumatic to make him take the veil; he was still capable of self-mockery. Could he accompany Charles on his summer travels to France? La Chartreuse deserved inclusion in the GGG. Georges had not replied, which should not prevent them seeing for themselves.

———————

Only a mock-up, five kilometres from the Charterhouse barred to visitors. The replica illustrated a medieval austerity beyond the comprehension of Daniel who rushed for safety to his banker in Geneva. Driving on alone, Charles regretted the shallowness of his brief intimacy with the Flight Lieutenant, too reticent among the extrovert set. The poems, barely leafed through, might have provided the understanding of disillusionment; Georges's must have been total, Charles's was partial, an absence of desire rather than despair. Why endure the gruelling punishment of cold and manual work at La Chartreuse when at a Benedictine Abbey with a large library he might write the historical studies for which he had never found time?

A bakery van blocked the road near an auberge made doubly attractive by the smell of fresh bread. Predictably, the innkeeper's wife mothered Charles, by choosing the room, food and wine; after serving the cheese, she shared a glass while enumerating the sites of the district.

The nearest could be visited before breakfast. Small Romanesque St Benedict's invited to a prayer in its medieval severity. The organ struck up and simultaneously a shaft of light penetrated the semi-obscurity; not illuminating a beautiful statue as long ago at St Stephen's, yet the clear steady ray was no less a sign in response to his fumbling mechanical prayer. A cathartic, overwhelming communication from the . . . Incomprehensible; wonderful like the 'Elsewhere' in the forgotten childhood experience, but shattering in maturity. His puffy eyes caused concern at the auberge, but Charles drove into the lovely morning with a novel serenity.

Serenity frayed with Robert, who took a perverse and active pleasure in creating mischief. The circumcised Muslim neglected Morocco's mosques for hotels near post offices to write innumerable 'witty' cards to the same acquaintances as friends he had none. His verbal diarrhoea excluded subjects of GGG or any immediate interest. He had driven Charles and Ralph during the war but now refused to help out; he simply ignored the fact that at his desired maximum speed of thirty kilometres the journey would last not weeks but months. Persistent misdirections finally imposed a parting of the ways at Barcelona airport.

On the motorways along the Mediterranean, accommodation was a struggle rather than a rest. Over breakfast in the Pyrenees Charles decided on a heroic leap to Laudorf; an uninterrupted 1,000 kilometres in the debilitating August heat dazed him into confusing brakes with accelerator. Mitzi wobbled into the opposite lane miraculously free of traffic. The shock released sufficient adrenalin to push on for a late supper with Herta.

She looked a fright, torn from bed to prepare a meal for a once again ravenous brother. The dressing gown hid the matchstick arms and legs, revealed by the summer dress at breakfast. Directing Red Cross ambulances kept her busy all day and in the evening she seemed afflicted with the exhaustion Charles had slept off. She parried questions about her health with macabre losses of life and limb in numerous accidents and closed the medical theme over the after-dinner drink. 'Now that I'm seventy, I've at last a good figure.'

Pitiful self-deception must be corrected rather than shattered. 'You nearly had to send an ambulance for me yesterday, would have served me right for my silly record-breaking. Moreover, a sandal strap chaffed and my foot is now swollen, so you make an appointment with your doctor to cut it off. You come along to hold my hand and then he'll have a look at you.'

She weakened claims of overwork at the Red Cross by predicting a heart attack if her brother insisted, but finally promised to consult the White Mafia at a convenient time within the week.

The physician who had misdiagnosed Max's fractured leg disinfected Charles's foot. 'Since cancer was suspected I haven't been permitted to examine the Countess though I was called when she had the flu. Last year an operation might have had some chance, but judging by her looks . . . She must be in considerable pain and it's admirable that she has taken on additional duties of Red Cross staff on leave, but for a district vice-president to be so terrified of an operation . . .'

Was she stupidly terrified or deliberately self-destructive? The physician's 'last year' was an open reproach, but Charles had argued then, apparently in vain, that there were easier ways to go.

As a delaying action Herta warned of a recent outbreak of rabies; when hare or roebuck approached Charles during his forest walks, he must run for his life. This bizarre reversal of roles seemed vindicated when she cried for help, standing on a kitchen chair under siege by a mouse, unconcerned by Charles's entry. Refraining from hostilities against the rabies suspect, he was to carry her to the phone and secure the kitchen door. The ambulance called reluctantly when she had been in terrible pain was ordered immediately for the mouse hunt; a burly conscientious objector, serving double time in the Red Cross, proved his heroism by disposing of the insidious enemy.

'This rabies *divertissement* does not divert from your appointment with Dr Miracle. He quite rightly ticked me off for not dragging you to his surgery last year. When I carried you past the mouse–dragon I felt a lump in the hole where you used to wear a stomach. Ask Hildegard to stay with you for a few days while I dash up to Vienna.'

'Hildegard wants a special diet and I haven't the energy for that. Visitors are a bore, not you Karli, you are family, all that's left to me.'

'Karli' from the suffering of Lis and Otto indicated protective anxieties; Herta suffered no less, but hers was an appeal that must be answered, the opportunity to assist that others had denied him. Cancelling the visit to Titi was a sacrifice, but missing her laugh unexpectedly expanded into a conflict of duties. 'Just when I need you most. Sorry, I needed you more after Mummy's death. Please don't think me ungrateful for your wonderful support last summer. But now I want to marry and your opinion is important.' The line seemed to have gone dead and then she added 'Kaliwali'. Extraordinary, she remembered the name she used as a baby, but she obviously claimed him thereby as a very special member of her family. But she understood that a sister suffering from the same illness as Mummy had priority; her description of the Californian-Irish Patrick was lovingly humorous. He was not as goodlooking as her ex-fiancé but so much more intelligent. He was in Vienna on an interpreter's scholarship. She hid her disappointment at 'I wish you had inspected him, not that an unfavourable opinion would have made any difference. He'll call you Kaliwali too. Sounds like one of those weird Australian names.'

———— ————

At St Benedict's Charles had decided to become officially what he had always been at heart; he had looked forward to discussing the conversion proper with Paul, but the story of the good Samaritan confirmed the superiority of practical assistance over ritual observance. Titi acted as intermediary, invited her confessor to dinner and both rang Laudorf to discuss the texts to be studied for conversion the following summer.

Still sensible in minor matters, Herta remonstrated against the length of the call, and started the following evening with 'The smears showed what you expected' that somehow made him responsible. The pathetic bundle of bones settled against her brother's shoulder to alternate between Germanic heroism and lachrimose self-pity, acceptance and rejection of the diagnosis. She must have it out with the White Mafia.

The physician grunted belligerently. 'The Countess is not above the half-truths of patients refusing to face facts. Indeed no operation is needed *now*, it's by far too late. The test wasn't necessary, but the written result might prepare her psychologically for the artificial exit she dreads so much; a few months, there is no choice. Let her eat, drink and smoke as much as she wants, it doesn't make any difference.'

Herta did not enquire about the interview, perhaps clinging to shreds of self-deception despite the pain and exhaustion that at last stopped her Red Cross work. She willed herself, however, into a drive to Pörtschach where she was invited for a fortnight by the hotel she had frequented since her youth. The owner took Charles aside, 'I know what we owe to the Fechtner/Tarburg patronage and I'll be delighted to have the Countess as my guest. But is she well enough just now?'

She obviously was not and on their return went straight to bed. The Laudorfs agreed with Charles on the need for a nurse, but Herta would hear nothing of such a silly waste of money. She was shaken by the death of Irene's husband from a brain tumour, too close an illness for comfort, yet comfort it oddly provided. 'I'll write her a nice letter. It might be consoling if I leave her Mother's solitaire. Surely you'll marry her now.'

'She wasn't too keen forty years ago and your hint is rather obvious. A letter of condolence for a successful rival is particularly tricky, so I just offer my shoulder to cry on.'

'You did that fairly expertly for me. Mother would have approved of Irene wearing the ring rather than my brat who gets the emeralds and pearls. You'd better take the prayer rug, the only decent piece Father didn't snatch from the Tarburg.'

The threadbare silk rug suited a decaying castle but not a utilitarian Athenian flat. 'Plenty of time in years to come' pleased despite the improbability.

Charles delayed the departure till two days before the CO opening and, therefore, left at dawn. Herta had insisted on preparing breakfast and though they embraced in the hall she followed him into the cold mist while he loaded the luggage. Forlorn and fragile she shivered in the dressing gown that hung loosely; she did not raise her hands as at the Tarburg and now not intuition but the eyes realised the finality of the leave-taking. Charles was opening the car door to hug her once more when the eldest Laudorf boy appeared out of the mist and said something to cheer her; she attempted a smile and the brave façade might crumble at the brother's shoulder. Compassion or cowardice lost the moment and the pathetic figure joined the memory of Mother's outstretched arms as an unforgettable reproach.

———————

Herta's writing was as shaky as Granny's towards the end.

'. . . Hildegard shamed Soph into looking after me. She acts the perfect daughter, but then she did the same with her father before suddenly abandoning him. She must therefore be encouraged as I couldn't manage on my own. I ask your consent to change my will in her favour, provided she sticks with me to the end. Perhaps the bribe wasn't necessary, but after her previous behaviour . . . You won't be cut off and the rug already belongs to you. I foolishly hoped you'd be around, but Mother and even Father would have disapproved of such selfishness. You can't leave your work for an indefinite period. If I make it to the summer we might be a united family yet . . .'

Heinz had shown the same consideration, but Herta was an only sister. Correct to notify him of the changed will, not that his consent was necessary. Soph deserved everything if she stuck it out. But having to bribe her into caring for her mother! He had no right to criticise. He hadn't even got out of the car to reassure her that he could come whenever needed.

'. . . Whoever said "The word *never* doesn't exist" need not have added "in politics". I've learned the hard way, have a tube and the attached nasties. I dictate this letter to Soph who spends a lot of time with me. The surgeon assures me I'll be home for Christmas, but do I want to? . . .'

Soph added, 'Mother is admirably brave. She talks fondly of you and hopes you'll marry Irene.'

Irene had gratefully acknowledged the offered shoulder, but the marriage was nothing but a dying wish for a peripheral happy ending. Closer and less fanciful, Soph asserted, '. . . Richard, my husband, came over for Christmas and immediately hit it off with mother . . .' Not a Herta expression, but she probably had become reconciled to her son-in-law.

His departure was, however, hardly the cause of Herta's death. Soph rang on a Wednesday evening. 'Mother was relieved from her pains yesterday.' She sounded rather relieved herself, naturally pre-occupied with the funeral the following Monday.

'Why didn't you ring immediately? Now it'll be difficult to fly to Vienna by Friday. Any idea about trains to Laudorf?'

Soph ignored both questions. 'We aren't expecting you. Richard isn't coming either. It's always difficult to get to Laudorf, and this winter rail and road are often blocked by snow. Not many will make it to the funeral. The Red Cross band certainly, as mother wished.'

Sensible not to be trapped in the snow for the sake of appearances. Herta would lie in a marble mausoleum though she was partly to blame for the disappearance of Mother's tomb. Soph was to order a wreath on his behalf and if he changed his mind he would ring back.

Comfort won the argument with convention valued by Herta and, no doubt, Christl had she been consulted. Daniel's selfishness denied any obligation and Soph gave the final absolution. 'Snow blocked the local railway most of the day. Only the Tarburgs, Laudorfs, Red Cross officials and the band attended, but there were many wreaths, yours the finest. Mother left you a considerable legacy as I had urged her.'

Charles refrained from correcting the impudence so soon after the funeral, but did so later by letter, when he explained his GGG duties during the summer. She agreed to a meeting at Laudorf in late August to finalise matters with the executor and then spend some days at the Tarburg; she was looking forward to renewing acquaintance with an uncle so fondly remembered from her childhood.

5

So fondly that she did not remember the August meeting which she had not mentioned to the Laudorfs. They were decidedly cool about Soph, goodlooking though too fat; she nursed her mother conscientiously but was in an unseemly hurry to dispose of Herta's belongings as if afraid . . . she had left behind the prayer rug as all knew that it belonged to Charles. The executor was on holiday and his substitute wondered why the Countess's brother had come on that particular date. Payment instructions could have been given in writing and the legatee was not entitled to any information about the estate except by court order.

——— ———

Charles and Friedrich rejected legal action advocated by Hildegard. 'Luckily you wrote that you were coming to the Tarburg. Letters to and from my godchild tend to go astray. She behaved monstrously and she shouldn't get away with it, but the jewels won't feature in the will; Herta dribbled them away in bribes so that her loving daughter wouldn't decamp. I have bigger baubles from my second husband which I intended for Soph, Norbert's wife got the Lechfurt lot and now she'll get all. Scheming little Soph is the big loser after all.'

'Be explicit in *your* will, Soph is a born inheritor.' Friedrich had always been shy with Charles, perhaps imagining a resentment over the affair with Eve; now, however, he was sympathetically concerned. 'I haven't my father's authority over Soph, but I am sorry about the smallness of the legacy. Thank you for not washing Tarburg dirty linen in public, like poor Uncle Rudi's sisters and son. I wish I could stop Soph talking on the BBC as Countess Tarburg, garden architecture is an innocuous subject but she is Mrs Travers.'

'She deflected my question about who owns Abbey Court by complaining about the difficulty of living with Aunt Helen, apparently obsessed with getting your father's *Notion of Justice in International Relations* published. Hardly the title of a bestseller! Odd to call a step-grandmother aunt, but then we all call Max's mother Aunt Valerie. She would have been delighted that I examine you in her very drawing room on the articles of Faith, though surprised that all the texts are in English.'

'Elementary, my dear Hildegard. Except on my brief visits to Austria, I haven't spoken or read any German since the Anschluss. Even with Father it was English in Australia and with Titi it's an amusing trilingual mixture, fairly impenetrable to outsiders. My tutoring and writing are in English and Canon Zobel luckily speaks it well enough.'

Like all Austria, they were glued to the TV when the Empress Zita, returned after sixty years of exile, put the interviewer in his place when he worried about how to address her; Your Majesty did not fit the network of the Republic. The old lady smiled condescendingly, 'As if that mattered, *mein lieber Herr*' signifying 'my good man' rather than 'my dear sir'. With such Austrian nuances Charles felt at home and he proposed opening a bottle of champagne.

——— ———

Divers Vienna municipal officers registered Charles's denunciation of the Lutheran Confession and he was ready for the Church to which he had always adhered. Paul had helped through school examinations and now as examiner forgave inadequate answers to perhaps deliberately complex theological questions. Charles knelt before the humble classmate for a sweeping general confession into which the co-conspirator from Samos refrained from probing. He gave absolution in preparation for the reception of the convert in the private chapel of the cathedral's Chapter House.

Only Titi and her husband Patrick witnessed the privileged ceremony. Kneeling before the altar Charles tried but failed to regain the Grace experienced at St Benedict's; confirmation as a Catholic was no less an anti-climax than becoming a British subject, which at least brought practical benefits. The spiritual had always been claimed and the official registration kindled no religious fervour.

A sin of omission must, nevertheless, be set straight, now that the trauma over Mother's grave had been overcome at Herta's. Charles must assume responsibility for the Grandparents' resting place he had so long neglected. The Convent had disappeared – not the fabric, like Mother's tomb, but as a religious establishment – for lack of novices. The new occupant, a foreign language school, might have a register of the former inmates' burial places but before facing another sepulchral calamity the only surviving family intimate must be consulted.

——— ———

Cemetery talk would have been tactless with Aunt Margarete looking so near her grave, probably the reason for her macabre reflections. 'My sister became increasingly perturbed, she had to be confined in

238

the clinic on the top floor. It was wicked of her to send you to those women in the Liechti.'

'I wouldn't dream of holding Aunt Olga responsible for what the concentration camp did to her.'

'You are a good boy to call her Aunt which you never did in her lifetime, but you know that it pleases me and it would please your mother if she looks down from Paradise though on earth she didn't encourage it, too far beyond Austrian social and religious taboos. Your grandparents weren't too happy with my visit, perhaps I reminded them of the Jewish streak in the Fechtners. This home is infinitely more comfortable than their convent, but they lived and died in congenial surroundings amongst their kind of retired civil servants. The emancipated Jews here are more amusing and immeasurably more tragic. Each withdraws into memories of his own perished world. Mine at least survives in you and that's why I leave all my belongings to you. My body goes to medical research, same as Olga's; saves unnecessary funeral expenses.'

The utilitarian solution precluded consultation about a REQUIESCAT unlikely to be IN PACE.

Renouncing the search for the Grandparents' grave benefited Lis's with a fine camellia arrangement because they had cried together at *Camille* with Greta Garbo; frustration, guilt and compensation combined into a floral tribute that moved the son-in-law she had never seen. Lis would, however, have approved of moustached Patrick Donelly whose Irish piety had been adapted to the Austrian pleasures, especially of the table which earned him and Titi the nickname the spare-tyre couple. He looked surprisingly Austrian and joined his wife and Charles in their language mish-mash and laughter. At an inn they attracted the attention of an elderly lady. 'Astonishing how little you have changed, Karl, since the days when my family hoped you'd marry my sister Dolly. Thank you for letting me hear real laughter once more, it has become very rare in our circles.' A sobering truth barely comprehensible to Californian Patrick.

His American practicality understood, however, that Herta's legacy would not outlast the expensive round of restaurants, theatres and opera, particularly after Charles's generous 'Donation to the Poor' on his conversion. Hawking an heirloom, ironically Tarburg and not Fechtner, differed embarrassingly from the discreet disposal of Mother's goblets; Patrick carted the prayer rug on his pushbike to the main carpet stores in the NO PARKING zone. Haughty Armenians and Iranians offended by tendering derisory amounts and in a smaller shop a swarthy Oriental offered even less. Rolling up the apparently valueless rug, Charles muttered 'Fuck' in Greek; the appropriate expletive from a mere foreigner was rewarded by twentyfold the previous sum; the rug was taken on commission and Charles was to call on the dealer's brother in Athens. 'Help from unexpected quarters . . .'

. . . came on the emotional level from Tania's husband. Dr Joseph Richter adored his actress wife – less excessively than Helen's worship of Father – and shared her love of travelling commemorated in slides he was restrained from showing. Though awed by Herta's coronet, he had stressed the urgency of treatment; where the professional had failed, Charles need feel no guilt. Forestalling an equal obstinacy from the brother, Joseph made an appointment with a leading oculist; the Professor confirmed the soundness of Charles's left eye, no change of reading glasses after ten years, while at the present rate of medical progress the right eye might yet be rehabilitated.

From the old Fechtner box in the Landtheater, by courtesy of Tania, Charles watched her fairly convincing Lady Windermere, yet Granny's 'She just doesn't know' still lingered indefinably. She overacted drawing-room plays more off- than on-stage and on an evening out the Donellys were not particularly impressed.

––– ––– –––

The CO Director could extend the compulsory retiring age in exceptional circumstances. Charles's unusual courses had acquired solid snob value among Athenians sufficiently wealthy to send their children to British universities, he was a sacred cow looking young enough to be displayed to inspectors from London without arousing suspicions about his age. Sloppy bookkeeping had, moreover, neglected contributions to IKA, Greek Social Security, and Charles was not yet eligible even for a minimum pension. He alone among the staff qualified for the public lectures 'British authors on Greece', together with a famous Byzantinist and Ralph, now President of WAA, the World Association of Authors. Mastering his initial trembling, Charles spiced *The Alkmeonids, Europe's First Political Family* with allusions clear to the prominent audience. 'Hipparchos, the original Minister of Culture, deserved assassination less than some of his modern counterparts' shocked the ambassadors, pleased the Conservative ex-ministers and drew prolonged applause.

––– ––– –––

'Your swipe at the Minister of Culture was fun but highly undiplomatic.'

'Can't a foolish lecturer rush in where diplomats fear to tread, dear Ralph?'

'Not when he depends on the grace and favour of the CO, Charles. With some twenty books published you'd better join the WAA. We are keen on liberty of expression, more so when leftish, unfortunately. I'd like someone to make up for Georges Arnault who was exceptionally civilised. He often regretted your friendship was not more permanent.'

'So have I, we had more in common than I realised. Writing and religion ranked low amongst my priorities in the 30s and sexually he couldn't compete with the Greeks. I made the wrong choice, I'm rather good at that. I've no real friends left here, Daniel has literally gone to the dogs. That bitch that tyrannises him at present is a great improvement on the previous hellhound but he became visible only in your honour. I hadn't seen him since the Chartreuse. On the phone he talks like St Theresa of Avila and Aldous Huxley rolled in one, was delighted that I wake up some seconds before anyone rings or calls. He wallows in my psychic potentialities, the Valois, dreams, thinks me an ideal medium. Yet is too lazy to find out about a Spiritualist Society as this would interfere with his dog routine. But we speak French which I like best, about Paris, old follies and he has an excellent historical dictionary. Still as a friend . . . Robert was equally peculiar in Morocco, yet I'm sorry he moved to London.'

'He bought an expensive flat, yet has no money for furniture. It's near a Buddhist centre, but he would have done better to sit at the feet of the Dalai Lama – India is cheaper. Christl is wonderfully unchanged, but you can't let your hair down with her. It's difficult to make new friends, but aren't you a bit stand-offish with the expatriates and your colleagues?'

'With the ex's I exchange the customary inanities at parties, my colleagues changed from distressed gentlefolk into distressing folk. More likely, I'm just becoming as antisocial as my father when he retired to England. The ladies in my class invite me to dinner, they cook well; the parents of my private pupils are certainly more intelligent but unsubtly condescending, so I am ruder than is strictly necessary. This greatly enhances my reputation among the *nouveaux riches* and I charge double fees. I'm quite friendly with a few diplomats, not intimate as with the Minister and his circle. Mimis is too intimate, endless boring recitals of sex. He wants me to move with him to Morocco, an inexhaustible supply of willing youths as every family produces its own football team from a couple of wives.'

'Not for you. You've always been in love with being loved, self-centred brute! You aren't cut out to end up as a dirty old man. England when you become senile, you have friends there, not to mention Irene. The things you like, opera, theatre, good food cost a lot of money. Just as well you've been commissioned to write a book on Algeria.'

———————

Algeria, long absent from the tourist map, promised intensive activities for Mimis on the long drive from Morocco to Tunisia. But to be on the safe side he persuaded Charles to relax first in the male brothel near the Atlantic coast. The place was boarded up and in the village some well-remembered boys directed the car to a small house. Madame was fatter, sad and stoic, feeding a young child. 'Not mine, my husband's youngest brother. After maman's death customers complained about thefts and the police closed the hotel. The restaurant on its own wasn't worth the effort. My husband works in Casablanca, I'm looking after the family here. Maman always said I was mad. No, thank you, I don't need any money. I had a good time with Moroccans, now I'm paying for it.'

Three times the car was stopped by villagers loitering with intent. Mimis waved but Charles drove on. Madame's fate was sad, the boys were bad and he wasn't mad to invite highway robbery.

Whether Madame had really married a Moroccan half her age stimulated Mimis into sex speculations and try-outs. In Algiers Charles became thoroughly fed up but he did not want to lose another old friend in North Africa. He went on his own to the kasbah which fifty years earlier had disclosed the gamut of Arab sensuality. Now filthy children in rags were kicking rubbish through the deserted alley to a gate where the misery of three blind beggars once again shocked Charles into emptying all his coins into their bowl. The stately St Georges was dwarfed by an unfinished building above the pool by which Father had warned Herta against the Tarburgs.

At the official exchange rate even the overcrowded buses were expensive so Charles walked to the cathedral, the symbol of Christianity's second predominance in Algeria. The portals were barred and a score of old people descended from a side door to the crypt, like persecuted Romans to the catacombs. On that Sunday, now an ordinary working day, the remnants of colonalisation all took Communion and Charles joined them with unaccustomed fervour. Parallels between the antique and modern decline and fall could no longer be discussed with Philip, the Minister and, best of all, Father, so a substitute had to be tracked down among the Athenian expatriates.

———————

Becoming a workaholic in his sixties, Charles attempted to write up the wealth of material during the busy academic year but still required the undisturbed quiet of the long vacation. Stelios nostalgically suggested the southern Peloponnese and once again they drove along the lovely coast, searching in vain for a beach not disturbed by a disco sign. The fishing villages were no longer sleepy and Aridio off the road was only investigated because of the unusual name among all those dedicated to saints. For maximum tranquillity Charles rented two rooms with a veranda above a rose garden; as peaceful as Laudorf, Herta would have liked it, she had tended her own roses well. Stelios could not outstay his welcome as he had lied to his wife about a customer in the country; she was ludicrously jealous, but then she was obese and he merely rotund. Before returning by bus to Athens his sightseeing enthusiasm revived at a sea cave where Charles waved his magical Tourist Office recommendation and was placed at the head of a long queue waiting for admission.

'When I am with you, Charles, I am treated with respect. With my wife . . . On our trip through Italy where you had suggested such a wonderful itinerary, she was only looking for a new kind of pressure cooker; she found one in Florence, wouldn't leave it in the car, and in a restaurant on the way back my younger boy dropped it. For her the journey was thus a waste of money, time doesn't count. It would have been so different with you.' Stelios affectionately laid his hand on Charles's, aware of the limits to their liking for one another.

Alone but never lonely, Charles relaxed instead of exploring ever-remoter regions for GGG, and was writing leisurely and therefore better on Maghreb history and culture. He intrigued fellow bathers by swimming out further than most when not engrossed in a book under his beach umbrella. He responded to approaches in four languages in which he kept the curious guessing his nationality, even joined them occasionally in the tavernas. The villagers soon adopted the quiet visitor, told him who had caught fresh fish and who caught clap from a tourist, which contributed in keeping Aridio sexually arid.

—— —— —— ——

But not the following summer in Morocco where Nordin unexpectedly combined sensuality with sentiment. He maintained that, true to the classical form Nur ed-Din, Light of Faith, he had to convert Charles to Islam, but his light shone brightest in worldly spheres. He possessed the usual good looks of his compatriots, but unusual tact and humour. Son of a prison guard, he told hilarious stories about crime and punishment, while the spontaneity of his tenderness was above pretension. He had just finished high school and like his fellow students he longed to be taken to England, but he would be happy to remain in Morocco to assist Charles with his books, first in French and soon in English. The local Director of Tourism gave substance to the fantasy by pointing out that Charles wrote about an equal number of western and eastern Mediterranean countries, that the Atlantic resort had an ideal climate, no pollution and to clinch the persuasion offered a comfortable new house at a cheap rent.

Nordin was certainly more intelligent and realistic than Stelios. Incredible though it seemed, he was probably even more attached – 'in love' sounded impossible at an age difference that might have restrained even Father. So was this a miraculous last chance or no-fool-like-an-old-fool? Experience had taught that his choice was bound to prove wrong, but the decision came from his 'heart that had died many years ago', the impressively sad boast of the Exeter tutor. Temptation was unfortunately resistible in the midst of regrets.

———— ————

Regrets vanished in the chalet Hildegard had bought above Salzburg. 'The Festival is particularly wonderful after years in Trieste, unbearably dull after I outlived a second husband. He at least died in bed and not dangling from a meat-hook like poor Norbert. Herta's fate was a warning to my brother; where she entertained lavishly he is careful, rightly as I won't contribute to the upkeep of that ugly pile. Do stay at least a fortnight, Herta accused me of having needles in my behind but you are worse on your annual race round the Med. Bring any of your friends, I am looking forward to finding out for myself why Ernst Häussermann is so durable among our theatrical celebrities.'

Ernst looked anything but durable, an unhealthy grey face over a pear-shaped body and his customary polite prudence was coloured by melancholic frankness. 'When I was thrown out from school I determined to succeed as much as you, not just because you were equally obtuse in Maths but also because your father owned the Landtheater. I grasped every opportunity however improbable, was lucky to be appointed cultural workhorse by the Americans and managed to make the minimum of enemies here. After I passed the *Matura* thanks to the *Lex Häussermann* I was actually proud to attend the annual old boys dinner forty years late. Some boys! More envious than I had ever been of you as I had achieved the Austrian dream, Burgtheater Director, Doctor *honoris causa*, Hofrat. Only two survivors from the Upper Chamber and you never attend; the others belong to a different planet. You look twenty years younger than I, just right for a world-weary prince in a Hofmannsthal play. I'm recasting *Jedermann* next year provided I live that long, probably the same horror as Herta and Lis. Here are two tickets for tonight and I hope you and your hostess will dine with me after the performance.'

Ernst obtained four tickets for *Idomeneo* with Pavarotti at the official but still considerable price, affordable when Titi brought the proceeds from a 'fuck' at the right moment. No prayer rug could cover for long the expense of Festival entertainment and Charles returned with the Donelly's to Vienna.

'One inheritance Soph didn't get her hands on. Margarete Horbitzer left me more than Herta after the depredations of her daughter. Compared to Philip and the Minister she was a pauper, but she could never do enough for me while I . . . I'm far from ungrateful yet I must give that impression. Paul will have a lot to forgive at my next confession. As Aunt Margarete was dissected by medical students, I can't put flowers on her grave so let's sublimate her memory into music. She would have approved of *Tannhäuser*, she remembered it was my introduction to opera.'

Blissfully free from gimmicks the superb performance greatly moved Titi, highly sensitive after a miscarriage. Without hope for children, the Donellys had followed a Church appeal and adopted a family in communist Poland, regularly sent food and clothing and had invited the two sons to Vienna. With the same practical Christianity, Titi and Patrick put their bedroom at the disposal of a provincial couple as accommodation was scarce during the Pope's visit; they themselves huddled on a narrow couch. Charles felt rather ashamed because none of his contemporaries would have trusted total strangers for the sake of religion. He had escaped to a cinema when Hitler addressed the jubilant mob from the balcony of the Imperial Palace, but he now joined the equally jubilant Viennese to receive the Pontiff's blessing from the same balcony. For a real happy end, however, Emperor Otto should have been standing there, but in this imperfect world . . .

Waiting for the flight to Athens Charles adapted the American of Patrick, the official translator, to formal English for the Papal press release. The almost sublime did not preclude the near ridiculous; customs stamped the receipt for a ring, which Charles passed back to Titi embracing her over the barrier so that she could claim refund of the sales tax. A pious fraud as the ring had consoled after the miscarriage and the refund would benefit the Polish family.

——— ———

In retribution the Greek customs unjustifiably prevented Mitzi's sale first to a colleague, then to the wife of the CO director and then even to a diplomat. Presenting wrecked cars to the Turkish authorities was forced by grim logic, handing over a serviceable vehicle to the chicanery of officialdom was galling. The car park ended with the CO employment which could not be extended beyond the age of seventy though the pension was still derisory because of past IKA contribution mistakes.

Mitzi was granted stay of execution till the end of September and her last summer was to be spent in northern Greece with Mimis. 'After embarrassing you in North Africa I know I'm only asked along for want of anyone better, but my varicose veins restrict the chase. Clutching at cultural straws is quite a change from what I used to clutch.'

His murder was briefly announced in the news bulletin and described with grizzly details in the press. Neighbours heard a commotion in the flat of the well-known socialite and saw two youths leaving hurriedly; Mimis was found strangled amidst scattered belongings and the bed was in disarray. Greek love of clichés did not excuse the absurd 'The police suspect foul play'.

Murder, suicide and illness had decimated Charles's circle and he was approaching seventy, the fatal age according to the horoscopes. The forewarning was recalled by a rare aural dream: AFERIM resounding three times in complete darkness, not threatening yet inexplicably reminiscent of UFARSIN in the Biblical writing on the wall. There was no Hebrew scholar at the Archaeological Schools, the confessional was not for the interpretation of dreams, but Paul could be asked on the next visit to Vienna. Daniel wallowed in gloomy speculations, but could not be prised from his dog routine to consult a rabbi, let alone for the summer jaunt.

The most suitable companion seemed a youngish colleague who had limited his Cambridge ambitions from an epic poem on the glory of antique Athens to one article about the failings of the modern city. Anthony was tall, blond and witty, but his lazy 'I'm sure it'll be all right' made him a doubtful assistant for guide book work. After a month of shallowness at close quarters, Charles longed for solitude at Aridio.

An elderly English couple had built a house overlooking the sea. Charles occasionally swam and dined with them, but mostly he sketched out a *Greece Debunked* which would be fun to write but hardly increase his popularity. But did he wish to stay in Greece? Where was less undesirable? Desiring neither country nor people was blessing, contrary to Robert's depressively negative Buddhist appraisal. The beauty of nature swept away bored resignation. The full moon silvering the olive groves tumbling from dark crags to the luminous sea sublimely translated Beethoven's Sonata to the eyes. The emotional vacuum gave the vision a singular poignancy but also the promise of new satisfactions on journeys of personal not professional choice. As a prelude Charles drove to deserted mountain villages outside guide book interest but connected by passable roads. 'No silly risks' and, of course, no driving on Assumption Day.

A letter from a new publisher was waiting in Athens. The proposals for an *Egypt* were hard to resist now that Charles was free to travel the whole year. Egypt ranked high as a personal choice, so work and pleasure need not yet be divorced. In the meantime Charles went swimming, further than the now badly polluted beach of the encounter with Stelios, who was not missed. In September quieter foreigners replaced the tape-playing mob, and Charles was reading when a hand was placed over his glasses and he was coyly asked to guess. He recognised the accent of an eager British Studies lady who suddenly discovered the overwhelming attraction of swimming. She was so colourless that her daily attendance hardly mattered, even when Charles occasionally talked with other foreign regulars under the sunshade. What she lacked in intelligence she made up in clumsiness – once wrenching off the car's door handle when Charles drove to her Piraeus home. Christian name terms were exacted for the hospitality; Loula served the meal lukewarm because carrying the excellent food from the kitchen and talking simultaneously was beyond her capacity.

The CO cultural season opened with a TV film on Delius. Loula and most viewers condemned the composer's ruthless exploitation of the musical student who was patiently scoring complex instructions. For Charles, artistic creation struggling against the overwhelming impediment of syphilitic paralysis rightfully disregarded the niceties of ordinary behaviour.

NIGHT

1

Mitzi's exploitation in her last week was restricted to the beach and dropping Loula on the return at her bus terminal before entering the motorway to Athens, empty of traffic at the siesta hour. On a hot afternoon Charles correctly proceeded when the traffic light turned amber, since a car suddenly racing out of a side-street and obviously violating the stop signal would have passed in front. Inexplicably, the open car slowed down in the middle of the crossing and the woman driver stared at Charles who slammed on the brakes.

A white-coated figure was kneeling before him, another was fiddling about with his eyes; Charles demanded that his oculist be called and insisted through the blurred imprecision of intermittent consciousness. He awoke in a soft embrace to a whisper 'It'll be all right, it's Janet'. His bellicose 'Who the hell is that?' faded into oblivion. Next he struggled with tubes till stopped by the disapproving grunts of a whitecoat reading a newspaper in a chair, clearly visible though Charles was blindfolded.

———————

A needle pierced the vein in his arm, was withdrawn and reinserted. He protested and was told gruffly to speak Greek and lie still as he was hooked to a drip. He couldn't have moved much since his leg or legs were weighed down, confusing like the shrill exchange whether cleaning took priority over breakfast; a clatter of plates and an admonition to drink his milk. In a spurt of energy he asked the silly woman the whereabouts of this desirable liquid which he eventually sucked up through a straw to wash down a hard rusk. Disproportionally exhausting, but a cacophony of voices prevented drifting back into unconsciousness. More cultured Greek declared 'Nothing to be done. Probably concussed'. Charles wondered that he understood the unusual word and also why another voice complained 'A nuisance he is on this floor'. The amber traffic light burnt in the darkness till a spoon with a lukewarm mixture of potatoes and rice was put into his mouth. He drank the sickly sweet orangeade because it was very hot. He had to shout repeatedly for a urinal which was then attached to his narrow bed, after a further struggle.

The mysterious Janet squeezed his hand. Identifying herself as the

Australian Consul, she claimed that his niece had authorised a private nurse. Not worth the trouble to trace the connection with Soph, but to the Consul's 'You had a very serious accident' he replied automatically 'What else is news?', then laughed at the silly expression. Why was he praised for being so brave when he was just abominably tired? He asked the Consul to ring Christl, the only number he remembered, and withdrew into comforting oblivion.

Daniel's voice, disembodied as for so long over the phone, described the room shared with three patients in the ophthalmic department in a large public hospital. Their quarrelsome wives fulfilled the functions of nurses, apparently off duty, but a white-clad female hunted down in a corridor condescendingly gave the information that the removal of the splintered sunglasses from the eyes required several hours. 'What's not in plaster or bandaged up is all cuts and bruises, while your nose is a very odd shape. Poor Charles, you must be in terrible pain.'

'Not a twinge, only a heaviness in my head. Sorry to disappoint you. Mitzi needs your attention more than I. Smashed up or not, she must be handed to customs within the week. They've been very tiresome and I don't want any more trouble.'

Despite Daniel's pathological aversion to officialdom, he promised with the help of the Consul and the Automobile Club to face the endless formalities. Awkwardly caring as long ago during Charles's jaundice, Daniel retrieved the keys of the flat from the bloodstained shorts to fetch money, pyjamas and toiletries.

Hand-patting seemed hospital etiquette when Christl, attended by her maid, came in the cool of the evening. She complemented the milk-rice dinner with some excellent cake and made unflattering comparisons with the hospitalisation when Charles had cracked his spine. Food and nursing, or rather the lack thereof, were appalling; worse were the constant inane chatter, jokes and guffaws which stopped abruptly when the foreign visitors were scrutinised. Christl's hat and gloves awed the hideous voices into adjournment to the corridor. She would obtain a private room the next morning when the matron was on duty. The niece confusion was due to his registering Titi as next-of-kin; the Consul had rung her in Vienna to obtain financial approval for a private nurse. Christl and subsequent visitors echoing the Consul in admiring his courage must have referred to hospital conditions, yet it was confusing and vaguely perturbing in his numb exhaustion.

He awakened to protracted clanking and crunching that mixed discordantly with the grunting and snoring of certainly more than three fellow patients. Impossible to tell in the suddenly frightening darkness soon pierced by the amber traffic signal, then peopled by white-coated figures. The male nurse reading a newspaper must have been imagined. Hand-patting, admiration, the call to Vienna indicated . . . Otto's eyes had been spared or he would not have borne his misery so long. Charles tested the bandaged face with the hand not immobilised by the drip. Confirmation would come in the morning, whenever that was. Then he saw his sunglasses lying as usual on the hall table.

The prick of a needle signified morning. Later a young voice introduced herself as Nitza, the private nurse, and explained the hospital's organisation whereby cleaning bucket, breakfast milk and occasionally doctors arrived simultaneously for the daily quarrel. The clanking proceeded from the nightly collection of garbage bags, the snoring was doubled by the patients' wives squashing their usually thinner husbands on beds not meant for two. Charles's joke about the progressiveness of mixed wards was beyond Nitza, but she demonstrated the minimal functions of the staff by washing off blood and dust where no cleaning had been required for medical purposes. She emptied and disinfected the urinal, also placed the emergency bell within reach though it was unlikely to be answered. A first posse of doctors changed the face bandages and a vague light flickered momentarily in the left eye, but not hope from the terse comment on the hardness of his skull. Nitza detailed the torn right eyelid over an empty socket; the left lid was bloody, swollen and closed. The second posse admitted an implant or transplant – difficult Greek terms – in the right knee, internal haemorrhages above the left, was astounded at the absence of pain and withdrew with the clucking of tongues reminiscent of the White Mafia in Palestine and India.

Charles in Goryland proliferated with Mad Hatters and Queen of Hearts. One confirmed the unsolicited continuation of the British Studies privately before conveying her son's disappointment at his tutor's absence. 'I was rather disappointed myself' was lost on her, but not the willingness to resume Ancient History the following day; Charles considered it unfair to endanger the boy's GCE exams. Christl would surely obtain a private room.

'Officially they've been abolished by our socialist masters except for . . . politicians. Your oculist is unenthusiastic in the ambiguous ways of doctors about moving you to a decent clinic, away from the actual surgeons. You were disinfected at the nearest hospital and dispatched to the one on the emergency roster. Neither had an ophthalmic department so you were finally transferred here. Though you were mostly unconscious you kept on demanding your oculist and the name of Greece's leading specialist overcame the prohibition of consultants, and as a special concession he was allowed to attend but not to perform the operation. The criminal lunacy to exclude a man of international repute when one eye is already lost.'

'And the other?'

'Badly cut, but the optic nerve is intact. Patience is needed. He'll visit you but won't remove the stitches in this hellhole. I'll leave you to your younger friends as I'm about to become a great grandmother.'

Charles kissed her hand to the audible gasps of the wives whose film education ignored civilised customs.

———— ——

Bad temper had replaced Daniel's momentary compassion. He sounded resentful, apparently holding Charles responsible for the chicanery of the traffic police and bloody-minded customs. The Automobile Club would not guarantee the exact hour for shifting the wrecked car, so he twice engaged a crane which was expensive. On the strength of a Hospital Certificate and with the Consul's help he had withdrawn money from Charles's bank and obtained the necessary papers in the nick of time.

Charles laughed hysterically. 'Without the "Saved" in-the-nick-of-time is not particularly felicitous. My horoscope's one positive prediction tested in so many hairraising circumstances succumbed to the fatal seventieth year. The warning was too vague to be of practical value. On an empty road, days before handing in Mitzi, months before my birthday, still disastrously correct.'

To ascertain, confirm, evaluate the damage – the occulist's precise English wavered – he required his large slit-lamp, but only after the surgeon had removed the stitches though this meant another week in the discomfort of the hospital. An unfunny understatement for conditions more suited to a penal than a medical institution emphasised by the pitiful bravado of the inmates. They gobbled up the chocolate shared out by Charles and probably helped themselves to more even minutes before an operation. Charles never touched the sweets brought in by most visitors, but the salads he wished for were difficult to convey and not available in the hospital. Nitza was given several unopened boxes as she had warned about the prevalent thieving, so easy as he was blindfolded. Before Daniel suddenly left for Geneva, a call on his banker not previously mentioned being apparently imminent, he entrusted Nitza with some banknotes which were placed in an envelope under the patient's pillow; when he handed the envelope to Loula to pay domestic bills it was empty.

Charles's digestion rebelled against the disgusting hash and mash, which he alone did not aggravate with chocolate. Enemas acted promptly, but on one occasion the first stirrings were delayed till after Nitza's departure. Charles rang the bell in increasing torment, finally unable to contain himself. Lying in his muck and misery he continued ringing until a shrill voice complained about the disturbance. Providing a bed-pan was apparently not part of her duties; he had a private nurse and the wives could have helped out. Charles cursed the wretched woman for her inhumanity and demanded the floor sister, but only a male nurse later washed him and changed the sheets in a time-consuming operation under the heavy plaster and avoidable had the bell been answered in the first half-hour.

The recent levelling down of medical services was punctuated during the night by the screaming of patients dumped in the corridors; the hospital was on the emergency roster, beds and above all attention were not to be found. From this nightmare of sounds Charles escaped into happier dream images. Mother sitting by his bed in the flower-filled room of the Vienna clinic, nurses eager to help. The horror of the first Turkish hospital and the incompetence of the second were not deliberate. Then Christl had arranged for as comfortable a convalescence as was possible in Greece. The hospital review was halted by a portrait. Filipino Lippi's profile of a young man under a red toque, a strange intrusion considering the magnificent Raphaels and Titians so often viewed at the Pitti. Unlike Clouet's Valois kings, the small portrait appealed to no subconscious memory or imagination but to a deeper, incomprehensible affinity.

Daniel had deprived himself explaining the inexplicable. Age forced Christl's retirement from the hospital's physical discomfort, but she was determined to secure the patient's spiritual comfort. The priest sent by the Consul seemed oddly reluctant to hear the confession in English, promised to return and never did. Religion had consoled more generously before the conversion!

Priests could not be coerced into saving a soul but doctors into releasing a desperate patient, provided he signed a special request. The oculist would attend Charles in the flat where the orthopaedic surgeon's assistant would remove the plaster though private visits were forbidden to state doctors. An ambulance was arranged for the morning, but Nitza predicted an afternoon transfer.

She was too sanguine since Reception possessed no influence with the independent ambulance pool fully occupied with collecting emergency cases. Anthony had taken over from Nitza when the CO Director belatedly paid a visit, presented a tape from the Organisation's music library, but, though informed of the interminable wait, did not offer to convey his oldest lecturer home, an easy task for his driver and security guard. Charles could not ask for the obvious and Anthony was afraid of a possible future employer. The endless evening frayed tempers and when the ambulance men at last called for the nervous wrecks, they had to be directed by their blindfold charge. Anthony was so unpractical that he had to be told to tip the men who carried Charles up to the flat, switch off the lights and place the urinal; as he had not emptied out the disinfectant, Charles accommodated the overflow by drinking up the glass of water on the night table. The unnerving reminder of the recent disaster due to immobility restricted the euphoria of solitude, though mere traffic noises reassured after the screams from the emergency beds, the snores from the regulars and the crunching of the garbage truck.

A police van removed Nitza who had dealt diligently with the problems of concussion, plaster cast and sightlessness. She helped the invalid patiently and herself imprudently: part of the students' fees and later of Loula's household money were missing. She conceded that she was the obvious suspect, but it was she who had warned of theft; nor was she so stupid as to risk a permanent well-paid job. She was, however, unable to resist an opportunity contrived by Anthony who alerted the police. When they failed to come, Charles rang the station and was abused for playing a hoax; Anthony's imprecision had given the number of a building site. Exhausting pleading and the Consul's intervention brought two detectives, who sympathised with the blind victim, yet after one officer had led away the shrilly protesting thief the other advised against bringing charges. The trouble was disproportionate to the amount, which was unlikely to be recovered. Informing the hospital was tantamount to a charge, so Nitza would rob patients till one of them beat her up. Anthony's reflections on Law and Disorder were interrupted by Nitza's phone call: for being let off so lightly she would forego three days' wages and when required she was willing to help out; she had left behind an apron, houseshoes . . . well perhaps when the grudge was forgotten.

To charge or not to charge . . . The accident had occurred near a suburban police station, which was finally persuaded that the plaster and bandages legitimately obstructed the course of justice. A polite officer came to take down a statement, and advised bringing a charge against the inept woman driver, an Arab who justified abandoning the unconscious victim by shock, though she herself was unhurt – a fact ascertained in the same hospital to which Charles had first been taken. He was desperately tired and had been warned about trouble when bringing a charge. This surely was a clear case for the public prosecutor, here at least justice would be done.

Between the two police visits Charles had briefed a new nurse, recommended by a CO colleague. She lacked Nitza's virtues, hopefully also her vice; she was elderly, worked in a hospital at night and deployed minimal activity in her double employment. Realising that 'Putting my feet up a little' was inadequate, she introduced a replacement whose pleasant young voice stated her willingness to undertake domestic chores. Persephone sounded worth a trial, but in the meantime Charles had expended more energy from a very limited stock in interviewing assistants sent by friends who had survived their care. The choice had depended on the quality of voice and Persephone's was as good as any.

———— ————

Persephone adjusted to alien needs within the flexible context of Greek nursing. Loula handled the domestic middle level with meek ineptitude, passing problems to her ward's most congenial CO colleagues. Mary Dimas organised the British Studies ladies into what Charles visualised as Pre-Raphaelite nymphs draped round his large bed for lectures which equalised originality of setting and substance. Incapacitated members of the Automobile Club were entitled to a small indemnity, which Mary obtained in record time, defeating the insurance company's red tape. Not, however, of the Social Insurance where the change from old age to invalid pension involved a complexity of cancellations, claims and medical examinations requiring a lawyer. The lady provided by Mary's husband, a Greek businessman, had specialised in Maritime Law, which probably contributed to the farcical delays, straining nerves and purse for half a year.

Charles owned no ships but an account and shares in Switzerland; with the same bank as Daniel who refused on his return any assistance when Mary revealed that 'the nervous Frenchman requesting help with the customs had been told about the indemnity, but would not listen'. Hotly denied, the ungracious irascibility precluded further responsibility. Anthony had not ruined his family because his father had already done so, nor were other foreign friends possessed of better common sense. 'Help from unexpected quarters' looked reassuringly like Uncle Sam minus the goatee, an amusing regular at Christl's parties. Plans for beach and opera never eventuated, but now Sam paid a visit and though he 'despised European forms and statements, if there is no one else to do the job, I'll do it'. He followed instructions painstakingly, but his New England caution came too late to prevent a disastrous investment. On a Sunday in October the stockbroker personally favoured an old but unimportant client to advise him of a highly profitable opportunity; the shares purchased Monday morning had lost half their value by the evening of the 1987 crash.

Irrationally, the financial loss prepared for the confirmation of the visual loss. The oculist postponed a definite verdict, supposedly because of post-operative scars, but finally found the remaining eye ready for slit-lamp examination in his surgery. After the repeated offers of 'Every possible assistance, transport for instance', the CO Director was 'not too happy about the afternoon appointment as the driver would have to be paid overtime', but was shamed into promising the car by Charles's readiness to shoulder the expense. Ten minutes later the Director's secretary conveyed regrets because the car had to fetch a VIP from the airport. Sam and Socrates Dimas, neither strong and both arthritic, carried plaster-heavy Charles down and later up the three flights of stairs but the CO's mean hypocrisy aggravated the stress of the crucial examination. The formal charade confirmed what had not been in doubt, though the oculist still avoided pronouncing blindness. The damage had been too extensive for further intervention, yet if money did not matter . . .

Certainly not when he could clutch at straws. Titi had contacted Erwein Erdöpany who demanded a detailed report, reluctantly given by the oculist – it was so delicate to describe a colleague's operation – while the state surgeon refused such an unscheduled 'extra'. Erwein consulted the Boston Eye Clinic which recommended two Germans and one Swiss specialising in 'Heroic operations'. In the meantime Charles had forwarded the report to a leading English specialist, whom he had helped in getting to know the Greeks. The reply 'Don't waste your money' was echoed by the Swiss; but Titi had succeeded in lining up the two Germans and two professors in Vienna within the last week of January.

This miracle of medical mobilisation had to wait till Charles recovered the use of his leg. Assured that no receipt was required for his illegal fee, the hospital orthopaedist became inordinately fond of patting the plaster which he regretfully replaced with bandages frequently changed though there was no wound. He finally relinquished his lucrative patient to an efficient physiotherapist, who restored the function of the knee by alarming grinding of bones.

Necessary implements turned into impediments on independent forays to bathroom and kitchen, after crutch and stick were exchanged for a white cane. Walking exercises along the banister of the large terrace – an enormous boon – had readied the legs for the commands of Athens's only foreign-trained instructress, who launched into standard sixty-hour courses for the blind; her 'basics' were sensible, but removal of all interior doors would have made the top flat even colder, while her haranguing Loula and Persephone on returning every object to a fixed place frightened the two into forgetting the place. The knee occasionally protested against endlessly repeated to-and-fro tapping on the terrace, yet the shell-shock trembling was revived by insignificant annoyances rather than hard work.

Annoyances accumulated into significance. Loula fetched and carried unnecessarily, as she was incapable of any decision, forgot what she had been told and, when she was at last persuaded to write things down, invariably lost the paper; the unfamiliarity with writing was multiplied in Persephone and devastatingly varied in an ancient former CO secretary who ably typed letters in three languages to Charles's numerous friends abroad but tended towards putting missives into the wrong envelopes. Charles's intercourse with the other flats had been restricted to struggling to extend the totally insufficient hours for central heating; the struggle was now resumed but was so indefinitely more exhausting without commensurate results. The landlady declared herself powerless to interfere, Loula had no backbone, foreign friends were rudely told off and the patient froze in between electric blankets, from which it was unsafe to move, especially to the bathroom. The owner of half the flats shed crocodile tears over the 'Terrible affliction' but when rung by Christl to see why Charles hadn't answered the phone – as so often out of order – she could not be bothered to climb the stairs.

Pinpricks enervated more than the instructress's perfectionism; she wanted her pupil to tap up and down the stairs without touching the railing, but if the ascent was arduous the descent was perilous. Lessons in the street aggravated Charles's trembling to tears because of the overwhelming effort required to zig-zag between garbage bags, motorbikes and cars parked on the broken pavement. The torture of street solos was abandoned, friends learned the simple rules for guiding the blind, applied by Sam on the long walk to Christl's New Year lunch. Concern was general but inexpert, few of the well-known voices needed identification but it was hard to say whom they were addressing in the disorientating babble. The attempt at social re-integration was too ambitious, but Christl had already provided more important religious solace.

———————

After the priest at the hospital had neglected his mission, she had tried for another curator of souls, but as Charles was neither registered nor dying she obtained only promises from the overworked Catholic clergy. She appealed to the Nuncio who entrusted 'this case or regrettable remissness' to an Assumptionist, a member of a small French order unknown to Charles. The link with the crucial Assumption Day was too evocative not to be conceded during several lengthy visits. Too experienced a confessor to contradict the penitent's acceptance of his affliction as Divine Punishment, the Assumptionist administered the Last Rites as Sacrament of Healing, for blindness as well as lameness since the knee was still in plaster. After the Ritual the priest displayed a kindred humour: the last recipient of the Sacrament improved spectacularly but then passed away; neither could be guaranteed. Making light of the repeatedly confessed death-wish was more charitable than sterile condemnation.

Charles attended Christmas Mass assisted by the Dimases who were wonderfully understanding when incense and music provoked uncontrollable sobs which climaxed in a prayer at the Assumption altar. Equally aware of material needs, Mary chose the gift on behalf of the CO staff, a tape recorder to vary the frantic search for foreign stations among the daily list of strikes, financial scandals, pop and folk waiting on the overcrowded Greek airwaves that triggered off the shakes. Deprived of reading, recorded books provided a welcome alternative and, though the CO tapes focused on teaching, Mary requisitioned the few novels. That the first played during a sleepless night was Graham Greene's *A Visit to Morin* could not be random coincidence but a tantalising glimpse of a Plan, incomprehensible and inexorable as the suffering of Herta, Lis and Otto seemed harsh punishment for whatever faults they might have committed. If blindness was merely a meaningless accident then suicide was the only logical way out, a release from tedious dependence. Morin chose between Faith and Belief, Charles between life and death.

———————

Friends abroad realised this more clearly than the acquaintances in Athens. The local intimates were deceived by Charles's self-mockery and too preoccupied with petty practicalities. Only Christl understood the fragility of the brave façade that occasionally crumbled before her motherly compassion. Distant well-wishers rallied in character: Titi above all with her organising talent; Tania with taped plays; Hildegard with a subscription to a braille newspaper, unfortunately unintelligible; Robert warned against suicide as it was preferable to suffer blindness for a few years rather than an entire reincarnation; Irene offered herself as an escort to any doctor world-wide; Ralph encouraged an autobiographical novel since *Greece Debunked* required impracticable historical research.

If research alone had been impracticable! The Lighthouse of the Blind recommended braille despite the complications of varying scripts. Charles's fingertips were found unusually sensitive and he laboured over the raised dots of the Greek and Latin alphabets to achieve the joy of reading, but the even harder punching out of bewildering symbols was unsatisfactorily restrictive. Another momentous choice as before about walking; abandoning braille allowed concentration on touch-typing. Two fingers had suited the final polishing of the transcript from handwritten to typed, but now revisions had to be perfected on tapes for an unalterable typescript. A blind university student supervised the memorising and manipulating of lower and upper keys until she overturned and broke a standing lamp displaced by Loula. For some obscure reason – the involuntary pun amused Anthony – the useful typist considered the smashing of the useless light a personal insult, yet the determined pupil persisted with solitary exercises.

Father would have approved the testing of his dictum, 'For an average intelligence nothing is impossible'. Concussion had not impaired the mental abilities, and self-discipline overcame the heaviness of the head. Physical disability had not absolved Charles from the obligation towards his student, who passed first in Ancient History. Charles could rely on his memory for tutoring, but for the annual GGG revisions editing assistance was needed though the material had been prepared using notes taken by Anthony on their journey. He needed the money but his intelligent co-operation constantly deviated into irrelevant gossip. Delius had been fortunate with an industrious music student, but Charles had to replace his frustrating amanuensis with a wealthy expatriate who knew that money had to be earned. The urgent work was dispatched before the deadline, the rest could wait for a return of sight if those German 'Heroic surgeons' succeeded.

————

Interpreting her duties compassionately, the Consul drove her Australian compatriot to the airport and, insisting on diplomatic privilege, settled him in the Austrian plane. The stewardess justified the preferential treatment by the passenger's accent; she unwrapped and cut up his lunch, speeded the transfer to a wheelchair and the passage through customs into Titi's arms. An inflection of voice, a touch of hand expressed clearer than tears the sympathy with the sufferings of her mother's generation.

The survivors continued in the supporting cast; Dolly's sister walked her childhood idol in the nearest park, constantly forgetting the illustrated guiding rules he had sent ahead; she became, moreover, entangled in the emptying of garbage tins, not as malodorous and noisy as the crushing of the rubbish bags in Athens but not exactly relaxing. She criticised the hump in his broken nose and the unbecomingly enlarged vein in the right temple. She shut up when Charles quoted 'Destroy what you adored' as she had received the solid education common in their set.

Paul pretended familiarity with this set by describing a ball he believed he had attended, though his schoolmate, who had opened with Marie Louise, knew better. They deplored the death of Ernst, the most successful of their class, though more modestly, of course, the Canon had been made a monsignore. Moving a congregation by a sermon was easier than giving spiritual guidance to the top boy of adulthood.

——— ———

Titi triumphed over German inflexibility at the intermediate stop where no wheelchair was provided to pass her charge through customs. She coerced an unwilling official into verifying that the passenger to the domestic air terminal at Cologne resembled the passport photo; not much, with an empty eye socket, scars and a different nose, but the flight was allowed to proceed.

By never taking no for an answer, Titi had achieved appointments with both eye surgeons on the same Friday, to fly back on the weekend as she could not absent herself from her office for more than one day. She had underestimated both her own and the invalid's adaptability, so Patrick had come along to deal with the logistics of the journey and also to stay behind if lengthy tests were required. He had studied at Bonn and had enlisted his former landlady to race them from town to town. Mutti partook of the opulent breakfast at the Cologne hotel, but though she claimed to know her way about she ignored the way to the clinic as well as the traffic lights on the motorway. Because of possible blood tests Charles had not eaten since the previous lunch in Vienna and the screaming of brakes on a very empty stomach made him tremble; he insisted on the removal of erratic Mutti from the wheel.

Patrick replaced her and later listened to her gloomy predictions in the vast hall of the Bonn Eye Clinic, where Titi steered the patient among the partly-sighted till they were admitted to the Presence.

Professor Langhaar simply ordered his assistant, Dr Nordwind, to make an exhaustive echogram; relaxed on a couch, the hardly perceptible electro-waves suited the surrealistic names of the doctors. A fairy-tale with a happy end, as the examination concentrated lengthily on the still existing left eye. 'Saved in the nick of time' after all?

An inadequate buffet completed Titi's tact till Langhaar had studied the report to which he now pointed with his glasses; a short slim man, his grey hair not long but neatly trimmed like his beard. Perched on the edge of a table he convincingly looked the part. Daniel had asserted that a dormant Cyclopean eye was activated *in extremis*; vestigial function, hallucination or psychic phenomenon gave comforting body to the precise German. 'The sounding warrants a cornea transplant in the left eye where shrinkage is minimal. No criticism of my Athenian colleagues, but a month or two earlier . . . There is at best a ten percent chance that an operation will enable you to cross a street, but not to read even with a magnifying glass. If you want to think it over and discuss it with your niece, you can let me know during my evening rounds.'

Even the slightest chance must be grasped and Titi must not be burdened with any responsibility. 'Nothing to think over, I'm ready when you are.'

The image remained unchanged, but the voice warmed to the subject. 'You could teach the Federal Government something about making decisions! I have operated on several Iranian soldiers whose eyes were as badly cut by Iraqi fragmentation bombs. Time is important and I'm attending a conference in a fortnight. You require a whole morning, up to seven hours, and my schedule is full.' The dramatic pause did not affect the benign image. 'Your courage deserves the sacrifice of a weekend. My assistants won't be pleased, it's Carnival, but all tests will be made beforehand and you are my private patient. The difficulty is finding a cornea, donors don't always die at the right moment.'

'My niece will join your staff in doing a donor in' was appreciated by her more than by the German physician.

Mutti enervated with accounts of ill-considered operations and misdirected Patrick. They were late for the Cologne appointment; the echogram was brief and the professor brusque. 'Your eye has begun shrinking and does not justify an operation. Coming in, you almost bumped into a similar case, severe lacerations by broken sunglasses. The poor chap lost both legs in the accident but he was brought to me within a month.'

Waiting for the car Charles 'saw' a young man in a wheelchair, a blanket over his legs, blue eyes staring.

Medical opinions frequently conflicted, but a victory dinner on such slender odds tempted fate. They were staying at a hotel as luxurious as the Dôme where Mother on returning from France had ridiculed ordering the most expensive dish; tactfully efficient Titi should have realised that this was not an occasion for *Sekt* – added to the other bills, three air tickets . . .

———————

They slept and laughed through the weekend in Vienna, to recover from past and prepare for future tribulations. Titi had made the appointment, but Tania and Josef took her ex-stepson to the fashionable professor who had only a fortnight earlier operated on both for cataract. A large fee was exacted before the superficial examination ending with a supercilious 'Keep body and soul together. In ten or twenty years we might transplant a whole eye.'

Josef's deference to a famous colleague was replaced by Patrick's no-nonsense for the fourth interview. He whisked Charles through the courtyards and endless corridors of the General Hospital where he had been judged unfit for military service. The courteous disorganisation, unchanged after fifty years, would now judge what hope remained. The echogram specialist in a distant wing had been notified but readily put aside her coffee and asked them to take her report back as 'through ordinary channels it would reach the professor somewhat later'. His assistant dealt kindly with this rule-breaking haste. 'The library is the only place where the professor won't be interrupted', yet after more corridors and waiting it was she who announced the verdict. 'The professor sends his apologies but he feels that I as a woman might convey the bad news more tactfully. I wish I could!' Another mother embraced Charles in tearful grief. Spontaneous compassion at a quarter the price of the equally unprofessional callousness the previous day. More stunning than human response was the neatness of the circle, a renewed glimpse of the Plan: his deficient right eye had saved him from the Russian front in the very place where his left eye could not be saved.

The shock struck him fully in the taxi. The driver tried to stop the paroxysm of sobs by a description of their route past the Imperial Palace, but awakening of memories failed as tranquilliser. The alto voice aroused, however, curiosity. To a whispered 'Is this a man or a woman?' Patrick replied, 'It is an Indian' which started hysterical laughter drying the tears before financial counterirritants. At his stockbroker's Vienna branch, Charles placed sales orders with an arrogance merited by unprofitable investments; the manager drove his self-possessed client to a bank and assisted with complicated transfers from America via Athens to Vienna and Bonn. A British Hospital Insurance, to which copies of the one favourable report were sent, covered the clinical expenses, but there were so many others. Business at last done, Titi's Filipino maid walked Charles round the block and vowed a novena for the success of the operation, a touching testimony to the universality of the Church.

Bonn confirmed that a cornea was ready and despite the demoralising score of three strong nos to one weak yes Charles's black humour never wavered.

——— ——— ———

Patrick's luggage consisted mainly of *Mozart Kugeln* for the Clinic staff. The delicious Austrian chocolates immediately sweetened the receptionist into allocating the largest single room and bath. A cocky young doctor was curtailed in his futile stabbing at the 'Unfortunately brittle veins', the monotonous refrain of the diabolical nurses in the Athens purgatory. No less a hierarch than Dr Nordwind pricked satisfactorily. *Kugeln* all round except for the banned house doctor. Patrick stacked a reserve of chocolate boxes for the night nurses and then took the popular patient – the 'gilded with chocolate' of the Zurich Banker revived in this Looking-glass World – for fresh air into the wood near the Clinic. 'Smaller but even more romantic than the Vienna Woods. Though those Kugel-addicts wouldn't inspire the sexy ballet in the . . . ?'

'Venusberg. My first and sixty years later my last opera. Langhaar's ten percent offers better odds than the Pope's staff sprouting again. But unlike Tannhäuser I don't repent my particular Venusberg, so this location is rather disquieting.'

'Titi will compensate with Elisabeth's prayer and I'll join the Pilgrims Chorus. For an on-the-spot sing-song I've roped in Mutti's son, a theology student. I am sorry I can't stay, but I have a seminar.'

Baths had required no assistance in Athens, but Clinic rules demanded supervision. In plaster-time females had washed the offending parts so that the knee-length pants placed on his bed evoked a Carnival masquerade rather than modern Venusberg prudery; the nurse, suborned by *Kugeln*, was free to avert her gaze while urging an end to the soak that relaxed the stress and prepared for the sleeping pill and injection.

Consciousness returned reluctantly. Tentatively he pressed a bell which was immediately answered. The glass of milk was an unpalatable as in Athens. The customary reddish darkness, occasionally enlivened by images of the dead, living and unknown, more often by geometrical designs, turned into a film of lavish interiors; over-furnished like Zeffirelli's *Traviata*. Puzzling, because this had not been the last film seen and Charles had ridiculed those vast galleries outdoing the Louvre. He dozed off and woke as always just before the phone rang. How did Kaliwali feel? Titi regularly used the childish endearment but never before followed by 'We love you very much, remember that.' Equally ominous, Patrick cracked a political joke that might well have waited. Black speculations subsided into drugged oblivion.

A cleaner made noises appropriate to her profession. His '*Guten Morgen*' she countered with 'Turk'. The image of an untidy woman recalled the Ankara hospital, the windows were certainly not so dirty but it was just as hot; from central heating, not the Anatolian sun. The guest worker linked the past possibility of paralysis with the present probability of blindness.

Professor Langhaar was relieved to be greeted with a quiet 'Tell me the worst'.

'We performed a keratoplasty, a cornea transplant. The retina was, however, too badly cut to be reattached so we abandoned the segment reconstruction.'

Big words for plain failure. 'You warned me and I still think I made the right choice.' Yet according to universal medical opinion the choice had never existed.

'You were remarkably brave making the decision and even more now learning that it was the wrong one. I have little experience of sightlessness, my job is to prevent it. If you wish I'll contact suitable institutions in Germany.'

'I prefer France' came without thinking as Charles had not yet considered institutions.

'I can help there too. My sister-in-law is in a convent near Cannes and I'll consult her. If you aren't too tired I'd like you to walk up and down the corridor with a nurse.'

Movement projected again the film of over-stuffed interiors and the fear of bumping into the surfeit of furniture quickly returned the patient to his bed. According to the radio, the Rhineland was as absorbed in the Carnival as pre-Anschluss Vienna. The *Traviata* décor gave way to the Ball in der Burg and Irene promptly phoned. She found the right tone of compassion, while soon afterwards Loula just sobbed and Daniel speculated on the imagery. Titi had obviously alerted the phone numbers left with her for an emergency which had now arisen.

Unlike Daniel's, the French of Frau Professor Langhaar was to the point when she enquired what kind of retreat her sister, a Dame de Sion, should look for. Through gratitude for personal attention a memory struggled to the surface. Not of Cannes where he had spent two hectic summers, but . . . the Convent in Jerusalem where a motherly Dame de Sion had consoled in the darkest despair. Was it part of the Plan that a sister of the same Order should console in physical darkness?

———————

The Professor's practical interest contrasted oddly with his lack of interest in the psychological aftermath of the operation. 'Unwinding of the visual memory' explained nothing. Why unwinding only after the second operation, why furniture when cars were the obvious cause of *Angst*? The Austrian levity of 'So you won't have me certified just yet' struck no answering chord.

Answers refused by science came partly from religion. Mutti's son, a leftish do-gooder, rammed down Divine Love; offensive even on a walk in the wood that uniquely sunny February. Stumbling over roots and stones was less perturbing than heavy furniture, and Charles compared his own to Tannhäuser's escape into the freshness of the spring forest. Not the music but the politics of the composer mattered, Wagner betrayed his revolutionary ideals and pandered to royalty. The attack became personal, against the inequity of a private room; though paid by an insurance to which the patient had subscribed for twenty years he had sinned against Equality.

Charitable theology redressed uncharitable theories. Conscious of his recent shortcomings, Paul had appealed to the Schotten to provide spiritual consolation to a former pupil through the Benedictine Order. The Prior of an Abbey near Bonn dealt patiently with an exasperated and doubting believer who questioned the Creed's Resurrection of the Body; surely not in its present imperfection, blind? Was, therefore, Reincarnation the answer? The prelate refrained from dogmatic rebuke by quoting St Paul: 'How unsearchable are His judgements, how unscrutable His ways.'

Australian ways seemed at first straightforward. Urged by the Athens Consul, her Bonn counterpart had announced his visit, postponed and finally cancelled because of ski and Carnival leaves. The offer of an Embassy car to the airport was withdrawn because of administrative complexities on Rose Monday, but the flight reservation had been confirmed. The receptionist, still under the influence of *Mozart Kugeln*, offered her car but the do-gooder objected to a curtailment of an employee's enjoyment of such a holiday.

The clerk at the airport found that the return copy of the ticket had been torn out, probably by mistake, the passenger had to check. When he was blind? Yes, because the copy was essential. No, it could not be used without the remaining ticket. Yes, the Australian Embassy had confirmed the reservation. No, the manager was absent, Carnival. The plane was full, so it was lucky that he could purchase a ticket for the seat reserved in his name.

The obstinate fool was abetted by the dogmatic do-gooder. The clerk was only obeying rules, he must not be forced into a responsibility for which he was not paid. The ticket would eventually be refunded.

In the mysterious billing of airlines the single flight cost more than the return ticket and Charles had only sufficient money because the charge for the operation had been halved, three hours instead of seven. As the Hospital Insurance would pay that expense, the reduction was no windfall but the seal of failure, now compounded by irresponsible stupidity. For the first time since the childhood flight to Marienbad Charles was airsick and then trembled in helpless dependence.

The official at Vienna airport just muttered 'Germans!' when he stamped the many papers required for a refund.

———————

Germans had made possible the blinding of Anton Bluhm. The deliberate gouging out of his eyes bore no resemblance to a car accident except in the result. Toni was the victim of Nazi inhumanity, deserted by all when he turned on the gas; inhumanity was not lacking from the accident, the unconscious victim abandoned, conditions at the hospital, but friends rallied, especially Titi who cared more than could be expected from any real niece. Had Soph at least pretended the slightest interest in her only blood relation, she might have qualified for yet another inheritance.

She was disqualified by a haemorrhage on the brain. 'Soph has been in a coma for a month, not the kind of news to tell you before your operation. She had time enough to make up for her past behaviour after I wrote of your accident. I don't share your Pay-As-You-Sin belief, you can't have done anything so dreadful. In Soph's case, however, it's so unusual at forty-five . . .' Tania was waiting for Charles with Vienna's only maker of artificial eyes to blow the glass. His wife explained patiently how the artefact was fitted into the socket and, worse, plucked out. The physical and psychological misery of imitating Oedipus brought on the trembling which exacerbated the clumsiness finally overcome by the lubricating tears of frustration. Tania's compassionate encouragement, not in her stage voice but patently sincere, swept away the last vestiges of the stepson's resentment.

They walked to Tania's flat, past the Votive Church that commemorated the escape of the Emperor Franz Joseph from an assassination attempt. 'No better place for an old Monarchist and recent Catholic like you, so I lit a candle before your operation. But now . . . Still, after this morning's ordeal I'll gladly join you in a prayer.'

Did his blindness show her the Way as Panagiotis's death had prepared his own conversion? Salvation at another's expense? Theological speculation was discarded in the laughter over the original misconception: the calculating intruder versus the precocious stepson.

Josef arranged a visit to the Home for the Blind near Schönbrunn where Charles had flirted with the son – illegitimate, but still of an Archduke. Though unaware of this quasi-Imperial connection, Tania declared after one glance at the inmates massed before the TV 'Not for you'. She bemoaned the closing of the Convent where the Grandparents had ended their days in congenial company. The Vienna cradle-to-grave cycle was unrealistic despite Tania and Titi. He would not abuse kindness and become a burden.

————

A burden imparted a purpose and Loula clung to it tooth and nail. Her husband had died after one year from a mixture of boredom and exasperation, a posthumous diagnosis based on Charles's own suffering. Yet she was indispensable for minor chores above Persephone's ignorance of English. Even less welcome a necessity was the lawyer, who had at last obtained the absurdly small invalid pension but no indemnity from the guilty party's insurance. On the contrary, for stating truthfully that the traffic light had turned amber, it was Charles who had been charged not the Arab woman who insisted it had been green; that she abandoned the victim did not seem to matter. The lawyer demanded witnesses though aware that her client had been alone. Had he no friends? They must at least testify to his careful driving, an acceptable generalisation when clients were excessively scrupulous. Daniel, Anthony and Loula asserted the appropriate before the examining magistrate who refused to take down Charles's statement, in longhand; better present a memorandum. The futility of the proceedings so enraged the accused that he let himself be persuaded by the lawyer to bring a penal action which would be amalgamated with the prosecution; and also a civil suit against the criminal driver's insurance.

Socrates would have warned against involvement with Justice but refrained from opposing his lawyer, who was to receive a disproportionate amount of any damages. Like all foreign friends Christl was ignorant of the Greek legal system; she commiserated but preferred nostalgia to present predicaments. Daniel still monopolised the phone at night, rarely bothered with a visit and despite his two cars – to beat Athenian driving restrictions – refused to take his oldest friend out of the terrible pollution. Breaking point came with Saint-Exupéry's 'The only blindness is that of the heart', shattering in its brutal incomprehension yet also laughable considering who quoted. The loss of French saddened more than that of a friend who merited this name no longer. Stelios regained it; he had made a bedtable and shelves and now closed his shop to drive Charles into fresh air; walking along the sea was bliss, talking about an unrealistic future a bore, the combination at best a stop-gap.

Mary and Sam filled the gap admirably but insecurely. A permanent Home had to be found; the few in Athens were inspected and discarded by Anthony. The Consul explored institutions in Australia, Sam did likewise in the States. Mary assisted with endless claim forms for the Hospital Insurance and the application for the Royal National Institute for the Blind rehabilitation centre at Torquay. Not sponsored by any National Health scheme, Charles was admitted at his expense but also his condition, a private room which necessitated personal intervention by Irene. Boarding school, a terrifying threat at fourteen, was a favour at seventy; to teach the prerequisites . . . ?

——— ———

Blindness revived the desirability of a monastic retreat. The blind monk in Eco's *The Name of the Rose* had managed well in the library of the Benedictine Abbey; except for murder and arson he might be imitated. Not in France as suggested by the Dame de Sion nor the Schotten as hinted at by Paul. Charles had lectured and written exclusively in English, so that language considerations dictated letters to the Abbots of Downside and Quarr.

'. . . I venture this request for a permanent retreat because of my unusual circumstances. I am working on an autobiographical novel, outspoken in tracing my conversion to Catholicism. Beginning and ending my intellectual and spiritual life with Benedictines seems an eminently Christian circle and I would gladly forego the comfort of private institutions. I could come for an interview in August, after rehabilitation at the RNIB Centre at Torquay . . .'

The prompt answers hardly differed.

'. . . We'll look after you during a retreat but can not accept guests as permanent dwellers. Please forgive me for not being more helpful . . .'

The Abbeys had been selected for proximity to Irene's farm, to which Charles repaired in early July. A CO colleague eased the stress at Athens airport but not at Heathrow. Unmusical wheelchairs are a depressing game; Charles was already seated when asked to cede the chair to a lame lady. He did, enquiring whether Europe's biggest airport could not muster a second conveyance. A sympathetic alto reminiscent of the taxi driver in Vienna was conjured up to wheel his charge through Immigration, where Irene was not waiting. Her name was called repeatedly, once even recognisably; the Indian attendant was given a description, meagre clues of age and height, summarised in 'A horse woman'. Legends of memsahibs inspired the Indian who spotted the lady within minutes. A long delay had been announced because of a strike in Athens, yet the plane was actually on time. Irene apologised, embraced, directed the psychic or merely intelligent Indian, and tipped him correctly in pleasing contrast to Loula's indecision.

Irene had hired a driver, the setting sun was hard on her eyes though tears probably presented a greater problem. Perhaps to steady her nerves she was sucking boiled sweets, preferable to cigarettes but Charles hoped that Devon had not switched from cream to lollies. Exeter evoked memories; the friendly holding of hands evolved into a long embrace when she installed him in her late husband's quarters: bedroom, study and bath. She hoped, however, he would not wish to be on his own too often. Meals were prepared by a cook-housekeeper and shared with an unmarried daughter; June was running the farm but found time to initiate her mother's friend into an electric typewriter, which he set into frantic motion while anxiously preparing for school.

———— ————

The Manor aggravated rehabilitation with a Victorian profusion of stairs and labyrinthine corridors. Potted plants within the triple porch impeded access to a baronial hall made unsafe by carved furniture between numerous doors. Irene signed papers, deposited money, negotiated a sweeping staircase and sharp corners before and behind doors leading to Charles's tiny room where she unpacked. The obstacle race had lowered morale which collapsed at high tea into an orgy of starch. The depressingly named cobbler, a hard pastry stuffed with potatoes, was perhaps tastier than shoe leather but no easier to cut. The accents of the three table mates were partly incomprehensible; kind intonations became impatient with the new-comer's obvious deafness. Worse than in the army and laughable after lecturing forty years in English, he was aurally as well as visually isolated. Returning inside with Irene tempted, was resisted and regretted on becoming lost in the formidable porch.

'The lady should have taken you back, but now that you are out here, would you like a walk? It's a lovely evening. I'm Aileen from Reception, Christian names only. You'll get used to the twenty or so Johns, perhaps not as you'll only stay a fortnight, a unique case. Intensive training starts tomorrow, without the usual week for set-tling in though you are somewhat older than the rest. Many trainees have residual sight, don't hesitate to ask for assistance.' Aileen was an outstanding surrogate mother; she showed him how to use the table in the centre of the hall as a landmark, but on this first evening guided him to his room. The draw-sheet on the bed sheet safe-guarded against drunken incontinence, alcohol was forbidden on the premises but the trainees frequented a nearby pub.

Getting sloshed seemed as unattractive now as in the army. Aileen's gentle 'unique' equalled the Sergeant-Major's exasperated 'irregular'. The odd man out metamorphosed into well-intentioned new boy during an anxious night.

No less anxious was the solo descent and search for the dining room to a Dickensian working-class breakfast. Persephone always poured his coffee, Charles now guessed wrongly and tea wetted his trousers; he had to change. Trembling he rushed up the stairs and through a door which closed automatically; no knob indicated an exit from the claustrophic hole. He tapped in mounting panic along crushingly close walls till fresh air accompanied 'You aren't the first to prefer the linen closet to your corridor. Just in case you want to hide again, the door does open from the inside. You made a remark-able get-away after nearly drowning in tea so let's begin at your room and concentrate on getting to the porch. I'm your mobility teacher.'

After initiation into the malice of nooks and crannies, Charles bewildered the Living Skills instructress by wanting to master eating rather than cooking, an art of which he had remained ignorant. She defended the established group cooking routine, echoed the Sergeant Major's 'irregular' but would consult the Director on social graces. The Communication Skills electronic typewriter seemed as con-sumer-unfriendly as June's electric; levers and buttons prevented following dictation from a tape. A manual model was reluctantly resurrected. Wood Carving class he refused; he could cut off his fingers without cutting up logs.

Aileen applauded 'this reasoned resistance to the mould. You are a breath of fresh air.' She showed him the railings that would help him through the garden when the staff had leave to see the Queen at the 300th Anniversary of William III's landing.

———— ——

'A letter from the Queen.' Aileen opened the envelope from Balmoral in the awed silence of Reception. The note from an equerry regretted that duties at the Castle prevented his coming to Torquay; the old acquaintance had rightly calculated the effect of the Royal Crest on the Director. 'Your instructors report excellent progress and unusual requests. Living Skills agrees to take dinner with you in private. Because of the celebration and a staff meeting you lost two afternoons, so I'm offering you an extra week on the house, still unsatisfactorily short. The President of WAA phoned, he'll visit you on Saturday.' The more title-dropping the better.

Best was Ralph's literate understanding. They had gained recognition with very different books, but as travels were out, Charles had to revert to novels though his first, *Stelios*, had been awful. Despite the Centre's skills, the technical difficulties were daunting. 'Don't overwhelm the reader with all the dramatic and sex incidents. What about reviving one in flesh and not only on paper or even add a new episode?'

'For fifty years I have led *you* into perdition, dearest Ralph. But when bowel movements become more enthralling than an orgasm it's time to desist.'

'Hurry up with that novel or I'll pinch that jewel.'

More in the familiar vein, the GGG Editor encouraged a personal account, *999 Reasons Not To Travel;* making fun of the inevitable mishaps in three continents would make amusing reading and warranted the effort. Were Gulden alive some financial reward would certainly have recognised Charles's cultural and historical contributions; the present publishers simply appreciated the perseverance after the accident.

'So they should! Nobody in Athens seemed suitable for *North Africa* till a lesser expatriate claimed he had lived in Algeria where he maintained many contacts. In the three weeks we worked together he did not provide one single answer to urgent questions but when he returned information I had given him as his own discovery I called his bluff and told him just to follow my instructions. He pretended to be offended and disappeared with all my notes, probably to sell them back to me. I've little patience with blackmailers and had to reconstruct my revision from memory. Anthony was kept to the grindstone by giving him my entire revision fee. I finished on the deadline but my trust in humanity was not improved.'

———————

The effort of tapping unaided through even the quietest streets prevented conversation, but in the blissful relaxation of a jacuzzi, after the weekly swim, Mobility listened with interest to an account of sightless visions. The film of dangerously over-furnished interiors subsided into blurred pictures in elaborate frames interspersed with precise family portraits and Lippi's *Young Man*; images of post-accident acquaintances surprised by an uncanny approximation. The stress of outdoor walks added little children, in constantly changing numbers and dresses but always just in front of the left eye to which sensations were restricted. Fantasies joining memories might appeal to a psychiatrist more than to Charles.

The staff were expertly patient but with the fellow-blind aims and attitudes remained unbridgeable. Robert's amiable eccentricity ani-mated the second weekend and the third brought release to Irene; she had come on two evenings so as not to coincide with other visitors. On the farm she tried to integrate Charles into her social fabric and also corrected his typing despite her 'dislike of anything academic'. Her set was affluent, arthritic, friendly and fiercely parochial; the similar social futility at Laudorf had made Charles neglect his brotherly duty, so was he now to endure it for his own sake? Herta had always expected a marriage with Irene, now indeed the most sensible solution, even emotionally when listening to the Noël Coward tunes of their youth. Her children were financially independent and would not keep her at seventy from the partner she had failed at twenty.

His two stepmothers likewise prospered, Helen probably now owned Abbey Court after Soph's death in the spring. Helen had notified Hildegard but not Charles; she had not even answered an invitation to Devon despite an assurance that his blindness would make no claim on her. Irene's existing and Charles's extinct family were discussed but a decision was postponed until Aridio.

———————

Aridio's Indian summer soothed away the tension of their journey. Their arrival in Athens had coincided with that of the Olympic Flame at the nearby stadium, to be flown to the Games at Seoul. Mary drove them from the airport as close as possible to the flat, but could not park. Irene conscripted a 'blatantly honest' sports enthusi-ast to carry the luggage under the direction of one incomprehensible and one blind foreigner. Within a few days Irene impressed Christl and Mary by being herself, Loula by making decisions.

The Hotel Aridio rewarded inclusion in the GGG with special attention. Charles insisted on two rooms, indoors at least he was able to manage on his own. Irene disapproved obliquely by starting a charm offensive against a solitary bather with whom Charles had exchanged smiles during previous stays because both kept resolutely to themselves. She failed with 'Sourpuss', but succeeded in preserving her charge from balls and boats when swimming, which they enjoyed as much as once riding. She read to him and enjoyed the seafood at tavernas, anxious to please by turning off the folk wailing.

A fortnight of the good simple life was too short for boredom but just right for the momentous decision: part of the year at Aridio, the locals were touchingly helpful, only the elderly English couple withdrew ungraciously from a possible burden. Some months would be spent at the farm, but Irene would also explore opportunities in warmer climes. Final arrangements would be made in Athens at Christmas.

2

By Christmas writing had replaced people. Mary moved to a suburb, Sam was overrun by American visitors, yet each reserved one evening for Charles; he hated putting them to work before every outing, but patient Loula was incapable of following banking and investment instructions. She and Persephone 'Killed with Kindness' but too slowly for the beneficiary. The ludicrous inadequacies of these female oafs were demoralising though amusing to relate; their clumsy administrations were restricted to the minimum, at the sacrifice of hot meals. The telephone remained the lifeline to Christl but not to Daniel; on a visit of goodwill he showed none but was more transcendental and tactless than ever. His 'It would have been so much better if you had become blind earlier' resulted in a second banishment. Morale sapped daily now collapsed, not to be restored in the cold Athens flat but perhaps in the comfort of Devon or the sun of Aridio.

Irene's weekly pep-tape and talking newspapers cheered, her physical presence would distract from writing. Charles hinted and Christl warned that he was a 'loner', so that he was granted a second solitary Christmas to consolidate nostalgic memories.

Childhood memories crowded a tape revised on a second recorder. The complexities of aural co-ordination incited him to type before a paragraph was properly formulated; belated changes in emphasis and style were scattered through the subsequent text in a disorder all the more frustrating in comparison with the ease of previous corrections. A British Studies lady read back the gibberish, difficult to disentangle for a first retyping; the new page was then amended by any amanuensis available. All claiming legible script largely illegible to everyone else. Eventual reconstruction from memory added stylistic divergencies to the technical. Anthony's 'Easy on history' echoed most publishers, with some envy added. 'That your last guide was translated into nine languages won't help this Rake's Progress. Play up the sex; you have some fine shockers, but cut down on the namby-pamby background.'

Yet the background had formed Charles's, justified his misjudgments and wholly explained his present misery. Without the expectations of the Dawn the disappointments of the Night lacked dramatic contrast, but most references to Father's part in Austrian politics were deleted.

Hildegard wanted them restored. 'I was fascinated by your father's arguments at the Tarburg that reforms might have saved the Monarchy. He would undoubtedly have played a part had Franz Ferdinand become Emperor. And despite Sarajevo he was the youngest under-secretary in the last Imperial government.'

'Too little too late, for Austria as well as my family.'

'Such a pity, for both. You'd have made a charming count, more so than my Austrian cousins. With a title you'd have become an ambassador and have married Marie Louise. I stayed with her during her last illness, at the time of your operation, and she admitted that for quite some time she had hoped your snobbishness couldn't resist a princess. She never understood why you awakened a mother instinct in other women.'

'Not my two stepmothers. Helen didn't even answer my proposal to meet at Irene's.'

'She died of cancer, soon after my godchild. Apparently in Germany, trying to find a publisher for your father's *The Notion of Justice*. That interloper Richard Travers "explained" that he first wanted to clear up the inheritance complicated by Helen's death abroad before announcing her demise. I rather resent his getting the Tarburg silver and furniture, not to mention Abbey Court. Perhaps a lawyer . . . ?'

'Not after my experience here, but Irene might get copies of the wills. It's wonderful to be talking to the only other survivor of the Tarburg/Fechtner tragedy, with more corpses than *Hamlet*. Do come soon again.'

'I'd love to be with you, but the pollution in Athens is bad for my asthma. You look absurdly young but I feel my eighty and like Aunt Valerie I'll wait for the Great Reaper at the Tarburg.'

———— ————

Titi continued the funereal mood. 'The Empress Zita was buried with the pomp and circumstance of a reigning monarch. Greatest show ever put on by the Republic. Anything connected with the Empire would be snapped up by Austrian publishers. If only you wrote in German.' She understood the impossibility of writing in a language unused for fifty years, though English seemed strange in a novel so far mainly set in Austria. She was fascinated to read not merely about the 'misdeeds' of her mother and Uncle Erwein but also of those of Kali Wali, whom she revitalised during a long weekend in Athens.

Irene attempted valiantly to extend revitalising intimacy over three months. Aridio's hotels were already doomed to package tours so that Charles booked into a larger new flat with his former landlady who would do the cleaning. The adjoining bungalow was occupied by her mother-in-law who unfortunately failed to die after saying farewell to relations and receiving the Last Rites; inconsiderate to the prospective mourners who stopped visiting her. This assured tranquility in the flat, but the mellow contentment of the Indian summer eroded in the noisy high season when ball-throwing brats made the beach unsafe.

The Rehabilitation Centre sent a detailed evaluation of the 'Able Gentleman with very definite views', more favourable a report than ever received at school. For a fortnight Sam brightened the scene, which was then darkened by some young Australians, acquaintances of Irene's daughter. Their accents and interests differed gratingly from Helen's and Eve's, though neither was glamourised by the passing of time. Charles's advice about a camping holiday in Turkey was sought and stopped by the Australians' accounts of gorgeous discos and frequent belly aches. He left them to Irene while he worked at the novel before enjoying several solitary meals of cheese and olives. Life had taught him to be alone; lonely he only felt in unwanted company. Irene persisted with trivia, the past and the weather were chewed over ad infinitum to be continued in Devon. Yet blindness left no choice; the Centre's short training was useless in the holiday crowd of Aridio and in August even the oafs escape from the traffic chaos of Athens. Total dependence imposed on Irene's hospitality.

———— ————

The warmth of Devon hospitality equalled the weather, but swimming in a neighbour's pool lowered the temperature less than the cold shower of Irene's table talk. Her 'Nothing academic' included the châteaux of the Loire recently visited by their hosts. 'The Bourbons I remember at least from the biscuits, but the Valois . . .' She wondered why her presumptive companion for life refused to accompany her on the social round though he remained politely entertaining to her guests.

A perfect hostess in all but talk, she restricted the GGG Editor to beaches, hotels and, of course, the weather. With Ralph she reminisced about Vienna, discussed intelligently one of his books and loosened the conversational restraints. She favoured the suggestion of writing every episode in the novel in the language appropriate to the setting, till assured that no publisher would accept a quadri-lingual *tour de force*. Ralph advised and counselled, admired Charles's struggle against overwhelming technical odds and encouraged him with a talking watch. Discouragement followed promptly with the dissolution of the Society of Blind Authors owing to lack of support. Every author for himself and publishers unlikely to take the blind hindmost.

Irene interrupted the writing with long walks till she sprained an ankle playing hopscotch with her grandchildren. Relying on the Centre's training, Charles tapped along the lanes, trespassed, was barked at but never bitten. Though he had refused their invitations, the neighbours tamed their arthritis for this energetic walker but few sustained his speed. Varying degrees of deafness led to hilarious misunderstandings during an occasional advantage of the greater over the lesser invalid.

Accounts mad and sad eased the estrangement Irene tried to reverse in the last week. Tea at an Exeter hotel where they had spent a night fifty years ago provided nostalgia but no basis for the future. 'How I envied the sophisticated "My heart died many years ago" of that lecturer here. When God wants to punish us He listens to our prayers, Irene darling.'

Retyping the manuscript made her aware of the significance he attached to *Tannhäuser* and she bought a recording of the opera with Lotte Lehmann. The last resort of her good intentions was not allowed to fudge the inevitable issue. Crying now over his selfish withdrawal would prevent future disappointment. Listening alone, the music filled the darkness with an astoundingly precise replay of the performance seen at Mother's side.

The reunion conceived by Herta's practical romanticism floundered in the clash between the practical and the romantic. Monastery and marriage demanded devotion or at least some belief; neither was required for the third English solution. Recommended by the Rehabilitation Centre, Charles was the guest of the Foundation for the Blind at Richmond and encouraged to form an opinion by sharing lunch with an articulate inmate, who summed up the institution fairly, 'Probably the best at the price. Well-managed charity, choosy about admissions, and therefore maintaining a good standard. Comfortably utilitarian, needs adjustments. My daughter cooks for me at weekends. I trust you have friends in London.'

Charles stayed for a few days with the wealthiest of these, who invited the others to fabulous meals and reminiscences. Ralph presided over a WAA conference in Africa, and in his absence Charles entertained with the expected tragic self-mockery and realised that no encore was wanted.

Unwanted, because an invalid upset the balance between work and play. The friends whose company Charles enjoyed were no more selfish than he had been, though he had made an exception for the Minister. Without the right companion there was no right place. The search round the world was a fantasy, Athens was a grim reality. Had Loula's heart been connected to her head instead of her feet, Charles would not have restricted her to the twice weekly of the faithful *British Studies* ladies. Persephone took him for walks, Mary, Stelios and lesser acquaintances occasionally drove him into air that could be breathed. Before their regular taverna evening, Sam attended to the correspondence, dwindling because essentials left little time for keeping in tenuous touch with the past.

Tucked between old letters was the sheet on which Charles had scribbled AFERIM, the mysterious word three times heard in a dream. Sam undertook to consult an archaeologist on his next visit to the States, but the solution came from his Jewish physician learned in Hebrew. *Afar* meant dust, the plural suffix signified 'Dust to Dust'.

The incomprehensible language of unknown forbears was less of a warning than the horoscope's 'danger near seventy'. As a judgement it had come to pass: dust were the friendships, loves, ambitions, the joys that compensated for the relentless struggle likewise predicted. Books, music, travelling had been pleasures before becoming part of a second-class career. He could have done better; he had refused opportunities after the cataclysm of the Anschluss. His choices had been wrong but had they really existed? Was Free Will predestined? Loula's Orthodox 'It is written'? Had physical and bureaucratic impediments warned against driving though it was essential for his work? A Higher Will had protected him in innumerable dangers and actual accidents, only to blind him through criminal negligence. Purgatory here and now instead of another life or place might be Divine Grace, but uniting the body with the spiritual Dust was tempting.

Suicide saved Uncle Karl from trial, the Auers from concentration camp, Toni from torture, Dolly from poverty; all acted under acute stress. His was chronic; millions suffered from blindness, but only few from blindness aggravated by education. The Minister and his circle of diplomats had welcomed Charles for his culture, now comprehended only by Christl. During their daily discussions of Art and History, they encountered as many fascinating moot points as she settled from the Encyclopaedia, but man does not live by telephone alone. Mary was a joy in literature, Sam in Opera, both were sensibly practical when available. Loula was disconcertingly available; without her Charles might not have survived, with her he did not wish to. Incapable of a 'yes' or 'no', she uttered a nondescript sound of enraging indecision, yet despite constant endeavours, she remained irreplaceable for the endless dealings with officialdom, from pension to faulty telephone.

Charles confessed his ingratitude and despair to the Assumptionist who was sufficiently concerned to resume his private visits. They agreed on the literary merits of Montherlant but not on his suicide after becoming blind; not even the altruistic motives in Greene's *Heart of the Matter* justified the deadly sin. Infinite patience was needed and Charles determined to set his own limits.

The liberation must not be botched up like Yvonne's poor mother jumping out of the window. EXIT in London refused advice, but Sam would try the Hemlock Society in New York. Remembering Aunt Margarete and her sister, Charles donated his body for transplants; his organs might prove more useful than the cornea he had received. Loula refused to fill in the 'un-Christian' forms, but Persephone obliged when assured of a legacy equal to the cost of a funeral. The body was not to be returned to the family; dumping the mutilated remains on an ex-stepmother, on a niece-that-wasn't-one or on the never-met widower of the real niece would have been too macabre a joke.

———————

Had Richard Travers provided a grave for Helen in Germany or England? Had her ashes been scattered like Father's? Irene obtained copies of Father's and Soph's wills from Somerset House; neither included the most valuable possession, Abbey Court, but Soph had bequeathed her 'Residual estate' to her step-grandmother who

apparently left no will. Dying slowly of cancer made intestate unlikely, so was the step-grandson-in-law the villain of this macabre farce
which engulfed the remnants of the Fechtner fortune?

Not merely the fortune but the Fechtner ashes disappeared without trace. Mother's with the family tomb, Father's and probably
Helen's scattered. What remained of Charles might as well be
dumped in the garbage, collected perhaps by the same truck that had
wakened him in the hospital of blindness.

——— ———

'The gory end will please the readers and is kind on your heirs.' Titi
tried shocking Charles out of his despondency which had become so
alarming on recent tapes that she and Patrick had flown to Athens
over Christmas.

'And you are my heir as you know perfectly well. How refreshing
that you are as sensibly callous as your mother. Soph or my nephew-
in-law might have "cleared up" or rather cleared off with the inheritance of an Australian living in Greece invested in Switzerland
and some catastrophic American shares, but it's simpler to instruct
my bank to transfer the lot to your account on submission of my
death certificate.'

'Our Swiss account is in the name of Patrick.'

His gentle snore halted the tax avoidance scheme. Titi had the
good sense not to laugh. Her husband was bored by technicalities
concerning an inheritance taken for granted, but falling asleep while
discussing the least onerous procedure . . . He had never been as rich
nor as poor as Charles who had deprived himself for the sake of a
comfortable old age but had always spoilt her mother and herself. No
longer could one look convey her condemnation of the unintentioned
insult, but Charles still had a hand and she squeezed it as on the
drive to the Bonn Clinic.

Titi's intuition never failed her, but she was not a great reader and
her interest in the novel was personal, not literary. Patrick was
naturally her first priority. 'As a punishment for the Sleeping Beauty,
I'll dictate him a letter to Ralph, my literary executor, who will
hopefully earn his fee by getting me published. You'll make the
payment from the Swiss transfer; you are more trustworthy than my
family. For local legacies to Loula, Persephone, Stelios, I've appointed Mary executrix of a will; she hates anything legal; how right
she is after my experience, but though my chattels here are peanuts,
it requires someone knowing English and Greek.'

The gold medals Charles had worn through so many misadventures though not at the last recalled the dead and *vanitas vanitatis* but

made suitable Christmas presents. Yvonne's Imperial Eagle held significance only for Titi, while her mother's St Christopher was appreciated by Stelios, and even more Marie Louise's Virgin by Loula. Patrick had slept himself out of Uncle Karl's signet ring, a petty postponement yet even the blind were entitled to a vengeful whim.

Laughter and tears with the Donellys over inheritance intricacies resumed over the literary obsession with Ralph. 'The story is unique, but so is the presentation, quite demanding on the reader. Publishers aren't too happy about that. All your books have been commissioned, but we'll have to hawk this one around.'

'Like Helen with my father's *Notion of Justice in International Relations*; even harder to get so abstruse a notion accepted. He worked on his undoubtedly learned tome for thirty years, I barely three on my novel, yet neither published in the author's lifetime . . . I'm weeding out Dawn before Night is finished, depending on the assistance available. Worse is the mechanical stress, tapes are inaudible or even break, a paper clip falls into the typewriter and once the ribbon slipped and I had two blank sheets to reconstruct. The malice of the inanimate objects *ad nauseam*.'

'Exactly what I mean, Charles. Such phrases are too . . . obscure.'

'In all my books and lectures I've used unusual expressions, perhaps stupidly proud of giving succinctly the precise meaning. It's more than style, it is me.'

——— ———

He did not change his style but eliminated what appeared laboured yet had come naturally; clarity before originality. After Ralph's departure, the aural memory was strained to the limit for the final shortened version; previous drafts were taped by those unimpeded by croaking, lisping and false teeth as every word was scrutinised before Charles retyped for the next rereading and further corrections, omissions, substitutions. Checking through the eyes of others was time consuming, imprecise, exasperating. The Lighthouse of the Blind recommend a scanner developed in America, reading type in five accents from Mid-Atlantic to Mid-Western; not, however, Greek script, and for lack of local demand no technician would be sent in the foreseeable future. Given the hostility of even the simplest gadget, Charles decided against the likely frustration from a costly and irreparable mechanism. 'Help from unexpected quarters' was personal but tantalisingly brief: a young Byzantinist preparing his thesis but eager to assist with any literary material. A steady amanuensis greatly facilitated work and he had just mastered all the complexities when he won a scholarship necessitating his departure for Turkey.

———— ————

The false light of literary, medical, personal and religious hopes flickered in the icy cross-currents. Dragging himself out of the warm bed to the cold bathroom admitted defeat in the struggle for more central heating. The blind expended twice the normal energy and Charles's dwindling reserves had to be preserved for the novel. Trembling impeded simple tasks like eating but not typing. He slept badly but did not increase the pills that left him dopy the following morning; moreover, brilliant inspirations crowded the nights, were recorded and discarded largely on the transfer to paper. The roseate glow now rarely soothed the darkness from which the gold-framed pictures disappeared; but in the streets little girls still obstructed progress, though they were often accompanied by short women in mourning or black headscarves. In moments of stress a snake raised its head towards the left eye, a nuisance without the panic caused by the viper at Pörtschach.

The BBC World Service fascinated with accounts of the Communist collapse but reception was often bad. Charles searched through the ethnic and pop screeching for the Greek news, dominated by strikes alternating from all to sundry. When the action against the woman driver who had left Greece was finally to be heard, strikers forced the clerk of the court to stop his notes and no future trial date was set; the nerve-racking drive through a chaos without traffic lights was as futile as the legal proceedings. The penal action so rashly brought by the lawyer had 'by an error of the court' not been amalgamated with the original charge; Charles was found not guilty on the prosecutor's initiative. A judge awarded full damages six months after hearing the civil suit but the insurance company appealed and the case was further complicated when the Greek Social Services made claims on the paltry award.

Acquaintances persisted with clichés of sympathy and unwelcome gifts of chocolate – appreciated, however, by Persephone. She had adjusted to the much-walk-little-talk routine when her husband, nicknamed Bocassa, became too ill to be left to his finite devices. The nurse replacement was a frenetic char arranging books and papers according to colour and size; for her Loula wrote in Greek a short list of telephone numbers 'never more than one digit wrong'. Stelios's emphysema affected his heart and on a walk through a tranquil grove he alarmingly suggested that if he dropped dead his blind companion would not find the way back. Christl grew frail and regretted that leaving the picture of her father's Derby winner to Charles had become pointless.

Loss of a last inheritance was one of the daily last straws. Yet blind Milton had created splendid poetry with the help of an intelligent daughter. More astounding because he was over eighty, a blind Doge of Venice conquered Constantinople with intelligent assistance. Death and circumstances had deprived Charles of intelligent friends; all were missed but the first would have been the ideal last. Blindness was the perfect foil to Otto's disfigurement in a companionship as natural in old age as once in youth.

——— ———

In another life? On a missionary visit to Athens, Robert proved reincarnation logically; how else to explain crippled or blind children? They had not served out their sentence, which was aggravated by suicide.

Persuasive but hotly contradicted by Sam the atheist who returned with the Hemlock Society's *Drug Dosage Table* and detailed instructions in *Let Me Die Before I Wake*. The prospective user joked about the choice of alcohol to increase the efficacy of the more easily available pills, best crunched up in yoghurt with honey. Despite an anti-nausea tablet, Charles's favourite champagne might bring up such a revolting accompaniment and he decided on whisky.

After final touches to the novel he prepared tapes for Irene, Ralph and Titi, to tie up ends not really loose. He felt bound to orderliness within the pattern beyond his control. Barely five, he had rewritten the *Trojan War* and in the last GGG revision he had rewritten the chapter on Troy. The visit with Anthony in the ultimate summer of sight had confirmed his childhood scorn of the legendary Greek heroes besieging that diminutive perimeter for ten years. The image of the disappointing hole in the rock ceded to the architectural splendour of Bursa; green and blue tiles merged into improbable convolutions till the snake aiming so persistently at the left eye turned into a tessellated work of art.

Art had been a major attraction of Catholicism, the Faith that intensified worship with the beauty of churches and ritual. Without visible props and despite the fine singing, Charles found it hard to concentrate on the Mass. The sympathetic understanding of the Assumptionist encouraged the confession of the intended end to his misery. 'Before my operation you gave me the Sacrament of Healing. Will you now refuse me Communion?'

The priest did not hesitate. 'The Body of Our Lord will help you to endure your purgatory.'

THE IKON MAKER

by Desmond Hogan

Pulsifer Press

'The first British paperback edition of the highly acclaimed novel' – *Time Out*

'Beautifully, concisely written, it is a seminal work, vivid and memorable' – Christie Hickman, *Woman's Journal*

'A beautiful tale . . . a moving and concise account of a mother's love and understanding' – *Gay Times*

'A fine, spare novel, and Susan's characterisation, in particular, is a triumph' – *Sunday Telegraph*

PAUL BOWLES BY HIS FRIENDS

edited by Gary Pulsifer

Peter Owen Publishers

This tribute to the writer and composer Paul Bowles contains contributions from, among others, Francis Bacon, Melvyn Bragg, William S. Burroughs, John Cage, Lawrence Ferlinghetti, Allen Ginsberg, David Herbert, Patricia Highsmith, James Purdy, Stephen Spender, Gore Vidal and Gavin Young.

'Magnificent!' – Hanif Kureishi

'Paul Bowles is the king of nightmare. Gore Vidal gives an interesting picture of Bowles's start as a writer. David Herbert gives the most alluring portrait of the lives of Paul Bowles and his brilliantly gifted wife, Jane. Ruth Fainlight's memoir of living in Tangier is alive with Jane's presence.' – Emma Tennant, *The Spectator*